'An extraordinarily accomplished début,' 'an unusual and un-usually good book,' 'first-rate first' are just some samples of the praise which greeted D W Smith's first novel, *Fathers' Law*. In *Serious Crimes*, DCI Fathers of Scotland Yard's Serious Crimes is again the protagonist of an exceptional crime novel.

At a weekend house party held by Sir Walter Granthelm, two of his guests are found dead in what seems like a suicide pact. As a result of the ballistics report, and what with Sir Walter's city connections, the international character of his guests and the previous year's theft of the Granthelm family silver, it is decided to hand over the whole case to Scotland Yard.

Which means Harry Fathers and, with his normal workload of corruption, armed robberies and the odd gangland death, he is just longing to have a bit more on his plate – especially as his wife has put him on a wholefood diet and all his best officers are about to be promoted.

This is not a straight-forward murder mystery; it is a subtle puzzle of wealth, greed, blackmail and antinomianism. It is also a novel of wit, character and suspense, which grips the reader from the first page to the last when the why- and whodunnit are finally revealed.

It is a superb successor to *Fathers' Law* and a gem in its own right.

D.W. Smith
SERIOUS CRIMES

MACMILLAN
LONDON

First published in the U.K. 1987 by
MACMILLAN LONDON LIMITED
4 Little Essex Street London WC2R 3LF
and Basingstoke

Associated companies in Auckland, Delhi, Dublin, Gaborone, Ham-
burg, Harare, Hong Kong, Johannesburg, Kuala Lumpur, Lagos,
Manzini, Melbourne, Mexico City, Nairobi, New York, Singapore and
Tokyo

British Library Cataloguing in Publication Data

Smith, Dan, 1951-
   Serious crimes.
   I. Title
   823'.914 [F]   PR6069.M4/

   ISBN 0-333-44117-6

Typeset in Plantin by Bookworm Typesetting, Salford

Printed and bound in Great Britain by Anchor Brendon Ltd, Essex

For Cora and Peter Weiss

CHAPTER 1

1

Anna Dark set to clearing the remains of last night's dinner party. The dining room was in perfect order already, as a result of work done after midnight. The main parlour had a pair of full ashtrays, some glasses and a mostly empty bottle of brandy, together with some marks on the coffee tables. She cleaned the tables, checked the floor and took the other traces of the socialising into the hall and put them on the tray she had left there. The light was colder and darker. The front door to Granthelm House opened almost due north. On the east side, the dining room and main parlour were warmed by the early morning April sun, but the hall, with its only windows facing north, never improved from a dim coolness. She shivered and went next to the music room, where one patch was beginning to be warmed by the morning. This was the room where most of the guests had spent most of their time once the meal was over. Wiping tables, picking ash off the floor, collecting ashtrays, bottles and glasses at a steady rhythm, it took half an hour to return it to order. The library would not need any clearing up, since nobody had been in there last night, and all she was left with to finish her pre-breakfast tasks, apart from setting the table, was the small parlour, facing north and slightly west, the coldest room in the house at this time of day. As she left the music room, Anna checked her watch. It was 6.50 a.m. – no need to rush, the family and guests would not be about for nearly an hour yet.

The door of the small parlour was locked. Anna clicked her tongue with irritation and puzzlement. It had no business being locked, and where was the key? She picked up the tray with the post-party debris on it and returned to the kitchen. Mrs Carrock was laying out what was necessary to provide breakfast to any taste – eggs to be fried, scrambled, poached or boiled; sausages, bacon and mushrooms; bread (white and wholemeal) to be toasted and croissants; butter and a selection of marmalades and breakfast relish; grapefruit halves and a large jar of muesli; three sorts of fruit juice; coffee and tea ready to be made. At 7.45 Mr Bolt would wake those who had indicated they would go to church; he would do it equipped with early morning cups of tea and quiet discretion. Breakfast would be ready from eight o'clock and the church-goers would finish and depart by ten to nine to walk to their worship.

Mr Bolt looked, Anna always thought, exactly as a butler should. Wearing white shirt, dark grey trousers and black unfancy shoes, to which he would later add jacket and a quiet tie, he entered the day alert, calm and apparently rested. Mrs Carrock, on the other hand, did not look like a cook in a large country house should. She wore tee-shirt, jeans and sandals, her long blonde hair piled up on top of her head, her face unmade-up and revealing that she had had either too much or too little sleep. Anna was dressed similarly, but unlike the cook she would shortly have to change into a dress and, like Mr Bolt, present the kind of smartness required these days of domestic staff – unruffled, yet unstarched.

'Eggs?' said Mrs Carrock to Anna as she entered.

'Just toast and coffee, thanks. The small parlour door's locked.'

Mr Bolt tutted as Anna had. He was sorting out his list of who was going to church. His employers, Sir Walter and Lady Sarah Granthelm, would go as they always did when they spent the weekend in the country. Their children, Madeleine and Walter, would therefore also go – as they never did except with their parents. Mr Rankley, doubtless to be found in Madeleine's bed (unless she were to be found in his), might go; Mr Waterford, in Walter's bed (no pretence here – Mr Waterford was not even assigned his own room when he visited), would definitely not. Miss Sheerley, Lady Sarah's niece, would accept the family duty to pray and give thanks, while Mr Homer (who might or might not be found in the same bed as her – Bolt had not quite satisfied himself yet about their relationship) had said he would not go. The American Mulhollands had also said they would not – Bolt had gathered that they belonged to some strange American Church – but their compatriots the George-Watkinses would, though not their son. Bolt gathered that the latter family hailed from New England, while the Mulhollands were from Florida. He felt there was some significance in this which helped explain the different ways they behaved. It might also be germane that Davis Mulholland was in business, while Michael George-Watkins was a diplomat. Keeping one eye on the pad of paper, Bolt pulled a key from his pocket and opened a corner cupboard, flicked his fingers over the bunches of keys hanging there, selected one and handed it to Anna, holding out the key she wanted.

It was difficult to get the key into the lock of the heavy door to the small parlour but Anna finally managed it. The room was curtained and dark. She clicked on the light, then blinked at what she saw and half withdrew. The room was occupied.

Ellen Sheerley lay perfectly motionless on one of the two large sofas which faced each other across a long coffee table. She was wearing the full-length, low-cut white dress in which the night before she had looked, so Anna and all the staff had agreed, breathtakingly beautiful. Her head rested on the arm of the sofa away from Anna at the door, her right arm caught between her body and the sofa back, her left arm flung negligently straight out, the hand dangling inches above the floor.

Slumped on the other sofa was Robert Homer. He was in his shirt, trousers and shoes. He lay as if he had fallen asleep while sitting, his feet on the floor, his head on the top of the sofa back, his body leaning to his right, his arms hanging down, one over the arm of the sofa.

Anna resisted the impulse to switch off the light and withdraw. This might be one of those moments which sometimes confront domestic staff, where discretion and delicacy are required. She tip-toed forward into the room.

'Miss Sheerley,' she said, and moved closer again to crouch and touch her ankle gently.

'Mr Homer,' she said and looked more closely at him. Then she saw his open mouth, his open, dreadful, blood-filled eyes and, as she stood up, the hole in his forehead.

For a moment she stood there. Then she began to back away, catching her foot on Ellen Sheerley's and half tripping. As she recovered her balance she looked more closely at the woman. Her face was peaceful, her eyes closed. As Anna peered at her, she saw blood on the fair hair at her left temple. The bunch of keys fell from her hand as she turned to run to the kitchen for Mr Bolt.

Granthelm House was an imposing, Victorian, three-storey construction in brick. In front of it was a sort of forecourt, lined by yew hedges. In the middle, a weathered stone cherub looked sadly down at the flower bed which encircled it. Several vehicles were drawn up in the forecourt – an ambulance, two marked police cars, two black Vauxhall Cavaliers, a black Rover 2300 and a red Ford Escort. More cars were parked in the smaller drive off to the right. Standing at the imposing front door was a uniformed police constable.

Detective Inspector Andrew Brain stood looking at the cherub. He was not happy. A tall, thin man in his early forties, wearing sports jacket, white shirt and tie, dark trousers and brown shoes, he had startlingly blond hair, blue eyes and pale winter skin. He was listening to the advice from his Chief Constable, a smaller man in his fifties, wearing a speckled brown suit which spoke of the country. They were outside in order to have a private conversation, standing well away from the house to be in the sun. It was 9.15 a.m.

'I'm not going to get in your way,' said the senior man, 'and you probably know the catechism as well as I do, but I do want you to be clear about the special nature of this case.'

'Murder is always special, sir,' said Brain in a gloomy tone that sounded like assent.

'Yes, of course, but the point is that Sir Walter is . . .'

He paused to gather a definition.

'Is Sir Walter,' suggested Brain.

'Quite so,' said the Chief Constable, 'with all that that implies, both in the City and the county.'

'Including the silver,' said Brain, even more gloomily.

'Indeed,' said the Chief Constable, his tone beginning to take on Brain's mordant air, 'which I think explains why he got me out of bed this morning to come along here. You know, of course, all too well what came of that.'

'We shan't forget that press coverage in a long while, sir.'

'Well, all that fuss: I'm not sure he was being entirely reasonable about it.'

'Not entirely, sir, no, but he is Sir Walter.'

'Quite so,' said the Chief Constable. He shoved his hands deep in his pockets. They stood in silence for a moment, reflecting on last summer's large and unsolved theft of silver from Granthelm House. 'The house party,' he said finally, 'includes an official from the American Embassy.'

'Ah,' said Brain, and tried his best to look respectful and thoughtful.

'Despatch,' said the Chief Constable suddenly.

'What I must perform with, sir?'

'Good man. I'll leave you to it. Murder and suicide: a nice job for a Sunday in the country.'

'Murder and suicide,' agreed Brain dolefully.

'That's your conclusion too, is it?' said the Chief Contable, with little of the inflection of a question in his voice. When Brain remained silent, he added, 'After all, the window was locked. And the door – from the inside.'

'So it looks, sir,' agreed Brain.

The Chief Constable eyed the Detective Inspector sidelong for a moment. 'What's your next step?' he said.

'Have a word with Dr Death, let the scene of crime boys have their go and get on with the interviews.'

'The order in which you take them may count for something,' said the Chief Constable looking at the chimneys.

'I understand that, sir. Though I thought I'd do the maid and butler first, since they were first to see the bodies, then the family, then the guests.'

'Yes, well, I suppose so, but try not to keep them waiting any longer than you have to. In and out as quick as you can. And you will remember the pronunciation, won't you?'

'Grant'm, sir, not Grant*helm*.'

'Quite. Well, good luck.'

As the Chief Constable walked to his car, Brain took another look at the cherub. It needed the birdshit cleaning off it.

3

Brain stood before the corpse of Ellen Sheerley. He took in the position of her body and limbs, the dried black blood at her temple, the beauty of her lifeless features.

Standing behind him, the local Home Office pathologist, Dr Albert, was droning on: '. . . usually say an hourly temperature loss in the vicinity of one point five degrees, fahrenheit that is,

11

I'm a bit old-fashioned in these things, which suggests death some time in the general area of midnight to three a.m. Hard to estimate precisely, no heating in the room but a reasonably warm night, probably slap in the middle of that zone, I'd say.' He coughed. 'There are a couple of other things you might be interested in. Noticed them when I took the temperature.'

'What's that then?'

Dr Albert leaned round him and bent over to raise Ellen Sheerley's dress with one gloved hand. It was loose and flowing and he held it high. 'There,' he said, indicating the back of the left thigh just above the bent knee.

Brain bent too and rested one hand, safe in its search glove, on the spot the doctor was pointing to.

'Drug addict?' he said. 'Or user, at least. Physically, she doesn't look like an addict. What else?'

Dr Albert held the dress even higher.

'No underwear,' said Brain, and turned towards the doctor making slight pushing motions with his hand. As the pathologist backed out of the way, the detective stepped carefully around the coffee table between the two sofas and approached the corpse of Robert Homer. The bullet hole was slightly left of centre in the forehead, less than an inch below the relatively high hairline. He peered closely at it and noted the powder burns.

'Contact wound,' he said.

He stood broodingly over the dead man for a moment, then stepped over the feet to look on the floor beyond the sofa. A black tuxedo lay there, dropped casually, a green velvet bow tie a few inches away behind it, and right beside the arm of the sofa, below the dead man's dangling arm, a .22 calibre automatic.

'Time?' he said.

Dr Albert took a couple of minutes to say that death had come to Robert Homer about the same time it came to Ellen Sheerley.

Brain walked to the door. 'When will I hear from you?'

'Well, I'll do it today, of course,' said Dr Albert, 'and get the report typed up tomorrow and sent on.'

'Call me with a summary when you've done it, can you?'

'Certainly.'

'Thanks.' As the doctor left, Brain took off his surgical search gloves and beckoned to the two scene of crime officers waiting with their equipment. 'All yours,' he said.

As the technicians began to unpack their bags to start work and the ambulance men appeared to remove the bodies, Brain walked into the hall. 'Strange wound, that,' he said to nobody.

<h1 style="text-align:center">4</h1>

They had all been awakened soon after 7.15 a.m., including those who had not wanted early breakfast and church. Bolt had asked each to go straight to the dining room. The gravity of his tone set the mood as they gathered in nightclothes and dressing gowns, even before Sir Walter stated expressionlessly that he was sure they would all be shocked to learn that two of the party were lying dead in another room in the house. As the words were said, they heard the arriving police cars scrunch on the loose chippings of the forecourt outside. Sir Walter had asked them to wait and gone outside to meet the police.

When he returned it was to say that each of them would be accompanied to their rooms by a policeman or policewoman, as appropriate, so that they could dress; that breakfast would then be served in the dining room and thereafter they would leave it only to go to the bathroom if necessary, whither they would be accompanied by an officer. He added that there would be no attendance at morning worship, that the police wanted to search the house and that he was intending to phone the Chief Constable.

His audience took this in, looking at each other somewhat uneasily as they made the inference to which only Madeleine Granthelm brightly gave voice. 'Of course,' she said, 'we're all suspects.'

'I would rather say, my dear—,' Sir Walter began carefully.

'Potential suspects, then,' his daughter interjected.

They had filed off in suitably gendered police company to dress. Breakfast was a quiet affair during which they were joined by a uniformed constable who stood stolidly at the door. After it the staff came in and sat together by one of the windows: Mr Bolt the butler, Mr Carrock the gardener and occasional chauffeur, Mrs Carrock the cook and Anna the maid who looked more ashen than the rest of the company and whose hand Mrs Carrock constantly and comfortingly patted. Madeleine Granthelm noticed, and walked down the long room to join them.

'Did you find them then, Anna?' she asked gently.

The maid's reply was cut off by a cough from the stolid constable who politely suggested that conversation about such things was best avoided. Madeleine shrugged and rejoined the others at the table where most were reading various bits of the Sunday papers brought by Carrock when he had walked down from his cottage with a police officer.

Slowly, conversation began, taking as its starting point something in the papers. George Waterford tried to discuss the review of a new play with Hannah George-Watkins, but unsuccessfully since she felt uncomfortable in his presence at the best of times and preferred to listen to her husband discuss the state of the Geneva arms control talks with Davis Mulholland. Out of duty, Lady Sarah, no more comfortable with her son's lover but equipped with a consuming sense of decorum that was triggered by such an obvious slight, took over the discussion of the play with the young man. As she became absorbed in it, the conversation moved to a general survey of the London drama scene which also drew in Brown Mulholland, a more relaxed American lady who did not share Mrs George-Watkins' prejudices. Peter Rankley opened the topic of football violence and hooliganism with Carew, the George-Watkins' eighteen-year-old son, and then moved to comparison of the rugby and gridiron codes, while the son and daughter of their hosts perched at one end of the long dining-room table and considered their plans for the summer.

The staff sat mostly silent, wondering at the ability of their employers' class to take such shocks in their stride, while the constable stood at the door and daydreamed. Sir Walter himself was for the most part absorbed in the City sections of the *Sunday Times*, from which he bestirred himself at one point when a car was heard to arrive. He left the room for a few minutes, returning to announce into a sudden expectant silence that the Chief Constable had arrived and settle back to his reading as the buzz of conversations picked up again.

A few minutes later they were interrupted. A tall, pale man walked in and announced himself as Detective Inspector Brain of the Guildford CID. He quietly apologised for their long wait and added that he merely wished to take brief personal details of each person – name, age, address and occupation. He then visited each person in the room separately, quietly asking his questions and noting down their answers.

14

When he had finished and left, the waiting continued. Madeleine attempted but failed to engage the company in speculation about Detective Inspector Brain – 'A misnomer if he's from Guildford,' said her father in a tone which ruled out further comment – and then returned to discussing the ever-declining merits of the French Riviera with her brother.

The door opened again, minutes after they had heard a car leaving. It was Detective Inspector Brain again. He began by repeating his apology that they had been kept waiting, and added that he was now ready to interview them.

'Would it be acceptable to use the library for that purpose, Sir Walter?' he asked. The owner gave an accommodating wave of his hand. 'Thank you,' said the detective. 'I'll call for you in turn. I hope to be quite brief with each of you. We shall take notes of the interviews and write them up as statements for you to sign later. There are three other things. First, I'm afraid that while I'm conducting the interviews, you may not leave this room except in the company of the officer to go to the bathroom or to come to the library. After you have been interviewed, please do not return here. This does not apply to Mrs Carrock who can prepare coffee and, later, lunch. But again, in the company of an officer. Second, I would ask you not to discuss anything relevant to the enquiry with each other until I've completed all the interviews. Third, I intend to institute a search of the house. I must ask if any of you object to having your rooms and possessions examined by an officer. I should add that if you do, I would seek a search warrant, which I have no doubt of obtaining.'

Nobody stirred.

'Good. The search will begin now, but as a matter of form we will include your agreement to the search in the statements we shall later ask each of you to sign. Thank you very much for your cooperation.'

He turned on his heel and left, accompanied by the other three. Peter Rankley broke the silence that followed by saying, 'He doesn't mince words, does he?'

'He sounds,' said young Walter Granthelm, 'like a surgeon before an operation.'

'And he's about to dissect us all,' said George Waterford, 'without anaesthetic.'

Lady Sarah interrupted. 'I think the point about coffee was well made. Would you, Mrs Carrock, please?'

As Mrs Carrock stood up, the constable said, 'There's an officer in the kitchen already, ma'am.'

'And perhaps the officers too would care for a cup,' said Lady Sarah.

'The ones who aren't busy rummaging through our things, anyway,' suggested her son.

George Waterford stirred uncomfortably and coughed as Mrs Carrock left the room.

'Dirty linen, George?' said Madeleine.

CHAPTER 2

1

Michael Kay kicked his bedclothes off and stood up. His head spun – the usual Sunday hangover. He stood for a moment in his tee-shirt and underpants, then spotted his cigarette packet on the table. There were still two in it. He lit one, sucked in the smoke, coughed and chuckled. Awareness of new possibilities filled his mind. Last night he had not found a woman to bring back to his two-roomed flat, and in that sense it had been a frustrating evening. But something much more important had happened, and that made it one of the best Saturday nights he'd ever spent. One bastard was going to be fixed. And there was money in it too.

It was not often that anyone like him could think he was on to something big and important, something to make him big money and let him be powerful. His first run-in with the law was when he was thirteen. Raised on a large housing estate in Tower Hamlets, he had turned easily to filching things from anyone and everyone before his twelfth birthday. It was something to do, exciting and profitable. He often had to run from the police as well as outraged shopkeepers and women who carried their handbags carelessly, but not until he was caught with a friend trying to chisel their way through a locked door in one of the tower blocks was he arrested.

Through the next four years there followed more arrests, convictions, deferred sentences and probation, the terms of which he consistently and inevitably broke until his first spell in a juvenile prison. He had graduated, through two spells in an establishment specialising in giving lads like him a 'short, sharp shock', to six months in a proper prison at the age of twenty-one. None of his crimes was large. Theft was a matter of a few pounds here and there, repeatedly. In prison he met a pair from his area who introduced him to house-breaking when they all got out. They took him along and taught him the rudimentary skills of selecting a house, casing it and entering without disturbing the neighbours. Corner houses were the best to enter – hi-fi, televisions, radios, home computers and cash the best to take. One night a randomly passing patrol car interrupted their exit from a house they were burgling for the third time. He hurled a ghetto-blaster at one of the policemen and got away. His two mates were copped. They didn't inform on him, but alone and shocked, he lost his nerve for breaking and entering for a time.

He had no explanations for his way of life. Probation officers and social workers had once tried to get one out of him, tried to get him to think and talk about himself. They had failed. Normally talkative and sociable, with views on anything and everything, he was silent about his own behaviour. He was in his teens then, and nobody had tried since. His parents whom he despised had long lost all ability to talk with him and any interest in doing so. He was not violent. He lacked the physique and the anger and the training for that. He had never mugged anybody, and in the company he kept, took pride in scorning people who did it. Battering an old lady, he reasoned, was one thing; honest theft was another. True enough, Michael, his friends would say, and one of them would offer him the chance of a couple of tenners for a few hours' work at the weekend, keeping an eye open for the old bill while watches were traded at the market.

To his everlasting surprise and fury, when he was twenty-three he was imprisoned for a crime he did not commit. It was because of watches. He was earning his score when somebody who didn't look in the least like a policeman grabbed the salesman right in the middle of his patter. As he was about to run, a hand fell on his shoulder and a voice said, 'You're nicked too, sonny.' He turned round and was knocked senseless by a single blow to the jaw.

As it seemed at the trial, though he was not sure because he found the proceedings hard to follow, the watches had been part of a consignment stolen from a large warehouse in one of a series of such robberies which the law had decided to end. For reasons he could not understand, and in an entirely unfair break with accepted practice, somebody had decided to round up the distribution network, at the small end of which was, among others, Michael Kay. It was outrageous. He – a casual labourer – had been put in the dock alongside the real thieves and the real fence. His story that he just happened to be in the market that day along with thousands of others – 'Why didn'cha nick them 'n' all?' he asked – was treated with derision by the Scotland Yard detective who was running the police operation. 'We got you bang to fucking rights, mate,' was the reply.

The policeman – a detective inspector, the highest rank Kay had ever dealt with, so the crime was obviously serious even if it wasn't down to him – had offered a trade: a friendly word in the judge's ear when it came to sentencing in return for a few names. Kay couldn't oblige: he had no names to offer. 'Your decision, kid,' replied the copper.

'But I didn't do nothing,' complained Kay.

The policeman had grabbed him by the hair, forcing his neck round at an ugly, painful angle. 'Nothing?' he said. 'Not never? If not this, something else. We got you. Tough.'

Kay was bitterly resentful. Selling was not even like stealing. Standing by while somebody else did the real work was not even like selling. And the bill never – but never – interfered with normal business in London's weekend markets – except this once. Keeping an eye out for the police was usually part of the ritual. They wouldn't make arrests, but they didn't like illicit trade on their patch. So you kept an eye out, and when you saw them coming you passed the sign and vanished. That way, honour was satisfied and everybody made an honest living. Except this once.

Even worse, when they searched him at the police station, they found a dozen watches on him. But he hadn't put them in his coat pockets in their cellophane wrappers. Somebody else had – probably the bastard DI. Everybody knew that the look-out didn't carry the merchandise; that too was part of the established pattern.

He got legal aid. He met the barrister assigned to him by the magistrates' court thirty minutes before the jury trial was due to start. The bewigged and gowned lawyer sat beside him on a bench and suggested a guilty plea.

'But I didn't do it,' said Kay. 'They've stuck me with receiving, and I didn't.'

'Well, so you say,' replied the brief with cultured calm, 'but the chances of the jury accepting that are distinctly low given the material evidence. A guilty plea will sit well with the judge when he comes to pass sentence. Prolonging the agony will only irritate him when the inevitable verdict is delivered.'

'But I'm innocent,' Kay insisted, 'and you're supposed to defend me.'

'The duty of counsel is also to advise, and my considered advice to you is to plead guilty. Well?' The barrister rose abruptly and appeared ready to walk away.

Kay thought he was going to walk out on him, leaving him to

19

go alone into court. 'All right,' he said quickly.

The judge sentenced him to eighteen months. The fact that Kay and three other minor characters in the drama pleaded guilty helped the prosecution to persuade the jury to hand down guilty verdicts on all the accused. Names made papers, including the name of the Detective Inspector who'd landed him there in the first place.

The barrister saw him briefly afterwards. 'There,' he said, 'what did I tell you? You've already done seven months on remand. Be a good boy and you've only two or three more to do. Nothing to it, eh?'

Afterwards Kay returned to occasional employment as a look-out. His failure did not seem to hurt his prospects for work in that line. He got together with his old mates for some more house-breaking. He did various odd jobs as they came up. Twice he helped in bank robberies, not at the banks themselves, but making sure that cars were where they should be for the lads to get away in. These bits and pieces on top of his social security payments gave him enough money to get by. He gambled a little – cards, dogs and the ponies. He had a few women, but none that cost him very much. He drank a lot and smoked, but took no other drugs. His small flat was as cheap as it looked.

One Saturday night he overheard a conversation which made him think. He recognised the faces, and at the sight of one of them his resentment at the injustice delivered to him two years before came flowing back. But when he heard what they were saying, resentment changed to vengeful pleasure. So this morning he felt powerful. He knew somebody from way back who had joined the police and who he had heard was now a Scotland Yard detective. If he remembered him right and if he hadn't changed, he was completely straight – the kind of idiot bill he needed now, the kind who believed police should be honest. He would get in touch with him somehow, and in return for a great deal of money he would put him on to something big, very big.

He drank some flat beer from a can he'd not finished the night before when he'd finally got home. 'Queen,' he said aloud, 'you're buggered.'

2

Sir Walter stood looking out of one of the two large windows in his main parlour. Here his guests and family had gathered as the police had finished interviewing them throughout a tense, long and tiring day. It was getting to the end of the afternoon, and still they had not quite finished. He put his hands behind his neck and pressed to relieve the tightness. He was a tall man, strongly built, a slight plumpness developing as he came into his mid-fifties, his pepper and salt hair thinning, his face dominated by bushy eyebrows above dark eyes. He wore a tweed suit over a check shirt and knitted tie. Even in these circumstances he carried an air of prosperity, confidence and power.

Davis Mulholland joined him at the window and stood with his back to it. The American wore a lightweight grey suit with a pink shirt and no tie. He was as tanned as a Miami-dweller should be despite his three months in England. A neatly made and fit man of average height, a little more than ten years younger than his host, the flavour of prosperity and power in his manner and style was sharper and more vibrant, the messages it transmitted as solidly based and clear as Sir Walter's, but differently encoded.

'I never get tired of admiring this room, Walter,' he said, 'the whole house, in fact.'

Sir Walter turned and surveyed the room. It was impressive. The walls were hung with original oil paintings which gave the room a textured, firm feel. Large enough to take two sofas and two groups of armchairs and still provide a spacious airy sense of comfort, it was in some ways the heart of the family home. Lady Sarah was sitting with a cup of tea in hand, refusing the 'something stronger' that Peter Rankley was pressing upon her. Madeleine sat with her mother, trying to talk about other things. The other Walter Granthelm sat in the window seat with George Waterford. They were reading the Sunday papers, not talking. The George-Watkins family were occupying one of the groups of armchairs. They were talking quietly and calmly. Michael George-Watkins had once been in an American embassy surrounded for four days by angry students the local government would not disperse – not Tehran, another. He had experience which would ease his passage through the day.

'Brown's in with the man now, is she?' said Sir Walter.

'Should be done soon, I guess. We'll make our move when he's

21

through with her. Maybe we should take this moment for a word.'

The American took Sir Walter gently by the elbow and they walked down to the far end of the room. Rankley saw and came over to join them. He was a large man of thirty-three who some years before had played second-row forward for a leading rugby club. His playing weight had been sixteen stone. Unable to make it to the very top, he had given up the game entirely five years before. Though he still looked impressively strong, he had since added twenty pounds of flab to his weight.

'I just wanted to say,' Mulholland began, 'that I think we're looking good.'

'Glad to hear it,' said Sir Walter.

'They're buying what we have to sell so I see no problems.'

'I'm more interested in being sure about the other transaction,' put in Rankley.

'Listen,' said Mulholland, 'if it's clear over here, it's OK everywhere else. You've put up the initial investment we needed from you, and the Bahamas handling point is all covered. Everything which needed buying is bought. We have a secure source of supply – I told you, Peter, about my discussion with Lima. They got a glut and it's a buyer's market at that level. We're gonna do better than our projections tell us. You've brought the distribution system under your control now, and there's a financial exit route which satisfies us perfectly. There was just the one area my people were worried about and, like I say, we're looking good there too.'

'What do you say, Sir Walter?' said Rankley. 'I'm only the middle-man in this.'

'What have I ever said?' replied Sir Walter. 'You know my views.'

'Hey, let's not go over all that again, OK?' said Mulholland. 'It's a necessary part of business. All I want to say is, we know where you stand now and the ship is looking pretty tight. It's taken a time to put this package together, granted, but we're all ready to go now.'

'You'll tell them tomorrow?' said Rankley.

'Sure,' said Mulholland, 'first thing. Hey, there's the lady.' He went to join his wife who had just entered the room. She was a few years younger than he, equally tanned, blonde and wearing a powder blue dress.

'Middle-man,' said Sir Walter to Rankley. 'You've got what you wanted, boy. Just be sure you can handle it.'

3

When Mrs Brown Mulholland left the library, Detective Inspector Andrew Brain called down a curse on the day, and a few minutes later added a blessing on Mrs Carrock as she brought him an unsolicited but deeply needed cup of fresh coffee. He smiled thanks at her and looked again at his notepad. The day's interviewing was completed. After the maid and butler he had moved on to Sir Walter and Lady Sarah, their two offspring, Walter and Madeleine, their two menfriends, George Waterford and Peter Rankley, the US diplomat Michael George-Watkins and his wife Hannah and son Carew, and lastly Davis Mulholland, another American, and his wife Brown. As he developed the timetable for the previous evening's dinner party, he had decided to leave several interviews to his detective sergeant: Mr Carrock, the gardener and chauffeur at Granthelm House who had not been present, and his wife who had left at midnight; six temporary staff hired in for the evening who had left at the same time; and three guests from the neighbourhood, Roland Briggs, his wife Susan and teenage daughter Belinda, who had all left shortly before one o'clock in the morning.

A little after that, Sir Water, Rankley, Mulholland and Homer had emerged from a long conversation in the main parlour. The three of that group who survived the night all averred that the conversation had been neither substantial nor private, and had ranged as such discussions do over wide ground from politics to sport. Sir Walter had been the first to leave it, coming out into the hall to say goodbye to the Briggses, but then returning. Some time after that, Homer had left the parlour and joined the rest of the party in the music room. Less than fifteen minutes later, the other three men had joined them. About then, Anna Dark had finished work and gone home. The five Americans – the George-Watkins family and the Mulhollands – had gone up to bed before 1.30, and at around the same time Robert Homer and Ellen Sheerley had gone out for a night stroll in the grounds. Nobody had seen them alive after that. Lady Sarah had gone to bed at around 2 a.m. just after Sir Walter had given Bolt the butler leave to go to his own sleep. Young Walter and George Waterford were the next to depart for bed, followed by Madeleine. It was then a little before 2.30. Sir Walter and Peter Rankley were alone for a final cigar and brandy and within thirty minutes they were both in bed too. Sir Walter had left the front door unlocked for Robert Homer and Ellen Sheerley. The small parlour had been left unlocked, as always, with the key on the inside; it had been used only briefly during the evening, and that was before the meal.

Thus the actors had severally quit the stage, leaving it bare for Sir Walter's niece and her boyfriend to return, enter the small parlour and lock the door. Then, presumably, one had killed the other and followed up by committing suicide.

There were some sticking points in this provisional story. All the timings matched for the period of the meal, through the point when the women left the men to cigars and liqueurs, until the men emerged, some to join the ladies and some to hive themselves off into a separate group. But then there were discrepancies in the estimates of how much time the four men spent in the main parlour. The three accounts Brain had from members of that group all understated the time compared to what most of the rest of the family, the other guests and Bolt recalled. Brain was inclined to trust the butler's account, since he was likely to have kept a close eye on the time throughout and was a thoroughly organised and efficient man in every respect. Besides, the others had been drinking heavily. On the other hand, it did not seem to matter very much.

Brain had also sorted out the relationships which knitted the group together. Rankley was Madeleine's lover, George Waterford was Walter's. Ellen Sheerley was the daughter of Lady Sarah's sister, Homer was her lover. Davis Mulholland and Sir Walter were doing business together – the latter's merchant bank providing finance for the former's venture in fruit importation. Michael George-Watkins was an acquaintance of Sir Walter's; he had not previously met Mulholland. Both Americans came with their families. The Briggs family had been invited largely so Belinda could provide teenage company for Carew George-Watkins.

The house-search had revealed one item of interest: a .32 revolver, well looked after, not fired since its last cleaning, loaded, and found in Robert Homer's suitcase. For the rest, apart

24

from a few magazines in George Waterford's possession of a kind not normally seen in Guildford and its vicinity, there was nothing either improper or unexpected.

The story line began to change when the scene of crime officers reported. They were troubled by some items missing from the small parlour: one pair of knickers, assuming Ellen Sheerley had been wearing them earlier in the evening; one pair of shoes (Brain had wondered about the stockings, but Anna Dark and two of the temporary staff had confirmed she had not been wearing them earlier); and one .22 calibre automatic shell. Brain shrugged at the news of the woman's clothing, but ordered another look for the second shell. When the scene of crime officers again reported no success, he joined them and spent twenty minutes suggesting the most unlikely places where it might have landed after ejecting from the gun. Patiently, they replied to each suggestion that they had already looked there. They were confident the shell was not in the room. Finally, Brain was too.

He had a man phone the hospital morgue. One possibility was that the shell had lodged in the clothing of one of the dead couple. It hadn't – so one of the shots had been fired somewhere else. Later, Dr Albert had phoned with a summary of the *post mortem* report. No surprises: each had died by .22 calibre bullet wound in the head. The shot which killed Ellen Sheerley was fired from a distance of about six inches, that which killed Robert Homer was a contact wound – the gun had been held against his forehead. The slugs had been sent off for a ballistics test. The pathologist had one more item of information: there was sperm in Ellen Sheerley's vagina, and also in small amounts on Robert Homer's penis – 'Consistent with sexual intercourse shortly before death,' as Dr Albert put it with, Brain uncharitably suspected, a certain amount of relish. He also confirmed finding traces of heroin in the woman's blood.

The phone call from Dr Albert had done nothing to relieve Brain's deepening gloom. It was bad enough to be called out on an off-duty Sunday to head an investigation, worse that it should be a double death, and worse again that it should involve Sir Walter Granthelm. The Chief Constable's morning advice had not been required for Brain to know that the case would be difficult. Even without the factor of Sir Walter, it had quickly begun to develop all the wrong signs. By late afternoon, the story appeared to be that a man and a woman had walked out into the grounds where they had sexual intercourse. He then killed her, carried her corpse into the house, locked himself with her in a room and committed suicide. He had apparently brought two guns with him for a country weekend, already intending murder and suicide, it would seem.

Even if the story made sense – and with a bit of effort that was not impossible – it wasn't neat. Brain sighed and left the library. He found Sir Walter looking grim in the main parlour and told him he would be back in the morning to search the grounds. Then he walked out to his car and, with a final look at the dirty cherub, left Granthelm House.

CHAPTER 3

1

Detective Inspector James Stevens was wearing a dark blue three-piece suit with a faint stripe, a pale blue shirt with a red and blue striped tie and well polished black shoes. He was, as ever, the picture of elegance, despite his stocky build. He had his hair cut and styled each week and smoked French cigarettes.

'You steaming great git,' he shouted. 'You idiot, you crud-head. Where the fuck did you think you were?' He was standing behind his desk, hands on hips, his face tight with fury and frustration, confronting Detective Sergeant Graves whose expression of pained self-righteousness marked his discomfort and displeasure at the abuse.

'You were in sodding Brixton, you clod, Brixton – what's that mean to you?'

'He was the one we wanted,' said Graves.

'He's nineteen and black,' roared Stevens, 'and you chased him half a mile down the fucking High Street. Moron.'

'He's coughed, guv,' said Graves, 'he's wearing it.'

Stevens sat down abruptly and waved at Graves to do likewise. The Detective Sergeant complied, settling his bulk unhappily on to the edge of the chair. He was six feet two and over fifteen stone, wearing a check shirt, knitted tie and dark grey trousers.

'That is not the point,' said Stevens more quietly.

'No,' chimed in Detective Inspector Queen from his desk on the other side of the room. 'The point, Graves, m'lad, is that these days you treat coons gently, especially in Coontown.'

'You keep out of it,' snapped Stevens.

'We've been looking for him,' said Graves, 'and I found him.'

'And instead of tailing him and seeing if you couldn't lift him quietly, you charged in and took him then and there. Where have you been for the last, what, six years?'

'I've been—'

'Have you read any newspapers? Have you watched the telly? I don't ask if you've read the reports and memos they send us – it's too much to expect that – but don't you occasionally have your eyes open?'

'Yes,' said Graves, getting angry at last, 'open enough to spot a

27

nasty little bastard we've been looking for and nab him.'

'But not open enough to see what part of town you're in?'

'Oh, he knew he was in Coontown, didn't you, Gravesy?' said Queen. 'Can't mistake the clothes they wear, for one thing. Snappy dressers, spades.'

'I've told you,' said Stevens sharply. 'Look, Graves, do you know how close you were to starting another sodding riot?'

Graves was silent.

'How many did you pick up in the end?' asked Stevens, as if he did not know. He cut Graves off again as the sergeant started to reply. 'Four, I believe. The one you wanted, and three who tried to fight it out with you, right?'

'They was obstructing,' said Graves.

'Smart bit of work, I'd say,' said Queen.

This time Stevens ignored his colleague. 'You were lucky there were only three of them and not three hundred. You chased him right down the High Street in full view of a thousand Sunday shoppers shouting, "Stop, police," you cretin. Why didn't you hand out printed invitations to a riot while you were about it, and a few petrol bombs to help things along, eh? Can you really not see that what you did was pretty bloody stupid?'

'Look,' said Graves, 'the idea is that we nab them, charge them, try them, get the conviction and put 'em away. That way, they get scared out of doing it again. If you're saying we've got to be too frightened to pick them up in the first place . . .'

'Let's not talk penal theory,' said Stevens. 'You had an alternative.'

'That's right,' said Queen, 'let my people go.'

'The alternative,' said Stevens, his voice rising as he glowered at Queen, 'was to pick him up quietly a little while later. The alternative was to think before you got on your size thirteen tippy-toes for a quick sprint through the crowds.'

'Look, guv,' said Graves, 'it didn't happen, right? There wasn't a riot. There was a collar and we got the rat we wanted, and that's all.'

'Three kids who didn't even know him – not mates, just bystanders—'

'And, being black, innocent bystanders at that,' said Queen.

'—butted in because they saw a white copper nicking a brother. One of 'em clobbered you, lucky there wasn't something lying around he could've really hurt you with. Though I don't know, lucky for you, maybe, but what about the rest of us?'

'Now look,' said Graves, with real pain at Stevens' goading, 'if that's the line you're going to take . . .'

'If the three of them were ready to have a go at you, what's to say another dozen might not have joined in, eh?'

'But they didn't,' objected Graves plaintively.

'But they could've,' said Stevens, mimicking Graves' tone. 'And you really don't see, do you? Look, I'll make it easy for you. If you ever do something like that again, it goes in your report and stays there, joining you on your way to Nether Wallop, all right? Now go away.'

Graves sat for a moment, then blew out a breath and stood up. He was red-faced from anger and hurt. 'Working in this fucking place,' he said bitterly. 'Sometimes I don't know, I just do not know.' He walked out, and the door would have slammed behind him except that the man who entered at the same moment caught the door as it swung.

Stevens shook his head, exhaled with emphasis and lit a cigarette.

'Well,' said the newcomer, 'what a pleasant way to start a Monday. All right,' he added, speaking to Queen, 'I'll see you first.'

Queen nodded and rose. 'Don't take it so to heart, Jimmy, dear boy,' he said. 'It's only human frailty. We can't all dress as well as you do.'

Stevens looked Queen up and down, a burly man, fourteen stone and five foot ten, wearing a charcoal grey suit that hung badly and shone at the seat, knees, elbows and sleeve cuffs, brown suede shoes, a white shirt and characterless tie, with mousy-brown hair that hung over his collar and ears and a bushy, drooping moustache. He looked at the newcomer – his immediate boss, DCI Fathers, four inches taller than Queen and a stone lighter, optimistically wearing a summer-weight, light grey suit with a subdued speckle in it, dark grey shoes, a tie quietly patterned in shades of brown over a yellow shirt, and with dark, well-brushed hair.

'Some of us can,' said Stevens gently, 'some of us can't. Some charge in with their eyes shut, and others ought to know when not to open their mouths.'

'Fair enough,' said Queen. 'Pansy it out if you have to, but it's not how I work.'

29

'Don't we know it,' said Stevens.

'And you wouldn't sit quietly by if I rubbished Pardoner like you did Graves,' Queen added.

Before Stevens could rise to this accurate jab, Fathers stepped in. 'Leave it out,' he said, 'both of you. You don't have anything to be proud of either, Queenie. You'd not like him cheering Pardoner on from the sidelines while you had a go at him, let alone what you actually said.'

Queen was silent; he had not realised how long Fathers had been standing outside the open door listening.

2

After fifteen minutes with Queen going over his investigation into a London gang running a protection racket and various other activities, Fathers called Stevens in. They spent twenty minutes discussing a rash of lorry hijackings and a gang which specialised in kidnapping – a consortium, Stevens called it. 'Very businesslike,' he said. 'Money from the first snatch financing the second, which they set up while the first is still running. A rolling programme with regular employment for the workers and lots of cut-outs between them and the board of directors. Two jobs down to them already this year.'

'Any word on who's boss?'

'Bosses,' corrected Stevens. 'No names, but the whisper is there's a group of them – three or four – who identify the target, set the plan, provide a safe place to hold the victim, and employ the foot-sloggers.'

'Any names there?'

'Working on it. Some hints. Making progress, but I'd rather not commit myself just now.'

'How strong is it, what you've got?'

Stevens fluttered a hand at Fathers. 'Putting it in police jargon, I'd say it's on the iffy side of dodgy.'

'OK. Keep me posted. Don't blow it by closing in too fast.'

'Course not.'

'And, James, in a bit, make your peace with Graves, all right? He was dumb, but how far you went – that was uncalled for. You owe him an apology, especially since you left the door open and let everybody know about it.'

Stevens looked at Fathers for a long moment. 'Yeah, I suppose so,' he said eventually, 'I'll smooth him over later, when we've both cooled down.'

'And don't blow your top again like that.'

'All right, 'nuff said.'

'Not till this afternoon, at least. Promise?'

When Stevens had gone Fathers settled to his eternally overgrown paperwork. He was almost an hour into it when the phone rang and summoned him to Chief Superintendent Bastin's office.

George Bastin was the senior officer in Scotland Yard's Serious Crimes Squad. He was an overweight six-footer nearing retirement age, and because of it more than ever inclined to take things easy. He kept the squad ticking over, rarely leaving his office in working hours except for meetings, never leading investigations himself, relying heavily on his two DCIs – Fathers and Cadwallader – to handle the real work. Whenever Fathers saw his boss, half his mind ruminated about age and change. About his own age – nearing forty, whatever that landmark meant – and about the change that would come when Bastin retired. Other changes were afoot too: Stevens, as competent a detective as Fathers had ever worked with, was looking for promotion to detective chief inspector, and would undoubtedly get it. At the same time, his best skipper, Pardoner, the same age as Stevens, was about to rise to DI. And below him, Yarrow – still 'callow Yarrow' in Fathers' mind, but effective for all that – had just put in for promotion to detective sergeant which he too would certainly get. If Fathers could keep Pardoner on his strength, the exchange for Stevens would not be too bad, and if Yarrow moved up to replace Pardoner, that would be reasonable enough. But so much change at once would be troublesome, especially since it meant several officers new at their rank settling in at the same time, which might encourage higher authority to intervene and give Fathers a DI or a DS who was more experienced – but heaven knew how good they would be. And who would replace Bastin?

Age and change, thought Fathers as he entered Bastin's office and compared his boss's current paunch to the tough, muscular look he had had only three or four years before – it comes to us all. Or would it be staved off by the raw diet his wife Sarah had put them on? Soon after Christmas she had decided that he was of an age when he finally had to start watching his weight and figure. Her point was cruelly emphasised by prodding his undeniably expanding waistline. Protests that the after-effects of Christmas gluttony would soon disappear as they always had were brushed aside. 'We are not going to be middle-aged slobs,' she declared as she took diet books out of the library, and determinedly increased the fibre and cut the cholesterol in their daily diet.

Near the end of February she announced that cooking food removed its goodness and did terrible damage to the body. 'Ye gods,' mumbled an anxious Fathers as she read out from one of her books how much dietary fibre was destroyed by cooking and what awful things happened to the amino acids when polyunsaturated fats were heated. Cooked breakfasts were out and salad lunches in as Sarah strove towards a target of 75 per cent of their food intake being uncooked and unprocessed – 'Only seventy-five per cent,' she said, 'there's no point in being extreme about it.' So each day, with his belly rumblingly full of fresh fruit, nuts, seeds, muesli and live yoghourt ('Pasteurisation is a mixed blessing,' was Sarah's curt response to his protest when even milk was banished), Fathers left home with a plastic box full of raw vegetables and salad.

The worst thing was that it worked. Fathers lost weight and felt sharper and more energetic than he had for years. But his prejudices were strong: he did not stop moaning and regularly dumped his lunch in the waste bin.

'Harry, how are you, sit down,' said Bastin. 'An odd one for you.'

'Oh,' said Fathers guardedly.

'Right up your street. Double killing, one of them faked as a suicide.'

'This is Serious Crimes,' said Fathers, 'not Murder.'

'Murder's a bit busy just now,' said Bastin apologetically. Fathers nodded, not wanting to think about the series of sexual attacks and mutilations which were absorbing the Murder Squad's full complement. 'Anyway, it was done in a room that was left locked on the inside, and I rather thought you'd be interested.'

'No.'

'Well, sorry, because it's on your plate. Here.'

Fathers flicked open the file Bastin handed him and looked briefly at its contents. He snapped the file shut. 'I saw this in the paper,' he said, 'but it said murder and suicide. Guildford plods've changed their mind, have they?'

'The Godalming lab changed it for them with the ballistics report. How're you fixed? Badly, I know – but how badly?'

'Queen and Stevens are both fully booked. What about Pot-walloper?' This was one of DCI Cadwallader's nick-names, bestowed on him by Fathers. The other nickname was Codswallop.

'Out of the question,' said Bastin. 'One DI and a couple of skippers out with that flu that's been doing the rounds.'

'I suppose I can give it today if I have to.'

'I rather think so – and more than today. You know of Sir Walter Granthelm, do you?'

'Heard of him, of course.'

'Of course. Chairman of one of the six largest merchant banks in London, member of umpteen other company boards, pillar of the City establishment, knighted by Mrs Thatcher – well, not actually by her, but you know what I mean. An old family, but very much today's man. There was something on him in a Sunday glossy a few weeks back – mostly about how he's Thatcher's type of businessman.'

'Huh.'

'Well, the locked room looks interesting.'

Fathers shrugged.

'DI Brain at Guildford is the man,' said Bastin. 'He wants help and you've been nominated.'

'What do you mean, help?'

'The murders happened on Saturday night, Sunday morning in a house full of guests, all of whom have now come back to London. He needs the Met's help to get round them and take new statements. When he took statements yesterday it looked like murder plus suicide. Now he knows different and it needs going over again.'

'Fair enough, but he knows the rules as well as anybody. Is it my case or what?'

'There's no rule says provincial forces have to give . . .'

'My rule does, and everybody else's. Is he handing it over or not?'

'You know that's why the provincials don't like the Met, don't you?'

'If he wants the Met's help, he can have it. All he has to do is

33

bell the right manors and supply a list of names and questions. They'll send a bod round soon enough. Or he can give it to the Yard – in this case, me – and I'll take it on. You know that.'

'I suppose so, Harry.'

'Or do you want us to spend our time doing everybody else's routine?'

'All right, all right.'

'I'll talk to him then, shall I?'

'Nicely if you can manage it.'

Back in his office, Fathers reread the notes on the case and phoned Guildford CID. DI Brain seemed to be in a state of deep gloom as they discussed the outline of the investigation, lightened only when he said there had been no sightseers so far.

'Much press?' asked Fathers.

'Some, but when you reckon it's a millionaire's niece, not a lot.'

'I'll come down this morning to have a look at Granthelm House and go back over the interviews you did.'

'I thought you'd be saying that.'

'It's a question, that if all the guests who were staying there live in London, then it doesn't make sense to run it from out of town.'

'No, and we couldn't run you from here, though you could run us from there any old time.'

'If you want a DC to go round a few addresses and ask questions by rote, you can have one. But not from me. For that, you can have the local manors. If you want an investigation, that's different.'

'I know, I know. I don't really mind.'

'So we'll work together then?'

'Yes, together, the Yard version of together,' said Brain. He put the phone down and, to his wall, said, 'Arrogant bastard – and welcome to it.'

Fathers went out into the squad's general office. He stopped at Yarrow's desk. The Detective Constable was talking on the phone and reading a report at the same time. 'Yeah, yeah,' he said impatiently. 'But no promises. Nine o'clock . . . Yes, I know it. See you then.' He put the phone down and snorted derisively.

'Who was that?' said Fathers.

'A small-time nobody, guv, who wants to be a big-time informer, a little git who's lived eye-deep in manure all his life and not grown anything but warts. Do you want me?'

'Yes, come along.' Fathers turned to where Pardoner sat.

'Skip, you too, please.'

In his office, Fathers handed the file on the Granthelm House deaths to Pardoner and sat with his feet on his desk as the Detective Sergeant read it and passed it to Yarrow. Pardoner was a capable detective, easily worth his imminent promotion, conscientiously strong on detail, with the important ability of working rather than jumping to his conclusions. His meticulous work was counterpointed by a flippant manner, something he had picked up from Stevens with whom, like Fathers, he had in common a university degree and a middle-class background. He was thirty-six, six feet tall, just over twelve stone in weight, dark haired, a neat and conservative dresser – today, a grey jacket, brown trousers and shoes, white shirt and a plain brown tie.

Yarrow was a different sort. Like Queen and Graves, he was from a working-class background. He had left comprehensive school with five O-levels, the minimum required for entry into the police force. Five feet nine inches tall, lightly built, with untidy blond hair and a pale complexion, he was wearing a grey leather jacket, shirt and trousers in almost matching shades of plum, a grey tie and grey shoes. His most notable features were his light blue eyes whose gaze, except when he was reading or writing, seemed never to rest on any object or person for more than the merest moment. The result was a shifty appearance, emphasised by his habit of looking sidelong at such people as senior police officers and suspects. He was a great deal more confident of himself than his eyes suggested, well able to hold his own at case meetings, and, in marked contrast to his early days on the squad, relaxed enough even with Fathers to crack jokes. As a detective he was well organised and determined, equipped with ambitious plans for his career and an earnest desire to please his superiors. His greatest quality was an excellent memory. Whether his recall was total, Fathers did not know, but it was certainly extraordinary, as he set out to prove immediately he had finished reading the notes.

'I read something about this geezer,' he declared. 'Not the usual guff about the big city gent. There was a robbery at this place last summer, a load of antique silver – valued at over sixty grand, I think.'

'Ever recovered?' said Fathers.

'Not that I remember. Might've been, but I didn't see anything about it.'

35

'Where did you read it?'

'Report that was circulated.'

Fathers nodded. As he had noticed before, the Detective Constable did actually read routine reports with close attention. It was unusual, and on several occasions had been extremely useful. He made a mental note to be sure it was in his recommendation for Yarrow's promotion.

'OK,' he said, 'so what do you make of it?' He gestured at the file in Yarrow's hands as he spoke, looking at Pardoner.

'Very interesting,' said Pardoner in a stage-German accent. 'Are they sure about the ballistics report?' he asked, switching back to his normal voice.

'So it seems. Brain told me that when he asked them to run the tests again, they said they'd already done them twice. And they're certain the slugs which killed the two were fired from different guns. Both .22 calibre, but different guns.'

'Humph,' said Pardoner. 'So it's not from Homer's other gun. And the one they've got is the one which killed her, but the shell they've got fits the slug in his head.' It was in the notes he had just read, but he always felt safer about a fact if it was repeated.

'Correct. So we want the extra gun and the shell. We also want to know about other keys to the room, and we want the lady's shoes and underwear. Anything else?'

'Motive.'

'Sex looks best. Or jealousy, maybe. The heroin might be an angle. Lots of background work on this one.'

'Well, well,' said Yarrow, 'what goings-on, what would Mr 'Udson say?'

'The better sort have their own ways,' replied Pardoner in a mild Scottish accent, 'and it's not for the likes of you to question them. Now then, cut along, the silver needs polishing.'

'Nah,' said Yarrow, 'it's been nicked.'

'What've you got on your plate?' asked Fathers.

'On my silver plate,' replied Pardoner in his normal voice, 'are Mr Stevens' kidnappings and that little matter of the Islington bank job.'

'Where are you with it?'

'The other side of nowhere.'

'Yarrow?'

Yarrow looked more uncomfortable and shifty than ever as he replied, 'I was working with DS Graves on that Brixton lot, but, er, well, he's sort of wrapped that up now, hasn't he? I don't know if he'll want a hand in the follow-up, he hasn't said, probably not recovered yet, er, you know.' He finished lamely, his eyes flicking from Fathers' face to the overhead light.

'Anything else?'

'Bits and pieces, not a lot, everything else was put on one side last week, if you remember. I was going to pick them up again, but if you want me on this I can leave 'em where they are.'

'Your bits and pieces,' said Fathers, 'mainly being the antiques you were helping DS Gordon on?'

'Yeah.'

'OK. I'll have a word with her about it. I don't want to let it go, or Arts and Antiques'll nick it back from us. Rustle up a car – one with a screamer so we can get through the crowds. We're going in ten minutes. Skipper, clear it with DI Stevens yourself, will you? He'll have to make do without you for a bit.'

CHAPTER 4

1

Yarrow used the siren freely and ebulliently to clear the South London traffic out of their way – it was something he still regarded as a treat – and the trip to Guildford took not much over an hour. They were in time to have a quick canteen lunch with Brain and his skipper, DS Cotton. The Guildford men, Pardoner and Yarrow all had sandwiches. Fathers had dutifully brought his salad and raw vegetable lunch with him and tucked in. There was an edge to the conversation, which Yarrow diagnosed as the resentment of a provincial detective at having to hand the case over to a Yard man. Fathers tried to make small talk to win Brain over, but it was not something Yarrow had ever seen his boss be particularly good at with strangers. The local man was clearly determined to be gloomy and touchy, and eventually Fathers let him be and switched the talk to the investigation. Brain had been back to Granthelm House that morning and warned Sir Walter to expect another visit, this time from Scotland Yard as well, explaining that the case had become more complicated when the ballistics test showed that the fatal shots were fired from two guns, only one of which had been found.

'How'd he respond?' asked Fathers.

'Interesting that,' said Brain, pausing to sip a cup of the canteen coffee which, to Yarrow's mind, was even worse than he was used to at the Yard. 'He looked really shocked. I mean, a man like Sir Walter, usually in charge of himself and everything and everyone around him – he went white and started to shake. Literally. Can't mean guilt, 'cause if he'd done it he'd know two guns'd been used and his reaction'd be rehearsed. Interesting. After all, they're still dead. Surprising if it's much worse to think that somebody's been murdered rather than committed suicide.'

'Mm. Though it means – well, it could mean – that one of his guests or staff is the killer.'

Brain considered Fathers' suggestion. 'True enough. But, you know, his reaction was pretty much instant. That's a thought would occur to you or me straightaway, but not necessarily to a civilian. Not absolutely at the moment he heard it.'

Fathers pouted with an expression midway between scepticism

and interest. 'Before we go,' he said, 'tell me about this silver robbery. Yarrow here recalled it from some report he'd seen. What happened?'

'Sixty-nine thousand pounds worth of antiques in solid silver. A family collection, begun by Sir Walter's father. Candlesticks, cutlery, tableware, some jewellery – but all of it unadorned silver, none of your encrusted gems and suchlike. Apparently, one of the features of the collection was exactly that – pure silver and nothing but, all very finely worked. Lifted one night last July, and whoever did it got in and out as clean as a whisper. Circumvented the alarm system, avoided the dogs . . .'

'Dogs?' said Fathers.

'Dogs,' repeated Brain. 'Three of them. Horrid great brutes they set free to roam the grounds at night. The gardener looks after them and keeps them at his cottage up the hill from the house. They'd been let out that night as usual but they must've been somewhere else.'

'House empty, was it?' asked Pardoner.

'Just the butler, up in his room in the attic. The family were away in London – usually are during the week – and the butler's the only staff who lives in the house itself. A window round the back was the way in and out. They cut the glass on the display cases which were in the hall and a couple of other rooms and that was that.'

'They?' said Fathers.

'Probably more than one, we thought, but it's not much more than a guess. Anyway, Sir W kicked up a terrible stink in the local papers. We had MPs and local councillors phoning up all over the place to find out how come we couldn't do anything about it. Actually, all that fuss got in our way and made the job a while lot harder, did he but know it. Then he got his insurance money and that was the end. We did all we could, but you know how it goes.' Fathers clucked sympathetically.

'Even had it on the sodding telly. Thought it could've been the butler and we kept a permanent tail on him for weeks, but there was no sign of anything. Word out all over the place, of course, but nothing's turned up. So we had to let it go in the end. Case officially still open, but actually closed. Nothing to do with this business, except that every time I look at Sir W I can hear him thinking nasty thoughts about it – and us.'

Brain and Cotton led the way in one car, the Scotland Yard men following, out into the country near Guildford, through small villages, up a narrow winding road through the woods, until they turned off and descended a steep lane. 'The vultures are here, then,' commented Fathers as they entered the lane, turning to look at the half dozen cars parked on the road. Several men were standing around chatting, and a couple ran to follow the cars as they entered the grounds of Granthelm House, but they were waved back by two uniformed constables stationed there for that purpose.

The lane went down the hill for almost a hundred yards, past three cottages and what looked like converted stables, before it flattened out into a shortish tree-lined avenue from which they emerged into the forecourt of Granthelm House. As Yarrow paused to decide where to park, Fathers said, 'Well, what do you think?'

Yarrow grunted noncommittally. Pardoner wiped the back of his hand across his nose and mouth and gave an exaggerated sniff. 'I fink it's the butler what done it,' he declared.

'Always best not to keep an open mind,' agreed Fathers, 'and it's so hard to find good help these days. Over there, Yarrer, and quick about it.'

As Yarrow parked the car, he asked, 'What shall I do then? Whip the butler round the back and do 'im over till he coughs while you sweet talk the upper crust?'

'I've got the thumbscrews here somewhere, I'm sure I have,' murmured Pardoner.

'We'll go through the introductions,' said Fathers, 'and then the skipper can hunt the thimble with the locals while I chat to the nobs and you take notes.'

The other two detectives grunted assent. As they got out of the car, Yarrow turned to Fathers and said, 'There is one point, sir, to which I wish to draw your attention.'

Fathers looked at Yarrow with amusement. Nearly three years in the company of Stevens and Pardoner had given the young man a taste for expressing himself strangely from time to time. 'Go on. To what do you wish to draw my attention?'

'To the curious incident of the dog in the night-time.'

'The dog did nothing in the night-time,' said Pardoner.

Yarrow clapped his hands together in delight. 'That was the curious incident,' he said grinning.

Brain caught the exchange as he joined Fathers and Pardoner. 'What was that?' he asked. DS Cotton stood off a respectful distance.

Fathers said nothing. Pardoner frowned: 'Yeah, come on, Elly,' he said, 'let us in on the secret.'

'It's Silver Blaze,' said Yarrow.

'Ah,' said Fathers.

'Eh?' said Brain.

'Silver Blaze,' repeated Pardoner.

'Oh,' said Brain.

'I think it's a Sherlock Holmes story,' said Pardoner.

'Right, skip,' said Yarrow, 'and you fed me the line something beautful. You were word-perfect.'

'It's his dirty secret,' explained Pardoner. 'In his spare time he reads detective stories. Trying to learn the trade, I think.'

'Nevertheless,' said Fathers to Brain, 'it is a point. Three horrid dogs, you said?'

'Oh. Yes, that's right,' said Brain. 'Cotton: go find Carrock.'

Cotton nodded. 'I'll ask his wife where to find him,' he said.

'Right then,' said Fathers, 'let's go and meet the other half. Try not to spit on the floor, OK?'

'Worry not,' said Pardoner, 'I brought the portable spittoon.'

'Just one thing,' said Brain. 'The hacks'll want a word.'

'Who is there?' asked Fathers.

'A few nationals, couple of locals, the PA.'

'Well, it's not too many. Bring 'em down and we'll have a quick word once we've introduced ourselves. See if we can't persuade them to go and get a coffee, and I'll offer them another word at your nick once we're through here.'

Brain nodded, went back to his car and had a word with his driver. Then he turned to the constable at the door. 'All right, son, we're ready now.'

The constable knocked twice and the door was immediately opened by a small, neat man in his forties. The detectives walked in.

'This is Mr Bolt,' said Cotton. 'Where's Mrs Carrock?'

'In the kitchen. Do you know your way there?' Cotton nodded and crossed the hall to a door which he opened and disappeared through.

'If you'll wait a moment,' continued the butler, 'I shall announce you.' His quiet voice and measured politeness instilled a silence on the policemen as he led them through one of two doors on the left of the hall.

The front hall of Granthelm House was large and airy, with a window on each side of the front door. There were six other doors off the hall, two each to the right and left and two at the back, one on each side of the sweep of the wide stairs.

'That's the small parlour, as they call it,' said Brain, indicating one of the doors to the right, 'where the bodies were found. The other door's for the music room, and you go through it for the library which runs the full depth of the house on that side. On this side, the main parlour, and there, where Bolt went, the dining room. The door my skipper went through leads down to a smaller dining room they use for breakfast when they don't have guests and to the kitchen, and that door on the right is the bog.'

The others nodded, looking round the hall at each door in turn, trying to take in something of the atmosphere of the house. Yarrow was almost audibly sniffing the air. The walls of the hall had oak panelling up to waist-height, and then a striped wallpaper above that. The ceiling was in white, with an ornate rose round the light fitting and delicate plaster work above each door. In the corner beyond the music room door – the far right corner as they looked at it – there was a niche in the wall where the telephone stood.

'By the way,' said Brain, 'it's pronounced Grant'm, not Grant*helm*. Just so's you don't do something vulgar like saying it the way it's spelled.'

'Thanks.'

'Reckon we're lucky it's not pronounced Mangrove Yacht-Warbler,' said Pardoner.

'They are ready to receive you,' said Bolt, re-emerging silently from the dining room.

'That's very decent of them,' muttered Fathers. Brain led the way in.

The dining room was very large. Yarrow guessed it must be at least forty feet by twenty. There was a large, oblong table in the middle with more chairs round it than he cared to count. Lunch had recently been eaten there. The remains of dessert and a half-empty wine bottle had not yet been removed, but the five people sitting at the far end of the table had been served with coffee. There were three men and two women. They watched the detectives enter but made neither sign of greeting nor expression of interest. Fathers stopped and looked at the group for a while. One of the men – large and formerly athletic, looking around thirty years old at Yarrow's guess – drank some coffee, then lit a cigar he had been toying with. Yarrow transferred his gaze to the young woman who sat next to the big cigar-smoker. She was blonde, and very good-looking. Her hair was cut fashionably and she was wearing light make-up. The shirt that was all Yarrow could see of her clothes was grey and buttoned to the throat. She returned his look and he flicked his eyes away to the man at the head of the table. He was in his fifties with a strong, lined face, pepper and salt hair, wearing a tweed jacket, white shirt and a striped tie. The young woman was on his left; on his right was an older woman, possibly in her late forties, thought Yarrow, slim and neat-looking, blonde and wearing a grey cardigan over a white blouse. On her right was a man in his twenties, wearing a yellow shirt under a green sweatshirt. One of the younger men, thought Yarrow, is Walter the son; the older man is Sir Walter; the women are Lady Sarah and her daughter Madeleine. His glance passed over them quickly and flickered back to the cigar-smoker who was looking back at him levelly, with an air which would have been defiant if it had less confidence, or which might have been contemptuous if it did not suggest its possessor had concerns which far outreached these interlopers.

And you've achieved that look and those jowls when you're no more than thirty or so, thought Yarrow: what a prat you must be.

Brain broke the silence by introducing Fathers to the group at the table and then naming each of them. The cigar-smoker was Peter Rankley.

'With the change in the nature of this case,' said Fathers, 'and because some of the people we must re-interview are now back in London, the investigation has passed into my hands. Detective Inspector Brain will continue on the case. With me are Detective Sergeant Pardoner and Detective Constable Yarrow. I shall be asking each of you to answer some questions in a while. I understand Mr Brain used the library for interviews. Would it be agreeable to repeat that today, Sir Walter?' He received a grunt of assent. 'Thank you. We'll call you as we want you, and I shan't keep any of you for very long. Please stay close at hand.'

With that he turned and left the room, the other detectives in his train, Yarrow closing the door behind him.

'Right,' said Fathers when they were in the hall. 'Let's have a look at the small parlour first, then the fourth estate, then the gentry.'

3

'Well,' said Sir Walter weightily when the five were alone.

'He was very brusque, wasn't he?' said Lady Sarah.

'Very tough,' agreed Rankley.

'Very manly,' said Walter, 'very much the policeman.'

'So we have to go through it all again,' sighed Lady Sarah. 'How extremely damn tiresome.'

'The names,' said Madeleine more lightly, 'I can't get over the names. So appropriate, they're really aesthetic. First Brain, now Fathers: comfort and authority combined, don't you think?'

'No comfort in that one,' replied Walter, 'but mucho authoritario, I'll grant you.'

'And Pardoner,' she continued, 'so Christian and forgiving.'

'You'll need that, will you?' asked Walter.

'On the other hand, Yarrow: appropriately proletarian to judge by the look of him.'

'Why proletarian?' asked her mother.

'Wasn't the great hunger march in the nineteen-thirties from Yarrow?'

'Jarrow, I think,' said Rankley.

'Not Barrow?' offered Walter.

'Whatever,' said Madeleine, 'but let's not labour the point.'

Her father slapped both hands on the table, grunted angrily and rose. He looked at his family and Rankley, then went and stood, hands in hip pockets, gazing through the window over his lawns to the downland across the valley.

'It may not be in his name,' said Rankley, 'but he had a slippery look to him – slug-like, I'd say.'

'Not all oicks are slugs,' said Madeleine.

'He may not even be an oick,' suggested Walter, 'not in the full and true meaning of the word.'

'Certainly slippery,' replied Rankley. 'Did you see his eyes? Never stopped moving.'

'Oh yes they did,' commented Madeleine coolly. 'When they

got to me they stayed still for quite a while.'

Rankley frowned. He did not like Madeleine's teasing, and he did not like Detective Constable Jarrow either, not one bit.

4

Fathers began with Anna Dark, the maid. She was nineteen and wore a plain white shirt, black trousers, sensible flat shoes. They were sitting at a large table by the window at the garden end of the library. Fathers sat with his back to the window, Anna opposite him, Yarrow at the end of the table to his boss's right with a large pad in front of him and a pen poised and ready.

Fathers began by tapping a couple of sheets of paper in front of him and explaining that they constituted the formal statement drawn up by the Guildford CID following her interview with DI Brain the day before. He intended to go through it with her, and if it represented fairly and accurately what she had to say, and after she had changed anything she wanted, she would be asked to sign it.

Anna Dark nodded. She was small and pretty and looked younger than nineteen but was self-composed if rather drawn. Her statement was concise. Apart from her personal details, it fell into two parts: the events of the Saturday evening dinner party up to soon after one o'clock in the morning when she had been given leave to go home by Bolt; and her discovery of the two bodies in the small parlour early on Sunday morning. Fathers slowly read out the first half of the statement, pausing at the end of each sentence with a quizzical look over his reading glasses to allow Anna to query or approve it. There were no queries. For the second part, he changed his approach, asking her to describe again how she found the small parlour door locked and what happened then. She described how Mr Bolt gave her the key on the bunch from the corner cupboard in the kitchen, how she went back to the room, opened it, went in, saw the bodies, saw the hole in Mr Homer's forehead and the blood on Miss Sheerley's hair.

'Then I ran back to the kitchen,' she said, 'and told Mr Bolt and he went to look.'

'Did you actually see where he went? Did you go with him?'

'No, I stayed in the kitchen. I was shaking all over and Mrs Carrock made me sit down. He said something like, "Let me see," so I suppose he went to the small parlour first, before he went to get Sir Walter.'

'All right. Now, have you looked into the small parlour since then?'

'No.'

'Let's go back a little, then, to the point when you asked Mr Bolt for the key. He got it from a corner cupboard, you said.'

'Yes, one of those triangular ones fitted into a corner, you know. He unlocked it and took out the bunch which has the small parlour key on it.'

'So it's kept locked?'

'Yes, all the time.'

'Where did he get the key to unlock it?'

'It was in his pocket.'

'Is that the only key?'

'Well, Jean has one, Mrs Carrock, and I suppose Sir Walter does, I don't know.'

'Fine. Now, when you went into the small parlour, while you were there or as you left the room, did you notice the key which had been in the door?'

'Um, no. I didn't look. I didn't think to.'

'It was just to one side of the doorway, between the skirting board and the carpet.'

'No, I didn't see it.'

'All right. Yarrow?'

Through all this Yarrow had been scribbling furiously. Now he looked up. 'Let me read some additional sentences for your statement, Miss Dark,' he said, 'and if they're all right we can add them to what you've already said, then you can look the whole thing through and sign. OK?' She nodded. 'Here goes then. "When I went to the kitchen I told Mr Bolt that the door to the small parlour was locked. He said nothing but made a sound I took to mean annoyance. He took a key from his pocket and unlocked and opened the cupboard in which the keys for the house are kept. He took out and passed to me the bunch on which the small parlour key is. He held the bunch by that key." Is that all right?'

'Yes, fine.'

'OK. "I did not look for and did not notice the key when I entered the small parlour or at any point while I was there." All right?'

'Yes.'

'Good. "I have not been back into or looked into the small parlour since I left it to tell Mr Bolt that the bodies of Miss Sheerley and Mr Homer were there." Right?'

'Yes.'

'Last one. "When Mr Bolt left the kitchen after I told him about the bodies in the small parlour, he said something like 'Let me see,' but I do not recall the exact words." How about that?'

'Actually, I think those were his exact words.'

'Are you absolutely sure?'

'Well, I *think* so. Not *absolutely*, I suppose.'

'Well,' said Yarrow, 'it's probably not worth changing it if you're not absolutely sure, in case Mrs Carrock or Mr Bolt remembers it differently, do you see?'

'I think so.'

'Shall we leave it how I read it out then?'

'All right.'

'Are you satisfied that it represents what you've said fairly and accurately?'

'Yes.'

'Good,' said Fathers, pushing the draft statement over to Yarrow who started to add his extra sentences at the bottom. 'Now, before we give that to you to read through and sign, is there anything that you would like to add to what you have told us?'

Anna shook her head.

'Anything at all, Miss Dark, however small. It might not seem important or even relevant, but if there's anything missing from your description of events it would be most useful to include it now – just in case.'

'You don't just want the truth,' said Anna, 'but the whole truth.'

'That's right.'

'Well, to the best of my ability, I've given it to you.'

'Fair enough. Now, you finished, Yarrow? Good. Read that through, would you, please, Miss Dark? Tell us if anything needs changing, and if nothing does then Yarrow will show you where to sign.'

Yarrow put the completed statement in front of Anna, who began to read with concentration. While she read, he contemplated the library. He was astonished there should be such a room in a private house. Bookshelves covered each wall from ceiling to skirting; they had even been fitted in tight around and above the

47

door from what the household called the music room. Four stacks of shelves stood at right angles to the wall opposite the door, forming five alcoves. In the first of these, at the far end from where Yarrow, Fathers and Anna Dark now sat, there were a pair of leather armchairs and two low tables set in front of a window; in the second, which had no window, were several piles of books on the floor; in the third, which did have a window, was an old roll-top desk with a straight chair; in the windowless fourth, were more piles of books on the floor and the sort of stool for standing on which is found in public libraries and some bookshops. The last, at the end of the room, was much bigger, with a full-width window looking over a terrace on to the garden. It was here that they sat. Yarrow wondered how long the library had been there, how many thousand books there were in it, how old the oldest one was, what it felt like to grow up in a house with its own library, how many of the books had been read by the current owners and their offspring, and for how many generations the family had owned the house.

He shook his head bemusedly at the thought of the wealth and the family continuity represented by the library. He was also struck by the fact that the room next door was called the music room. This family not only had two parlours but an extra room, which looked to his eyes like a fancy sitting room, which they had designated for music. The only musical things about it, as far as he had been able to gauge while waiting there for Fathers to complete his instructions to Pardoner and Brain, were a grand piano and a very expensive-looking stereo system together with a record cabinet and storage places for cassettes. But he could imagine the family and guests gathering to listen to a specially brought in string quartet. The room was decorated throughout in white, had a patterned carpet rimmed by highly polished flooring, and the walls were hung with impressively framed paintings – Yarrow counted more than twenty of them, mostly landscapes, two seascapes, three portraits and a pair of abstract designs. One of the portraits he had recognised as Sir Walter and Lady Sarah. Multiple French windows let in the maximum of light and gave on to a garden which sloped away from the house down to a large lawn at the end of which was a high stone wall fronted by a long hedge. Perhaps in the summer, thought Yarrow, they would listen to the quartet on the lawn.

The maid stopped reading and indicated she was satisfied with the statement. Yarrow came out of his reverie, stood up and went round to lean over her shoulder. 'So, can you sign here, please . . . and here?' he said. He gave her his pen and she began to sign as he instructed. 'Thank you. And here again, right up against the last word. Oh, and would you just initial these bits here . . . and here . . . and that one. Just so that those mistakes don't distract anybody's attention when they come to read it. Thanks, that's lovely.' He sat down again.

Fathers leaned forward and put his elbows on the table. 'Has anybody told you how the nature of this case has changed?' he asked.

'No,' said Anna. 'How?'

'Yesterday, the police were working on the assumption that what we had was a murder and a suicide.' Anna nodded. 'Today, we're working on the assumption that it was a double murder.'

Anna paused and expelled a breath before speaking. 'You mean, they were killed by someone else?'

Fathers nodded.

'Why?'

'Why have we changed our minds or why were they killed?'

'Um, both I suppose.'

'We've changed our minds because of the evidence, and we don't know the motive.'

'But that means it was somebody who was here over the weekend.'

Fathers smiled inwardly. So much, he thought, for Brain's assumption that civilians don't immediately see the nasty implications that detectives make it their business to spot. 'It seems likely,' he said, 'though it's not the only possibility. So now you understand why I want you to help me form an impression about the household, the weekend guests and so on.'

'Good heavens,' said Anna.

'We'll take some notes, but they won't be written up into a statement and we shan't ask you to sign them, or hold you to them in any way. Do you understand?'

'You mean it sort of has a different status to what you've just been asking me about?'

'That's right. Of course, if you tell me any downright lies, that would still count as obstruction, but if you give me opinions and in time I decide I don't agree with them – well, that's a different matter. Clear?'

Yarrow had sat in on several of Fathers' interviews over the nearly three years that he had been a member of the Serious Crimes Squad, and was repeatedly struck by his boss's skill in them. He found it hard to know where he stood with Fathers – what the DCI thought of him, whether it amounted to approval – and he had never truly liked his boss, even if he had learned how to get along and even make jokes, but he had a deep respect for him. He studied Fathers' methods closely, and was convinced that one element in his success, which had given him the reputation of being one of the very few detectives who really could break cases by a flash of inspiration, by pure deduction and brainwork, was his ability to develop an almost intuitive feel for the circumstance in which a crime had occurred. He had the knack of unobtrusively appealing to witnesses' sense of themselves as possessing judgement and slowly seducing out useful observations.

Fathers asked first about the two victims: 'Were they lovers?'

'Well, we thought so.'

'We?'

'The staff, on Saturday night. We thought so. But we weren't sure. They were given separate bedrooms, but I didn't think they meant to keep to them.'

'What other, er, couplings were there?'

'Um, the George-Watkinses and the Mulhollands, of course, they're married couples. And Miss Madeleine and Mr Rankley, and then young Walter and Mr Waterford.'

Fathers flicked an eyebrow.

'Yes,' said Anna, 'he's gay.'

Fathers nodded and cleared his throat.

Fathers' diffidence about homosexuality seemed to encourage Anna, for she immediately launched into praise of both Walter and his lover, of how friendly they were and approachable, how little they presumed upon the staff in general and Anna in particular. 'They often say gays are the only men who really understand women,' she concluded brightly.

'Could be,' said Fathers noncommittally. 'What about Ellen Sheerley, now?'

'I sort of felt she was a bit wild, you know? But really nice. And, of course, ever so good-looking. She was really stunning last night, bit daring too.'

'What do you mean?'

'Well, you know.' It was Anna's turn to be diffident, drawing back from what she had been about to say.

'You mean the way she behaved?'

'Oh no, not at all. Well, only a little bit. But I really meant, you know, how she was dressed.'

'What about it?'

'Well, it was a beautiful dress and everything but, well, if you want me to say it straight out . . .'

'Please.'

'. . . it was really quite low-cut and she wasn't wearing a bra.'

'Oh.'

'The men were all kidding each other about it – the men who were serving, I mean – you know, trying to catch a quick peak when they stood at her shoulder to serve, then telling each other back in the kitchen and sort of claiming points for how much they saw.'

'Sounds fun,' said Fathers drily.

'Oh yes,' said Anna seriously, 'that and the gossip is half the fun of serving at these do's.'

'A bit wild, I think you said?'

'Just an impression, what with her Porsche, and her clothes, and her manner and everything. Like, I'm sure she knew what the men were up to on Saturday and I'm certain I saw her actually give one of them a bit of a show, you know? Deliberately, I mean. It's not like she didn't have anything there, you know, anything for them to see.'

Fathers raised his eyebrows and pursed his lips.

'But it was sort of fun,' Anna said, almost defensively, 'it's not like she was really, well, flirting with them or something, just being a bit outrageous, not that anything would come of it. I always thought with her that, well, she really had a good time in life, do you know what I mean? One of those people who have the energy and the guts to dare an awful lot and to get away with it.'

Anna stopped and thought with her eyes cast down.

'I suppose maybe she didn't get away with it, this time.'

'What do you mean?' said Fathers.

'Oh, well, I suppose I'm a bit of a Protestant at heart. I sort of meant that maybe that wildness carried her astray and she got – she got killed.'

'Astray?'

'Or into something she couldn't handle.' She looked at Fathers.

51

His face was entirely expressionless – she took it for scepticism. 'Oh I don't know. The truth is that you asked for impressions and opinions, and I'm giving them to you, but that's one of those feelings you can have about someone or something, and when it comes right down to it, you don't really know why you feel it, but it's there and it won't go away. Do you know what I mean?'

'Oh indeed I do,' said Fathers emphatically. 'But did she give you any grounds for it? For example, did she come here with different men?'

'Oh no, Mr Homer was the only man she ever brought here – at least while I've been on the staff.'

'Which is since last July?'

'Yes.'

'Or did she talk about wild parties or some such?'

'No, not as such. I mean, she would talk a bit, not to me, you know, but while I was in the room and you can't help overhearing, about parties she'd been to or was going to, but she never said anything that implied they might be – well, wild or anything.'

'So it's an impression you gained from her manner?'

'Yes, that's it, from her whole way of being.' Anna paused for thought again. 'There is just one thing,' she said, 'though it doesn't really mean anything.'

'What?'

'Well, from something Miss Madeleine said one time I gathered she – Miss Sheerley, I mean – used to go with Mr Rankley.'

'Would that be while he has been having his affair with Miss Granthelm, or before?'

'Oh look, I mean now you've said you're not going to write this up into a statement and hold me to it, it would be so easy to say that, yes, it was since he and Miss Madeleine have been going together. But if I said that, it would be something that might be true, but I don't actually know.'

'With that qualification, that you don't actually know, what do you actually think?'

'Well, you see Mr Rankley and Miss Madeleine are a longstanding scene. I'm not sure how long, but at least three years, I'm sure. So I sort of assumed that therefore if Miss Sheerley and Mr Rankley had a thing, it must have been something on the side for him.'

'Sounds reasonable. Why did you say it doesn't mean anything?'

'Well, that's normal behaviour, isn't it? I mean, fidelity and all that, it's not really demanded, is it? And all that stuff about stealing your best friend's bloke – or your cousin's – it doesn't carry the, you know, the impact that it used to.'

'Long ago.'

The maid grinned.

'Anything else in that line?' asked Fathers.

She shook her head.

'So how about Robert Homer?' he asked.

'It's awful to say so,' said Anna slowly, 'but I didn't really like him.'

'Why not?'

'Oh, he only came here a couple of times, so I didn't really know him, but he was a bit flash, do you know what I mean? A little bit too obvious with his money. A bit like Mr Mulholland actually – he's one of the people who left yesterday – but without the charm. What I really mean is that I'm used to serving wealthy people at table and clearing up after them and so on, but what I'm used to is county wealth, old wealth – he was City wealth, and new.'

'Sir Walter is City wealth, in a sense.'

'Not in the sense I mean.'

'I know what you mean.'

'It wasn't anything specific, but – well, you asked for my impression and that's what it was.'

'Unfavourable?'

'Definitely.'

'Mr Mulholland, though, you like?'

'Yes, I suppose so, Mr George-Watkins too.'

'And their wives?'

'Well, Mrs G-W is a little – tight, I suppose is the word for it. Her skin looks tight on her face, her lips look tight, she walks that way and talks too. Mrs Mulholland is – well, she's just a little bit too much the other way, do you know what I mean? Sort of effusive and American.'

'I know.'

'Nothing wrong with that, mind, but it's a bit odd when somebody starts to tell somebody else's maid about what her therapist said.'

'What did her therapist say?'

'Oh it was some of that I'm all right, you're all right guff that used to be fashionable.'

'Did it?'

'Long ago.'

Fathers grinned. 'How do you come to be working here?' he asked.

'I beg your pardon?'

'If you'll forgive me for saying so, you seem to be cut out for something a bit, well, a bit more than a maid.'

'Nothing wrong with being a maid. It's a living, and not such a bad one.'

'I do apologise if I've offended you.'

'No, you haven't really. It's just that it's what some of my friends say. To answer your question, though, I'm filling in time. I've got a place at York to read English. I was going to go up last October, but, well my father died, if you must know, early in July last year, and I felt I couldn't just leave my mother. I'm the last one to leave home and I thought it would be too much. So I got the place deferred for a year and looked round for a job and they needed a permanent maid here.'

'I am sorry to have raised it.'

'Don't bother, you didn't know.'

'In my day, York had a very good reputation for English. Does it still?'

'Oh yes, I was very pleased, it was quite a hard offer, but I got the grades.'

'What was the offer?'

'A and two B's.'

'And you got it?'

'Better. I got two A's.'

'I'm impressed. I knew, you see.'

'Fathers knows all,' chimed in Yarrow who was fascinated. Higher education was another of the worlds about which he knew nothing except from the outside. Anna smiled. Yarrow was hoping Fathers would now ask what it was like to work at Granthelm House, but he didn't. Instead, he stood up and thanked Anna for her time, and for being so open with him. Yarrow saw her to the door and went to look for Mr Bolt. Anna told him the butler would be in the kitchen. As they came out of the music room together, they found Peter Rankley in the hall.

'Will you be wanting us soon?' asked Rankley.

'As soon as we can,' replied Yarrow without stopping.

'I did have an appointment in town,' commented Rankley.

'When for?'

'Four.'

'I'm sorry, sir,' said Yarrow, 'but you won't make it.'

'As if you cared,' said Rankley.

Yarrow stopped at the door that led to the kitchen. 'Murder is murder, sir,' he said quietly.

CHAPTER 5

1

Michael Kay was dejected after his brief phone conversation with the man at Scotland Yard. He had managed to get through to Detective Constable Elliott Yarrow, who sounded just as prissy as Kay remembered him from years before. They had grown up on the same estate, and though Kay and his mates had never been successful, many were the times they had tried to break into the Yarrow flat. On the phone, Yarrow had been condescending, dismissive, overflowing with disbelief that somebody like Kay could have information worth paying for. But he had at least agreed to a meeting, and that was something. Kay was determined not to let this opportunity go by.

He went to his favourite boozer for a quick drink which turned, as it usually did, into a long, slow one. He spotted a man, a trader, who had been asking about fur coats – and as he had happened to hear about a consignment of so-called seconds which had just come available, he took him aside and in return for ten pounds passed the news along. By closing time he had blown the tenner on drinks for himself and one of his few straight friends who, being unemployed as well as straight, was always short of money. At two thirty he weaved his way out of the pub, checked his cash and decided to get a meal. As he stopped to light a cigarette, he saw somebody he recognised getting out of a car. He was about to hail him when his fuggy brain clicked and reminded him not to. It was Queen, the bastard who had dropped some watches in his pocket to send him inside all that time ago: the Queen he had seen last Saturday night talking to the sort of man a Scotland Yard detective should not be seen with – the Queen he was going to nail.

He decided to tail him. He had no experience of such things, but thought that if he stayed on the other side of the road he could manage it, despite the effects of the drink which in any case were beginning to clear, as his blood pumped itself up with adrenalin. Sod that Yarrow, he thought: I am going to line up this bent bill for him, and the superior little sod can pay through the fucking nose for it. He followed Queen round the corner, then nipped back as the detective took a quick look up and down the road before ducking into a shop doorway. After a minute, Kay wandered past it on the opposite pavement, trying hard not to look as if he was looking at the doorway. He needn't have bothered: Queen had gone inside. Kay nodded to himself. The building was not actually used as a shop, not for retail anyway. It was a small wholesale clothing outlet, run by the man Queen had been with on Saturday night. Better and better, thought Kay. It was a warm day, nice enough for hanging round to see how long Queen stayed there. He belched beerily. Well, eating would have to wait. There was a newsagent's further down the street, and Kay went in there to get a packet of cigarettes and a copy of the *Sun*. Then he went and took up station leaning on some railings obliquely opposite where Queen's car was parked.

He began with page three. He was one of those men who seem to think it's possible to see more of a photograph by tilting it. Once he had done that, and realised he was not going to get a look down the girl's knickers however hard he tried, he turned to the sports pages. He found a pencil to mark some likely-looking horses in the late afternoon races – he'd only get to the bookies' and back them if this business was over in time, though – and then read the cartoons and the readers' letters. The main feature of the day was a confession piece from a rock star who was long since past it. He described the groupies and how they flung themselves at him, how he'd got into a sex and drugs orgy at the country home of an earl known for his charitable work, and how his first marriage had broken up. For tomorrow, the paper promised even more shocking confessions about the rock star and a woman called 'wild Mary'.

Kay checked his watch and then took another look at page three before starting to read the paper from the front. He had just about finished it all apart from the horoscope when Queen came striding round the corner, got into his car and drove off. Kay folded the paper into a pocket and strolled back to the corner. There was a large Jaguar parked outside the shopfront, which suggested that the boss-man was in. Within a minute two men came out, shook hands, one getting into the Jag and the other walking in Kay's direction. He checked his watch and began to walk towards the other man. They crossed just as the Jaguar moved off and then Kay was alone. When the man on foot was well round the corner, Kay turned and retraced his steps. He came to the corner carefully and took a quick look round, but the other man was nowhere to be seen. He breathed a sigh of relief and walked quickly on towards the café which had been his intended destination over an hour ago.

After he had ordered his meal, he looked at his stars for the day. 'Beware new personal ties,' it said, 'and watch out for an old acquaintance who might cause new complications. But business is looking good. If you get the chance, take it.'

2

The butler was a small, understated man, his short dark hair neatly combed back from a widow's peak, his skin pale and smooth on a bland thin-lipped face with dark eyes. He sat down with neat and maximally economical movements, folded his hands on his lap and waited for the questions. Fathers went through the same routine as he had with Anna. First the personal details: Bolt was forty-four, and had been butler at Granthelm House for a few months more than six years. He was divorced and lived in a flat in the converted attic of Granthelm House. Then the events of Saturday night: his account did not differ in the slightest degree from what he had said the day before or from Anna's account, though his memory for times was rather more precise than the maid's. He had been given leave to stop work a few minutes after 1.30 a.m. and had gone straight to bed. He had set the alarm and put his light out at 1.53 a.m. precisely.

'You have a very good memory,' said Fathers.

'For late nights, sir,' said Bolt with a slight twitch of his mouth, which Yarrow thought might have been his version of a smile.

Fathers moved on to the Sunday morning and Bolt described how he had given the small parlour key to Anna. 'Was the cupboard door open?'

'No, sir, it was locked. I unlocked it with the key which I have for it, which I always have on me in my pocket.' To demonstrate, he pulled out a small bunch of keys from his pocket and held one out. 'That's the one, sir.'

'Is it the only key for that cupboard?'

'No, sir. Mrs Carrock has one and so does Sir Walter. He keeps it in his desk here in the library.'

'Show me, will you?' said Fathers rising.

Bolt stayed in his seat. 'I don't actually know where in the desk he keeps it,' he said. 'It's a desk with numerous small compartments, some of which are hidden and opened by shifting a particular panel.'

'I know the kind you mean.'

'And I'm afraid I don't know how to open them, nor in which of them Sir Walter keeps this key.'

'Well, I'll have to ask him. So you gave her the key she wanted and a few minutes later she came back.'

'Yes, sir, at a run. She looked very upset.'

'What did she say?'

'The exact words, sir, I don't recall, but the drift was that there were two bodies in the small parlour, two dead bodies.'

'She said two dead bodies, did she?'

'Bodies or dead bodies, sir, I'm not entirely sure.'

'And you said?'

'I think I said, "I'll go and see."'

'And then you went to the small parlour?'

'Yes, sir, and looked in through the door which she had left open.'

'Did you go in or just look in?'

'I didn't cross the threshold, sir.'

'Then?'

'I went to get Sir Walter.'

'What did you say to him?'

'I said there was something he should come to see, something urgent.'

'Did you say what it was?'

'No, sir.'

Bolt and Sir Walter had hurried downstairs and to the door of the small parlour. 'Sir Walter went in, sir, carefully so as not to disturb anything, and then he said, "Look, they've been shot. Call the police."'

'Was that all he said?'

'Yes.'

'How far did he go in?'

Bolt paused for a moment to consider. 'As far as the coffee table between the two sofas, sir.'

'Then he told you to call the police, and you did so.'

'Yes, using the phone in the hall.'

'And Sir Walter?'

'Joined me there, sir.'

59

'When you'd finished the call.'

'No, sir, while I was telling the police the address.'

'And then?'

'He told me to wake the guests and ask them to go to the dining room, which I did.'

'Thank you. Now, I just want to come back to the business of the key. First, did you see the key to the small parlour door? Not the one you gave Anna, I mean, but the other one?'

'No, sir. I saw the bunch I'd given Anna, lying on the floor just inside the room, but I didn't see the other key, which should have been on the inside of the door.'

'It was lying on the floor.'

'I'm afraid I didn't notice it, sir.'

'Are you sure?'

'I'm sure.'

'Did you have occasion to notice it on Saturday evening?'

'It was in the door at seven when I checked round to make certain everything was ready for the evening, but I had no reason to check it again before I went to bed.'

'All right. Now, when you went to bed, what did you do with those keys you have in your pocket there?'

'Sir?'

'Did you leave them in your trousers? Did you put them on a bedside table, chest of drawers, what have you?'

'On my chest of drawers, sir.'

'Did you lock the door to your flat before sleeping?'

'Yes, sir, I always do.'

'And last night was no exception?'

'No, sir.'

'Even though it was late and you were tired?'

'It's routine for me, sir, automatic.'

'Fine. One last thing. Was the cupboard where the keys are kept in the kitchen locked on Saturday night when you went to bed?'

'Yes, sir.'

'You're certain?'

'I am, because when the temps and Mrs Carrock all left on Saturday – that was at midnight – I noted down on my pad the hours that each one had put in. I keep that pad along with certain other papers – bills and the like – in that same cupboard. I then closed and locked the cupboard.'

'And you did the same when Anna left about an hour later?'

'No, sir, I simply told her to remind me in the morning to write her hours down.'

'So the cupboard was locked from midnight until you opened it to get the small parlour key for Anna?'

'It was. To the best of my knowledge.'

'Thank you. Yarrow?' Fathers pushed the statement across to him. Yarrow went through the business of reading out the amendments he wanted to make to Bolt's statement. Bolt listened carefully and verified them all. Then Yarrow wrote them in and passed it to Bolt who read the statement carefully. At the end he nodded, and Yarrow showed him where to sign.

As he had with Anna, Fathers now altered the terms of the interview, explaining about the change in the nature of the case and the need to hear the butler's impressions about the people in the house over the weekend. Bolt nodded and twitched an eyebrow as he absorbed the implications of this information and the accompanying request.

Of Homer, he said, 'Since you push me, sir, I have to say he was very sharp, sir, rather flash – as Miss Granthelm put it, rather *nouveau.*'

'When did she put it that way?'

'Last night.'

'Who was she talking to?'

'Her father.'

'When was that?'

'Shortly before the party assembled for cocktails, sir.'

'A bit before seven thirty then?'

Bolt nodded.

'And you agree with that assessment?' said Fathers.

'Frankly, sir, yes.'

'Something you didn't quite like about him.'

'Yes.'

'Something in his style.'

'That's right. Nothing I knew against him, if you understand. I suppose one shouldn't speak ill of the dead . . .'

'For a detective investigating murder,' said Fathers, 'I can assure you, Mr Bolt, that there is no rule more frustrating.'

'I understand, sir. Frankly, Mr Homer was not a man I would ever want to trust.'

'Did Sir Walter agree with Miss Granthelm when she passed

this remark yesterday evening?'

'Well, I didn't have the impression that he expressed any strong disagreement.'

'Did he express any disagreement at all?'

'He, er, suppressed the subject, sir, rather than responding directly.'

'I see. Did Mr Homer come here often?'

'This was his third visit, sir. The previous occasions were in the summer and the autumn of last year.'

'Thank you. How about Miss Sheerley, now? What can you tell me about her?'

Bolt frowned and pursed his lips slightly, took a breath and expelled it before answering. 'She is – was – very beautiful, of course. She was, socially speaking, very desirable, much in demand, so I understand. At a certain level, so to speak, she lived a very full life. She was very charming – to everybody – helpful when she could be; extremely nice, in fact. But there was, if you understand, an edge to her.'

'An edge.'

'Yes – not that she was unhappy, you understand, but she wasn't positively happy, which is what she wanted to be.'

'Don't we all?'

'I suppose so, sir. She never gave up trying to be happy, but it did seem to be an effort. You can't get happiness by constant effort, really, can you, sir?'

'I suppose not. Bit wild, was she?'

'Not wild, sir, I think that's putting it a bit strongly, but intent on a good time, over-intent, perhaps.'

'I gather she was a frequent visitor here.'

'Oh yes, sir. At least, during my time here she has been. Her parents are abroad and Lady Sarah and Sir Walter have been rather second parents to her.'

'How many times has she been here since Christmas, for example?'

'Well, she was here for Christmas with the family for a few days, and again after the New Year's celebrations in London were over. Again at the end of January for a weekend, and in March, and this time.'

'Was that sort of frequency typical?'

'More or less.'

'Now,' said Fathers, 'what about her and Mr Homer?'

Bolt's mouth twitched a couple of times. 'I rather think they were, sir, but I'm not entirely sure.'

'Ah. Was she here on his previous visits? You said this was his third time here.'

'That's correct, but no, sir, on neither of those occasions was Miss Sheerley in the party. In fact, the first time there was only him and Mr Rankley, apart from Lady Sarah, Sir Walter and Miss Granthelm.'

'And the second time?'

'A much larger affair, sir, but Miss Sheerley was not among them.'

Fathers did not think he could get Bolt to indulge in gossip about his employers, so he moved on from Sheerley-Homer to see what Bolt could offer about various other relationships in the party. 'Miss Granthelm is with Mr Rankley, is that right?' he asked.

'Yes, sir, for quite some time now, though whether it will lead to marriage is not clear. Some years back, I understand Miss Granthelm was on the edge of marriage, but it came to nothing. Not with Mr Rankley. That she was on the edge of marriage with, I mean.'

'While Mr Granthelm,' said Fathers, 'now who's he with?'

Bolt's mouth twitched and pursed. 'Mr Granthelm makes no bones of the fact that he is homosexual, sir, and he has a longstanding relationship with Mr Waterford.'

'He's come out – that's the expression, isn't it? – has he?'

'Yes, sir, and insists on sharing a room openly with Mr Waterford when they spend a weekend here, whereas, for example, Miss Granthelm and Mr Rankley maintain the fiction of separate rooms when her parents are here.'

'And what do Sir Walter and Lady Sarah think about that?'

'About which?'

'Their son and Mr Waterford.'

'They acknowledge and permit it, sir, without accepting or endorsing it, if you understand. All is tact and discretion. We are careful in what we say.'

'Careful.'

'Yes, sir.' Bolt's mouth twitched again. 'For example, the expression, queer as a bottle of chips, would not be permitted, whereas gay and homosexual would be – if the subject were to arise.'

'Tell me about Mr Waterford,' said Fathers.

'I don't know much, sir. I'm not sure what job he does, if indeed he does do one. He talks a lot about the stage, literature, films and so on. He's very amiable, seems to be from a better background, public school and so on.' Bolt's mouth remained still, but his right eyebrow arched slightly. 'Rather a nice pansy, really.'

Fathers wrote 'nice pansy' on his pad. 'Mr Rankley?' he said.

'An executive in some sort of estate agents, I believe, in London. Very well off. Very.'

More questions could not draw Bolt further on the subject of Peter Rankley, so Fathers switched to the George-Watkinses. Bolt regarded them as very pleasant, though he thought the son rather brash – 'Very American, sir, unlike his parents.'

Fathers moved on to the Mulhollands. 'Very American, sir,' said Bolt, with more emphasis than he had used when applying the same term to the young George-Watkins. 'I understand he is a business associate of Sir Walter's. I gather some venture in the Bahamas may bring them together. They are from Florida. They were here a few weeks ago and this is their second visit. Very generous they were on the last occasion, very generous.'

'Generous?'

'It is the custom,' said Bolt carefully, 'to give some tangible expression of appreciation for the service which guests enjoy from the staff on their visits, quite the custom everywhere, and Mr Mulholland was very generous in that sense, sir.'

3

As Yarrow accompanied Bolt out of the library, he was met by Pardoner. 'Hang about, Elly,' said the detective sergeant. 'Daddy may not want the next one straightaway. We've found summat.' Yarrow nodded, thanked Bolt and turned back into the library.

'Nifty set-up, this,' commented Pardoner as they walked past the stacks of books.

'I dunno,' said Yarrow with a yawn, 'money after all, I ask you, is it worth it?'

'Yes.'

'Too right.'

'Something up?' asked Fathers as the pair hove into his view.

'We've found it,' said Pardoner simply. 'Or them rather.'

'What?'

'One pair of frilly k-nickers, a pair of shoes and a cartridge case looking suspiciously like a twenty-two.'

The three men left the library together, with Pardoner leading. 'In the trees beyond the garages,' he said. 'Gawd, you should see the cars. Fan-bloody-tastic. Homer had a Britannia, the Sheerley woman a yellow Porsche and Rankley tools around in a spanking new Morgan. Young Granthelm has an old MGB, and Madeleine a Ferrari. Mum and Dad have a Wolls, a Wange Wover and a yummy little Aston for wunning awound in.'

'Britannia?' said Fathers.

'Bristol Britannia,' confirmed Pardoner. 'Amazing car.'

'Stylish?'

'Super élite, clotted cream, pots of money stylish. Worth megaquids that one, I can tell you.'

'So Homer wasn't short of a few bob,' commented Fathers.

As they emerged from the house, Pardoner pointed to where DS Cotton stood with another man. 'That's Carrock,' he said.

'Well, let's go see a man about a dog,' suggested Fathers, and the three changed course and joined the gardener and the local detective.

'Mr Carrock,' said Fathers, 'I'm Detective Chief Inspector Fathers. We have a couple of questions to put to you.'

'So the officer told me,' replied Carrock. He was in his early forties, a tall, strong man with an out-of-doors complexion, balding fair hair, wearing a check shirt, jeans and muddy work boots, standing with hands in pockets and a cigarette in his mouth. When he spoke, the cigarette bobbed up and down between his lips.

'You look after the dogs,' began Fathers.

'Three of them,' said Carrock, 'two dogs and a bitch, all Alsatians.'

'What did you do with them on Saturday night?'

'Ah. They was kept in the pen. Didn't want to let them out, see, in case a couple of the guests should want a little stroll, when they'd not want to be torn to bloody shreds, eh.' The cigarette ash fluttered down as he spoke. Yarrow was making notes on his pad.

'Were you told to keep them locked up, or did you do it off your own bat?'

'Nah, it's the way, see. I was told once, when I first started here, that any time there're guests for a do like Saturday's I should keep 'em locked up, so I don't need telling special. There's the staff too. They know old Bolt and my missus, of course, and they probably wouldn't go for Anna neither, but the temporary help they hire just for the evening, the dogs'd go for them, I reckon.'

'And the family.'

'They know them. We make a point of that – they all come up and say hello to the dogs every once in a while so the look of them and the smell's familiar.'

'But not the guests?'

'It'd confuse them, I reckon. Anyway, not worth the trouble when you can just keep 'em penned.'

'So, Saturday night as usual on such occasions, they weren't let out.'

''S right.'

'Sorry, Yarrow,' said Fathers. 'Nice try.' Then he caught a look on the Detective Constable's face. 'Got a question, have you?'

'If you don't mind, sir,' said Yarrow.

'Fire away.'

'Do you remember the night of the silver robbery last year?' asked Yarrow.

'Do I?' said Carrock. The cigarette had burned down to its filter tip, and he spat it out. It landed by Yarrow's feet.

'What did you do with the dogs that night?'

'Oh, they was out as normal. Only Bolt in the house, see, the family were all away, London and wherever.'

'What time did you let them out?'

'Last thing before I went to bed, just like normal. I suppose that'd be around eleven or thereabouts.'

'Are they good guard dogs?'

Carrock chuckled. 'Ask the gentleman,' he said, indicating Cotton.

Cotton smiled in turn. 'He means a time in, oh, May last year, was it?'

''S right,' said Carrock. 'They caught some lads messing around and near as anything tore 'em limb from limb.'

Fathers looked at Cotton. 'Just some innocent malarkey, we thought, sir,' Cotton said. 'Three local lads breaking in for a dare, so they said. Not into the house, mind, just the grounds, but the dogs caught them and they ended up in hospital with a good

66

fright, their bums full of anti-tet, and a mass of stitches. They howled to wake the dead.'

'What with the barking 'n' all,' added Carrock, 'I'm surprised we had to call the police. Could've heard it from here to Guil'ford.'

'So you've no doubt they're effective guard dogs,' persisted Yarrow.

'None at all,' said Carrock.

'And when you let them out in the evening, what do they do? I mean, do they go round together or what?'

'Oh, they play around a bit, see, hunting and messing about. When I get them in the morning they're usually all together, and when I let them out at night they all race off together too. Dunno what they do in between, though.'

'One last thing,' said Yarrow. 'Are the grounds fenced in?'

'Well, there's a wall all the way round the south side, that's back of the house, and then over on the east that wall continues on up and like turns in and runs up to the gate up the avenue there. On the west side, we've replaced the wall with a wire fence. You can't see it from this side because of the hedge, but I keep it trimmed on the other side so it's perfectly visible. And that goes right up to the road there, up above those cottages, which are all part of the grounds, see. Then there's more walls, separating the cottages' gardens from each other, and another one which goes right round the stables where me and the wife live.'

'How high are the walls round the south and east?' asked Yarrow.

''Bout nine feet. Got them broken bottles on top, too.'

'Thanks. I'll write up what you said about Saturday night into a statement and somebody will come and go through it with you and ask you to sign it.'

Carrock nodded, pulled out another cigarette, lit it and threw the match he had used on the ground.

4

'So this is where it happened,' said Fathers, 'and a nicer spot for it he couldn't have picked.' He was standing at the edge of a small grassy clearing amid some trees where Ellen Sheerley and Robert Homer had made love a little over thirty-six hours previously.

Immediately after which, presumably, she had been shot. A pair of women's dress shoes – more slippers or sandals than proper shoes, reflected Fathers – had been neatly placed at the foot of an old blackthorn. Not far away, in some longer grass, lay a pair of knickers, the spot marked by a little pennant. And to the edge of the clearing, another pennant marked where the ejected cartridge case lay.

'As far as she's concerned,' said Pardoner, 'it's where it all happened. First the sex, then bang.' He paused and thought about the unintentional pun. 'Sorry,' he muttered.

'Any signs of a third party?' asked Fathers.

'No. I quartered it when they told me they'd found the shoes, and we approached from the outside in. That's how we found the knickers and the cartridge case. No obvious signs of anybody else having been here, but then again the first plod here might've obliterated them, not that you can blame him. He's got to put his feet somewhere.'

Brain was standing at the other side of the clearing. 'No blame there,' he said, 'but it's all a bit odd, isn't it? I mean, Homer was definitely shot in the small parlour, so if somebody else killed Sheerley, he'd then have to persuade Homer to go back with him, one of them carrying the woman's body, into the house – and then shoot Homer there. Hardly seems likely Homer'd do that.'

'In which case,' said Fathers, 'the likelihood is that they came here, started to screw, flung shoes and pants wherever, finished and then he shot her.'

'What a callous sodding bastard,' commented Pardoner.

'Neither one seems very likely to me,' said Fathers.

'But it's got to be one or the other,' objected Brain.

'Hey-ho,' said Fathers. 'I don't think I like the smell of this case.'

'Huh, it was bad enough yesterday before the ballistics test came through.'

Fathers nodded. 'All the doings,' he said.

'I'll make the arrangements,' said Brain, 'and meanwhile we'll keep looking for the second gun.'

The three Scotland Yard men walked back to the house as Brain went to his car to radio through instructions to send out a photographer and a technical assistant to record and examine the scene of sex and crime. As they came out of the trees, Yarrow seemed very subdued. He was walking with his head down, apparently deep in thought. Fathers couldn't believe it was the effect of the place they had just been in or the thought of the murder committed there. The first time he had seen death at close quarters was while he was in his probationary year as a uniformed constable. It had been a motorcyclist who had skidded on a wet bend in Stoke Newington. It was before crash helmets were compulsory, and PC Fathers had taken one look at the bloodied, destroyed head and vomited uncontrollably. On very bad days he could still recall how the fragments of shattered skull looked and how he had reacted, but he had seen too much since to retain that early sensitivity. Yarrow too would have seen many similar sights, both on the beat and as a plainclothes detective. So what was bothering him now?

'Good move to ask Carrock about the night of the break-in,' said Fathers, breaking Yarrow's contemplation.

Yarrow looked up, visibly unhappy. He clicked his tongue and looked away. 'Something's bothering me,' he said. 'Something about the robbery. I can't think whether it's something from that report which I can't quite remember, or something I've seen since we got here. It just won't come together.'

'Relax,' said his boss, 'and it'll come to you by and by.' Yarrow nodded.

'One thing I thought,' offered Pardoner, 'is they were lucky only the silver got nicked.'

'All those paintings, you mean?' asked Fathers. 'Yes, but they'd be pretty bulky to carry away, even if they cut them out of the frames. There's not just the ones in the music room – must be about half a dozen big ones in the dining room, and Brain tells me there's another lot hanging up in the main parlour. All originals, so he says.'

'Mind you, guv,' said Yarrow, 'you can't just put sixty-nine grand's worth of antique silver in your hip pocket and vault over a nine-foot wall.'

'I suppose not. It was a proper job, wasn't it?'

'And very selective,' added Pardoner.

'And if there was just the two of them,' said Yarrow, 'they'd need to make a couple of trips.'

'But,' said Pardoner, nudging Yarrow with a grin, 'the dogs did nothing in the night.'

'Well,' began Yarrow defensively, but Fathers cut in.

'No, it's a good point, whether about Saturday night or last year. But that's not what's bothering you?'

'No,' said Yarrow. 'Something else.' He lapsed into silence again.

'Tell you what, skip,' said Fathers as they went in the front door, 'can you rustle up some coffee for us, and while you're doing that ask Mrs Carrock where she keeps her key for the kitchen cupboard where they have all the house keys, all right? Get her to show it to you. Also, just for interest, find out where the alarm system is controlled from. After that, wait for the technicals and see they do their stuff, then why don't you hitch a ride to the station and take the train back to town? No need for you to hang around here when you can be fixing up to turn Homer's flat over.'

'Will do,' said Pardoner.

'Go find Sir Walter, Yarrer, and tell him we're ready, OK?'

CHAPTER 6

1

Sir Walter Granthelm did not enjoy having somebody else in charge under his own roof. He did not like the pushy London detective who had been sent down to handle the investigation, nor did he have a favourable impression of the man's assistant who sat taking notes, now and again directing a distinctly suspicious look at him. Slippery, he decided, was a good description of this young fellow: Rankley was right. Nor did he enjoy going over the statement he had already made to the police. The fine points of detail which the man Fathers insisted on bringing up were, in his impatiently and repeatedly stated view, unnecessary.

'What does it matter exactly what time we came out of the main parlour?' he snapped. 'Good god, man, it was a social occasion. I wasn't keeping a close eye on the clock.'

'Yes, yes, if Bolt says different, take his word for it,' he said in response to Fathers' persistence. 'I shan't fight for my recollection. It hardly counts, does it?'

'I've no idea what precise words he used when he woke me. I was asleep, d'you see?'

'Is this really necessary?' was his reply when Fathers asked whether he or Bolt got to the small parlour first.

'Close enough to see they were dead,' he said when Fathers wanted him to describe exactly how far into the small parlour he had gone.

'You could see the bullet holes, could you?' asked Fathers evenly.

'The hole in Homer's head, yes, and the blood on Ellen's hair. Do you enjoy picking at other people's pain like this?' But Sir Walter's snappiness revealed no sense of grief at either death.

'And then?'

'I told Bolt to phone the police and followed him out of the room.'

'Immediately?'

'As good as.'

'There's no such thing as *as good as* immediately,' said Fathers pedantically. 'Either it was immediately or it wasn't.'

Sir Walter shrugged and pulled a pipe and tobacco pouch from his jacket pocket. From the pouch he took a pen-knife and started to attack the contents of the pipe-bowl with it. Fathers leaned down the table to where a heavy glass ashtray sat and pushed it along to Sir Walter.

'Did you gaze at the bodies for a few moments, perhaps?' suggested Fathers.

'Possibly,' said Sir Walter, concentrating on emptying the pipe-bowl into the ashtray.

'What does "possibly" mean?' said Fathers. 'Did you or didn't you?'

'I suppose I may have.' He rapped the pipe on the ashtray and examined the now clean interior of the bowl.

'May have?'

Sir Walter did not reply.

'So you didn't follow the butler out immediately,' said Fathers. 'It was a few moments after.'

Sir Walter remained silent.

'May we take that as a statement of fact?' persisted Fathers. 'You stayed in the room for a few moments and . . .'

'Yes,' said Sir Walter. He took tobacco from the pouch and began to fill his pipe.

'Did you at any point see or disturb the key to the small parlour? The one which had been or should have been in the door, I mean?'

'No. I did see a bunch of keys there, on the floor just inside the door, but that's all.' Sir Walter completed filling the pipe and began to tamp the tobacco down with the handle of the pen-knife.

'You didn't see a single key lying there by itself?'

'No.'

'Now, that bunch of keys you saw – did you recognise it?'

'Yes.'

'As?'

Sir Walter took a lighter from his pocket and lit his pipe. When it was going properly, he blew out a cloud of smoke which hovered between him and Fathers, and finally replied, 'As the bunch, or one of the bunches, Bolt keeps locked up in the kitchen.'

'Where in the kitchen?'

'Corner cupboard.'

A slight draught from somewhere edged the cloud of smoke in Yarrow's direction. Yarrow looked up crossly and flapped his hand to drive it away.

72

'Who has keys for that cupboard?' asked Fathers.

Sir Walter blew some smoke out of the side of his mouth towards Yarrow. 'Myself, Bolt and Mrs Carrock.'

Yarrow blew the smoke back towards Sir Walter who rewarded him with a glare. Yarrow's flickering eyes gave Sir Walter the satisfactory feeling of having won that exchange.

'Where do you keep your key?' asked Fathers.

'In my desk.'

'Who else knows it's kept there?'

'I don't know. Bolt, I assume, and probably my wife. Perhaps my son and daughter. I don't know – you must ask them.'

'Would you show me, please?'

Sir Walter rose, sighed, blew some more smoke over Yarrow and wordlessly left the table to walk up the library to the middle alcove. Fathers followed him. Sir Walter slid back the roll-top, opened a small drawer, put his hand in and pressed something. A piece of panelling flicked open to reveal a small compartment. It was empty save for a key. He took it out and showed it to Fathers.

'Are you sure that's the key, Sir Walter?'

'Yes.'

'Don't put it back, please,' said Fathers. 'I'd like to try it to be sure.' He did not add that he also wanted it checked for fingerprints. Sir Walter handed him the key with a shrug and Fathers led the way back to the table at the end of the library. Yarrow had opened one of the windows.

Fathers began again. 'While you were with Mr Homer, in the dining room after the ladies had left, and later as well, what did you talk about, do you remember?'

'Not really. Nothing special. He is – he was – interested in the horses, and we talked about that. Too interested, as a matter of fact.'

'A gambling man?'

'Yes.'

'And you didn't approve?'

'Approve? Not my business.'

'But you say he was too interested in the horses.'

'In my view.'

'Did he get into debt with his gambling?'

'I don't know.'

'But you say he was too interested in the horses.'

'That was my impression.'

'Based on what, Sir Walter?'

'Based on very little, Mr Fathers. It was my impression of the man. He could recount the detailed form of a very large number of horses. I didn't think he had gambling debts – I don't know either way. I thought he simply showed too much interest in the horses.'

'Too much for what?'

'For normality.'

'And that's what you talked about with him and Mr Mulholland, and later Mr Rankley too?'

'Among other things.'

'Such as?'

'The news, the pound, the weather, shares. Usual sort of thing.'

'Mr Homer has visited this house before, hasn't he?'

'Yes.'

'Often?'

'No.'

'When?'

'Autumn, summer.'

'How did you meet him?'

'Ellen introduced us.'

'When?'

'About ten months ago, I should think.'

'Last June, then, shortly before his first visit here?'

'I suppose so.'

'And he first came here in which month?'

'July.'

'With Miss Sheerley?'

'No.'

'And the other visit, in the autumn, was that with her?'

'No.'

'He became a friend, did he?'

'Not much more than an acquaintance, really. Can't really think now why he was invited those two times. Maybe we thought Ellen was coming, asked him down too, and then she couldn't come.'

'They were having a relationship, were they?'

'An affair, yes.'

'Apart from the horses and gambling, what was your opinion of him?'

Sir Walter considered his pipe which had gone out. As he

74

picked up his lighter from the table, he replied, 'Nice enough. Didn't know him all that well, as I say.'

'On Saturday evening, did your daughter discuss him with you?'

Sir Walter finished relighting his pipe and blew a long stream of smoke up and away over Fathers' head. 'Discuss? – not really. She did pass a comment, somewhat slighting.'

'Saying?'

'She described him as rather *nouveau*.'

'What did you do?'

'I don't encourage such talk about my guests.'

'Do you think she was right?'

'She's not usually far out in such matters, though perhaps a little over-sensitive to them.'

'She didn't like Mr Homer?'

'You must ask her.'

'I will. By the way, what did Mr Homer do for a living?'

'He was in commerce of some kind, ran a trading agency and probably had one or two other interests. I don't know the details.'

'Did you have any business connections with him?'

'No.'

'How about his family?'

'Don't know anything about them.'

'Now, what about Miss Sheerley, what's your opinion of her?'

'Nice girl,' said Sir Walter and lapsed into a grave silence which Fathers did not break. 'Her father's a diplomat, you know, in Kenya at the moment. She often came down for weekends. Fine girl.'

'What did she do for a living?'

'Private means.'

'Ah. What about her private life?'

'She didn't talk to me about it.'

'You knew about her relationship with Homer, though.'

'Yes.'

'Any others?'

'No.'

'None at all?'

'I don't know. She didn't tell me the names of her menfriends.'

'Were there many?'

'If you are implying she was promiscuous, the answer is no.'

'I'm not implying anything, Sir Walter, I'm merely asking.

75

You don't know of anybody else specifically with whom she had a relationship?'

'No.'

Fathers shrugged. 'Did you know she took heroin?'

Sir Walter was silent for a long minute. 'Impossible,' he said finally, looking down at the table.

'No, it's confirmed by the *post mortem*.'

Sir Walter looked levelly at Fathers. 'Then that is news to me,' he said, 'sad news.'

Fathers looked at him for a while. 'Yarrow?' he said.

For the third time, Yarrow went through the business of reading out his proposed amendments to a statement. It was much harder than with either the maid or the butler, not because Sir Walter queried everything but because he gave no sign of listening. Yarrow had to ask him twice if he agreed that the amendments were fair and accurate representations of what he had said. Then Yarrow added them at the end of the statement and gave it to Sir Walter who, without reading it, signed at the bottom with a pen from his inside jacket pocket.

'Don't you want to read it, sir?' asked Yarrow.

'No.'

'It is advisable.'

'No.'

'Then please would you also sign here at the top, and here right in tight where the last sentence ends. Are you sure you don't want to read it first?' Sir Walter signed where indicated with impatient jabs of the pen and handed the statement back. The interview was over.

As Yarrow rose to accompany Sir Walter from the library, Fathers handed him the key. 'Check it does fit the cupboard, would you?' he said. 'Before you get Lady Sarah.' Yarrow took it carefully, holding it by the part which fitted into the lock. Fathers nodded approvingly. Yarrow didn't need telling.

2

When Yarrow sat down with Lady Sarah at the library table, he turned to Fathers. 'The key fits, guv,' he said and handed it over. Fathers nodded, slipped it into a small envelope and then began on Lady Sarah. She was calm and extremely polite, the simple elegance of her clothes and hair matched by her gestures and speech. She answered Fathers' questions with grace and efficiency, occasionally speaking slowly, either for emphasis or, Yarrow wondered, perhaps for his benefit as if she thought she was dictating her answers to him.

At about 10 p.m. when the cigars were served she had led the ladies into the music room where coffee and liqueurs were available. They had chatted desultorily of this and that until they were joined half an hour later by some of the men. After a while, the fug of cigars and cigarettes had driven her out on to the terrace where she was joined from time to time by others of the party. She had occasionally come back into the music room to top up her drink or detach somebody from a conversation to join the group outside. She had not seen Sir Walter during this time, or Mr Homer, Mr Mulholland and Mr Rankley. She supposed they were talking business, since she knew that her husband and the American were engaged in assessing the prospects for some sort of joint venture – 'Probably Mr Mulholland's idea and our money,' she said, 'usual sort of thing' – and she had gathered, she wasn't sure how or who from, that Mr Homer was also involved. 'They do some business together, I understand,' she said in answer to Fathers' question, 'and I believe that's how they met originally.'

'Mr Homer and your husband, you mean?'

'Yes.'

When Fathers sought her opinion, she expressed the deepest fondness for Ellen Sheerley and a polite refusal to say anything about Robert Homer. 'I didn't know him, you see,' she said, 'so I didn't have an opinion about him.' She did not really know what line of business he was in – 'trade of some kind, but I'm really not sure' – and she neither knew his family nor had heard anybody talk about them. He had to be satisfied with that, and then set to probing what she knew about Ellen Sheerley's social life. Lady Sarah believed it to be a model of propriety – 'as far as anything is with young people these days,' she sighed.

'What do you mean by that?' asked Fathers.

'Oh, just that they take a different attitude about certain things.'

'Like?'

'Well, their relations with each other, obviously.'

'You're talking about their sexual relations?'

'Yes, not that I disapprove. I neither approve nor condemn.

77

It's different, that's all. Attitudes have changed with the times.' She finished with a slight dip of one shoulder, an arching of an eyebrow and a slight pursing of the lips – as close to an actual shrug as she ever would come, thought Fathers. Then she smiled and added, 'You see, Mr Fathers, I was married even before swinging London became the thing, so I'm from a different world really from the one they move in today.'

'And drugs?' he said.

'I beg your pardon?'

'Do they take a different attitude about drugs?'

'I'm sure you know that as well as I, Chief Inspector,' said Lady Sarah, 'but if you are asking whether Ellen involved herself in that aspect of it, I'm afraid I don't know for a fact, but from everything which I do know about her I would entirely doubt it.'

'Perhaps a little experimentation, now and again,' suggested Fathers.

'Perhaps,' she said, 'but that would surprise me, and anything more serious would be quite a shock.' Fathers decided not to shock her.

He finished by asking her about the small parlour key. She knew where the bunch was kept in the kitchen, and knew that her husband, Bolt and Mrs Carrock each had a key for the cupboard, but she did not know where Sir Walter kept his key. 'I've had no occasion,' she explained, 'no need to know.' This time Yarrow had no amendments to make to her statement which he passed over to her. She read it carefully, nodded her approval and signed where he told her to.

After Lady Sarah came her son. Walter had an engaging look, and was slightly plumper than he had seemed when Yarrow had seen him sitting in the dining room. He moved and spoke lightly and had the same manner as his mother. He was twenty-seven years old and lived in London, working for a large publishing company.

His account of Saturday evening matched his mother's, except that he had emerged from the dining room some thirty minutes after her – 'That's all I can ever bear of those men-only hog sessions,' he commented. He had talked sociably with the guests in various combinations and, soon after his mother left the party at 2 a.m., he had gone up to bed with George Waterford. He gave this information without reflection, but there was a challenge in the tilt of his chin. He had no idea what was talked about in the main parlour, nor did he have the slightest interest. He recalled Ellen Sheerley and Robert Homer saying they were going out for a walk around 1.30; he had not seen them again. He had known her for many years and liked her, but in the years when she had become a frequent visitor to Granthelm House he had been away most of the time – first at university and then living in London. Although she had also lived in London, they had not seen each other there at all – only when visits to his home coincided. Otherwise their paths did not cross, since they moved in quite distinct social circles. He expressed the clichés of distress at her death. Robert Homer he did not know well and, after deftly checking with Fathers that it was all right to speak ill of the dead, was prepared to add he did not like him either. 'Teeny bit bumptious,' he said when Fathers pressed for a reason, 'fast money.'

'Fast? Do you possibly mean, maybe a little shady as well?'

'I wouldn't know,' said Walter Granthelm quickly.

'But that was your impression, was it?'

'No. I just mean the way he lived, what little I saw of it, was quite money-fixated. I didn't like it.'

'Do you know how he made his living?'

'No.'

'How did he meet your father?'

'I don't actually know, but I'd always thought it was through Ellen. I don't think it was because he and Madeleine were shacking up. Or at least, it was around that time, but not through Madeleine, I mean.'

'And how long did that relationship of theirs last?' asked Fathers. Yarrow was struck, this time as often in the past, by how easily Fathers absorbed a new piece of information and gave the impression he had known it already.

'Oh, several months, till he chucked her last autumn.'

'Mm. Now, Miss Sheerley and Mr Rankley were also . . .'

'Yes, in fact it's all rather a sore point with Madeleine. She didn't like Peter two-timing her, and she didn't like being given the boot by Homer either. Especially because he then carried on with Ellen. She's been a bit snappy with Ellen ever since. Christmas was not pleasant, I can tell you, what with that, and a certain frostiness between my father and her.'

'"Her" being Miss Sheerley or your sister?'

'Ellen. Don't know what it was about, though.'

Walter knew nothing about Homer's family background and nothing about the keys of the house and where they were kept. He had, as he pointed out, left home. He read through his statement with a good grace, signed it and offered to get his sister himself.

Before Madeleine Granthelm arrived, Pardoner turned up bearing a tray with coffee pot, cups and saucers, milk, sugar and biscuits. 'Sorry this took so long,' he said. Yarrow poured the coffee – black with no sugar for Fathers, very white with two lumps for himself.

'Anyway, it's all done and I'm off. The cupboard's sturdy with a good lock – no sign it's been forced or picked open. The alarm system is BergSafe Three: fully functioning and Bolt showed me the certificates from the last three checks – they're done six-monthly. I phoned in and Bunn's going to meet me at Waterloo with a couple of techs and we'll go straight round to Homer's pad and destroy it. He's fixing the warrant now. Fortunately, he lived alone – our Greek chum, that is.'

Yarrow looked quickly at Pardoner, interest and puzzlement simultaneously etching themselves on his forehead, but he said nothing.

'Fine,' said Fathers. 'We've just got the two more interviews, then we'll have a word with Brain and the hacks and toddle back to town. Check in when you're done with Homer's place and we'll have a drink before finally knocking off, OK?'

'Right. Brain's got something for you to see, by the way. A photograph, he said. He apologised for not having shown it you before we came out here.'

Fathers nodded. The provincial policeman would not like having been inefficient, and he wouldn't like apologising directly to Fathers for it. The apology sent via Pardoner was supposed to suffice.

As Pardoner left, Madeleine Granthelm arrived and sat down. She had her mother's slimness and her father's height. She was stylish, good-looking with a good figure, and very attractive. Yarrow found it hard to keep his eyes off her and on his notepad. She paid him no attention, alternating her gaze between Fathers and her hands clasped in her lap. After allowing her to express shock at the death of two lovely people, Fathers went through the events of Saturday evening. The same scenes of ladies withdrawing to leave gentlemen with cigars and later being joined by some were unfurled. Her father had appeared on the scene for the first time a few minutes after the Briggs family left at about one o'clock. Some time later the party began to break up definitively as the Americans all decided to go to bed. Her mother, brother and George Waterford had left them around two and she said her good nights soon after, leaving just her father and Peter Rankley in the music room.

'What time was that?' asked Fathers.

'It was a little before two thirty when I switched off the light, and I suppose that getting ready for bed took about ten or fifteen minutes, so it was about ten or quarter past two probably when I left Peter and my father in the music room. I was wearing a watch, but I don't remember looking at it.'

'Mm. And what time did Mr Rankley get to bed?'

'I don't know.'

'He didn't wake you up when he got in, you mean?'

'No,' said Madeleine straightforwardly. 'I mean that he didn't get into my bed. We didn't sleep together last night.'

'Why not?'

Madeleine leaned back in her chair and looked steadily at Fathers. 'What business is it of yours?' she asked coolly.

'There is no need for you to know that,' replied Fathers with equal calm, 'but I do need to know your answer to my question, please.'

'We just didn't, that's all. Sometimes we do when we're here and sometimes we don't. That night we didn't. All right?'

'So it's not unusual for you not to sleep together when you're here?'

'It's neither usual nor unusual,' she said with a touch of her father's asperity. 'Sometimes we do . . .'

'And sometimes you don't,' Fathers chimed in. She smiled. 'I don't apologise for the necessity of these questions,' he continued, 'but I do understand your reluctance to answer. It's perfectly normal. Unfortunately, they are necessary and so are your answers. You liked Miss Sheerley and Mr Homer, did you?'

'Yes.'

'In fact, just now you described them as lovely people, I think,' said Fathers. She nodded. 'Although yesterday evening you passed a rather negative comment on Mr Homer, describing him I think as rather *nouveau* – is that right, Yarrow?'

Yarrow made a show of flipping back through his notepad.

'That's right, sir: "rather *nouveau*".'

'Who told you that?' she asked sharply.

'That doesn't matter,' said Fathers. 'Did you, in fact, say it?'

'Well – it's true, but it doesn't mean to say I didn't like him. I was just commenting. I actually thought he was very nice, but he was just a bit *gauche* sometimes, that's all. He was actually very vibrant and I found that quite appealing, but it had this other side to it and he could be a bit tactless about money.'

'You knew him well, then?'

'Not really, not well. But he's been here before and I've met him a few times in London at various do's.'

'So you've never met his family?'

'No.'

'What did he do for a living?'

'That was a bit – well, not mysterious, but unclear – at least as far as I was concerned. He used to say he was in international trade, but I don't actually know what it meant. He has shares in this and that, including a couple of rather nice restaurants, I think. But I don't really know.'

'I gather he was interested in horse-racing.'

'Was he? I didn't know.'

'Despite having had an affair with him.'

She blushed. 'It wasn't really an affair,' she said after a moment. 'Just a quick fling.'

'On the rebound while Mr Rankley was having an affair with Miss Sheerley, perhaps?'

'Not on the rebound, no. I didn't know police business was a matter of tittle-tattle and gossip.'

'How did you feel about Mr Homer when he ended your affair?'

'I – it wasn't an affair, it wasn't . . . important enough to merit that description, nor long enough.'

'And when it ended, how did you feel?'

Madeleine shrugged. '*C'est la vie*,' she replied with what Yarrow thought was entirely artificial brightness.

'And how did you feel?' insisted Fathers.

'Not very happy and not very sad. These things happen, you know. It passed the time – for a very short while.'

'And how did you feel about Miss Sheerley having an affair with Mr Rankley?'

She blushed again and bit her lip. 'I wasn't happy,' she said, 'but it finished and well – all was forgiven.'

'It ended in the autumn, didn't it?'

She nodded.

'How did you get on with Miss Sheerley after that?'

'As I said, all was forgiven. We got on fine. Perfectly. She was a very nice girl and I've always liked her.'

'So the fact that she had a relationship with your lover and you had one with hers did not in any way affect your relationship with her?'

Madeleine looked hard at the detective, and when she next spoke, the Sir Walter in her came out strongly: 'Mr Fathers, either this is all unnecessary, in which case please stop it, or you are implying I had a motive for their murders – in which case we can stop this interview right now and continue it only with a lawyer present and only if you formally decide to hold me.'

Fathers looked at her in silence for a long time. Yarrow tapped his pen on his pad in an even slow rhythm. She looked irritably at Yarrow who avoided her gaze and instead watched her hands which were now gripping the edge of the table.

'I'll note that comment,' said Fathers finally, 'and remind you that you are at any time entitled to request the presence of a lawyer, in which case we'll continue the interview at the police station.' He paused to let the words sink in. 'Do you want to do that or shall we continue here?'

She waved her hand at him. 'Go on,' she muttered.

'I'll also remind you,' said Fathers, 'that one or two of your earlier replies were rather misleading. You say you didn't know him well, but in fact you did.'

'Not really well.'

'Well enough to have slept with him.'

She remained silent.

'Do you wish to change any of your other replies?' asked Fathers. 'You still say you didn't meet his family?' She nodded. 'You didn't know what he did for a living?' She shook her head. 'And you didn't know he was interested in horse-racing?'

'Well, yes, all right, I did know that.'

'He gambled?'

'Yes.'

'Successfully?'

'Occasionally.'

'He wasn't in debt?'

'No, Rob always had plenty of money.'

'How did you meet him?'

'Through Father. He introduced us one day in town when his stupid secretary got his lunch dates mixed up and we both went out with him.'

'How did they meet?'

'Rob said it was business. But I don't know what kind.'

Fathers nodded, then asked her about the keys. She knew where the house keys were kept, and knew who had keys to the cupboard in the kitchen. She also knew her father kept his key in his desk in the library and that it was in a secret compartment.

'Do you know how to open it?'

'Yes. I've known for years. Discovered it when I was ten years old, I think, messing around on a wet afternoon.'

After the business of amending her statement was complete and she had read and signed it, Yarrow accompanied her out of the library and looked for Peter Rankley. He found him in the main parlour reading a newspaper. Before he could say anything, Rankley rose with a grunted 'At last' and strode into the library. He sat down heavily opposite Fathers and said, 'Well?'

As Yarrow sat down he could feel Fathers' tetchiness, but his boss smiled, apologised for keeping Rankley waiting so long, and began gently to go through the account he had given to Brain the day before.

Rankley went on as he had begun, without bothering to control his irritation. According to him, he had not at any stage noticed the time on Saturday evening and thought it of no account. He claimed forgetfulness of what had been discussed with Homer, Mulholland and Sir Walter in the main parlour, but was emphatic that it was not about business. 'Why should it be?' he said. 'None of us is doing business together.'

'No?' said Fathers lightly. 'I understood different.'

'Mulholland and Sir Walter are,' said Rankley with such a confident air that it did not sound as if he were contradicting what he had just said, 'but they didn't talk about it.'

'And Homer and Sir Walter,' suggested Fathers in a tone that almost made the comment into a question, but not quite.

'No,' said Rankley, 'not that I knew.'

'And you with any of them?'

'No.'

'How did you meet Homer?'

'Through Ellen.'

'Was that while you were having your affair with her?'

Rankley paused, his neck and ears turning red. 'That's not true,' he said.

'Oh I think it is,' said Fathers quietly.

'Just a passing fancy,' replied Rankley. 'Nothing came of it.'

'What does that mean?'

'It was casual, soon over, not serious.'

'But you did sleep with her.'

'Yes.'

'How well did you know Homer?'

'Not well.'

'What'd he do for a living?'

'He ran some sort of trading company. I don't know the details.'

'Ever meet his family?'

'No.'

'Did he ever talk about them?'

'I think his father's a stockbroker, lives near Esher.'

'Not far from here, then.'

'Not far, no.'

'Did you like Homer?'

Rankley shrugged his large shoulders. 'Not especially, didn't dislike him, though.'

'And Miss Sheerley?'

Rankley shrugged again.

'You liked her well enough,' said Fathers, 'to have an affair with her.'

'It didn't last,' replied Rankley. 'I liked her, but we didn't get on well enough for anything serious to come of it.'

Fathers finished by asking about the key, about which Rankley expressed total ignorance. Fathers nodded and turned to Yarrow, who passed Rankley the unchanged statement to sign. He read it, signed it and stood up.

'Thank you, Mr Rankley,' said Fathers. 'Most helpful.' He smiled at the look of puzzlement which greeted his closing comment.

CHAPTER 7

1

The farewells were perfunctory and barely polite. Neither the Granthelms nor Rankley met the eyes of either detective as they acknowledged Fathers' request that, if they were planning to travel any distance, they should first inform him or DI Brain. Halfway up the lane Yarrow stopped the car. ''Scuse me a moment, guv,' he muttered and turned round to get his briefcase. He walked over to the converted stables where the Carrocks lived. Ten minutes later he was back. 'Just seeing a man about a dog,' he commented as he restarted the engine.

They found Brain in his office, talking on the phone. He looked up as the pair of Scotland Yard men walked in and waved a photograph at them. Fathers took it and looked at it with Yarrow. It was a picture of Robert Homer, slumping dead on the sofa in Granthelm House's small parlour. The bullet hole showed clearly, about halfway up the forehead, almost exactly above the point where his left eyebrow ended at the bridge of the nose.

'So give it a spin,' said Brain into the telephone. 'You've got the warrant, haven't you?' He listened for a moment, then snapped, 'Just do it.' He hung up. 'Antiques,' he said. 'A dodgy dealer's secret warehouse.'

'Oh yeah,' said Yarrow with interest. 'Who is it?'

'Yarrow's dropped antiques to come down here,' explained Fathers.

'It's a lad called Pillbury.'

'Oh, I know him,' said Yarrow. 'Think you've got him this time?'

'Ach,' said Brain. 'Probably not. You know what he's like – enough whispers to burn your ears off, a thousand warrants, and never a glimpse of anything he shouldn't have. Mind you, I'm never sure if he really is a bad 'un, or whether all that talk is just the other dealers niggled by the rings he runs round 'em. Now, the photograph. May not count for much, but the hole's in an odd place, and the *p.m.* says the angle of entry was very steep.'

'Right, Yarrer, on the sofa,' ordered Fathers. Yarrow complied, sitting on one of the spare chairs, checking the photograph

86

to arrange his body as Homer's was. 'All right. Now, sit upright.' He held his finger to Yarrow's head, at the spot where Homer had been shot. 'Bang.' He pushed hard with his finger and Yarrow jerked back as if he had been shot. His head rested on the chair-back in almost exactly the same position as Homer's. 'Now top yourself.'

'Oh it's all too much,' said Yarrow as he sat upright again, holding an imaginary pistol to his head. 'I can't go on – bang. Strange way to hold it.'

'What're the classic ways to end it all?' asked Fathers sitting down in the other chair. 'In the mouth or the temple, or holding the gun with two hands directly in front, thumbs on trigger, or with one hand holding it upside down.'

'Could be done,' said Yarrow. 'You turn and duck your head a bit as you squeeze the tit, suddenly taking fright and all, or it slips.'

'Quite believable,' said Brain. 'But if you were knocking somebody off and going to fake it as suicide, and you whip the gun out when the bugger's off guard, wouldn't you make it look like one of the classic methods?'

'Oh dear,' said Fathers. 'This is getting complicated, isn't it?'

'Nah,' said Yarrow. 'He sees it coming, jerks, but too late.'

'Contact wound,' objected Fathers.

'He's too slow,' replied Yarrow. 'Slight movement before the shot's fired. Or the killer does it so fast, he can't get it exactly right. Gets the gun to the head, but it's a fast movement and he only gets one chance.'

'Mm, could be,' said Fathers. 'What d'you think?'

'Could be,' agreed Brain. 'I don't know. Just thought it was worth mentioning, that's all. After all, if it's meant to look like suicide, why bother to walk off with the gun in your pocket? Why not drop it where it looks realistic?'

'Nerves,' said Fathers, and simultaneously, 'Panic,' said Yarrow.

'So why use the second gun at all?' persisted Brain.

The Yard pair were silent for a while. Then Yarrow said hesitantly, 'Maybe Homer's still got the first one. I mean, maybe he done her in and then somebody else did him – for revenge like.' He paused and cast a swift look at Fathers.

'Maybe,' his boss grunted noncommittally.

'But, I mean, does it matter if it was meant to look like suicide? We know it's not. We know we're looking for a killer – so what else do we want?'

'The gun. Maybe you're right, but we do need that gun.'

'I've got some more men lined up for tomorrow,' said Brain. 'We'll keep going till we've covered all the grounds.'

'You're sure it's not in the house?' said Fathers.

'Yes,' replied Brain shortly.

'Fair enough. You haven't got to Homer's family, have you, yet?'

'No. Been looking, but I can't get a line on them. They haven't come forward either, even though his name's in all the papers.'

'Rankley says they live in Esher. Father's a stockbroker.'

'He didn't say yesterday. I'll get on to it. Before you go, by the way, should we make sure we've all got copies of the statements? The Briggses and the temporary staff were seen today by a lad of mine. They've all signed on the dotted.'

'Right. Maybe Yarrow and your secretary can sort out the others while you and me go see the press. Are there many there?'

'Still a coupla nationals, two locals, PA, and a couple of radio bods and a TV crew. Have you got anything to tell 'em?'

'No. I'll cobble up an introductory statement, and they'll ask a few questions, and I'll mainly say, "No comment," and that'll be that.'

2

'The whole matter,' said Sir Walter Granthelm, 'is ill-conceived and in its execution has been amateurish in the extreme.' He was standing beside Peter Rankley's Morgan sports car, into the boot of which Bolt had just put the ex-rugby forward's suitcase. He had waited until the butler had gone back into the house with his usual generous tip before broaching the question of business. 'I want no more of it.'

'Look,' said Rankley, casting an eye at the constable still standing by the door, 'if it makes you feel any better, I don't understand it any more than you do . . .'

'No it does not make me feel better,' snapped Sir Walter.

'. . . but that's no reason for going off the wall,' continued Rankley, heaving his bulk behind the steering wheel and closing the door with a neat click. 'There's been some simple mistake somewhere.'

'Your mistake.'

'No, not mine. Look, you are as committed as we all are – this is not a recoverable investment at this point, there is no turning back, as well you know, and anyway there's no need to worry.'

'No need to worry,' echoed Sir Walter scathingly. 'How can you say that, you arrogant, inexperienced cretin, when you understand no more than I do what the hell's going on? What do you know? Have you ever been involved in a deal of this scale or of this nature? No you have not. Do you know the possible risks and pitfalls? No. Do you understand the world in which you're operating? It's not to be found in a land economy textbook, you know. The entire investment is in danger because of Mulholland's whim and your ineptitude.'

Rankley pulled the starter switch. The engine roared as he pressed the accelerator. When it settled down to ticking over, he said, 'It was not a whim and there is no ineptitude. If you'd calm down for a moment, you could see that. Davis said it all last night. We are, as he might say, in a go situation. From now on, it's only profit. The weekend has upset you. That's understandable, but don't go jumping into any ill-considered action.'

'You're warning me, are you?' said Sir Walter grimly.

'I'm offering some advice which you'd do well to take. The deal is sound. Every problem has been resolved, every eventuality covered, nothing can go wrong and nothing will.'

'I should never have agreed to it in the first place.'

'But you did – eagerly, if you remember – and you're in too far to pull out. Don't even think of it.'

Sir Walter turned on his heel and stalked into the house. Rankley shrugged, engaged the gears and was gone. As Sir Walter closed the door on the noise of the car, Madeleine came down the stairs.

'Is everything all right with Peter?' she asked anxiously. 'I don't like it when you two bicker.'

'That is the most ridiculous car for a man of that size,' said her father angrily.

'Oh, that's all right then,' said Madeleine.

'Thanks, guv,' said Pardoner and Yarrow in chorus, accepting the pints their boss put on the table. They were sitting in Fathers' favourite pub, fifteen minutes' walk from Scotland Yard and therefore not as packed by other policemen as the ones which were closer.

As Fathers sat down, DI Stevens came in, looked round, spotted his colleagues and walked over. 'All looked after?' he said, casting his eye at the full mugs on the table.

'Here, let me,' said Fathers, standing up. 'The usual?'

Stevens nodded, pulled a stool over and sat down. 'How's it been going?' he asked.

'Bordering on the tolerable,' said Pardoner. 'A nice juicy one for the annals.'

'Double murder yet,' said Stevens. 'City magnate, high society girls, Americans, a locked room in a country house. What more could you want?'

'A solution,' said Fathers, returning with Stevens' whisky.

The four took sips from their respective drinks. Then Stevens and Pardoner pulled out cigarette packets and after a desultory gesture at offering them to the others, each lit up.

Yarrow was a non-smoker. He had started to smoke when he was nine, and given up for good when he was seventeen. Pardoner, he reflected, was a restricted smoker. Although the Detective Sergeant always carried cigarettes on him, he resisted the temptation until his first visit to the pub in the evening, and then smoked like a chimney in order to compensate for his earlier self-control. Stevens, on the other hand, was a proper smoker, but with a difference. Though trying to reduce his intake, he went through a packet and a half of Gauloises each day. His method of cutting down was predictably idiosyncratic: instead of buying fewer or restricting his smoking hours, he smoked less of each one. Now, for example, he lit up and then rested the cigarette on the ashtray, letting it smoulder there. As he took part in the conversation, he would forget about smoking and let the cigarette burn down to the end. Sooner or later he would want another puff, notice his first one had gone out and light up a second, which would get the same treatment. Yarrow doubted if the Detective Inspector averaged more than two or three puffs a time. Fathers was a rather different case. For several years he had been, in principle, a non-smoker of cigarettes – which meant that he smoked at times of particular stress or discomfort and at social occasions. After Christmas, however, he had changed and was now, in principle, a non-smoker of cigars – which meant that he smoked at times of particular pleasure, such as when the working day was ended, as well as snitching other people's cigarettes when the need was on him. He got a packet of cigars out now, selected one and lit it with Pardoner's matches. He exhaled, so that the cloud of heavy smoke hung over the table, and as he sighed with satisfaction he caught Yarrow's look.

'All right, Yarrer,' said Fathers, 'I'm not Sir Walter – I won't blow it at you.'

'You do an' I'll blow it right back,' replied Yarrow. 'I've dealt with the quality now, mate, you watch out.'

'And did you find it at all improving to associate with better circles?' enquired Stevens.

'Nah,' said Yarrow, 'all they do is screw in the grass, take 'eroin, shoot each other and blow smoke atcha. Smart birds, mind.'

'Well,' said Stevens, 'as a behavioural analysis of social classes A and B, I doubt that could be bettered, though you did leave out making money and spending it. What's this about smoke-blowing?'

'Sir Walter got narked with me,' explained Fathers, 'and took it out on the lad by blowing a few lungfuls of pipe-smoke at him. Yarrow blew it back like a good boy, but it didn't seem to help the man's temper.'

'Surprising that,' said Stevens, 'you'd think it'd sort him out no end.'

'Childish too,' muttered Yarrow.

'So who did it?' asked Stevens.

'If we knew that . . .' said Pardoner, leaving his sentence unfinished as he drank some more beer. 'Nothing of interest in Homer's flat,' he added.

'Where'd he run his business from, then?' asked Fathers.

Pardoner shrugged. 'The only papers in his flat are personal – tax and so on. But his company – he called it Agamemnon Trading, by the way – is registered at that address and the tax stuff has allowances for him using his home as his office. So I suppose he worked from there, but there's nothing like company books and what have you.'

'Did he use a secretary or anything?'

Pardoner shrugged again. 'I haven't been through everything yet by any means. We'll see.'

'First thing in the morning,' said Fathers. Pardoner nodded. 'No, second thing,' Fathers corrected himself, 'after you've had a word with our other house guests – the Mulhollands and the George-Watkinses and this Waterford johnnie.'

'I rather think,' said Pardoner, 'that you should do the G-Ws yourself.'

'Oh?'

'Senior Yankee diplomat and all that. Protocol, you know.'

'Probably right at that,' sighed Fathers. 'OK, I'll do him and his lady wife, and you do Waterford and the people with the funny first names. Brown and Davis: which is which?'

'Brown's the missus,' said Yarrow.

'Mrs Brown, you've got a lovely daughter,' sang Stevens. 'Anybody want another?'

'I'll have the other half, thanks,' said Fathers.

'Me too, ta,' said Pardoner.

'No thanks,' said Yarrow, 'I've got to nip off and see a grass in a minute or two. Quality in the afternoon and shit in the evening.'

As Stevens went off to the bar, Fathers turned to Pardoner: 'Check the statements through with them and then sound them out about the keys and get everything you can about how well they know the others, especially Homer and Sheerley, how they met. Ask Mulholland what business he's doing with Sir Walter. Also, when you've got that lot under your belt, Sheerley's flat, her flatmate if any, other friends.' Pardoner nodded. 'You, m'boy,' Fathers added to Yarrow, 'can start going into the background. Routine checks to begin with. Don't forget Mulholland's American. Talk to Drug Squad about Sheerley. And the gun that's been found: I want its history. But first thing in the morning, get round to Sir Walter's office in the City and sound out his secretary.'

'About him and Homer?' asked Yarrow.

'Got it in one. I'll try to see at least Mr G-W in the morning and we'll see if we can have a pow-wow shortly after lunch. See how far we've got, if anywhere.'

Stevens arrived with the new drinks and handed half-pint glasses to Fathers and Pardoner. 'So how's it feel?' he asked.

'Not good,' said Fathers, 'though that doesn't mean anything.'

92

'What's the theory then?'

'Don't have one.'

'How about these chickens?'

'Some chicken,' rumbled Pardoner, blowing out his cheeks and trying to look and sound like Churchill, 'some neck.'

'But no theory?' said Stevens. 'No explanation?'

'I have devised seven separate explanations,' said Yarrow, 'each of which would cover the facts as far as we know them, but since we know fuck all, what's the use?'

'Where did that one come from?' asked Fathers.

'That's "The Adventure of the Copper Beeches",' said Yarrow, 'changed a bit, though you probably didn't spot that, not knowing the original and all.'

'What do you do, Elly?' asked Pardoner. 'Learn some up the night before and just wait for the right time to drop 'em into the conversation, all casual-sounding, or do you remember them without trying?'

Yarrow shrugged, embarrassed. 'Some of them just sort of stick out when I'm reading,' he said.

'Seven explanations,' said Stevens, 'and I'll bet they're all to do with sex.'

'That's the most likely, isn't it?' said Fathers. 'What a tangle: the Granthelm woman with Rankley; Rankley with Sheerley; Sheerley with Homer; and Homer with the Granthelmette.'

'Not to mention the gay couple,' said Pardoner.

'All at once?' asked Stevens.

'Makes you think, doesn't it?' said Fathers. 'Stop it, Yarrer, you'll go blind.'

'There's the business of the locked room, too,' said Stevens. 'Adds a certain *je ne sais quoi*, eh?'

'Now that's where *I've* got seven separate explanations,' said Fathers, 'all of which would fit the known facts. I've a feeling with this one, unless we get something on the guns, that we're going to approach it arse first.'

'An appropriate mode,' commented Stevens with a wink.

'I mean by looking into the background and digging up a motive.'

Yarrow brightened up considerably at this. He, after all, had been given the task of going into the background. 'If it was sex,' he said, 'worth remembering who knew where the key was.'

'Who?' said Pardoner.

'Sir Walter, Madeleine, Bolt and Mrs Carrock,' said Fathers.

'And maybe Rankley from Madeleine,' added Yarrow.

Fathers nodded. 'Of course, that's only who says they know where the key's kept.'

'It might be nothing to do with sex,' said Pardoner.

'That's why Yarrer's off to the City and you're asking Mulholland about business – and why the single most important thing to look for when you go through Homer's stuff is anything that will give us a line on his work.'

'Brain might help us there via the family,' suggested Pardoner.

'Could be.'

Yarrow stood up. 'Thanks for the drink, guv,' he said. 'One thing, who was Homer?'

'The poet, you mean?' said Fathers.

'Oh,' said Yarrow blankly. 'Poet. Dead is he?'

'A few thousand years ago.'

'So he wasn't English?'

'Greek.'

'Greek?'

'Yes. Why?'

Yarrow paused. 'You know I said I was trying to remember something,' he said.

'Yes.'

'There was a whisper about a Greek we came across a coupla weeks ago – you know, while we've been looking into the antiques thing. I mean, they just call him "the Greek", and we thought that meant he was Greek, if you see what I mean.'

'Seems a reasonable inference,' said Fathers. 'What of it?'

'It was to do with silver – that's why when I was thinking about the robbery at that house and after the skipper said something which sort of sparked the connection . . .' He let the sentence tail off when he saw Fathers' sceptical look. 'Do you think it's worth just looking it out, then?' he asked diffidently.

'You never know,' said Fathers. 'In this business, you do not never know.'

Yarrow nodded and left. 'Bright kid, that,' said Stevens when the detective constable had gone.

'And getting brighter all the time,' agreed Fathers.

'Why don't you ever let him know then?'

Fathers considered Stevens' question for a moment. 'It'd be bad for his soul,' he said. 'Anyway, I do let him know. I just don't let him know as often as I know he wants me to let him know.'

'Tricky stuff, that psychology,' Stevens observed.

'How're you feeling about the Promotion Board Friday?'

'Bad for my soul,' said Stevens.

CHAPTER 8

1

Yarrow reached the Bricklayers' Arms pub close by Roman Road in Bethnal Green a few minutes after nine o'clock. A Monday night, so trade was not brisk. He had no trouble recognising Michael Kay standing at the bar, and the four other men in the room had equally little trouble recognising Yarrow as the old bill. What is it, he wondered, which makes it possible for perfectly honest Londoners to spot a cop a mile off, and means they have to shut up immediately? But are they perfectly honest? He walked up to the bar. 'What'll it be then, Michael?' he asked abruptly.

'Bitter, please,' said Kay, 'with a Bell's to chase it, since it's on expenses.'

'Two pints please, missus,' said Yarrow to the landlady. To Kay he added, 'It's not on expenses till I'm sure there's something to all of this.' He accepted and paid for the beer in silence, pocketed his change and walked over to a table in the corner. Kay joined him.

'Cheers, mate,' said Kay.

'Mate?' said Yarrow. He drank from his beer. 'This the grot-hole you usually drink in, then?'

'Do us a favour,' said Kay. 'I didn't want to meet in any of my regular places, case we were seen.'

Yarrow grunted and drank some more. This was close to where he had grown up. He remembered Kay well – a kid from the same estate, a few years younger, always getting into trouble. He had looked up Kay's record after he got back to the Yard from Guildford, and nothing in it surprised him. 'What's it all about then?' he asked.

Kay lit a cigarette and began to tell him. He started with a long rigmarole about where he had been on Saturday night and who he had been with. Yarrow sighed, only half-listening, wondering and doubting whether this was going to be worth it. His mind slipped from Kay and his course from one pub to another on Saturday, and he thought about where he had been that afternoon.

The books in the library: Yarrow could still not get over them. And the view from the library window – to his perception, as

96

rarefied and strange as the possession by one individual of some thousands of books. Not that the fact that such a view existed was strange, only that there should be people who lived in a house from which it could be enjoyed. At the back of Granthelm House, a rich lawn sloped away steeply from a large terrace before levelling off into a plateau mostly hidden from the house by bushes. Beyond that, the downs stretched away – that day, in spring sunshine. Yarrow pondered views: from the eighteenth floor of the tower block in which he had been brought up, the view over the docklands had been spectacular in its own way, but there was a heavy price to be paid for enjoying it. The lifts had no indicators, were out of action through either vandalism or breakdown for half the time, and smelt permanently of urine except when the odour of vomit dominated. The phones in them, for use in emergencies, were connected to an office that seemed to be invariably unoccupied. When a flat on the floor below his family's was broken into by having its door smashed off its hinges, the police found nobody who would acknowledge having heard or seen anything. He had come home from school more than once to find bits of the door jamb chiselled away, presumably by kids trying to break in. His father had always fixed it afterwards – it wasn't worth waiting for the council to come. Joining the police had been Yarrow's passport out of that country; his younger sister had married at eighteen to get hers. His parents were still there, desperately seeking but never finding an alternative to the modern flat in the modern block which the council had been so proud of twenty years before, which they had been so pleased to move into before their world had collapsed with inflation, his dad's unemployment and the steady disintegration of the inner city and all its amenities and services.

The view from the eighteenth floor had been spectacular, especially at dusk. But between the view and the viewer was the reality of daily life. The view from the Granthelms' terrace was spectacular in a different way – softer, less cluttered, not angry. And the reality of life – except for rare interlopers like Yarrow – did not get between the view and the viewer: it connected them in a relationship of wealth, ownership and confidence.

Yarrow snapped out of his reverie: 'Who did you say?'

'Ah,' said Kay with satisfaction, 'I thought that'd get you

going. I said Detective Inspector rat-face Queen and Jacko fat-arse Pascall.'

'Go on.'

'So Jacko says he'll see rat-face right, and rat-face says they can do business.'

'Those their exact words, are they? "I'll see you right" and "We can do business".'

'Near enough.'

'What's "near enough" mean?'

'Well, Jacko says, "I'll see you right, Queenie," and he says, "You're on, mate."'

'Word for word?'

'Word for effing word.'

'What else?'

'Nothing else. They talked about this and that for a bit and then pig-eyes gets up to go and says, "I'll keep you in touch if anything breaks," and Jacko says, "Make sure you do." And then Queen says, "But you get it sorted out fast," and Jacko says, "OK."'

'And where are you sitting all this time, or were they shouting it from the stage?'

'Like I said – were you dreaming or something? – they were sitting in the corner and I was standing by the wall just round where they couldn't spot me. See, I saw them together and I thought, 'allo-'allo, what's going on 'ere then, a plod an' a crim sitting cheek to bleeding cheek, so I strolled over like to get an earful. An' I did an' all.'

Yarrow finished his beer. 'Another?' he said, walking to the bar without waiting for the answer. He returned with two fresh pints.

'Still no Bell's?' complained Kay. 'What's wrong? What more d'you want?'

'A whole lot more,' said Yarrow in his most dubious voice. 'Queen's the one who nicked you, isn't he, for the watches? Receiving: big time stuff that for a ponce like you.'

'He was gardening,' said Kay, outraged. 'Anyway what d'you mean – ponce? Fucking hell.'

'You pleaded guilty.'

'Fucking mouthpiece said I should. Said there was no way I was getting off and I might as well not fight it and then the beak'd be lenient. Shit-head. The stuff was planted all the same.'

'Makes it worse if you reckon he fitted you up,' commented

Yarrow. 'Getting your own back, are we, by telling a little pork pie to get him in the shit? Come on, Michael, you'll have to do a bit better than that.'

'If that's your attitude, I'm off,' said Kay. But he made no move to go. 'You gotta bent screw hanging about with Jacko Pascall – you don't need to bother why I'm telling you. So what if it's a chance to dish that fucker? All right – I'm no grass, most times if I'd heard something like that I'd've kept my mouth shut. Since it's Queen, I want to see him done for it. Fair enough. But it's true all the same, God's my witness.'

'When were you last in church then?' sneered Yarrow. 'Of course, if you're no grass, you'll not want paying for this.'

Kay stayed silent.

'Or will you?' asked Yarrow.

'I want my whack.'

'Straight between the ruddy teeth, sunshine, if you're messing about on this.'

Kay bit back a retort and took a long drink of his beer. 'Saw them again this afternoon,' he said.

'Oh yeah.'

'Yeah. I was just passing. Saw Queen go into Jacko's place on Duffy Street. 'Bout an hour later he came out, and then Jacko comes out straight after him.'

Yarrow toyed with his beer for a moment, then took a sip. 'I can check where he was this afternoon, you know,' he observed, 'and I can make your life a misery if you're sodding about. What time was it?'

'Two thirty to three thirty,' said Kay confidently, 'give or take.'

Yarrow nodded. If Kay was prepared to risk him carrying out his threat, there could be something in it. Kay had never been particularly clever, or especially brave. It didn't seem likely he'd have the guts to risk Yarrow's wrath, nor the smarts to work out a way of deceiving him. 'Tell me about Pascall,' he said.

'What? Ain't'cha got it all on file, then?'

'I can look it up tomorrow,' said Yarrow, 'easy as I looked you up today. But save me the trouble. He's a loan-shark, isn't he?'

'That's how he started.'

'What's this place on Duffy Street you mentioned?'

'He's in the rag-trade now. It's his legit side, if you can call it that. Dozens of Pakky bints beavering away in their ratty little homes for next to nothing, and then they hand the stuff over and

Jacko wholesales it. Duffy Street's where he keeps his stock.'

'But he's still into loan-sharking, isn't he? Still his main line?'

'Yeah, but plus a lot more. Like when he gets some silly cow properly hooked, if she's young enough he puts 'er on the game to earn the interest for him.'

Yarrow nodded. These were good days for loan-sharks. A family got into money trouble, and Pascall or one of his people would hear about it. Next thing, a friendly visit, usually to the wife, and an offer of help. A hundred pounds, my dear, just to help you out with these bills, and then you can pay it back – let's say ten pounds a week over thirteen weeks. Of course, sweetheart, you've got to keep up with the payments, but if they get a bit difficult for you, have a word and we can probably sort something out. With most, especially the ones on social security, the unemployed, the one-parent families, the repayments simply broke the back of the weekly budget. Just to pay the interest, the loan had to be topped up – and then the borrower was on an ever-descending spiral. Pascall used the repayments to provide the top-up loans and took the allowance books for security, or one of his men turned up with the mailman when the giro arrived to make sure the repayment came out first. Even in families where the husband worked, the wife might need to borrow. Whether the man were employed or not, the woman would usually keep it a secret. If it was a working woman who borrowed, the shark took first bite from her pay packet. And when the troubles had built up to become unbearable, and she was thinking about shop-lifting the basic necessities, a way out would be offered: prostitution, usually. Good days for sharks, the 1980s.

'And then,' said Kay, 'he's got this crew of heavies to pick up the interest from the difficult ones. And he's used them for protection and to muscle in on a couple of clubs and what-not. Dunno what he isn't into.'

'Diversification, they call it,' said Yarrow. He paused thoughtfully. Kay should be given his chance, just in case this was genuine. 'Big fish, Michael. You sure you want to go on with this?'

'I can look after myself.'

'Don't make me laugh. If this is for real and Jacko hears about it, he'll send a couple of chums after you with pickaxe handles – not that they'd need them.'

Kay shivered. 'Yeah,' he said, 'but that's down to you, isn't it?

Because I'm not going to talk about it.'

'You make sure you don't,' said Yarrow, 'not to anybody but me. Not anybody – d'you understand? Not if the Metropolitan Commissioner comes calling and says he's taken over the case. You got me?' Kay nodded.

Yarrow stood up. 'I'll check it out then and get back to you.'

'How'll you find me?'

Yarrow walked over to the bar and bought another pint of bitter and a double measure of Bell's. He took them back to Kay. 'Don't worry,' he said, 'I'll find you.' He paused before leaving. 'When you called me, did you know Queen's my boss?'

Kay looked at him, shocked.

'Well, you do now. Don't worry, though. I got another boss above him who's straight as you like. They say he fixed a bent one some time back. I'll have a word with him. Without mentioning your name. But if this doesn't check out, you're gonna have a tough life. Get me?'

Kay nodded and drank his whisky.

2

Fathers arrived home a little after nine o'clock. Sarah greeted him with pleasure as he closed his front door. 'Hey,' she said, 'you're back sooner than you said. I was just about to eat. Shall I put something together for you or have you already eaten some disgusting crud?'

'Not a crumb of crud has passed my lips all day,' replied Fathers. 'How long've the kids been in bed?'

'They're probably still awake.'

'I'll go say good night. I'd love something to eat if you've got the stuff out.'

He went upstairs. Gary was asleep and had already kicked off his blankets. Fathers tucked him back in again and smoothed his son's hair as he wriggled and complained in his sleep. In her room, Samantha was still awake. 'Dad,' she said as he came in, as if she was picking up a conversation they had left off a few minutes before, 'do you think I will get into St Anne's?'

Fathers sat down on her bed. Samantha had been refused a place at the secondary school of their first choice and her parents were appealing against the decision. 'Yes,' he said, 'I do – but I only think it, mind you – we've talked about this and you know your mother and I can't promise it. But we'll do our best and I think we stand a very good chance. The first year isn't full up yet – we know that because I asked the head – and they have the more advanced maths course and the other ones don't. So I think it's a very good chance. It'll be a couple of months to wait before we have the actual hearing, but they do this sort of in-between stage that's not so formal, and I really do think they'll let you through then.'

'That's soon, isn't it?'

'Yes, though we don't know the exact date.'

'And will you be there?'

'Yes, I'll do everything I can to be there, my love, but you know your mother could do it by herself if need be – if I have to be in court or something.'

'Yes,' said Samantha, 'I know she could.'

'She can do anything.'

'Yes, mothers can do anything,' said Samantha, repeating the title of a picture-book she and her brother had had when they were little.

'Good night.'

'Good night, Dad.'

He kissed her and tucked her in. As he got to the door she said, 'Another hug,' so he went back and gave her one. As she wrapped her arms round his neck, she whispered, 'And have you only eaten raw food today?'

Fathers chuckled and disentangled himself. 'You can do anything too,' he said. 'Good night. See you in the morning.'

Downstairs in the kitchen, he put his arms round Sarah and kissed her. 'Sam's a-worrying,' he said.

Sarah traced the small scar by his mouth with her finger and nodded. 'And you've been drinking and smoking,' she said. 'We'll just have to wait and see, but it's harder for her.'

She kissed him again and he started to grin. 'What is it?' she said.

'I thought so,' he said and stood back from her. 'Confess.'

She looked at him out of the corner of her eye and turned away from him. 'Oh no,' he said, and grabbing her by the shoulders he swung her back to face him. 'As my little DC said today, Fathers knows all – or did he say I know best? Never mind. Just confess, it'll do you the power of good.'

'It was wholemeal bread,' said Sarah defensively, breaking away from him again.

'Don't gimme that,' said Fathers. 'It was a peanut butter snack, incompletely disguised, I might add, by the toothpaste with which you slyly brushed your teeth, hoping I wouldn't notice.'

'One sandwich,' muttered Sarah, 'and it's the third degree. Your job's getting to you, Harry. I'm worried.'

'So what happened,' asked Fathers, refusing to be put off, 'to all that stuff about fruit and nuts when you want to eat between meals?'

Sarah turned and looked him in the eye. 'I felt like peanut butter,' she said with defiant emphasis.

'That sort of day, was it?'

'Oh, so-so. Some kid shat all over some books in the children's library, that was the only highlight. How was yours?'

'Double murder. I was down in Guildford most of the time.'

'Oh, that country house thing? I thought the paper said it was murder and suicide.'

'We've changed our minds.'

'And they've called you in to take charge?'

'Well, the locals asked for some help and it ended up with me being put in charge.'

'Don't gimme that,' said Sarah, mimicking her husband's earlier tone. 'They asked for some help, and you said nothing doing unless you could run the show.'

Fathers shrugged. 'What're we having?'

'Yesterday's leftovers, topped up a bit, in pitta bread.'

Fathers smiled.

'Don't,' said Sarah beginning to laugh. When she had introduced the first change in their diet that January, wholemeal pitta bread had started to figure large. This had provoked Fathers into referring to Sammy Salad, Tommy Tomato, Beatrix Beetroot and so on. It was a silly joke, especially when they repeated it in infinite variations – and he and Sarah loved it.

'Anything on the box?' he asked.

3

Sir Walter Granthelm sat with his wife and daughter in the breakfast room watching the nine o'clock news. His son had returned to London an hour ago, straight after the evening meal was finished. He watched the news without real attention. When it was over Madeleine flicked the 'off' switch and brightly remarked that at least there had been nothing about them in it. Her father nodded. 'Small mercies, my dear,' he said. He rose and walked to the door. 'If you'll excuse me.'

He walked through the dining room into the hall and paused. The small parlour was firmly locked, the key removed by the police for forensic tests, a strip of sealing paper like masking tape stuck across the door from one jamb to the other in such a way that it would be impossible to enter the room without leaving a trace. He looked at it and shuddered, the memory of his brief look at the two dead bodies on the Sunday morning coming back to him with an intensity that made the nausea rise in his throat. As he crossed quickly to the music room, he thought of the calm policeman, pressing him for an account of *exactly* how long he had remained in the small parlour before joining Bolt at the phone. Fathers, he thought, will be a problem, and pressure could probably not be put on him the way it could on the local CID over the silver. The London man was an altogether different sort from the Brain fellow.

He crossed the hall and went to the drinks cabinet in the music room. Thankfully, it was fully stocked. Bolt must have found time to replenish the supplies after they had been plundered on Saturday night. He picked out a tumbler, poured a brandy with a splash of soda and took a long drink. It fought for a moment with the nausea, and won. He topped the glass up and walked more comfortably to the stereo. He flipped his fingers across the casettes, found Handel's *Messiah* and put it on. As he walked back to the box of Dominican cigars beside the drinks cabinet, he stopped for a moment to consider the portrait of himself and Lady Sarah, done five years ago, sitting in this room before the open window with the lawn sloping away behind and the downs rising up in the background. The artist had taken liberties with the landscape, lengthening the lawn and bringing the downs in closer than they truly were to make them more dramatic, with sky lit as in an early summer evening, the sun's rays slanting across to highlight the side of their faces. They sat on straight chairs, each with their hands in their lap, half turned to each other, half to the viewer, as if interrupted in private conversation. The painting combined intimacy with an awareness of family position.

Sir Walter looked at himself and his wife for several minutes, then shook his head and got a cigar. He nipped the end off, warmed it with the lighter from his pocket and put it in his mouth as the first wisps of smoke began to curl gently up. The taste brought his nausea back. He took the cigar from his mouth and frowned at it with distaste. He sipped some more brandy, which again drove the bile down. He sat down in his favourite chair, resting the cigar on the ashtray at the side table, and relaxed into the music.

The problem with Fathers was not just that he was intelligent, though he was obviously that. Nor just that he was determined and tough, though he was clearly both of those things too. After all, he did not head the hierarchy. At the rank of detective chief inspector, he supposed, a man has attained some seniority, the right to act on his judgement, the responsibility to run much of his work. But there were higher ranks who could control, limit, overrule him, however tough he was or determined or clever. No, the problem was that he appeared to be out of reach. That afternoon, during the seemingly endless wait for the peremptory summons which finally came from the shifty young fellow, Sir Walter had phoned a friend, a director of a daily newspaper. He had asked about Fathers. Fifteen minutes later he was called back. His friend had consulted the paper's senior crime reporter who, unfortunately, had been lyrical in Fathers' praise. The detective had registered many outstanding successes and had a long list of judges' commendations for the efficiency of his work. He had been five years at his current rank – which meant he had got it young, and further promotion was his for the asking, so the reporter was reliably informed, any time. Sir Walter's friend explained that, understanding what thought lay behind the enquiry, he had asked discreetly about Fathers' response to pressure. The reply had been so blunt he had noted it down almost verbatim and now repeated it: 'You won't find anybody to do him down,' the reporter had said, more or less. 'One of the Sundays went gunning for him a couple of years back over a botched kidnap case which hit the headlines – some rock star's daughter. But they got nowhere – nobody else would take it up – and the truth is it wasn't his fault anyway. Rumour has it he badly annoyed the Home Office around the same time and they wanted his blood, but the Yard backed him up and that was the end of that.'

Sir Walter had moodily thanked his friend and hung up. The Home Office might be a line to pursue, but he had no direct contacts there. It might be worth a few questions, perhaps a look through *Vacher's*, to see if there were any familiar names in useful positions – after all, civil servants tended to be mobile between ministries, or there might be an old college man. But if they were not people with whom he was in current or recent contact, approaching them on a matter like this in which he had no legitimate business interest might be complex, even counter-productive.

Sir Walter's thoughts drifted off Fathers and on to Rankley. That young bastard, he thought, with the arrogance and the apparent belief that he invented ruthlessness which marks out the new men in business and in politics. Not that ruthlessness itself was an issue – in so many cases such people turned out to be soft once the pressure was really on: it was the air of it they carried with them which grated so. He banged his fist on the arm of his chair in fury at himself for having turned to Rankley in the first place. It was that which had allowed the oaf to suck him into the deal with Mulholland. He downed his brandy and relit his cigar. The nausea came back immediately. He stubbed the cigar down angrily into the ashtray and ground it out. Then he rose and returned to the cabinet to get a refill. To Rankley, he thought, there is no obvious solution. The man is half right: there *is* cause to worry, but there is also no turning back. Fathers on the other hand: something might be possible there. There must be somebody he knew who could help; there always was.

CHAPTER 9

1

Michael George-Watkins' office was large and plush, dominated by a picture of President Reagan which was offset, even undermined Fathers thought, by several reproductions of eighteenth-century English political and social cartoons. The diplomat's welcome was friendly and communicated a readiness to help. He was a large man, taller and heavier than Fathers. He was in his late fifties, and not in good physical shape. Shoulders which might once have been broad and square seemed to have hunched, sloped and folded in towards his chest. His skin was so pale it was almost a genuine white, speckled at his hands and wrists, deeply lined on his face. Heavy bags under his quiet brown eyes gave him a look that reminded Fathers of an ageing hound. His short-cropped hair was a mixture of grey and white. He carried his right hand awkwardly and limply; the tops of his middle and fourth fingers were missing, and he extended his left hand to shake Fathers' right.

Fathers had spent most of the morning with Bastin and Cadwallader – not an unpleasant session, but in Fathers' view, entirely wasted. As Bastin neared retirement, he had developed the habit of taking up his senior officers' time with meetings that appeared to Fathers to lack any real purpose. This one had been dubbed a policy meeting. The previous week it had been personnel development. Before that it was crime prevention. In Fathers' mind, the policy of the Serious Crimes Squad was to solve as many serious crimes as it could and jettison the rest as quickly as possible. Personnel development was a concept he neither understood nor cared for. And crime prevention was the business of local manors, not the squad. Cadwallader made it worse by appearing to enjoy the meetings, and even suggesting topics for future ones. Uncharitably and, as it happened, inaccurately, Fathers suspected that his colleague's reason for liking the meetings was to avoid involvement in the operational details of his team's work. He believed that, now he had passed the age of fifty, the other DCI in the squad was given to taking it easy. The truth was that Cadwallader thought they were administratively useful. He found they helped his daily work. But

Pot-walloper was one of many colleagues over the years for whom Fathers had no respect. The reason was simple and had nothing to do with success or failure at clearing up crime: in Fathers' first two years as a DCI, he had successfully dumped into Cadwallader's team a batch of what he considered to be inefficient detectives – one detective sergeant and three detective constables. It was one of his few successes in office politics, though he did not brag about it since he wanted to retain the option of repeating the exercise. He rightly had a low opinion of himself as a bureaucratic in-fighter, so he had only contempt for anyone he could best. Only with Queen had he been unsuccessful. Pot-walloper had dug his heels in and refused to accept him. Queen had been a DI when Fathers arrived at Serious Crimes at the same rank, and there he had stayed. Fathers had given up trying to shift him.

Rather than be interviewed behind his large desk, Michael George-Watkins sat in a leather armchair set at right angles to a matching sofa on which he indicated Fathers should sit. 'There's some coffee freshly made,' he said. His voice was deep and sonorous, carrying an air of easy authority. 'Would you care for some?' Fathers accepted and thanked him, and the diplomat rose ponderously and walked over to his desk where he pressed a button on his intercom and summoned coffee. His secretary brought it in just as he was sitting down again. She poured it into fine coffee cups, smiled, checked she was not wanted to sit in on the session and left.

'Now,' said George-Watkins, 'how can I help you in this bad business?'

Fathers pulled from his briefcase the statement written up from the notes made of George-Watkins' interview with DI Brain two days before. 'I'd like to go through this with you, sir,' he said, 'and if you think it's a fair and accurate representation of what you wish to say, I'll ask you to sign it. Then there's a couple of background points I'd like to go over with you.'

They made swift progress. There was nothing in the statement which the diplomat wanted to change. He knew nothing about any keys to the small parlour or a cupboard in the kitchen. He had met Sir Walter initially through work and then later at various social gatherings. Last weekend had been his second visit to Granthelm House. The previous time he had met Lady Sarah and Madeleine, but not young Walter or any of the other guests who were there on his second visit, except for the Briggs family. 'I rather think,' he said, 'that they have been invited on both occasions so their daughter could provide some company of the right age for my son, though how successful that effort was I can't say.' Apart from Sir Walter, he had not met any of the weekend party anywhere else besides Granthelm House.

Fathers thanked him and offered him the statement to read and sign, which he did. 'Now what were those background points?' he asked.

Fathers tucked the statement into his briefcase. 'Did you discuss with Mr Homer – or any of the other guests, for that matter – anything to do with his business? We're having trouble pinning down exactly how he made his money.'

'Ah, well I was left with the impression that he ran some sort of trading company and that he was doing – or had done – some business with Sir Walter. That's rather inexplicit, I'm afraid, but beyond that I can't help you.'

'Was there any talk about business of any kind over the weekend?'

'Oh indeed there was. I understood that when Sir Walter, Mr Rankley, Davis Mulholland and the unfortunate Mr Homer withdrew to the drawing room, they were going to discuss business.'

'The main parlour,' said Fathers.

'I beg your pardon,' said George-Watkins, 'the main parlour, indeed, I mis-spoke myself.'

'Did somebody actually say they were going to discuss business?'

'Yes: young Rankley.'

'Mm. At any other time were matters of business raised?'

'They were. On the Sunday afternoon in the, er, main parlour, when the police interviews were nearly over, Davis Mulholland took Sir Walter and young Rankley aside and they talked of this and that.'

'It was business, was it?'

'It was.'

'You overheard?'

The diplomat contorted his shoulders into a close equivalent to a shrug and waved his left hand in a cross between embarrassment and self-deprecation. 'I didn't eavesdrop,' he said, 'but I did overhear.'

'Would you tell me, please?'

'I heard mention of Lima, which I gathered was a source of supply, of the Bahamas which were referred to as a handling point, though perhaps it's another source of supply since Mr Mulholland talked of having bought everything they needed there, and in general of trade – you understand, of buyers' markets, distribution and a financial exit route.'

'What would that last mean?'

'A way of repatriating profits. You understand, if you're an American enterprise engaged in international trade, you don't want the profits you make when a commodity finally reaches its market to remain in that country – unless you have other investment plans, that is. Let me illustrate. Suppose that Mr A is not selling goods from country X to Mr B so that he can then sell them in country Y, but rather the two of them are jointly financing the purchase in country X and the distribution in country Y, with all the costs of transport in between. Then the profits on sales in country Y would be split between them proportionate to their intitial investment. At that point Mr A would rather like a way to get his winnings home. Do you follow me?'

'I think so.'

'So without going into the details Mr Mulholland was expressing confidence that that aspect of their business together was satisfactorily arranged. In general, he seemed to be saying that various problems, to which he did not specifically refer, had been solved and that the deal could be brought to fruition.'

Fathers paused and thought for a moment. 'They were making no secret of their discussion, then,' he suggested, 'if you heard all of this without, as you say, eavesdropping.'

The diplomat moved his right arm so that the hand flapped slightly. 'A car crash, Mr Fathers, left me with several disabilities,' he said, 'but it did not affect my hearing.'

'Nor your memory, it seems.'

'Nor my memory.'

2

Fathers had meticulously planned the rest of his day. A session with Pardoner and Yarrow at two o'clock would be followed by three hours of paperwork. Together with a phone call to Brain, a quick report to Bastin on the Granthelm House investigation and the bits and pieces which always came up and got in his way, that would let him leave the office by seven. After dinner he would be able to go through the evidence he was to give in a major trial on Wednesday.

He was to be called first thing in the afternoon. It was a case with seven defendants who were charged with twenty-nine robberies of sub-post offices in the previous three years. The investigation had consumed a lot of his time and effort, identifying what appeared to be two separate groups of three – two to do the actual robbery and one driver – as one group of six, with a seventh who decided which jobs to do, set them up and appeared to take the lion's share of the money. Fathers' testimony together with some forensic evidence would be the key factor linking the two groups to each other and to the seventh man. The previous Friday, the prosecuting counsel had warned him that a leading QC had been briefed to act for the seventh defendant. His obvious tactic was not simply to try and unhook his client from the other six in the prosecution case, but also to show that the link between the two groups of three was mythical. It was therefore essential that Fathers be utterly confident of his evidence. The defence barrister would challenge Fathers' facts, attempt to make him look unsure of them, place alternative interpretations on each and every one of them and, if given the slightest opening, reduce him in the jury's eyes to a hopelessly incompetant investigator.

On the other hand, by the time Fathers appeared the groundwork would have been well laid. The jury would have fully absorbed the fact that the methods were precisely the same in every robbery: two masked men would enter the shop both armed with shotguns, one also carrying a heavy mallet. The one without the mallet would fire a single round into the ceiling, and the other would use the hammer to smash the glass on the post office counter. The shop assistants, any customers and the post office workers were all invariably stunned by the noise and violence of the first three seconds' action. The result was that money from behind the post office counter and from the shop till was handed over meekly. The skilful deployment of intimidation meant that in not a single instance had anybody suffered physical injury – though three heart attacks, several bad cases of nerves and a phobia about entering post offices could all be blamed on the gang.

Fathers' plans for the day went up in smoke. Almost literally – because the cause was a blaze at an industrial estate in Kilburn.

When he got to his car outside the Embassy his driver told him DS Graves urgently wanted to talk to him. Fathers called him up, to be told of a fire the previous night at Drews' warehouse.

Fathers cursed silently. The warehouse was on a list drawn up by DI Stevens of places which might have been used for storing the merchandise stolen in the lorry hijackings he was investigating. Today, he'd gone to Birmingham to talk with the local CID about three other possible storage sites.

Moreover, Graves reported, Queen was out and they couldn't raise him on the radio. Fathers decided to go himself.

3

Detective Sergeant David Pardoner sat at the dining table in Ellen Sheerley's smart flat feeling uncomfortable. The woman who sat opposite him was young, beautiful, aristocratic and composed. She had long dark hair, and was wearing a white jacket over yellow shirt and trousers. Her name was Victoria Crane – 'Though my friends call me Tory, and that's how I sign myself, actually' – and she was the third and youngest daughter of a viscount. She had shared the flat with the murdered woman for nine months. She had come back from the private art gallery where she worked, especially for Pardoner and Yarrow. The latter was currently searching through Ellen Sheerley's belongings. This fact did not disturb the Honourable Miss Crane's composure at all – not visibly, at any rate. She had made them both coffee. She answered the Detective Sergeant's questions with care.

'No, Ellen didn't work. She had means enough of her own and no particular bent to do this or that.'

'How'd she spend her time, then?'

'Oh, the usual sort of thing. Parties, plays, getting around, keeping in touch.'

'Robert Homer was her boyfriend, was he?'

'Yes.'

'For long?'

'Mm. I suppose getting on for a year now.'

'Do you know how they met?'

'No.'

'Did she have other boyfriends?'

Tory Crane tilted her head and looked at the policeman.

'Apart from Peter Rankley, I mean.'

She absorbed the implication of this comment for a moment, then said, 'Occasional fancies, maybe.'

'Many?'

'Some.'

'How many's that?'

She smiled. 'I didn't keep count. Is it important?'

'Yes.'

'Why?'

'I'm afraid I'm not at liberty to reply to that,' said Pardoner. He paused and sipped his coffee. 'I suppose if you think about it you can work it out.'

She thought about it and worked it out. 'Ellen is – was – very attractive,' she said, 'and not slow to find men attractive.'

'What was her taste in men, Miss Crane?'

'You sound like a gossip columnist, Sergeant.'

'Possibly, but I'm not. This is a murder enquiry and I would like you to answer.'

She gave him a look which reminded him of a cat arching its back. 'Do you enjoy picking through the details of a dead person's life like this?'

'Not especially. I wouldn't do it if it weren't necessary. Would you mind answering?'

'Well, I don't think she had a specific taste, if by that you mean young or old, tall or short.'

'All sorts then?'

'If I say yes, you'll take that and make it sound awful. If I say no, you'll ask me again if she had specific tastes. So I think I won't answer.'

'You don't have to worry how it'll sound. At this moment there's no importance to appearances, least of all for Miss Sheerley and Mr Homer. Anyway, as I said, I'm not a gossip columnist. I'm not going to publish anything.'

'If it comes to a trial, you'll doubtless bring it out then. Have you heard the expression, *Nil nisi bonum*?'

'Yes, and like every other policeman I wish it'd never been invented. If you knew how many killings go unsolved – which means how many killers don't get caught – because people want to protect the victim's reputation, then you'd understand.'

The cat arched its back again. 'I think,' she said carefully, 'that the problem is that your question is the wrong one.'

'What's the right one?'

'I don't know. Isn't it your job to ask the questions?'

Pardoner grinned. 'Ve ask ze qvestions,' he said with a nod. 'You said you didn't keep count. Is that because there were so many men you lost count or because you didn't really know?'

'Because I didn't really enquire.'

'Would you say she was promiscuous?'

The cat looked ready to spit, but was probably too well-bred to go through with it. 'There you go, you see. No, I wouldn't say she was.'

'But she'd have more than one man on the go at a time.'

'Yes, as you know if you know about Peter.'

'And there were others.'

'Yes, but I don't think I ever met them, not while I've been living with her, anyway.'

'Did she talk about them?'

'Not really.'

'How did you know about them, then?'

'I mean, she didn't talk about them in detail, but you can always tell when somebody's off to meet a man, and I might ask then, for example, if she was going to meet Rob, and she'd say no, but wouldn't say who it was, and I wasn't nosy enough to find out who. Sorry.'

'But not promiscuous you say.'

'No.'

'What does promiscuity mean to you?'

Tory Crane gave every sign of giving this question serious thought. 'I don't actually know,' she said after a while. 'What does it mean to you?'

'Not sure I know either. I suppose it's to do with a sort of dividing line that's defined by numbers.'

'I think Ellen didn't cross that line.'

'How about drugs?'

If Pardoner had expected to shake her composure with this question, casually asked, dropped in without build-up, he was disappointed. She shook her head decisively. Pardoner looked at her sceptically. 'You mean you lived with her for nine months and didn't know she took heroin?'

'She did not.'

'Indeed she did. Not enough to be an addict it seems, not yet anyway, but she used it all right.'

'I don't believe you.'

'Why would I lie, Miss Crane?'

'How would I know?'

Behind her, Yarrow entered the room and gave her a discreet cough. He was holding something between forefinger and thumb of his right hand – a little packet of something white. Pardoner looked questioningly at him and he nodded. 'Good quality too,' he said.

'Well, Miss Crane, it appears Detective Constable Yarrow has just found some heroin.'

She turned round to look at the grinning Detective Constable, turned back to Pardoner, and the cat finally spat. 'Shit,' she said. 'Stupid, stupid, stupid. Shit.'

Pardoner ran his hand through his hair. At last, he thought. He leaned back in his chair, folded his arms and looked steadily at her. She returned his look for a moment, then looked down at the table for a long time, then stood and walked down the room to gaze out of the window over the river. 'And she told me,' she added.

At length she returned to her seat, taking a cigarette from a packet on the coffee table as she passed and lighting it with a lighter from her jacket pocket.

'Well,' she said as she sat down, 'that wasn't very clever was it? I'm afraid it's taking this *nil nisi* bit too seriously. What do you want to know?'

'Let's start with the drugs.'

'I suppose, technically, it's an infringement, isn't it?'

'What is?'

'Well, I mean the fact that the smack's here. You could do me for possession.'

Pardoner shrugged. 'We'd have to be feeling really nasty to try that on,' he said. 'Assuming you found it in Sheerley's room,' he added to Yarrow who was leaning against the door jamb. The other detective nodded. 'Well then,' said Pardoner, 'it's like a standard drug bust where lots of people're living together. It'd only be the occupiers of the rooms where the stuff was found that we'd actually charge.'

Tory Crane had regathered some composure by now. 'Well,' she said, 'soon after we got this place, I found out Ellen was mainlining.'

'When did she start?'

'I gathered she'd been doing it for quite some time. She always

115

claimed she had it under control. Just took the occasional hit.'

'Did you think she was right?'

'I was never sure. It's nasty stuff, heroin, isn't it? I mean, worse than snorting once in a while, or smoking dope.'

'Did you ever try it?'

'No, I never have. I've tried coke and dope, but I don't actually enjoy the sensation, just like I don't like being drunk.'

'Where did she get her supply from?'

'I'm not sure, but – well, this isn't more than a guess, but I think she got it from Rob sometimes.'

'Why?'

'Why do I think that, you mean? Oh, it was just some comments she passed. I can't remember exactly what she said now. It certainly wasn't an explicit statement that she got it from Rob, but that was what I half-concluded.'

'Half-concluded.'

'Yes.'

'Let's back-track now, shall we, Miss Crane? Would you like to change your statements in any way about her menfriends and your knowledge of or about them? As I said, I doubt we'll think of charging you for possession, and I'll ignore your comments about your experiments with illegal drugs, but do think hard about the possible consequences of not telling us everything you know and having us coming back, pestering you more and talking about obstruction.'

'Yes, well I wasn't misleading you. Last autumn I think Ellen broke up not just with Peter Rankley, but also with somebody else she'd been going with for quite a while, somebody I'd never met. I got the impression it might've been a politician – you know, somebody of power, somebody with a public position, so it had all been very discreet. But I don't actually know that. I'm just trying to help you as much as I can.'

'I do appreciate that.'

'And for a little while this year, there's been somebody else as well as Rob Homer. I forget his name now, but I think it began with a D.'

'So she didn't keep that secret.'

'No, although I think it was only his first name she ever mentioned. He was quite rich from what she said, and he's American, but that's all I can recall.'

'Began with a D,' said Pardoner. 'David?'

116

'Mm. Maybe. I'm just not sure.'

'Donald? Derek?'

'No, it was one of those names which could be a surname.'

'Davis?' suggested Yarrow from the door.

4

Fathers' afternoon was frustratingly slow but fruitful. The fire had been a serious one, starting in Drews' timber warehouse during the night and threatening to engulf a paint factory alongside. In the event, the factory was saved but the warehouse and a small machine tools plant on the other side of it were burned to the ground.

By the time Fathers arrived, the various fire experts and scene of crime officers scouring through the still smoking remains were certain the fire had been started deliberately and in the warehouse. Drew himself and the night-watchman were being questioned alternately by DI Edwards of the local CID in an empty office borrowed from the paint company. Fathers sat in. After a while, they conferred. They both had the same impression: the night-watchman was telling the truth in his professions of innocence, but Drew, while he might not be lying, was worried about something and wasn't telling the whole truth. The obvious line to pursue in this case – as in any other arson – was insurance fraud. Drew was in for a tough time, and his manner showed he knew it.

At the same time there was another line: the watchman had provided descriptions – hazy, to be sure, because it was at night – of three teenagers, as he took them to be, whom he had seen in the vicinity not long before the fire started. A local resident, out walking his dog just before midnight, had come forward to report also seeing three teenagers at the same time as he had first smelled the smoke from the burning warehouse. He had seen them under a street light and provided excellent descriptions. Better, he recognised one and provided a name. The Local Intelligence Officer quickly provided identifications of the other two. They were followed to their homes as they came out of school and, with their mothers in attendance, brought to the police station for questioning.

As Edwards and Fathers were leaving the site, they were

approached by two reporters – one from a local paper, and one from a national. Edwards confirmed that the Fire Brigade and CID both suspected arson, adding that enquiries were in hand and several leads were being pursued. Then the Fleet Street man took Fathers to one side. 'What're you doing here?' he asked.

'What're you doing here, come to that?' replied Fathers. Malcolm Hardy was a senior reporter who would not normally bother with something as small as this, unless he happened to have an inside line on Stevens' investigation, which was barely credible. 'Demotion?'

'No, I was up this way for something else, and the office called me when the news came over the wire. Anything to it?'

Fathers shrugged. 'Nothing on the record,' he said, 'and probably nothing at all.'

'I see you're on the Guildford case.'

'For my sins.'

'Sir Walter's having you checked out.'

Fathers looked at his shoes for a while. 'Is he now? Through whom, may I ask?'

'Me for one.'

'What did you tell him?'

'All the dirt.'

'Spoke to you himself, did he?'

'No, he got a prat called Pindar – Lord Pindar – to call me. Wanted to know, among other things, how susceptible to pressure you might be. I said for a fistful of tenners you'd see anybody right.'

'Who's Pindar?'

'He's on our board, one of the reasons we're going down the hole.'

'He said he was asking on Sir Walter's behalf, did he?'

'No, but we reporters, we have our ways. I'd already seen on the tapes that they'd brought you in, so I took a wild guess. Called Pindar's secretary, pretended to be grand, and asked if Sir Walter had just been talking to his lordship, because there was a matter the three of us were involved in, and Sir Walter and I had agreed to talk to Pindar about it, but I wasn't sure which one of us was meant to call him. So the secretary says, yes, his lordship's just had two calls with Sir W.'

'You're obviously very hot stuff, Malcolm.'

'I thought you should know. I don't like that sort of thing.'

'Me neither. Thanks – I owe you.'

'Keep in touch, then.'

At the police station, Fathers joined Edwards to question the teenagers about their previous night's activities. The local DI was a tough-looking man in his mid-forties, just under six feet tall, broad-shouldered, strong, with big hands which when bunched into fists looked quite terrifying. His hair was short and greying, his gaze steady, his face slightly pockmarked and distinguished by a much-broken nose. He was exactly the sort, Fathers considered, to make short and efficient work of three adolescent males. Edwards took them one at a time. Fathers asked no questions, but was introduced on each occasion: 'And this is Detective Chief Inspector Fathers of the Serious Crimes Squad at Scotland Yard.' Edwards did it quite well, lowering the pitch of his voice and slowing his delivery just enough not to be overdoing it. It had a visible effect on each boy and his mother. This was serious. A man was there from the Serious Crimes Squad to prove it. His presence loomed as intimidatingly as Edwards' fists and face as the boys tried to explain what legitimate reasons they had for being in the vicinity of a major fire just when it started.

After the first two interviews and the contradictory stories they elicited, a local detective sergeant reported the technicians had found fragments of what they thought was a small home-made fire-bomb. Edwards and Fathers raised eyebrows at each other but said nothing. The conclusion was obvious: this was probably a means of arson out of reach for the three teenagers. But young firebugs are not unknown. The third boy provided a third alternative to explain what they were doing there. When they had left the interview room, Edwards grinned and suggested they have another go at Drew and let the boys sweat it out for a while. The timber man had been brought to the police station, but the change of environment seemed to have calmed him rather than increased the pressure. He gave a cool display of incomprehension in response to Edwards' emphatic assertion that the police knew how, when and where the fire was started and had a pretty good idea why.

Edwards and Fathers returned to the three boys. They each changed their stories when Edwards said he knew they were lying, but still none of them matched. There were now six alternatives. If the boys hadn't started the fire, they had been up to no good of some sort which they were afraid to admit to the

119

police or to their mothers. Edwards had them all brought into the same room. In a dead-pan voice he recounted each of the stories, then quietly told them it was all a pack of lies and they had one minute to tell the truth or he had no alternative but to hold them, possibly overnight. One of them stuttered out the truth: earlier that evening they had managed to steal six large cans of lager from an off licence, had gone to the industrial estate to drink them and get a little tight, and had just been leaving when the fire started. They had stayed to watch it, seen the Fire Brigade arrive and then left the scene to get to their homes. The other two mumbled their agreement with this confession which brought different responses from the three mothers. One remarked that it was all a lot of fuss about nothing. One remained silent, biting her lip, her hands shaking. The third leaned over and cuffed her son back-handed on his ear. 'Stupid bugger,' she said. Fathers felt equal sympathy with all three reactions.

Edwards sent them back to their separate interview rooms. He explained the situation to the desk sergeant who listened grimly. 'Will you authorise a caution, sir?' he asked.

'Of course,' said Edwards, 'but put the shits up them first.' He took Fathers into his office. 'What do you think?'

'They're telling the truth now.'

'Yeah. So Drew's the main candidate, you reckon.'

'Maybe. Bear down on him, in any case. Something nasty's been in that woodshed. It may be nothing to do with our case. The place went on our list for the same reason all the others did – a smell of something dodgy, but we're not certain there's a connection.'

'Yeah, I remember putting this feller on your list when one of your lads was phoning around the manors.'

'So you might do well to hint at something other than the insurance fiddle – or as well as that.'

'Usual thing, then,' said Edwards. 'Generally terrorise the bastard and see whether anything crawls out of the cracks.'

CHAPTER 10

1

'Right,' said Fathers, 'what've you got for me?'

They were sitting in his office. The time was getting on for six o'clock, and Fathers needed to hear from Pardoner and Yarrow so that he could go properly equipped to the review meeting with Bastin. All three had cups of coffee, and once they had made the ritual noises of disgust about it, Pardoner began his report. The Mulhollands had changed nothing in their statements before signing them and knew nothing about keys. Davis Mulholland was doing business with Sir Walter who was providing the finance for a new trading enterprise through the merchant bank of which he was chairman.

'Did he mention Peru?' asked Fathers. Pardoner shook his head. 'Or the Bahamas?'

'No. He says it's to import fruit from Florida. You know, strawberries all the year round – that sort of thing.'

'How awful,' said Fathers. 'They won't be a luxury then.'

'You can get 'em in the supermarkets already,' said Yarrow, 'from Israel.' Fathers was not mollified.

'They both know Rankley,' Pardoner continued, 'though not very well, likewise Madeleine and son Walter. They hadn't met any of the George-Watkinses before the weekend. And they both say they didn't know Homer or Sheerley.'

'On the other hand,' said Yarrow.

'On the other hand,' said Pardoner, 'the Honourable Miss Crane says Sheerley was in the sack with a rich American whose name might have been Davis.'

'Really,' said Fathers.

'But she didn't produce the name herself. Elly suggested it to her. And she was still a long way short of certain about it. And there must be other rich Yanks in town.'

'OK,' said Fathers, 'how about Homer's business life?'

'Progress,' replied Pardoner. 'We've got a secretary bird. He used her for routine work over the past ten months or so. He ran a trading agency, mostly antiques, artefacts, that sort of thing. He didn't have any transport of his own – just hired trucks and whatever as he needed to, or sent things by airfreight. Still no proper company books or records. I dunno where he kept them but I'll keep looking. And I've been on to one of the transport companies he used. They specialise in the fragile end of things. You know, perfect handling guaranteed, a hundred years of not breaking more than ten things a day. They say that over the past two years they've done a lot of business with him. They're searching out the details and we'll have them tomorrow. We got two other company names from the secretary lady. I'll follow up more tomorrow.'

'Did Homer buy and sell,' said Fathers, 'or did he just see to getting the stuff from one place to another?'

'A bit of both,' replied Pardoner.

'How about his finances?'

'Pretty good. His personal bank account's got an overdraft, but the bank manager told me Homer was a careful investor with quite a lot of income from shares and the occasional killing on the stock market. The company account's very strong for the sort of operation it was. About sixty grand. The secretary tells me Homer'd been building it up for some big deal he was about to close.'

Fathers registered that fact with raised eyebrows and then Pardoner moved on to Ellen Sheerley. 'Seems to have lived a very gay life. Plenty of menfriends, though her mate 'n' I quarrelled over whether she was promiscuous or not. Didn't work, lived well, broke up with somebody last autumn, was getting into the sack this year with this Yank, Homer was a regular fixture. And Elly found the smack like we told you. The flatmate reckons it may've been Homer who supplied it. And that's that.'

'How about Waterford?'

'Couldn't find him.'

'Oh?'

'The address he gave Brain is his parents'. But he hasn't lived there for years. His mum gave me another address, but he left before Christmas, and his parents' home is what they have there for forwarding his mail. I got the impression there'd been a bit of a tiff before he moved out. So I called mum again, and she said pretty huffily that she didn't know where he lived now and didn't give a damn, ungrateful little you-know-what. I tried the younger Granthelm, of course, but he was never in his office when I phoned and he hasn't returned any messages. I thought I'd roll round his place later on.'

'Yes. I don't like the sound of that. Oh well – maybe nothing. Yarrer?'

'Sir Walter's secretary,' Yarrow said, 'is not a bird. She says Sir Walter's had appointments several times with Homer since last summer. There are two groups of them: one in the summer, and one in the last thee months. Between August and Christmas, they didn't see each other – or, if they did, she didn't make the appointments for them.'

'So,' said Fathers, 'Mulholland's in commerce and knows Sir Walter. Homer's in commerce and knows Sir Walter. Some people think Sir Walter and Homer are doing business together. Everbody agrees Sir Walter and Mulholland are doing business together. Sir Walter and Mulholland say they aren't doing business with Homer yet Homer's seeing Sir Walter frequently. Interestinger and interestinger. Where does that get us?'

'Back on the manor,' said Yarrow, 'we'd sort it out with a bunch of fives and a knee in the goolies.'

'Call for Queen?' suggested Pardoner. Fathers repressed his grin as a senior officer should. Yarrow's smile was weak and didn't need repressing. Pardoner was crestfallen.

'Go on,' said Fathers with a wave of his hand.

Yarrow reported that there were no entries in criminal records for any of the house party or the staff. The Drug Squad did not have Ellen Sheerley on their list and thanked him for the information which they would follow up. The worst thing known about any of them was that Rankley had picked up eight parking tickets in the period since Christmas. The Mulhollands had been in Britain since mid-January and he had telexed the FBI in Washington asking for any information known about them.

'Where did the parking offences occur?' asked Pardoner. Yarrow wordlessly handed him the pad on which he had noted the details. 'Ah-hah,' said Pardoner.

'What?' said Fathers.

'I spy a breakthrough.'

'What?'

'Could be coincidence, of course, could be nothing to do with anything.'

'Get on with it.'

'All Rankley's parking offences are within, oh, say ten minutes' walk of Mulholland's flat.'

There was a pause as the three detectives looked at each other. Fathers noted that Yarrow appeared to perform the feat of looking at him and Pardoner simultaneously. Don't his eyes ever get tired? he wondered.

'So,' said Fathers finally, 'Rankley and Mulholland say they . . .'

'Please don't go through all that rigmarole again,' begged Pardoner. 'We get the general drift.'

'It'll be worth a good look, that,' said Fathers. 'Yarrow, that's yours.'

'Right, guv.'

'Get over there and see if his car's a regular visitor. It's pretty distinctive, after all, and the wardens would probably remember it. Nice work, skipper, by the way. And it's not likely he's been booked every time he's been there. Anything else?'

Yarrow shifted uncomfortably in his chair. 'I, er, well I looked into that Greek business,' he said.

'And?'

'Well it was silver, and the whisper was that it was a large shipment out of the country. It was in late July.'

Fathers looked at Yarrow with interest. 'You've got a feeling about this, haven't you?'

'It adds up, guv, because I also checked on Sir Walter's silver collection. It's well known, you see. He's never had the crowds in at Granthelm House, of course, but it's been put on display twice – once in Guildford and once in London as part of a much larger exhibition. So it was catalogued. It's all eighteenth-century English – plates and goblets and suchlike together with some necklaces, rings, brooches and bracelets.' Yarrow was eager to convince, speaking fast. He paused for breath. Fathers nodded encouragement.

'You see,' Yarrow continued, 'if that came on the market in Britain, then sooner or later it'd be spotted, but it hasn't been and they've had nine months now. And if they melted it down – well, first of all, they'd get much less than its value made up, and second, they'd have the extra cost of exporting to some market where unhallmarked silver could be traded more or less openly. But if it was exported intact – without melting down, I mean – then in Germany or France they could find buyers, because the collection's only well known over here. And since Homer was in trade, and now the skipper says that most of it was antiques and suchlike – well, it all adds up, doesn't it?'

'Circumstantially speaking,' said Fathers, 'it certainly does.'

'And you see,' added Yarrow, 'the insurance value that's put on it was sixty-nine grand, but that doesn't mean they'd get that when it was traded. They could get much more. The value's been put on it by an independent assessor, but it's not been tested out in the marketplace, has it? I asked one dealer this afternoon and he reckoned that if somebody sold it in carefully chosen bits and pieces, here and there, he could probably bring in twice that much.'

'Is Gordon still here?' asked Fathers.

'She was when we started.'

'Let's have her in.'

Yarrow left the room and returned a minute later with DS Gordon. She was in her mid-thirties, one of two female detectives on Fathers' team, Cathy Gordon was the same height as Yarrow, strongly built, with dark hair and an oval, imperturbable face which perfectly matched her character. Before Fathers could say anything, Yarrow, too hot on the trail to be put off by politeness, interjected, 'It could give us a motive, see.'

'Not for Sheerley,' objected Pardoner.

'She could've been in on it,' said Yarrow. 'She and her uncle weren't getting on so well recently, according to most people bar him.'

Pardoner made a sceptical face.

'It's a possibility,' said Fathers dubiously, 'though double murder in return for theft is overweighting the scales of retribution a bit. But at any rate we can look into it. After all, Sir Walter's one of the ones who knew where all the keys are kept. Cathy, has Yarrer told you about this Greek business?' She nodded. 'Has he told you who he thinks it is?'

'Homer,' she said.

'See if you can put a firm name to him, will you, love?'

'If I can, darling,' she replied. She hated being called 'love', 'dear', 'sweetheart' and the various other endearments by which men address their female colleagues, but she was smart enough to make her point without making too much of an issue out of it. 'That all?'

'Yes. Thanks. Pronto, OK?'

'By yesterday,' she promised.

'Pillbury,' said Yarrow suddenly.

'What?' said Fathers and Gordon together.

'He's got a warehouse in Guildford,' said Yarrow to Gordon, and to Fathers, 'and he's the bloke Mr Brain was talking about over the phone when we got there.'

125

'I don't remember,' said Pardoner.

'It was in the evening,' said Fathers, 'after we'd finished.'

'I'll see if I can put them together,' said DS Gordon.

'That would begin to get very neat, wouldn't it?' said Fathers when she had gone.

'Maybe,' said Pardoner, 'but I still don't like it for motive.'

'Business deal gone wrong,' suggested Yarrow, 'and maybe the girl just got in the line of fire, so to speak.'

'Or else was in on it from the beginning,' said Fathers.

'But look,' said Pardoner, 'you're talking about a businessman.'

'That doesn't mean he's incapable of killing,' said Fathers, 'far from it, in fact.'

'No, I don't mean that. I mean the opposite really. Supposing Homer did pull a fast one. Somebody like Sir Walter must be used to that – having it done to him and doing it to other people. I mean, what is good business except pulling a fast one? I just find it hard to imagine him reacting like that.'

'Well, maybe,' said Fathers. 'Anyway, we're a long way short of closing this one out. For one thing, we still lack that second gun. No news from Brains, I suppose?'

'No, though we've got a line on the first one,' said Pardoner. 'Part of a consignment of target pistols reported stolen in 1982.'

'So it's been swanning around for five years.'

'Yeah. I've asked Bunn to see if he can track it, but not much chance, I reckon. Odds are the second one came from the same consignment.'

'Well, we'll see when we find it. Good work, both of you. Let's keep at it.'

2

Yarrow shifted uncomfortably in his chair. He had stayed in Fathers' office when Pardoner left. Fathers was now looking accommodatingly at him.

'I, er, I've something to tell you, guv,' said Yarrow. Fathers indicated he was ready to listen. 'You remember I was talking on the phone yesterday morning to somebody,' began Yarrow.

'And last night when you left the pub, it was to go and see a grass.'

'Yes, well I saw him.'

'And he came up with something?'

Yarrow paused a long while. Finally he said quietly, 'He says Mr Queen's on the take.'

Fathers looked levelly at Yarrow. The silence in the room was intense. From the general office outside he could hear the sound of a typewriter – Pardoner, presumably, writing up his day's report. He had been fearing something of this kind for some time. Not necessarily with Queen, possibly with any of his detectives.

'It's Jacko Pascall,' said Yarrow. 'Not the grass, the bloke who's oiling Mr Queen, I mean.' Fathers nodded. 'He saw them in a pub and listened in on what they were saying. And he saw Mr Queen go into a place Pascall has on Duffy Street yesterday afternoon, and after he came out Pascall came out. So they was meeting.'

Fathers took in a deep breath and blew it out before asking, 'And what did he overhear in the pub?'

'Pascall said, "I'll see you right, Queenie," and Mr Queen said, "You're on, mate."'

'Anything else?'

'Mr Queen said he'd let Pascall know if anything broke, and Pascall said fine, and Mr Queen told him to get it set up fast.'

Fathers nodded and sat in silence, thinking about how to limit the damage. Yarrow broke into his thoughts: 'What're you going to do? Give it to the CIB?'

'Leave it with me,' said Fathers. 'Who's the grass?'

Yarrow shook his head. 'He'll not play with anyone else,' he said, 'only me.' Fathers looked at him broodingly.

'And he'll want some money,' Yarrow added. 'Not a lot, but some.'

'Of course he bloody will,' said Fathers angrily.

'Do you want me to follow it up?'

'No,' said Fathers after a while. 'You've no business doing that. You've got enough on your plate what with checking out the parking plods, and you've the statements to get from the George-Watkins woman and boy, and you need to find time to get on with the antiques business with DS Gordon.'

'What're you going to do, then?'

127

'I really doubt there's anything in this,' said Fathers after another long pause. Yarrow's look had a deep disappointment etched into it. 'I'd know already if something like that was going on, or likely to. Do you think we don't keep tabs on everything like that? But have another word with your man. Don't tell him I'm sceptical. Get him to agree to speak with somebody else about it, somebody from internal enquiries. I won't have you handle an investigation into a senior officer in your own squad.'

'What if he says no?'

'If it comes to it,' said Fathers, 'I'll order you to tell me his name and you can take your choice what to do about that.'

Yarrow looked at Fathers for a long time, his eyes unusually steady. It was Fathers who looked away first, his glance dropping to his desktop.

'All right, guv. I'll ask him.'

'See you do.'

3

Some of the paperwork Fathers had to do simply would not wait. After seeing Bastin for thirty minutes he forced himself to settle at his desk for three hours. He did not tell Bastin about what Yarrow had said; there was no need for him to know yet. It could possibly be handled without referring it higher up. But if Queen was being that indiscreet, the chances of somebody else seeing or overhearing him in the company of Jacko Pascall were obviously high. If it did break, there would be hell to pay. And to live through.

He was depressed both by the information and by the way he had responded to Yarrow. But it was the only way. If Yarrow's grass would agree to talk to somebody else about it, so much the better. He would get the name, and there it would end. He would give the man some money and, depending on his feel for the situation, either let him believe that an internal enquiry was going ahead or else scare him off.

What if the man refused to play? It was the ordinary thing: not only did detectives like to keep their informants to themselves most of the time, but the informants preferred it that way. There was less chance, then, of their activities getting back to anybody who might track them down one dark night and deal with them the direct way. If Yarrow's whisper thought like that, would Fathers then go through with his threat and order his Detective Constable to tell him the name? A direct order like that could not be refused without risking severe displeasure. At the least, it would probably be impossible to keep Yarrow on his team and his chances of promotion would be dished for some years to come. That would be a shame for the lad and a loss for his section. Moreover, a disgruntled Yarrow might tell his colleagues what lay behind his sudden transfer and his lack of promotion. The first effect of that would be to corrode his team's relatively good morale and spirit. Or Yarrow might obey the order under protest, lodging a written explanation of his reasons in the files. It might be possible to lose it, but Yarrow was probably too smart to let that happen. There would be little chance of keeping it from Bastin, and how would he react? Conceivably, he would go along with Fathers, but there was a risk he would not, or that he would appear to do so but allow a negative note to creep into his personnel report. At that point, not only Queen's but also Fathers' position would be at risk. Fathers crossed his fingers, touched wood and silently expressed the fervent hope that Yarrow's grass would agree to talk to somebody else. There might be no other way out.

His depressed, flickering thoughts ruined his concentration as he ploughed his way through the most urgent paperwork with a grim determination. Among the things he put to one side was his recommendation on Yarrow's promotion. That would have to wait to see how this business turned out. But for that it would have been uniformly positive, a pleasure to write: it would have catalogued Yarrow's most important contributions to various investigations, his qualities of diligence, good judgement and the astonishing feats of memory he regularly performed, and in general his growing confidence and development as a detective since he had joined the Serious Crimes Squad. It would also have mentioned his personal amiability and calmness under stress, but it would not have referred to his ever-shifting gaze or his occasional difficulties with written reports and syntax. It would have concluded with a warm and unqualified recommendation for promotion to detective sergeant. Fathers sighed and shifted the file to the bottom of his 'pending' tray. When he had done everything which had to be done immediately, he put it in his 'out' tray, and collected from his filing cabinet the material he needed to study for tomorrow's trial.

He was haunted by Yarrow's news as he drove home, as a result of which he very nearly crashed and came close to scraping the wing as he turned into his front drive. He entered his house and went through to the kitchen. Sarah was doing the last bits of clearing up before she went to bed. On the table was a plate of salad. The clock said 10.55.

'One thing about this raw food diet,' said Sarah icily as he came through the door, 'is that at least the food I prepare no longer gets cold waiting for you.' She did not look at him and carried on about the kitchen.

Fathers thumped his briefcase on to the table. 'I'm sorry,' he said.

'You were going to be home at seven, and you were going to see the kids before they went to bed, and we were going to eat together.'

'There was a fire, arson, out at Kilburn, then a couple of meetings which wouldn't wait and some bureaucracy which has waited too long. I had no choice.'

'You could've phoned.'

Fathers was silent. Forgetting to phone home was one of his commonest sins.

'I thought we were getting somewhere on that,' Sarah commented. 'It seems I was wrong.'

Fathers again held his silence. There was no defence.

'You are the giddy bloody limit,' Sarah said. She was holding a pepper mill in her hand and banged it hard on the dresser. But her voice remained calm and cold. 'You know how much I hate it when you don't call if you've got to change your plans. You know what an unreasonable way it is to treat somebody you live with. Don't you?'

When he remained wordless, she repeated herself. 'Don't you?'

She got a cloth and wiped up the pepper which had come out of the bottom of the mill when she banged it. 'Don't you? We've been through it countless times. There's nothing more I can say about it. Why do you keep on doing it?'

'Oh for Christ's sake,' he said finally, 'I was going to phone you when I got back to the Yard and say I had a couple of hours' work still to do, but then Bastin wanted to see me to go over this double killing business, so I had to see Pardoner and Yarrow first, and then something came up that's . . . well . . .'

'There's always bloody something,' Sarah hissed at him. 'Good sodding night.'

She left the kitchen. Fathers took off his jacket and looked at the salad, feeling hungry and unable to eat. He went to the corner cupboard and poured himself a large measure of whisky. Then he sat at the table and looked at his food for a while as he drank. In the end, he began to eat.

CHAPTER 11

1

Yarrow wandered disconsolately through the streets and squares behind Harrods. The morning sun was summer hot and he took off his jacket as he walked. He had slept badly, dreaming that he stood in front of Fathers, holding a huge wad of ten-pound notes and saying, 'I took them from Mr Queen,' to which Fathers replied, 'Give them to me, lad, give them to me,' and when Yarrow complied his boss tucked them into his wallet and went off chuckling. He awoke tired and dispirited. It was a relief to find at the Yard that Fathers was not coming in. He decided to go in search of traffic wardens, and after checking in at their local centre, went out hunting the one who was covering the patch which included the Mulhollands' flat.

He was puzzled by Fathers' response to the news about Queen – and by the disappointment in his own reaction. Disappointment at what? It was inconceivable that his boss was also on the take, perhaps receiving a cut of anything Pascall gave Queen. He tried to dismiss the message of his dream as being a reflection of his worst fears, not something which made any sense in the real world. He did not entirely succeed. Perhaps Fathers meant to cover up for Queen. Yet that was not only out of character – Fathers was rumoured to have grassed long in the past on a colleague who was taking bribes and fiddling the insurance companies for their reward money – it also went against the well-known fact that Fathers didn't like Queen, regularly blocked his promotion, and had made several efforts to shift the DI out of his section. If Fathers' reaction stemmed from something else, why had he wanted Kay's name? Yarrow understood Fathers' refusal to let Yarrow investigate a senior officer in his own squad. But the normal practice was not to ask for the name of a private informant unless it was absolutely necessary. Was that the case now? Even if Yarrow didn't follow up himself, he could be an intermediary between Kay and whoever handled the investigation without revealing Kay's name.

What about his own reaction? Why had he told Fathers Kay wouldn't talk to anybody else, when it was he himself who told Kay not to? Was it his worst dream fears already asserting themselves? Or an unconscious refusal to let something he'd started be taken out of his hands? In the unofficial book, that was one of the worst mistakes a detective could make, and he hoped he wasn't guilty of it. If neither of those two things, what was it? He had felt right at the time, even if he didn't know why, and afterwards he justified it to himself with the thought that Kay might indeed refuse to deal with anyone else. So what would happen if Fathers actually did order him to reveal Kay's name? If he refused, that would be that as far as his promotion and most of the rest of his career were concerned. If he complied under protest, that would annoy Fathers, and he would not only be relegated to routine foot-slogging tasks instead of going along on the big cases, but would probably lose his chances of promotion equally effectively. If he complied without protest – what was wrong with that? Could he really believe Fathers would not act professionally and honestly at all times?

Lost in thought, he almost walked straight into the traffic warden he was looking for. She was writing out a ticket for an Alfa-Romeo and didn't notice him. He stopped himself just in time and perched himself on the wall a few yards from her. He started to whistle 'Lovely Rita'. She whirled round in annoyance and he stopped. They looked at each other for a second, the irritation disappearing from her expression. She was in her early twenties, with dark curly hair under her cap and large brown eyes. Despite the uniform, she was very attractive. Yarrow realised his mouth was open as he looked at her and he closed it with a snap.

'That's my name,' she said with a half smile.

'I know,' said Yarrow, getting out his warrant card and showing it to her. 'Rita Thomas, number 1147, that's why I was whistling it. I'm looking for you.'

'Oh,' she said and smiled again. 'I'll be with you in a tic.' She turned back to her task. She was about five feet four and slim. Her accent was west London working class, he noted, and her voice was low but clear. She taped the parking ticket in its plastic cover to the handle of the driver's door and stood back to admire her handiwork. 'I do like booking swanky cars,' she said, turning round. 'I'll do the rest, all right, but it's the flash ones which are the fun. What can I do for you then?'

'You and your mates have booked a particular car quite frequently over the last little while,' said Yarrow, 'and I wanted to talk to you about it.'

'Sure,' said Rita Thomas, 'but not here – I don't like being

133

around when the driver comes back. Some of the blokes do, and a few of the women as well, 'cos they like to be all righteous. But I don't. It can be a bit unpleasant. Let's go round the corner. There's a bench there, if you like.'

'Love to.'

'Actually, her name was Meta,' said Rita as they walked.

'Whose name was Meta?'

'The woman in the song.'

'What? The Beatles' song?'

'Yeah, didn't you know? I thought everybody knew that. She booked one of 'em near their recording studio and apparently they got talking. So they did a song about her, but they chickened out at the last minute and called her Rita instead.'

'Wouldn't have been believable, that,' said Yarrow, 'a meter maid called Meta.'

'That's what they thought, but it was true.'

'I didn't even know there was such a name as Meta.'

'You do now.'

'Live and learn.'

They got to the bench and sat down. Rita took off her cap and shook her curls. Yarrow looked at her and they exchanged smiles.

'It's about a D-registered black Morgan,' Yarrow began, making the effort to get his mind back to the reason for his presence there. 'It's picked up eight tickets since Christmas – that's better 'n one a fortnight. And we're sort of interested in it.'

'Oh I know that one,' said Rita. 'It's owned by a great big bloke, looks very well off.'

'Bit of a prat really,' said Yarrow.

'Yeah, that's the one. You're wrong, by the way, it's got nine tickets since Christmas. I booked it just now.'

'Oh yeah? It's around here a lot then, is it?'

'Mm. He doesn't live here, but he seems to be round a couple of times a week, maybe more some weeks. Parks wherever he can – sometimes legally, sometimes not.'

'Does he come alone?'

'Usually, I think, though of course it's just the car I see mostly, so he could come with somebody else a lot of the time and I'd just not notice.'

'But you have seen him with somebody else?'

'Oh yes,' said Rita. She turned to face Yarrow. He had a nice even face under his untidy blond hair, and she caught a glint of something in his pale blue eyes before they flicked away from engaging with hers and appeared to focus briefly on various objects on the ground and in the trees across the road. She smiled and rested an arm on the back of the bench. 'One time I saw him with a woman – quite tall and very good-looking, lovely clothes she was wearing, blonde.'

'That's his girlfriend,' said Yarrow.

'Really? That's not the way they walked together.'

'When was that?'

'Febr'y?' suggested Rita.

'Any other time?'

'Not with her, no, but a couple of times I saw him with another bloke. Smaller, dressed pretty sharply, darkish – not black, I mean, but you know, black hair and a dark complexion. They didn't arrive together – came in separate cars, you know, then walked off together. Ooh, you shoulda seen the car he had.'

'I have,' said Yarrow.

'What is it then?' Rita challenged him.

'Bristol Britannia.'

'My, aren't you detectives clever? What sort of crime is it?'

Yarrow looked at her and cocked an eyebrow.

'Oh, you can't tell me – it must be serious, then.'

'No, even if it was nicking a couple of quid I couldn't tell you.'

'Oh,' she said, sounding disappointed.

'The Morgan's here now, is it?'

'It was just now.'

Yarrow stood up. 'I think I'll go have a look. Um, there's one thing.'

'Yes?'

Yarrow's nerve failed him at the last minute. 'Oh just that – well, don't talk about this, will you? They'll know that I came to see you 'cos I checked first to make sure someone would be around here, but don't tell them what I asked you about. Please.'

'Not if you don't want me to,' she said, and looked at him steadily. Yarrow's nerve recovered itself.

'Er, well, I'm sure I'll want to ask you more questions about this,' he said. 'Maybe get a statement.'

'Right.'

'So, maybe, well if you're free I could buy you a drink after work and we could talk about it some more.'

'Well,' she said, and Yarrow's heart sank, 'what I like to do, see, when I knock off is get home and have a bath and put my feet up.' He nodded dismally. 'So if you'd like to pick me up at my flat after I've had a bite and a bit of a rest, you could take me for a drink then. Say, seven thirty.'

'Oh, right, good. Where?'

She told him. 'Have you got a car?' she said.

'Yeah. A Nissan.'

'I hope it's legally parked.' There was a mock sternness in her voice.

'Course it's not,' he replied grinning. 'Where round here can you park legally?'

'Oh dear,' she said. 'A white one, a sports car?'

'Oh no.'

'Oh yeah. I booked it ten minutes before you found me.'

'Oh well, small price to pay.'

'But I thought you lot always used official cars.'

'Normally, but I couldn't get one quick enough just now, so I used my own. Never mind. See you half seven.'

'The Morgan's parked just round that corner on the other side of the road,' she said, pointing.

'Yes,' he said, beginning to walk off in the opposite direction, 'but I'm more interested in the bloke than the car.'

'I suppose so. 'Bye then.'

''Bye. My name's Elliott by the way.'

Yarrow felt considerably bucked by their conversation. His worries about Fathers and Queen were far from his thoughts and a foolish grin spread across his features as he walked off. Rita watched him go, and smiled with pleasure when she saw a little skip in his walk. He was nice.

2

Fathers was met outside Court 11 at the Old Bailey by Gregory Allen, QC, the prosecuting barrister.

'All your homework done, Mr Fathers?' the barrister asked cheerfully. Fathers nodded. He was panting slightly from having hurried. 'Well, I'm afraid we're going to keep you waiting for a bit.'

'Oh sod,' said Fathers. 'I'm behind enough with everything as it is. How long, do you think?'

'Hard to say, I'm afraid. Winston's been enjoying himself this morning so we're running behind time.'

Fathers nodded. Winston Jessop was the QC hired by Loader, the seventh defendant.

'He's got a cross to do now,' continued Allen, 'then there's another witness and then it's you. It depends on him. I'll ask if you like. He was rather gung-ho this morning though. Actually, all three had a go at Rogers from Kingston this morning, but Winston especially. Deplorable performance. By Rogers, I mean – Winston was very much on song.'

'Cracks appearing in the delicate fabric of the DPP's case?'

'No, I'd hardly go so far, but the defence have obviously conferred with each other and they started launching little raids this morning. Rogers wilted at their first burst so they put up a concentrated barrage and he didn't do too well. Odd really, he'd seemed very calm and gave a good account when I had him. Don't they put you lot through your paces in training, give you a taste of hostile barristers and so on? I'd've thought a detective sergeant should do better.'

'Jessop's pretty high-powered,' said Fathers with a shrug. 'Can be quite a shock when it happens, even if you've got some experience.'

'Yes I suppose so, not that I've had that experience, of course. However, I'm not worried. You know that he'll go for you, of course.'

'He has to, and for Urban.' Stanley Urban was the Home Office forensic scientist who would be giving evidence immediately after Fathers. 'If he doesn't, there's no separate defence for his man.'

'Quite so. Ah, there he is. I'll sound him out.'

Fathers watched the two barristers confer quietly. Jessop looked over Allen's shoulder, nodded at Fathers and murmured something. Fathers turned away, and saw Queen hovering twenty yards down the corridor. He held up a warning hand. Queen nodded.

'He says he'll not be very long with the first cross,' said Allen returning, 'but he won't commit himself on the second. Best I could do. Good luck.'

'Thanks.' Queen approached as Allen went into court. 'Let's just go round the corner, shall we?' said Fathers. They found a window seat and sat down, Queen lighting a cigarette. Fathers

137

took the packet and picked out a cigarette for himself. Queen held out his lighter as he took the packet back and waited for his boss to say what was on his mind.

'I told you to be careful,' said Fathers quietly. 'You've been seen.'

'Who by?'

'Seen with Jacko on Saturday night and Monday afternoon.'

'Who?'

'And overheard.'

Queen puffed on his cigarette and was silent.

'He said he'd see you all right and you said, "You're on."'

Queen briefly arched his back. 'True enough,' he said. 'I did. I made good progress. Who saw us?'

'Don't know.'

'Who told you, then?'

'You don't need to know. Not a local, though. Yard man.'

'It'd be easier if I knew,' Queen said.

'No. It'd become more complicated than it is.'

'Someone on the squad, then, someone in our section?'

'No.'

'Drug Squad? Flying Squad?'

'Stop it.'

Queen shrugged. 'I suppose you've got your reasons.'

'So be more careful in future. And be quick. Tell him you need something straightaway, token of good faith or something.'

'Got to let it sink in first. Can't hurry it.'

Fathers stood up. 'As quick as you can, then.'

'Right. Don't worry about it. It'll come through OK.'

Fathers sighed. He'd had a bad night. Sarah's icy hostility had deepened the gloom begun by the conversation with Yarrow. At breakfast, Sarah had maintained her distance from him, and the mood of the morning affected the children, quietening them and making them as brusque with him as she was. He had phoned in to the Yard to say he would be working at home preparing for his court appearance, for he couldn't afford to be interrupted as he would be at his office. Unfortunately, he never found it easy to work at home during the week. As Sarah often pointed out, he could do it at night and at the weekend. But during office hours in the week it always felt fundamentally wrong to be at home, even if he was busy. The few times they had taken their summer holidays at home, he had been impossible – as fidgety and hard to satisfy as a child on a wet afternoon. The previous evening, the mood at breakfast and the usual difficulty of working at home when he should be at the Yard combined to prevent him from settling to his preparations as he knew he had to. It wasn't till around noon, when the imminence of his departure for court gave his adrenalin a spurt that focussed his mind, that he could concentrate.

He sighed again. He had had to call Queen and speak to him privately before the trial. But it was the worst way to prepare for it. He rose and went to the witness room.

3

Fathers returned from the Old Bailey just after four thirty, dumped his briefcase in his office, scanned a pile of urgent messages and went to the canteen for a cup of tea and a sandwich. He saw Stevens sitting at a table with Graves and made his way over to them.

'Hi,' said Stevens. 'How'd the evidence go?'

'So-so,' said Fathers. He sipped his tea.

'All righty then,' said Stevens to Graves, 'we'll wait till the traffic's died down and then you can go and collect chum Drew and bring him down to West End Central. We'll chance our arm with him.'

'I'll go set it up then,' said Graves. 'See you.'

When Graves was out of earshot, Fathers said, 'You've made your peace with him then?'

'Yeah. Quick to blow up, quick to cool down, you know what he's like.'

'You, James, are the one that blew up.'

'Well, true, but you take the point. We're friends again which is what matters most. How *was* court?'

'Jessop had a go at me,' said Fathers, chewing on his cheese sandwich.

'Oh, who's brought him in? Loader?'

'Yup.'

'The mysterious seventh man.'

'Not so bloody mysterious once Urban gives his evidence.'

'True. That was a handy bit of carelessness on Loader's part.'

'Assuming Stanley plays it straight. I'll have his guts if he pisses this one down the drain.'

'It's not likely, is it?' asked Stevens soothingly. 'He's only done it once.'

'Yeah, I know, and that was several years ago, and truth to tell it was very complicated and the evidence was actually a bit dicey. All the same, he had a reasonable hand and he screwed it up. I didn't see it, of course, but I've heard the details and, well, have you ever seen him in action?'

'Coupla times.'

'You know what he's like then. He doesn't say, "This is . . ." – he says, "The probability is that this is . . ." I've even heard him say, "The presumption is that this is . . ." Take any jury and half of 'em decide "probability" means he's guessing, and as for a "presumption", that's the same as taking liberties. He doesn't say, "The test showed that . . ." – he says, "I have concluded that . . ." He doesn't realise that juries know people are fallible but think scientific tests aren't.'

'What you mean is he's too precise, too honest even.'

'It's not a question of honesty, it's a question of knowing how to communicate. Ah well, we shall see.'

'I take it from all this,' said Stevens, 'that Jessop really did have a go at you.'

'Well, he had to, of course. Loader's defence is different from the others'. Jessop doesn't give a toss if they go down as long as he can disconnect Loader from them – and the two key witnesses to do it with are me and Urban. Given that, I suppose he wasn't too rough. He got a bit het up at one point, but that was during Allen's examination.' He bit into his sandwich again and looked at it with a frown. 'We'd fixed it up for his questions to lead me into the forensic evidence, you see, so as to establish it in the jury's mind before Urban came along to muddy it up.'

'Wizard wheeze, that. Right up Greg's street.'

'I know. But Jessop spotted it immediately and jumped to his feet and objected to this and that all over the place. I plaintively said that since I'd been asked how the connection had been established, I had to refer to the evidence we had available, and sod the fact that they hadn't yet heard from the boffin himself. So then Jessop asks that the question be ruled out of order.'

'What did the beak say?'

'Oh he took our side. I got the feeling he knew what we were up to, though.'

'That probably means he'll sum up for the prosecution.'

'Yes,' said Fathers reflectively. 'I hadn't thought of that. Anyway, next thing, Jessop asked that I stand down while they take Urban, so Allen got up to say there's no reason for that – after all, the jury will more clearly understand where the forensic evidence fits in if they hear me first, and then they can judge the scientific stuff on its own merits. Points out that I'm not giving a scientific opinion, just explaining why we decided Loader was the man and how that clinched the connection between the two gangs. And m'lud says that sounds all very reasonable and why don't they get on with it. Jessop quietened down after that.'

'I'll bet he did. How about the cross?'

'He was after proving that I hated Loader's guts and was aching to pin something on him.'

'Can't argue with that.'

'James,' hissed Fathers, 'not in public, please.'

Stevens chuckled. 'So he wanted to show your judgement was affected.'

'Yes. So I immediately went back to the forensic evidence to show how right I was, and he said he didn't want to hear it, and I said it was a relevant part of my answer to his question, and on we went, round and round. It's all about showing that the links between the other six and Loader are very tenuous and that I'm not to be trusted. He'll try to do the same with Urban. If he can just plant that seed of doubt in the jury's mind he's got a fighting chance of an acquittal. So he had no option but to have a go at me.'

'Very philosophical. In the end, d'you think he succeeded?'

Fathers paused and then gulped down the rest of his tea. 'Only the jury knows.'

'How about the other six?'

'I think they're pretty much done for. Their mouthpieces didn't put up much of a show.'

'And there's no chance of breaking the link between the two teams – between the one that was caught on the job and the one that wasn't?'

'No. The evidence against all of them is very strong. United they stand and that's how they'll fall. How'd you get on in Birmingham?'

Stevens wagged his head from side to side before replying. 'Two definite noes and one maybe. The Kil-burned warehouse is very interesting though.'

141

'You liked Drews', did you?'

'Enough to keep it on the list after our first several trawls through. It was a bomb that started it.'

'They're sure?'

'Yes. They've found all the bits they need. A clock, some fancy wiring, a detonator, a little gelignite, some gunpowder strangely enough, a little combustible material, and a lot of petrol cans surrounding the whole thing. The gelignite blows the cans to bits so the petrol pours on to the dry wood and paper. The gunpowder gives it an extra whoosh and up it goes. There's a couple of firebugs who've done it that way before and we're after them now.'

'A method like that and it won't be insurance fraud,' commented Fathers.

'That thought had already occurred to me.'

'So you're getting out the old thumbscrews for chummy, are you?'

'Well, it might be a short-cut.'

'Could be right. What d'you think? A falling out among thieves?'

'Something along those lines. Of course, it could be something entirely different, the which we wot not of so far, but then if we put the frighteners on Drew hard enough he'll probably want to cooperate. Edwards is coming down to lend a hand.'

'Ah-ha. Hard man, soft man.'

'Well, you've got to admit he's perfectly cast for the part, especially with Graves in tow.'

'I'd confess to anything if I had to face a pair like that, anything.'

'Excuse us, guv.' It was Pardoner, with Yarrow a few yards behind.

'Skipper,' said Fathers. 'Sit down. Yarrer, you too.'

'We gave up waiting for you,' said Pardoner, 'and came for a cuppa, but we can use the time if you don't mind.'

'Good idea,' said Fathers. 'I'll just get some more gnat's pee.'

When he returned with a second cup of tea, Stevens had gone. He sat down and gestured to Pardoner to start.

'Developments,' said Pardoner. 'Number one, Homer sent off a pretty good-sized consignment at the end of July. It wasn't marked down as antique silver, but then it wouldn't be, would it? It was in two batches, actually. One to Paris, the other to Milan.

We're checking up on it now. Shouldn't take more than a year or two to get the replies.'

'Good,' said Fathers. 'Anything else?'

'Elly,' said Pardoner.

Yarrow seemed reluctant to speak at first. His hesitancy reminded Fathers of how the young DC had been in his first few months at the Yard. Sod it, he thought, and I know why.

'I saw Mrs G-W and the boy,' Yarrow began. 'Nothing there. But Rankley's car's been parked near Mulholland's flat much more often than he's been booked for it. He was there today, in fact. And soon after he left, Madeleine Granthelm arrived.'

'Did she now?' breathed Fathers. 'Who else was there?'

'I don't know,' said Yarrow. 'She arrived about ten minutes after Rankley left. I waited another half hour. Then I gave up and went to see the George-Watkins missus and boy. I didn't know that I'd gain anything by staying.'

'No,' said Fathers, 'but it could be worth keeping an eye on that place. This gets more interesting all the time.'

'There's more,' said Pardoner. 'Homer visited there at least twice – or at least his car was seen in the neighbourhood. Could be coincidence, of course. He could've been visiting somebody else in the area.'

'We're getting rather overloaded with coincidences, though, aren't we?' said Fathers. 'At any rate, we know Rankley and Mulholland are lying about how well they know each other. There's also a tie-up between Mulholland and the Granthelm woman. And possibly between him and Sheerley. We're going to find out what was in Homer's consignment of last July. Oh, we're beginning to make things add up. Lots of things. Maybe too many.'

'Fully a three-pipe problem,' said Pardoner, 'eh, Elly?'

'Right,' said Fathers. 'Yarrer, first thing in the morning, you get out and skulk around Mulholland's place looking inconspicuous and not like a copper. Skipper, you set up a proper rota so that Yarrer doesn't have to spend more than tomorrow morning doing that. I want an eye kept on that place round the clock. Use some of our strength and some from the local manor. I'll talk to them if need be.'

'Tail 'em?'

'No, I can't justify that, not yet anyway. Yarrer, tomorrow afternoon, heavy spadework on Rankley. Skip, press the Eyeties and the Frogs for an answer. By the way, anything back from the FBI?'

Pardoner shook his head.

'How about Waterford?'

'I'm told he's off in a van with a bunch of scruffs, putting on a revolutionary play in the sticks. When I get the itinerary, I'll nip off and see him.'

'Right,' said Fathers, 'let's hop to it.' But as the two rose to go, he caught Yarrow's sleeve and held him back. 'What'd your grass say?' he asked when Pardoner had gone.

'I haven't had time to ask him,' said Yarrow.

'OK.'

Yarrow did not hear the relief which lay behind Fathers' response.

On his way up to his office, Fathers took a decision and felt better for it. When he got there the first thing he did was pull out Yarrow's file. He began to write his comment on the DC's promotion, and he wrote it as he had intended to before the news about Queen and Jacko Pascall. When he had finished, he sighed. It could make things more complicated, but it was the right thing to do. He felt pleased with himself.

4

Pardoner sat on a stool at the breakfast bar, sipping the coffee Stephanie Clay had heated up, trying not to look at her. She was another beautiful, aristocratic-looking friend of Ellen Sheerley's. Her name and address had come from the dead woman's diary and address book. He had called her at the advertising agency where she worked, and she had suggested it would be more convenient for her if he came to her apartment after work. He had not expected her to be taking a shower when he arrived, or to answer the door dressed in a towel. She had at least replaced that with a white towelling bathrobe, but it was too short for his peace of mind and too loosely tied at the belt.

'It was a terrible shock,' she said for the third time since she had opened the door to him, 'but I'm not sure how I can help you.' She sat on the stool beside his.

'Do you mind if I smoke?' he asked.

'Not at all. Actually, I was just going to say the same thing. I'll get an ashtray.' She got down and walked to the low coffee table in the connecting living room. Pardoner watched her go, then averted his eyes as she bent down to pick up the ashtray.

'What we're doing,' he said when they had both lit up, 'is constructing a profile of the two victims. It's part of the routine in a case like this. I gather you were a friend of Ellen Sheerley's and saw her quite often, and that's how you can help us.'

'I see. Look, this coffee's awful, do you want something stronger? No? Well I do.' She walked round to the other side of the bar and got what she needed to make herself a stiff gin and tonic. 'Go on.'

'Actually, I think I will. Just a small one.'

'I've got a lager in the fridge if you like.'

'Please.'

She went to the fridge, got out a can and some ice for her own drink and returned to her stool, collecting a glass for him on the way.

'Obviously, the first thing to know about is her boyfriends,' said Pardoner pouring his beer, 'over the last year, say.'

'Well, there was Rob Homer, of course, poor man.'

'Yes. And?'

'That chap who used to play rugby – whatsisname.'

'Peter Rankley.'

'That's him. Can't imagine what she saw in him. Anyway, it finished a while back.'

'And?'

'Her uncle – Sir Walter Granthelm, though I think that's over too.'

Pardoner sipped his drink. 'Are you sure?'

'I think so, pretty sure, why? Oh, I see, didn't you know?'

'We've heard something to that effect,' lied Pardoner smoothly, 'but nothing more than rumour, gossip really, which we can't put too much reliance on. But you're sure, are you?'

'Pretty sure.'

'Why?'

'Well.' She sipped her drink while she reflected. 'For example, one time last autumn we came back from a do in Sussex on the Monday morning and I dropped her here when I went in to work. I think Tory was doing something – some man probably – and Ellen didn't want to interrupt. Anyway, she was still here when I got back in the evening. And I was going out and she was

145

wondering what to do and looking a bit irritable and fretful when the phone went. I answered it and it was for her. He didn't say who he was, but I thought I recognised the voice as Sir Walter – I've met him a few times, you see – and I think she may have used his name, not with the title, of course. Anyway, next thing she was getting into battle-gear and making sort of suggestive comments, so I just assumed – well, you know.'

'You took her to mean she was going to spend the night with him?'

'Of course.'

'Though she didn't say so explicitly?'

'No, I suppose not. All but.'

'Was there anything else? You said, for example, that you thought the affair – if it was one – was over. Why's that?'

'Well, once when I was round at her place, she telephoned him. Asked for him by name, I mean.'

'When was that?'

'Mm, January, I suppose. Anyway, she was obviously told he wasn't there because she got quite angry, saying how she'd called dozens of times and he was never there, and then she left a message, and put the phone down swearing about the secretary.'

'So she was calling him at his office?'

'I suppose so.'

'Did she say anything to you about it?'

'Well, just the stuff about the secretary, and she called him a mean bastard actually.'

'That was all?'

'Well, she said something about how he'd better watch out.'

'Did she explain what she meant?'

'No. I didn't ask.'

Pardoner drank some more beer. 'Any other men?'

'From time to time, I suppose, I don't really know.'

'Anybody new this year?'

'Not that I know of.'

'Oh. One thing, do you know how Homer took all this?'

'What – you mean her and other men?'

'Yes.'

'I don't think it was a problem. I mean, they were going for quite some time, since Easter last year or thereabouts, I suppose, but I don't think it was really serious, if you know what I mean. They had no *plans*, as far as I knew, anyway.'

146

'You don't think he was jealous?'

'She never said so.'

'One last thing, Miss Clay. Where'd she get the heroin from?'

She looked at him steadily for a moment, then tossed off the rest of her gin and tonic.

'We know she used it,' he said. 'The *post mortem* showed that, and we found some in her flat. But we don't know where she got it from.'

'Nor do I.'

'Did you know she used it?'

'Well, not heroin specifically, but I knew she used something. I assumed it was coke.'

'How did you know?'

'Oh, she was often smacked out at parties and things.'

'You recognise the signs, do you?'

She eyed him warily and shrugged. 'I suppose so.'

'But you don't know where she got it from.'

She shrugged again. 'From Rob maybe. At least the coke – he always had plenty of that.'

He finished his beer and stood up. 'You've been very helpful, Miss Clay, thank you very much, and for the drink too. A word of advice.'

'Yes?'

'Ellen Sheerley wasn't on the Drug Squad's lists as a heroin user. She is now. They'll be checking around.'

She smiled. 'Thank you, Sergeant, that's nice of you, but I don't need it.'

'Fair enough,' he said. 'You may have friends who do, though. Goodbye.'

CHAPTER 12

1

The temperature had dropped by several degrees, the sky was grey, the breeze was cold and the weatherman had said there might or might not be rain as the day wore on if not earlier. Wearing a tracksuit jacket zipped to the top, jeans and training shoes, and equipped only with a notepad, a pen and a flask of tea, Yarrow arrived at the public garden opposite the Mulhollands' Knightsbridge flat at eight o'clock. On the left breast of the tracksuit top was an insignia he was particularly proud of: on a jet black background, a silvery white bird raised its wings so they almost met at the top; in the middle a garish yellow fist appeared to thrust out from the emblem.

He found a bench from which, between trees and through a gap in the hedge, he could clearly see the Mulhollands' front door. While he kept his watch, he looked around the square from time to time, but there were no traffic wardens in sight. Rita and her colleagues were prowling elsewhere this Thursday morning. Last night he had taken her out for a drink at a riverside pub in Chelsea. They had quickly dropped the pretence of further questioning under which the date had been arranged. When it began to get chilly towards ten o'clock he drove her back to her Fulham flat. Without innuendo, she invited him in for a drink. They talked until midnight, at which point she announced it was time for bed. Yarrow did not have so high an opinion of himself that he thought she meant it was time for them to go to bed together. This saved him from disappointment when she walked him to the front door, and saved her from having him press the issue. Their goodnight kiss was affectionate but brief. Before going he explained he expected to be busy the next two evenings, and proposed a film on Saturday. She accepted straightforwardly and he used a biro to write her telephone number on his wrist so they could confer about what to see and when to meet.

Sitting on his bench, Yarrow felt the contented afterglow of the evening and was relaxed and comfortable despite the cold. By ten he had finished the tea, but had not used the notepad. His contentment was beginning to evaporate, and he cast a self-critical frown at the Thermos flask. The problem with the tea was that he now wanted to use a lavatory. There were, of course, no such facilities in the garden, so he sighed and gritted his teeth. The more he tried not to think about it, however, the more he wanted to go. Unfortunately, there were occasional passers-by who, this being Knightsbridge, might either remonstrate with him or even call the police if they saw a strange young man relieving himself on a Council tree. How come it's all right for dogs and not humans, he wondered, disgustedly eyeing the turds on the path. At ten thirty, Mrs Brown Mulholland left the flat and walked in the direction of the Knightsbridge shops. At eleven fifteen, finally unable to bear it any longer and willing to risk anything, Yarrow went behind a large tree and relieved his bladder. Zipping up, he ran back to his bench, hoping he had missed nothing. It's hard to urinate looking over your shoulder, but he thought it unlikely there had been enough time for Mulholland to leave unseen. At twelve ten a taxi drew up by the flat and Mrs Mulholland got out, holding two big plastic carrier bags which suggested she at least had had a fruitful morning. At twelve twenty Yarrow was approached by two men wearing donkey jackets with orange strips across the shoulders on which were stencilled official-looking words.

'Fancy helping out with the gardening, then?' said one of them. It was DC Bunn. He introduced the other as DC Selby, borrowed from the local CID.

Yarrow cast a glance at the sky. 'Thanks, Rabbit,' he said, 'but no thanks.'

'Anything happened?'

'Not a lot.' Yarrow showed Bunn his notepad. 'I'll leave you to it. Ta-ta.'

2

Among the message slips on Fathers' desk when he returned from the trial on Wednesday evening were two from Sir Walter. They talked by phone Thursday morning.

'I wish to know,' said Sir Walter briskly, 'what your man was doing here on Tuesday and again already this morning — a different one – asking questions of my secretary.'

'They were asking questions of your secretary, Sir Walter,' replied Fathers evenly.

'Evidently,' said Sir Walter, pronouncing each syllable with exaggerated care. 'On whose authority?'

'Mine.'

'It is not good enough, Mr Fathers, for you to send a man round here to bother my secretary.'

'You think I should have come myself, Sir Walter? I'm afraid that's not how we work.'

A long silence followed this response. Fathers wondered whether Sir Walter would give him heat or ice in return. It was ice: 'My point is that I was not informed, nor was my permission requested.'

'We don't need your permission to interview members of the public,' responded Fathers sharply. 'It's a public duty to assist the police in the course of our enquiries, and it is our duty to carry out our enquiries as quickly and efficiently as possible.'

'It is not good enough, Mr Fathers. You will be hearing about this, I give you fair warning.'

'Thank you, Sir Walter, I'll look forward to that. Was there anything else?'

'Don't take it quite so lightly, Mr Fathers,' said Sir Walter gently. 'I am not without influence.'

'This is a murder enquiry,' said Fathers, 'and if that's all, I'd like to proceed with it.'

'Not so hasty, please. I want to know what she said.'

'That's between her and us,' said Fathers, 'though I suppose you're quite at liberty to ask her for yourself.'

'I want to be sure there are no misunderstandings.'

'Thank you for your concern, Sir Walter. If anything puzzles us, we always know where to find you. Is that all?'

'There is one other thing. I'm taking this opportunity officially to inform you that I have a business engagement which takes me out of the country for the weekend.'

'Ah. Where are you going?'

'Brussels. A financial conference.'

'Thank you. Are you travelling alone?'

'My wife will accompany me.'

'When do you go, and how, and for how long?'

'I fly on Friday afternoon from Gatwick. I return on Sunday afternoon. We shall be staying at the Hilton. The conference is in the European Parliament. Now, is there anything else you wish to know?'

'The flight numbers, please, Sir Walter.'

'My secretary has them.'

'Thank you. You've been most helpful.' Fathers caught an irritated grunt as Sir Walter transferred the call to his secretary.

When he had the details he needed, Fathers made two phone calls. The first was to the Yard's international liaison section, to ask them to arrange with the Brussels police for Sir Walter and Lady Sarah to be unobtrusively watched during their stay in that city. The second was to Detective Inspector Brain at Guildford.

'Is the lady still at the house?' he asked after they had said 'hello'.

'Yes.'

'Do you still have people there?'

'No, we've finished, and there's been no big press interest since the weekend so we've seen no reason to keep somebody there.'

'Can you find a reason for going back today and tomorrow?'

'I expect so. Why?'

'They're off to Brussels for the weekend. I'm not going to try and stop them. But I want to know what kind of luggage she takes with her.'

'Whether it's just enough for a weekend, you mean, or something longer?'

'Precisely.'

'OK. No problem.'

'Your search got nowhere, then?'

'Not a sausage,' said Brain lightly. 'I'd've told you if we had. We finally finished yesterday. There's no second gun on that property, nor just around it – not in the house or the grounds, and not in the Carrocks' place either, we went over that. I suppose we could always say we need to search the house again, just to be absolutely sure.'

'Good idea.'

'Though, to be honest, I am absolutely sure. We didn't miss a thing on Sunday when we did the house. There's been no second gun there at any point since we first arrived.'

Malcolm Hardy stopped his Ford in the parking area in front of Granthelm House and whistled to himself in mock awe. It was a place and a half, all right, just as the society columnist had told him. On the other hand, neat though everything else was, the cherub needed cleaning.

Hardy still resented the telephone call he had received on Monday from Lord Pindar. He had twice before been trapped into conversation with his lordship. After the first time he had told his wife that Pindar was an arrogant, prematurely senile, offensive twit. After the second, he added that he was opinionated, garrulous and ignorant of everything to do with newspapers. Moreover, he had a regard for the ethics of his profession, and, though too smart to bring down his editor's wrath by refusing to help Lord Pindar when he sought to use his influence to get inside information, Hardy did not see it as his job to act as a personal intelligence service for arrogant twits, even if they were directors of his newspaper. That was why, when Hardy met Fathers at the site of the Kilburn fire, he told him about the enquiry from Sir Walter. It was also why, when he sensed a story, not only did the lord's interest not deter him, it acted as a positive attraction.

Hardy built up to it slowly, partly because of other tasks, partly because he spent some time talking to colleagues and doing a little phone-and-legwork to establish some background on the Granthelms and their friends. When his editor asked what major story he was preparing – not because he knew Hardy was working on one, but because that was his way of saying good morning – he muttered, 'This and that,' and winked. The editor took that to mean a big story was in the making and that, not unusually, Hardy wasn't going to tell anyone much about it until he was good and ready. Sensing a scoop, the editor asked no more. However, the background work Hardy did was not particularly revealing. There were few items of any interest: one was that Sir Walter Granthelm was rumoured to have had some kind of money trouble the previous year, the result of an unsuccessful flutter on coffee in the futures market. There was no scandal about the family: the murdered woman and Sir Walter's daughter had both appeared in the newspaper's society column a couple of times going about their innocent business of parties, opening nights of new clubs and charity balls, and the son was forthrightly homosexual. That, of itself, was no longer the stuff of which good copy was made, though it would help enrich the story if and when the case eventually came to trial. There was also a hint, no more, that maybe Sir Walter and his niece had dallied together for a while. Only a hint, but possibly useful, thought Hardy.

He did not take the story just to spite Lord Pindar. Even without being able to lay his hands on anything really juicy, the work would not be wasted. If the police did bring charges, good background would become extremely useful. The trial would be big – it had all the right ingredients: high society, a man of wealth and power, a double murder, a country house. On Wednesday evening he phoned Lady Sarah to get her agreement to see him, and then Detective Inspector Brain at Guildford to check the police had no objection. Approval for the visit was laconically given: 'We've finished there ourselves,' Brain said. 'You won't be getting under our feet.'

'How's it going?' asked Hardy.

'So-so. It's in the Yard's hands now, as you probably know. What's your interest?'

'General background. Readying up for the ninety-first trial of the century.'

Hardy knocked at the front door. It was opened by a nice-looking maid. He explained who he was and asked to see Lady Sarah. The maid left him at the door, and returned a minute later to say Lady Sarah would see him in the main parlour. She showed him into it, taking his raincoat. He was left alone for some minutes, during which he took the opportunity to remind himself of several things: first, not to smoke; second, to get Lady Sarah's confidence – today he was not the hard-nosed reporter, but the friendly and honourable purveyor of truth; third, therefore, to be as unremarkably courteous as he could, at least until the point when he sprang his little surprise, and even then if he could manage it. He wandered round admiring the paintings and furnishings. As he waited he heard the telephone ring. When Lady Sarah entered the room, she seemed, though polite, rather disturbed. She showed him to an armchair by the fireplace and sat down in another opposite him. As she did so, he opened by thanking her for agreeing to see him and expressed his condolences on the violent death of her niece, sympathetically suggesting that this must be a terrible time.

'Indeed it is,' Lady Sarah replied. 'I've just had the police on the phone. I thought they'd finished yesterday, but now they want to come back and start all over again – inside the house, would you believe? They did the house on Sunday. I thought we were rid of them.'

'They told me they'd finished here yesterday,' agreed Hardy. 'That's why I thought it would be all right to come down. I know it's a bother for you, but better than having everybody crawling all over the place at once.'

'They're still looking for the second gun, the man said, and they've decided they might have missed it on Sunday.'

Hardy was writing in his notepad. 'They were doing the grounds these past few days, were they?' he asked.

'That's right.'

'So they reckon two guns were used, but they've only got one.'

'Right again. That's why they decided it was two murders, rather than one and a suicide.' She paused, swallowing, visibly taking in what she had just said. 'Oh heavens, it's so upsetting. I'm not sure which would be worse, actually.'

'Which would be worse?' repeated Hardy.

Lady Sarah looked at the reporter for a while. He was not at all bad, she decided. A man in his forties, slightly greying hair, medium height and build, not overweight, respectably dressed in suit and tie, a round open face, a quiet voice with, she thought, a bit of West Country in it. He was not at all like what she had feared when he had phoned and, although she felt she had to see him, she had prepared herself to give him very short shrift indeed. He remained silent under her inspection. He knew pretty well what was going on in her mind, and was hoping it would come out on the right side.

'Which would be worse out of double murder or murder and suicide, I mean,' she said at length.

'Oh I see. Well, I suppose that if it were murder and suicide they wouldn't have come back on Monday. I suppose you had to do the interviews all over again?'

'Yes. Look, it's nearly lunch-time – would you like a drink?'

Hardy smiled. He was in. To press his advantage home, he replied, 'Thank you very much, but I really oughtn't to. Driving back, you know, and with the police coming round, well, it wouldn't really do, would it? But don't let me put you off having something.'

'Thank you. If you won't join me in a drink, might you care for a cup of tea?'

'Very kind,' nodded Hardy.

Lady Sarah got up and pressed a button discreetly placed beside the mantelpiece. 'Please feel free to smoke if you wish to,' she said as she sat down again.

'No thanks, I'm trying to give it up,' lied Hardy.

'Good luck with it. Now, how can I help you?'

'Well, this is all just background, really. Can you tell me about your niece? Please don't if it bothers you – or keep it short if that's easier.'

Lady Sarah's reply was interrupted as the door opened and the maid came in. 'Ah, Anna, I'll have the sherry now, please, and Mr Hardy will take some tea.'

'Thank you, ma'am,' said Anna, and left, gently closing the door. She went to the kitchen first to pass on the order for tea to Mrs Carrock.

'She's hitting the sauce bottle a bit,' commented the cook irreverently.

'Well,' said Anna defensively, 'being left here to cope with all of this. It's a bit much for anyone, I should say.'

'I saw you'd put an empty gin bottle in the rubbish,' said Mrs Carrock unrelentingly. 'Had a bit of a session last night, did she?'

'It wasn't full,' said Anna.

'No, but it was on Tuesday. I saw Nuts getting it out of the box.'

Anna said nothing. It was true, she reflected as she went to get the sherry, that Lady Sarah had swayed her way to the dinner table on both of the last two evenings. But it was a big and lonely house when you were the only person in it, especially at a time like this, she thought, momentarily forgetting to count herself, Bolt and Mrs Carrock as persons. She took the sherry bottle from the cabinet in the music room, then carried it back to the kitchen together with a glass. When she had poured the sherry out, she said to Mrs Carrock, 'We need another bottle of this too.'

'See what I mean,' said the cook.

When Anna got back to the main parlour with the tea tray and the sherry Lady Sarah and the reporter were in full swing. Lady Sarah did not interrupt her flow, except to beckon Anna to bring the tray in and put it on a table beside her. She was describing

Ellen Sheerley's family. Anna poured the reporter's tea and took it over to him. As she left the room she heard cars arriving and opened the front door. 'Detective Inspector Brain,' she said as he walked up, 'I'll tell Lady Sarah you're here.'

Lady Sarah told Anna to bring the detective into the main parlour, and rose as he entered.

'I do apologise for the necessity of this,' Brain said, in a tone which Hardy thought remarkably unapologetic, 'but it has been put to me that we simply must repeat Sunday's search in order to be quite sure we missed nothing.'

'I would have preferred to consult my husband,' she replied evenly.

'I'm sure, but as I've said all along, there could be no question of not getting a search warrant if it came to that.'

'Quite so. Where do you wish to begin?'

'I'll have a word with Mr Bolt, if he's here, and start with his flat at the top. We'll work our way down.'

'Anna will show you where to find him. Thank you, Mr Brain.'

When the policeman had gone she sat down again. 'What a discourteous man. He didn't even acknowledge you.'

'Oh, we know each other,' said Hardy equably. 'He knew I'd be here, of course.'

'Of course,' she echoed with, Hardy thought, a bitter edge to her voice.

Hardy re-established the equilibrium by asking for more details, mostly irrelevant from his point of view, about Ellen Sheerley's family. After a while, he changed topics, first checking he had got it right that she and Sir Walter had married in 1958, and then broaching the first of a trio of increasingly sensitive matters. How she responded to the first, and how he handled it, would determine her reaction to the third when he dumped it in her lap.

'Your daughter Madeleine,' he said. 'Now, she's not married, is she?'

'No.'

'But she's, er, having a relationship with Peter Rankley, the ex-rugby player.'

'That's right.'

'Marriage in the air, do you think?'

'I really don't know, Mr Hardy.'

Oops, thought Hardy, sailing a little bit close to the rocks.

156

Lady Sarah, however, gave no sign of displeasure. 'My daughter,' she continued, 'is very much her own person, as so many young women are these days, and she will doubtless make up her mind in her own time about starting a family.'

'Of course. Time enough, after all. She's only — what, twenty-five?'

'That's right. Time enough as you say.'

'You were married at nineteen, though.'

'It was the fashion, I suppose, young marriages, and I've not regretted it for a moment. But fashions change — in more ways than one.'

'As you say. Well now — your son, he's not married either, is he?'

'No.'

'In fact, it's reasonably well known that he's homosexual.'

'He makes no secret of it.'

'And what do you feel about that?'

Lady Sarah sat and reflected for a while. If he had asked what she *thought* about it, she could have answered more easily.

'We brought our children up to be able to make their own choices,' she said at length. 'Walter has made his. We accept that it is his choice, just as it was his decision to work in publishing rather than, for example, to follow my husband into finance.'

She left it there.

'Are you disappointed, Lady Sarah?' asked Hardy after a time.

'No. For the most part, publishing is a perfectly reputable trade.'

Hardy smiled. 'I meant,' he said, 'are you disappointed by the fact that he's openly homosexual?'

'Better than being in the closet, I should say,' replied Lady Sarah with her own smile.

'Then are you disappointed by the fact that he's homosexual, leaving aside whether it's open or not?'

Lady Sarah's eyebrows arched and her head tilted. It was, Hardy thought, the upper-class equivalent of a shrug. 'Disappointment is not an issue,' she replied. 'He seems happy enough. For a mother, that's what counts most.'

'And for his father?'

'I'm sure it counts most too.'

'Does it bother you that neither of your children are married?'

'Marriage for the sake of it or to please your parents is not really

157

a likely recipe for a successful relationship or a happy life, do you not think, Mr Hardy? I suppose I would like to have grandchildren one day, but it's not my greatest ambition. I don't yearn for the day when I have my offspring married off. I'm not Mrs Bennet, you know.'

'I beg your pardon?'

'Jane Austen's Mrs Bennet, in *Pride and Prejudice*.'

'Um, well, what is your greatest ambition?'

'Oh really, Mr Hardy.'

'Well, I just wondered if you had one,' he said apologetically.

'No, not really, I don't need to, you see. At the moment, my main hope is to be rid of all this business and to be able to enjoy my own house without seeing policemen rummaging everywhere.'

'Quite, Lady Sarah, quite.' Hardy paused. This, he thought, was about the right moment. He made a show of twisting in his chair, crossing and recrossing his legs. 'There is one other thing, and, well, I hope you won't think ill of me for raising it.' Lady Sarah remained silent. 'We've heard that another paper has got hold of a story which it's trying to substantiate at the moment. If it manages to, then I can assure you it will give it as big a splash as it can, and I doubt it will worry very much about trampling on anybody's sensibilities. The only thing which might head it off is either if the lawyers decide it has a bearing on this murder business – you know, it could be affected by the whole *sub judice* thing – or if somebody else got in first with the story and treated it rather more gently. Do you see what I mean?'

'Well, I think I follow you, Mr Hardy, or I would if you came to the point.'

'Of course. Lady Sarah, the thing is, well, is it true that your husband and Miss Sheerley were having an affair?'

Lady Sarah was, reflected Hardy, made of stern stuff. She did not reply immediately, but her silence was not a retreat. She engaged his eyes with hers until he had to look away. She sat tight-lipped, and if he detected a slight flush on her cheeks, that was the only visible reaction.

He had seen this tactic used by reporters on his paper's society column. What happened was that the column found out that Lord Somebody was having a fling with the Honourable Miss Whoever. A reporter then phoned Lady Somebody to explain in gentle tones that it was well known that her husband was a philandering toad, and that the *Daily Something-else* was about to go to press with the story. So, suggested the reporter, why don't we just cobble something together to try and limit the damage? In her relief at having found a friend, the wife could then be relied on to say something which would make excellent copy and, when printed, do far more damage to her emotional peace than simply slamming the phone down. The difference between that and what Hardy was now doing was that he had no story about Sir Walter and Miss Sheerley having an affair – only the weakest hint of a possibility. He was on a fishing expedition.

'I can tell you,' said Lady Sarah finally, 'that there is no truth in that story whatsoever.'

'Ah.'

'If, as I suspect, that is the real reason why you came down from London, your journey is wasted and your visit is now over.' She got up and pressed the button by the mantelpiece.

'Well, if that's the way you prefer to play it, Lady Sarah,' said Hardy, also rising.

'I advise you not to go to press with such an ill-founded story, because if you do I imagine there is a strong chance that my husband will sue.'

'Well, that might not deter the paper which got the story first. Most papers write libel costs into their annual budgets.'

Lady Sarah folded her arms and stood silent.

'I can take it from you, then, that there's absolutely no truth in the story, can I?' asked Hardy. 'If the other lot come out with it, we can print a report to that effect, yes?'

'It would be better for you simply to drop it.'

The door opened and the maid reappeared. 'Mr Hardy is leaving now,' Lady Sarah told her. 'He needs his coat.' Her manner was as frosty as anything Hardy had ever seen. The maid mutely closed the door as she went out.

'Well,' he said, 'if that's what you'd rather, but once it gets into the public domain, you know, it's fair game. Should I tell our lads to go to press saying it's not true, or what?'

'I do not intend to continue this conversation.'

'I do apologise, Lady Sarah, you know, but the story is there.'

'Where have they got it from?'

Hardy breathed out lightly. There was something, then. Perhaps. 'I'm not sure. One of her friends, I suppose.'

'Whoever it is is mistaken.'

Perhaps not, thought Hardy. 'If you would just say something attributable,' he suggested, 'then if and when it does come out we'll have something to go on.'

'Everything I have said is attributable, as you put it. There is no truth in the story.' The door opened. 'And here is your coat. Good day, Mr Hardy.'

As Hardy got into his car he wondered if he had been very foolish or very smart.

4

When Yarrow got back to the office he was still wearing his jeans and tracksuit top. 'Watch out,' said Detective Sergeant Graves, 'yellow-fist's arrived. Bruce Lee – hung-ta!' With the shout he gave a poor imitation of a karate kick in the direction of Yarrow's groin.

'No, skipper,' said Yarrow, 'you've got it wrong. It's like this: h'yah!' His much louder yell was accompanied by a jab of his right fist which stopped a fraction short of Graves' ample belly.

'That's as maybe,' responded Graves, 'but Daddy and the gentle Pardoner want you. They're in the holy of holies.'

As Yarrow walked by, Cathy Gordon looked up. 'You were right, Elly: took some doing, but I've finally got it definite that Homer was the Greek. I've already told Pappa.'

Yarrow was still smiling when he entered Fathers' office. Pardoner was looking out of the window. Fathers was speaking on the phone and waved Yarrow to a chair.

'Yeah,' said Fathers into the phone, 'just wave Homer at him and see what he says . . . What? . . . Well, it's worth a try. Anyway, I'll be in touch later. I think we might want a review meeting. Could you get up here tomorrow? . . . Right, thanks, I'll get back to you, 'bye.' He looked at Yarrow as he put the phone down. 'The skipperene's told you you were right, has she?' Yarrow nodded, still feeling pleased with himself. 'Good work.'

'Erudite johnnies, your modern underworld,' commented Pardoner.

'It's antiques, you see,' explained Yarrow, 'classy line of business.'

'Brain's going to see what Pillbury has to say about it. He's thinking about charging him with receiving in connection with the silver robbery.'

'At the moment,' said Pardoner, 'it'd be a bit of a try-on.'

'That's why he's thinking of doing it,' said Fathers. 'The man's wearing five other charges of receiving, so Brain reckons they can offer him a sixth and see if he'll trade some information. Anything happen at Mulholland's?'

'No,' said Yarrow. 'Wife went shopping, that's all. Nobody else in or out.'

'Well, we'll keep our beady on it for the time being. You got that all fixed up, skip?'

Pardoner nodded.

'And you're pushing Paris and Milan for an answer?'

Pardoner nodded again.

'Good. I doubt if it'll really give us a motive, though. The business of Sir Walter and the Sheerley girl seems more promising, especially now his secretary's confirmed what the Clay girl told you about the phone calls. Keep pressing on that, skipper. See if you can dredge out something a bit more substantial, juicy even, about her social and sex life. I have a feeling that's where the answer lies, if anywhere.'

CHAPTER 13

1

Through the afternoon, Fathers sat at his desk doing more paperwork. The sheer volume of ex-trees which paraded through his 'in', 'pending' and 'out' trays seemed to increase exponentially year by year. Less and less of it seemed essential to the task of catching criminals, and every now and again some smart bugger would invent a new bureaucratic system for the whole Yard. Everybody had to learn new categories and classifications, mistakes abounded in the first weeks of the new system, and the tide of paperwork rose ever higher.

His distaste for paper-pushing almost invariably made it hard for Fathers to concentrate on this aspect of his work. But today his focus was also disturbed for other reasons. Though he had eased his conscience by writing Yarrow's recommendation, there was still the business of Queen and Pascall. Unless Queen could extract some cash from Pascall in the next few days, the whole thing was likely to blow up in their faces. Then again, with Yarrow's promotion beginning to go through the machinery, it reminded him that Stevens was up before the Promotion Board tomorrow. And Pardoner in a month's time. Yarrow would follow on, probably a month after that, by which time Stevens would have moved to another part of the Yard and Pardoner would either have filled his shoes or be on his way too.

As for himself, Fathers had no real desire to seek a promotion. For one thing, the higher the rank, the greater the load of paperwork. But he had always taken his career seriously, and had now been a detective chief inspector for longer than he had stayed at any other rank. Was it time for him to make a move too? Bastin had twice mentioned it since Christmas, and Stevens had teasingly suggested he was going to overtake him if he didn't look out.

Also disturbing his concentration were his thoughts about the Granthelm enquiry. The lack of the second gun, and the fact that the first one had only Homer's fingerprints on it, meant they had had to put their effort into background work so that they could build a sense of possible motives. A lot was emerging in the background; nothing was gelling into a clear motive. He thought

162

about the classic list: means, motive, opportunity. Until they found the second gun, they had nothing to trace down the line till they found how it got into the hands of one of the people staying that weekend at Granthelm House, all of whom had opportunity. So 'means' had a question mark beside it, as did 'motive', while 'opportunity' had too long a list of names.

A phone call gave Fathers the text of a telex message from the American Federal Bureau of Investigation. Neither of the Mulhollands had a criminal record, but their names did appear in FBI files with a note that all queries and information about them should be directed to the Governor's Special Narcotics Investigation Unit in the State of Florida. Fathers called the telephone number which the message gave. To the woman who answered, Fathers explained who he was, where he was calling from and why. He was immediately connected to somebody else, a man to whom Fathers repeated his explanations and who responded that he had no personal recollection of the name Mulholland, but that he would look it up immediately.

It was fully ten minutes before the man came back on the line. 'OK,' he said, 'apologies for the delay. It took me a while to find. Score one for the Feds, I guess. Now, Mulholland's name has arisen in the course of our enquiries, but I don't have anything here that gives us anything more than that. I guess you need to talk with Bob Flores who put the name on our lists and gave it to the Bureau too.'

'Thank you,' said Fathers, 'can you transfer me to him?'

'No, but I can give you his number. He's working out of Miami at this time.'

'Oh, I'm sorry, I thought I was calling Miami.'

'No, the other end of the state. This is Tallahassee. OK, so here's the number.' He read it out.

'Thanks,' said Fathers.

'You're welcome.'

But when Fathers called the Miami number he was told that Flores was out. He left his name, number and a message.

While Fathers fretted, Pardoner's pressure on the Milan and Paris police paid off, but he was not there when the call came through. Cathy Gordon took it, and after a few minutes' conversation called Yarrow over. The call was from Captain Rutello of the Polizia Criminale in Milan. Through the Liaison Room interpreter, he explained that some progress had been made in tracing the consignment that the London police were interested in. It had been delivered to a major antiques dealer in Milan who had then sold it off to four other dealers – two in Milan, one in Genoa and the other in Venice.

'You understand,' said the interpreter for Captain Rutello, 'the man has been cooperative with us. He has displayed his records. It was, as you suggested, all antique English silver artefacts. Of the two dealers in Milano to whom he sold a certain proportion of the consignment, one has himself succeeded in selling all he bought. We are now seeking his customers, all of them private buyers. The other has not sold everything. We have descriptions of what he retains, and the names and addresses of his customers. We have also, of course, passed on the enquiry to our colleagues in Genova and Venezia. Their urgent assistance is promised, and we expect positive results. However, I am myself in a position to provide you with a description of the unsold items. Are you ready?'

'Hang about while I get our list, will you?' asked Yarrow. He put the phone on Pardoner's desk and went to his own, flicking through the pile of folders on it till he came to the one he wanted. He returned to the phone and sat down on Pardoner's chair. 'Right you are,' he said. 'Shoot.'

Back came descriptions of two matching silver platters, a set of six silver goblets and three unmatching silver trays.

'That's them all right,' said Yarrow at the end. 'Can you hang on to them?'

'Yes, if the items in question are stolen, we can do so. As we find more, so we shall take them into our possession and inform you.'

'Good. Now, the bloke who took delivery in the first place, you said he was cooperative, didn't you? So you don't think he fenced it?'

'I can offer no conclusion. It is, of course, possible that he bought them honestly, but equally possible that he knew the provenance of the silver, or at least knew he was purchasing illicit goods. He himself naturally claims the honest alternative. Perhaps you should question the man who sent it here.'

'No, we can't do that. He's dead.'

'Ah. Well, I can certainly question this dealer myself and assess the results. But he has the air of one I would expect to be capable of handling such pressure. How did your man die?'

'Murdered. We came across his involvement in this silver robbery and we're following up on that to see if maybe it'll give us a motive, not that I'm suggesting your man in Milan's the one we're after.'

'Well, perhaps not, but the arm of Italian crime is long as you may well know. In any case, if I suggest suspicion is falling his way, it may increase the pressure.'

'You'll let us know.'

'Of course.'

'Thank you very much indeed for your help.'

'It is my pleasure. Goodbye.'

Yarrow put the phone down and went to see Fathers. 'Sir Walter's silver did go to Milan,' he said.

'Certain?'

'The bloke read me a list of what's not been retailed yet.'

'Right. So Homer was a tea-leaf – or at least a fence. Maybe he set it up himself, even if he didn't actually stroll in and take it.'

'He was perfectly placed either way, guv. He knew the house, knew where the stuff was kept, knew about the dogs, had a chance to look over the grounds.'

'But Carrock said that, although the dogs were kept familiar with the family, so to speak, they didn't bother with ordinary guests.'

'Well, you know when I went to get Carrock to sign his statement?' said Yarrow. Fathers nodded. 'I asked him about how to deal with three big brutes like them. And he reckoned that if you put out some choice meat up near his house, you could keep the dogs busy for a while and get away with murder anywhere else. He didn't say it, but if you did that you could put some kinda drug in the meat, as well, just to be on the safe side.'

'And, again, knowing when the dogs usually came out and where from would be more than a bit useful, whether Homer did it himself or just set it up.'

'One thing, guv, is that they don't have warning signs up about the dogs. And those kind of dogs wouldn't bark for the fun of it, only if they saw an intruder and went for him. I mean, otherwise they'd wake the neighbourhood every night. So if you were casing the place – I mean, if you didn't have inside knowledge or anything – you wouldn't hear the dogs or see 'em, would you? And if you went in to have a look around one night, well you'd hear 'em about half a second before they got you.'

165

Fathers looked at Yarrow for a while. 'Right,' he said, 'so inside knowledge is the key. Homer either did it or set it up. Do you still feel it gives us a motive?'

Yarrow shrugged. 'The wop reckoned it was an Italian job. He's going to lean on the dealer who took delivery in Milan and see what comes out.'

'Well,' said Fathers, 'everybody wants their own criminals to be guilty. Question of national pride, you know.'

2

The early evening was chilly and darker than it should have been because of the low, heavy clouds. Sir Walter Granthelm parked his Rolls-Royce on a double yellow line, got out, locked the door and walked up the steps to the Victorian building. The front door was opened before he could ring the bell. 'Walter,' said Mulholland with a smile of welcome. They shook hands. 'Good to see you. Come on in. Peter's already here.' He led the way through the hall and into his ground floor flat. He helped Sir Walter out of his coat and hung it on the ornate hall stand. The sitting room into which he showed Sir Walter was large and plush, with two large sofas and three armchairs. Peter Rankley was sitting in one of them. He stood up with words of welcome. Sir Walter nodded as he walked to one of the other armchairs and sat down.

'What'll you have?' asked Mulholland.

'Scotch.'

'Straight up?'

'Thank you.'

Mulholland poured a generous measure into a tumbler and handed it to Sir Walter who did not wait for his host to open the proceedings and had no time for small talk.

'The pressure, gentlemen,' he said, as Mulholland and Rankley sat down, 'is building. Today a reporter turned up at my house, clearly in the process of preparing a major feature article, and intent on digging up every piece of dirt he can. The police have returned *en masse* for another search through the house, not that they will find anything, of course, there being nothing to find. My office was again visited by a detective asking questions of my secretary. He was, apparently, after two things. He wanted to know about phone calls I've received from that damn girl and, Peter, he wanted to know about contacts between you and me.'

'Sir Walter,' said Mulholland, 'I appreciate your problem, but I'm confident we can ride this pressure out.'

'The point is that at present you have no plans to ride it out. You intend to go ahead according to your own schedule. That's why I wanted to meet. To persuade you that you are wrong – that we should, in fact, ride it out as you say, rather than pretend that nothing has happened.'

'I can't see . . .' began Rankley.

'I don't expect you to,' said Sir Walter. 'You will remember the view I took. Well, let that be. But from the moment the police decided it was double murder instead of murder and suicide, the situation changed. The man who now heads the enquiry has, by all accounts, and I have done some discreet checking via the press and through the Home Office, a great reputation for efficiency and an unequalled record for clearing up difficult cases and bringing them to trial. The scandal rag interest would have been personally difficult, but in a business sense no problem. When that is combined, however, with the interest of the crime reporters and the involvement of this Fathers, then we are facing a potentially severe hindrance. The police at Guildford are, to a definite extent, within my reach. I cannot control them, but I can exercise influence and exert pressure. The Scotland Yard CID, however, outreaches my grasp. I have looked and can find no way to put a discreet stop on Fathers, not even through the brotherhood.'

'Now, look,' said Rankley, but he was cut off again.

'No,' said Mulholland, 'Sir Walter has a point, a strong one. Retrospectively, we may have left our corrective action a tad late. I think I'll approach my principals for a judgement on this. Will that satisfy you, Sir Walter?'

'If you approach them with strong arguments for a judicious delay – then, yes it will. Not long, but long enough for us to be out of the glare of publicity and away from the eyes of Scotland Yard.'

'A month?' said Mulholland.

'I hope that will be enough,' said Sir Walter.

'It's too long,' said Rankley. 'There's too much hanging on this. We can't wait that long.'

'If you are in over your eyes,' said Sir Walter, 'that's your problem. If I have an assurance, Davis, that you will approach your people with that argument I have no further problems.'

'You've got it,' said Mulholland.

Sir Walter rose. 'Thank you,' he said, 'then I'll be going.'

'Did the police object to your trip this weekend?' said Mulholland, also standing.

'No, they wanted the details, but no objections.'

'Good,' said Mulholland. 'Good in two ways. One, because it would've been inconvenient if you had to delay. Two, because it means they're not too worried about keeping a close eye on you.'

Sir Walter shook hands briefly with the two others. 'I'll see myself out, thank you.'

Rankley and Mulholland waited until they heard the sound of the front door closing, then both crossed the room to the window and watched Sir Walter walk down the steps and along the pavement towards Knightsbridge.

'You can't be serious,' said Rankley.

Mulholland raised his eyebrows at him.

'About delaying I mean.'

Mulholland patted his arm. 'Of course I'm not,' he said. 'The first load is already on its way. You forget that once Sir Walter has had his little meeting, he has no further active part to play. As far as he's concerned, the only thing left for him to do is wait for his share of the profits.' He sipped his drink, then went to draw the curtains. 'Unless the police take it into their heads that he aced those two. If they're pestering his secretary, maybe that's the line they're taking.' He shrugged. 'Too bad.'

3

As Yarrow had promised, he was able to find Michael Kay without difficulty. But Kay was unwilling to talk in his local pub, even though in his casual clothes Yarrow did not look like a plainclothes policeman or stand out in any other way. Kay finished his drink and took the detective out into the street. 'Somebody might recognise you,' he said. 'Let's go to the Duo.'

'What's that?'

'Club.'

Yarrow shrugged with distaste. 'All right,' he said, 'I'll drive.'

168

'Nice wheels,' said Kay as they got into the white sports car. Yarrow ignored him.

The Duo turned out to be a strip club on the edge of Soho. Kay appeared to be a member because they were able to get in paying only one entrance fee each, instead of the usual trick of one payment to 'join' and a second to enter. The room into which Kay led Yarrow was large and dark. Seating was at round tables, served by two topless waitresses who brought drinks from the bar by the door. About half the tables were occupied, entirely by men, some alone, some in groups. At the far end was a stage with a catwalk leading out to the middle of the room where there was a circular dais ringed with alternately flashing red and yellow light bulbs. A spotlight shone on a woman who was taking off her leather clothing and moving almost in time to the disco music. Kay walked towards a table from which he could get a close view of the stripper, but Yarrow took his arm and steered him firmly towards one against the wall. As they sat down he looked at the stripper. Removing her clothing was made more difficult by the fact that she was carrying a whip, which from time to time she lashed on the floor. The strip, thought Yarrow, was a challenge – for her at least – but the tease was non-existent.

A waitress arrived at the table. 'Two beers,' said Yarrow.

'And a Bell's,' said Kay quickly.

She brought the drinks and asked Yarrow for £7.50. 'How d'you make that up?' he asked, reaching for his wallet in his hip pocket.

'Two quid for beer and three fifty for shorts,' she replied.

'It's only a half pint,' said Yarrow, giving her the exact money.

'Did you want pints then?' she asked, dropping the money into a pouch at her waist, and registering with a toss of her head that he had not given her a tip.

'No.'

'Lucy coming on?' asked Kay.

'Later,' said the waitress. 'Two turns time, I think.'

'You should be up there yourself,' said Kay. The waitress walked off. 'She's something, Lucy is,' he added.

'Turns you on, does it?' asked Yarrow with a sneer.

'No, I mean she's really good, Lucy, not like this slut.'

The woman on the stage had removed the last item of clothing and was pretending to masturbate with the handle of the whip.

Various suggestions were being shouted at her by the audience.

'How's it going?' asked Kay. He got out a cigarette and lit it. 'You got anything for me? I been looking into it some more.'

'Oh?'

'Asking around, like. A lot of right people know Queen's on the take, it's all over the shop.'

'I've got a word of advice if you're asking around about Queen and Jacko Pascall,' said Yarrow.

'Yeah?'

'Don't.'

Kay was silent for a while. He watched the stripper pick up her clothes and do a strange skip and run along the catwalk, accompanied by scattered applause and more shouted suggestions. He picked up his whisky and tipped his chair back. 'I can look after myself,' he said.

Yarrow leaned over, grabbed a handful of shirtfront and yanked Kay forward so that his chair crashed down on to its front legs, the cigarette fell to the floor and the whisky spilled on his lap.

'Can you?' asked Yarrow quietly. He turned round and waved his hand at the waitress. She came sluggishly over. 'Another Bell's please, miss. My friend just spilled his first one, over-excitement you know.'

'I saw,' she said and went to get the order.

'One of me could make mincemeat of a stupid ponce like you,' said Yarrow, 'and there'll be three of Jacko's, with dusters and pickaxe handles.'

'You didn't have to do that,' said Kay, using his handkerchief to mop the whisky off his trousers.

'I'll take you outside and give you a taste, if you like,' offered Yarrow. 'Not because I don't like you, but for education. I'll take you to pieces in ten seconds flat and leave you there, but you'll get up and walk away after a bit, which you'll be lucky to do if Jacko sends his funny friends for you.'

'Well,' said Kay defensively, 'you've got the training and all, haven't you?' He pulled out a second cigarette and lit it.

The waitress came up with the whisky. Yarrow gave her four pound coins. She did not even make a hint of a gesture of looking for change before she walked off.

'The point is, matey,' said Yarrow, 'that so do they have the training, in a manner of speaking, and you don't.'

170

'All right,' said Kay when he had gulped half the whisky down. 'I wasn't going to ask any more anyway. I just wanted to know a bit, you see. I thought it'd help.'

'It does,' said Yarrow. 'It's stupid, but it does help.' He got his wallet out again and extracted a twenty-pound note which he folded and passed to Kay. He put his wallet on the table and drummed his fingers on it. 'As they say, Michael, there's more where that came from. That's for starters. A token of good faith. My boss wants to talk to you.'

'Queen?' said Kay sharply.

'No, calm down. My real boss, his boss too.'

'You told him?'

'Not your name. Just passed the word on. He wants to talk to you.'

'You said not to talk to anybody else but you.' Kay downed his whisky and passed the glass to Yarrow. Wearily Yarrow held it up and waved it above his head.

'I did, that's true.'

The waitress came up and took the glass from Yarrow's hand. A young woman walked out to the dais. The music changed and she started to move to it. She was dressed as a parlour maid in a country house might be.

'So what's changed your mind?' asked Kay suspiciously.

'My boss has.'

Kay watched the new stripper while he thought. The waitress arrived with the whisky and Yarrow gave her a five-pound note. 'Change this time,' he said. The waitress shrugged and put a pound coin and a fifty-pence piece on the table. Yarrow pocketed them. He took another twenty-pound note from his wallet which he then slid into his back pocket. He curled the note in his fingers and waved it in time to the music. 'That's all there is for tonight, Michael,' he said. 'You've run me right out of the ready. But there's more if you want it and will work for it. What d'you say?'

'I dunno,' said Kay. The stripper had dropped her dress on the floor and was down to an old-fashioned bodice with frills at top and bottom, and black stockings in very high-heeled stiletto shoes.

'That Lucy?' asked Yarrow.

'Nah, she's ten times better, hundred. This one's not bad, mind, but Lucy's special.'

'Know her, do you?'

171

'Lucy?'

'Yeah.'

'No.'

Kay drained his beer, stubbed out his cigarette and lit another one. He watched the stripper some more. 'I dunno,' he said again, 'I don't like it. I mean, I know you from way back, I reckon you're straight. But somebody else – I mean, I trust you. What if I said no?'

'I'd tell my boss,' said Yarrow evenly. He took a first cautious sip of his drink. 'This beer's been watered.'

'And what would he say?'

'I don't know.'

'What do you reckon?'

'I don't know.'

'What do you think I oughta do?'

'If you don't wanna do it, don't. Let's see what he says.'

'OK, yeah, tell him no then.'

Yarrow stood up.

'Hey,' said Kay, 'aren't you going to wait for Lucy?'

'No thanks, Michael, thank you for inviting me to share your entertainment, but no thanks. I'll be in touch. Don't ask any more questions, all right?'

'All right.'

Yarrow walked to the door. A large man in a dinner jacket blocked his exit. 'Don't come back, will you?' he said.

4

Fathers was working late, not anxious to go home and face more of Sarah's iciness. He had told her at breakfast that he would not be back till very late. She had sniffed and thanked him for telling, with an emphasis that dripped sarcasm. At nine thirty his telephone rang. His caller introduced himself as Bob Flores and asked how he could help Fathers in the matter of Davis Mulholland.

'I'm not at all sure if you can help,' said Fathers, 'but if I can take a moment to explain, then perhaps we'll see. Is it convenient now, or would you prefer another time?'

'No,' said Flores, 'this is as good as any. Go ahead.'

'Davis Mulholland and his wife were guests at a house last

172

weekend where a double murder occurred. The host was a London financier, Sir Walter Granthelm, and the deceased are his niece and her boyfriend.'

'Sure, I think I saw mention of it in the papers here. Isn't this the murder in the country house, two dead bodies inside a locked room?'

'That's right. The thing is, we have no useful forensic evidence, so we're looking around for whatever we can find. One obvious task was to check with the FBI about the Mulhollands, and they've referred us to you – not you personally but to your unit, who gave me your number. So can I begin by asking what the Mulhollands' background is, and what's your interest in them?'

'The specific interest is in him,' said Flores. 'Let me give it you in broad. Davis Mulholland is a food shipper, mostly imports and domestic distribution. He runs a middling company with seven freighters, two cargo planes and a trucking fleet for statewide distribution. Trucking is how he started, doing pretty well for several years, then some time back – maybe six, seven years now – he put up a lot of new capital, bought two planes and a couple of ships and moved into a different league. Now, there're three reasons why we're interested in him. Number one is simply that he's an importer with his own vessels and planes. Drug trafficking is a major industry in Florida, especially down this end, and it slips its fingers into just about every pie. One thing the big men are particularly interested in, of course, is staying one jump ahead on the methods they use to get the drugs in. So just about every medium-size transport company is on our lists and we try to take a good look at each of them. Number two is that the pattern of getting along OK and then making a sudden leap with big new investment is characteristic of companies in which the mob's investing. Sometimes it's part of the operation, and sometimes their legit side. You follow?'

'Yes indeed.'

'OK,' said Flores, 'now reason number three is more substantive. Again, I won't bother with details. Various employees of Mulholland's either have convictions for drug trafficking, or arrests without convictions, or are pretty well known to have had connections with the drug trade. It's not a whole lot – maybe twenty in a company with a hundred fifty employees – but they're all in what would be key positions if he *were* running drugs, you get me? So we figure Mulholland is a pretty likely candidate, but I have to say we have nothing hard on him. Now, is that any help? Have you come up with anything to maybe mesh with that?'

'Well, not really, I don't think,' said Fathers. 'Tell me, he's on your lists for those reasons, but you don't have anything firmer to go on, is that right? I gather you haven't traced a shipment to him or anything like that.'

'You're right. They're signs that might mean something, but it could be a false trail. He has the right smell, but what've we got? He ships food, but it can't be true that all food shippers are drug traffickers too. He raised a lot of sudden investment, but it's been known to happen – and even if we're dubious about the particular bank he raised it from, well, it does a lot of respectable business as well. Not every customer can be in the mob. And he employs ex-cons: in Miami, it's hard not to. It's socially responsible to give those folk a chance. You know what I mean?'

'I do. Let me put in my twopence worth. The thing is Mulholland has definitely lied to us. He says he's here doing business with Sir Walter Granthelm – the financier – but he also says he hadn't met Homer, the murdered man, before the weekend, which probably isn't true, and he says he's met one of the other guests only a few times and that they're not doing business together, and that's definitely not true. They meet two or three times a week and they've been overheard talking business together.'

'What kind of business is he doing with this finance man?'

'He says it's arranging food imports here from Florida, so we can all have strawberries in mid-winter.'

'Sounds good. You have any more details?'

'Something very vague. The man who overheard him talking business with Sir Walter and this other guest said it was to do with some sort of trade which involved Peru as the source of supply and the Bahamas as a handling point. It doesn't seem to fit in with fruit from Florida. Does it mean anything to you?'

'In my part of town, Mr Fathers, it means only one thing.'

'Oh?'

'Cocaine.'

Fathers sat silent for a while taking this in. Finally he said, 'But I thought Colombia was the main source.'

'So it is, but it grows just as well in Peru. They produce maybe

174

eight, ten billion dollars' worth a year.'

'Christ.'

'That's wholesale price, of course, the street value's many times that much.'

'Jesus.'

'We're talking very big business. And it would make a lot of sense for Mulholland to bring a financier in on the deal.'

'For investment, you mean?'

'Partly that, but mostly to get the proceeds out of the country.'

'Yes. That was part of the conversation our man overheard.'

'Who is your man? Is he reliable?'

'You tell me. He's an American diplomat. Should be reliable, don't you think?'

'Really,' said Flores. 'If this all hangs together, I don't know if it'll help your murder enquiry, but it should help your narcotics division. The Drug Enforcement people over here have been warning the Europeans for two years to expect a major influx. There's a lot of over-supply in the Americas, and you are the obvious target market. And I'll add one thing. It's my own personal feeling. I don't think Mulholland is one of the real big guys in the whole business, more a sort of rising, middle-level executive. Opening up a new market might be very much his level of operation.'

'Well, Mr Flores, you've certainly given us something to think about. I don't know if it'll produce a motive for our murders. Personally, I think sex holds the key to that one. Where do we go from here?'

'One thing, Mr Fathers, if I may. Just out of interest. Your mention of the key brings it to mind. What about this locked room?'

'Oh that's no real problem. Four people definitely had access to the spare key, and there might be others who haven't admitted it. Anyway, it wouldn't be hard to take a wax impression of the key and get a copy made up. So in principle, there's lots of candidates. That's why we're spending most of the time looking into each person's background.'

'Sure. Mr Fathers, I'm thinking that, if my boss approves it, I would like to come to England. I'm not sure if I could help you out a whole lot, but I think you can help me.'

'I'm sure we'd be very happy to accommodate you, Mr Flores.

When would you come?'

'Let me get back to you. How long will you be at this number?'

'Not long, but I'll be here tomorrow.'

'OK, I'll see if I can get approval. Talk to you soon.'

'Goodbye, and thank you.'

'No, sir, thank *you*.'

Fathers put the phone down and looked at it sombrely. Cocaine, he thought. Merchant banking. Antiques. Sex. Shit.

CHAPTER 14

1

Fathers, at home at seven o'clock on Sunday evening, tapped thoughtfully with a pencil on the list in his hand. The case was maturing nicely: just two more possibilities to eliminate and it would be all tied up. He jabbed his pencil decisively at one of the names, his mind made up what to go for, and took off his glasses.

'Right,' he said, 'Miss Scarlet, with the dagger, in the study.'

Gary held up the card with Miss Scarlet's picture on it.

'I've got it,' said Samantha. 'I'm making an accusation. The revolver, in the lounge, by Colonel Mustard.' She reached over for the murder envelope and, masking it from the others' eyes, took a look at the contents. With silent triumph, she turned each of the cards over.

'Gracious,' said Sarah, 'what would they say at the Yard if they knew their brightest light was regularly outclassed by his daughter.'

'They'd say it runs in the genes. That's that then. Time for some reading, you two. I'll put away.'

There were many things on Fathers' mind as he packed the game away. They had been chasing each other round in his thoughts all weekend. The Granthelm case was not so much maturing as multiplying. Flores had phoned back on Friday to say he would arrive in London on Monday morning. He was to assist Fathers in the murder investigation, assess Muholland's London activity and have talks with the UK Customs and Excise and the Drug Squad. A visit to the Mulholland flat by Rankley and Sir Walter had been reported. Fathers spent some time negotiating Home Office approval for telephone taps on all three men – one for Mulholland's flat, two for Rankley's home and office and three for Sir Walter to cover both homes and his office. Not to his surprise, the request to bug Sir Walter disrupted the usual smooth willingness to approve any such operation. Eventually, of course, he had prevailed, but at the cost of repeating himself several times as he was referred up the line in the Home Office hierarchy.

At lunch-time he had been phoned and invited out for a drink by Malcolm Hardy who wanted to pump him for background on the investigation. To lubricate the wheels of privileged information the reporter offered the suspicion that Sir Walter and Ellen Sheerley had been having an affair. Once he was sure Hardy had no firm evidence, Fathers declined the invitation. But it was another curl of smoke: it was increasingly hard to believe there was no fire underneath it. Friday also brought word from Paris that some of Sir Walter's silver had turned up there as well.

During the afternoon, Yarrow approached Fathers with the news that the informant on Queen and Pascall wouldn't talk to anybody else and that he wouldn't willingly pass the name over. Fathers had nodded and told Yarrow to get on with his current task in the Granthelm case – looking into Rankley. He would consider it over the weekend and they would talk about it on Monday. He suggested Yarrow make one more try before then. Meanwhile Stevens, looking unusually stiff, had gone for his Promotion Board interview. Fathers had not seen him afterwards to ask how it had gone, and he did not know any of the members of the board well enough to feel comfortable asking them. So he wondered and fretted over the weekend, hoping for Stevens' sake that all had gone well for him, and for his own sake that Stevens' promotion would be denied.

His personal life had hit a trough and then picked up considerably. On Thursday night, he got home at ten thirty to find their neighbour's teenage daughter in occupation. Sarah had gone out somewhere – the cinema, presumably, though she had not told the baby-sitter and left no note for him. He paid the girl for her work, got himself a salad supper and sat watching the snooker on television. It was after midnight when Sarah returned. He had become both anxious and angry and it showed on his face when he turned to her as she walked in.

'Now you know how it feels,' she said. He nodded, and then began to find it amusing and started to smile. Her own expression went from defiance through irritation to amusement. 'I deliberately picked a film in town,' she said with a smile, 'just so's I'd be back really late.' She took her coat off. 'It was a good film,' she added, 'that French one that we said we'd try to go to about a month back.'

'I am really very sorry,' he said after a while. 'I know you hate it and I know it's very wrong of me, and I try to remember to call. I do, really.'

'It's just the feeling of being left to one side,' she said gently. 'I

178

don't think I'm afraid for you any more. It's just being there at your permanent convenience, whenever you don't have anything more important to do. It makes me so bloody angry, being treated like a hobby you take up whenever you've got a bit of free time. You can't really know what I mean because it doesn't happen to you. You're not a woman, not a mother and housewife. How can you feel it, understand how much I feel it? So I decided to let you have a little taste of it.'

'All I felt, really, was anxious. I didn't think of it being a film in town and the time it takes to get back.'

'No, you were angry too,' she said, 'I could see it on your face when I came in. You're angry at me for not being there when you want me to be – and that's how I felt on Tuesday, except that I'm used to it and it's not too bad if you'll only bloody phone.'

'You've howled at me often enough when I've phoned.'

'Yes, but I don't feel it so much. I get it out of my system quicker. You were angry, weren't you?'

'All right, yes, I was angry.'

'Good.'

'Is it good for my soul?' he asked.

'I'm sure it is,' she replied. 'Shall we have a nightcap? Whether it'll be so good for your soul that your mind will act on it, only time will tell.'

'What'll you do next time I do it?' he asked, pouring two brandies.

'Pick up a sailor in Soho,' she said taking her glass and adding some soda. 'Cheers.' She eyed him over the top of his glass as she drank, waiting for his reaction. He sombrely returned her look.

Sarah's evening out made Fathers feel tight and anxious as he went home on Friday evening, wondering what she would do next to drive the lesson home. But it seemed to have relaxed her. She did not return to the topic of his delinquency again. Though the weather was wet and windy they had a good weekend, despite his distracted mood. Saturday night they went out to eat with Sarah's sister and brother-in-law, and Sunday evening they were planning a quiet meal together.

As Fathers finished putting the Cluedo away with the other games in the sideboard, the phone rang. It was Pardoner. 'Shit,' said Fathers.

'Good evening to you too, guv.'

'Sorry. What is it?'

'We've had a call from Brussels. Sir Walter's on a plane for Geneva.'

'Shit,' said Fathers again. 'What about his missus?'

'She's on her way back here.'

'Are they sure?'

'Yes. Luckily they had their bloke follow them right into the departure lounge. They're checking the hotel for any extra news now and say they'll get back on to us if there's anything.'

'Have you alerted the Liaison Room?'

'Yes. They're getting in touch with Geneva now. We want him followed, presumably?'

'Yes. We also want to know about any other flights he's got booked. I'll come in, but talk to them yourself if I'm not there in time.'

'OK. See ya.'

Fathers went to find Sarah to explain. She was in the kitchen doing some washing-up while Gary and Samantha sat at the table, reading, sipping milk and nibbling digestive biscuits. Sarah read her husband's face before he said a word.

'Oh sh—rats,' she said.

He nodded. ''Fraid so. It's important, but it shouldn't take long. I'll be back in an hour or so, or I'll call you.'

'I'll keep my fingers crossed,' she said.

He kissed Gary and Samantha good night and left.

2

Yarrow got out of the lift on the fourth floor. It was seven thirty. The disinfected smell of hospital assailed him. He wrinkled his nose with distaste; it always made him wonder what sick, decrepit and gory odours were being covered up. He followed the signs for the ward he wanted and found the sister in her office. He flashed his warrant card at her: 'Kay,' he said.

The sister looked at Yarrow with a worried face. 'In the second section, on the right-hand side,' she said.

'He's all right?'

'A broken rib, a broken nose, two broken teeth. But, yes, from your point of view, he's all right.'

'What's that mean?'

'He can talk.'

'Thanks,' said Yarrow and left the office.

She followed him into the ward. 'Only while visiting hours last,' she said. 'Fifteen minutes.'

'Of course,' replied Yarrow. He found Kay's bed and sat down in the chair beside it. Kay looked up from the magazine he was reading, saw who it was, and returned his attention to the page. 'I warned you,' said Yarrow without ceremony.

'You pathed the fucking word,' said Kay. He spoke with difficulty, breathing through his mouth because of his broken nose and lisping because of his broken teeth. His cheek was swollen under the bandage and one eye was forced almost shut.

'I warned you that if you went around asking questions, he'd catch up with you, didn't I?' said Yarrow. Kay kept his good eye doggedly focussed on the magazine. 'I looked for you, and everywhere I went they all said the same thing. You'd been there all right, asking about Queen and Pascall. Ran out of places to try in the end. So I thought of hospitals and pinned you down this afternoon. Last night, was it?'

'Hit me with a bleeding plank,' said Kay, looking at Yarrow at last. 'Didn't give me a bleeding chanth.'

'I told you they wouldn't.'

'What do you mean, "they"?'

'Pascall's crew, of course, what else?'

'It wathn't them. You should know. You pathed the fucking word.'

Yarrow paused for a moment. 'Who was it, then?' he asked.

'Who d'you fucking think it wath?'

Yarrow examined his hands. 'I didn't pass the word,' he said.

'Then how did that rat-faith know it wath me?'

'Queen,' said Yarrow.

'Rat-faith fucking Queen,' confirmed Kay.

'I didn't tell him, or anyone,' said Yarrow. 'He knew because you'd been asking around too much. Poor silly bastard that you are.' He stood up abruptly. 'Don't worry. I'll nail him for you. You can have a century when you get out.' He turned and left, nodding to the ward sister on his way out.

Kay watched him go with bitter scepticism. A hundred pounds would be handy though, if Yarrow could be trusted. He returned to his magazine.

On his way out, Yarrow used the stairs instead of waiting for the lift. He was shivering with anger as he emerged from the hospital. He checked his watch: he'd be about half an hour late meeting Rita.

3

When he got to the Yard, Fathers was surprised to find both his detective inspectors there, as well as Pardoner, Gordon and Bunn. Only the last two were supposed to be there; the other three were all doing unarranged and unpaid overtime. He took Pardoner into his office with him. Pardoner reported quickly and efficiently.

'Geneva,' he began. 'They've phoned back and they'll have two men on the spot when Sir Walter's plane arrives – which is in about twenty minutes. They're happy to help out but they'd like a word with you: the man you want is Captain Gerrell. I've got his number.'

'OK.'

'I've given them a description, of course, including what clothes he's wearing – Brussels gave us that. And a photo's being put on the wire for them.'

'Good.'

'Brussels: like I said, they followed the Granthelms right into the departure lounge. It was only when they said goodbye to each other and went to different planes that they realised Sir W was not coming back here tonight. So they waited to make sure he boarded the Geneva plane – just in case he was being really smart – and called us. Lucky I was here.'

'Diligence is its own reward, skipper.'

'Bollocks.'

Fathers waved an admonishing finger at the Detective Sergeant who grinned and asked, 'What d'you think, guv? Is he bunking?'

'A man like Sir Walter,' said Fathers, 'it's hard to believe, really. But even if it's not a rabbit, it's a naughty. Anything more from Brussels?'

'Not yet. But they said they would.'

'OK. Does the man you're dealing with speak French or Flemish?'

'French.'

'Good, then I can talk to him direct when he gets through. I'll

182

call Geneva while I'm waiting. D'you know what he wants, this Gerrell?'

'He didn't say.'

'Probably a hint as to how big this is. Where's the number?'

Pardoner handed it to him. 'One thing,' he said before he left. 'I caught up with Waterford yesterday.'

'Oh? Where was he?'

'St Albans, putting on a play called *Dark Harvest*. I asked him to describe it and he said it was about the long-term effects of nuclear war and poverty in the Third World. A nice evening's entertainment, if you ask me. I tell you that, because it was the most interesting thing he said. He obviously likes young Walter – loves maybe – and can't stand the rest of them. Not a bad bloke actually, not when you make allowances for the fact he's scruffy, left-wing and queer.'

'So?'

'Leave him out of it, I reckon. Doesn't move in anything like the same circles as Sheerley or the Granthelm girl. Innocent bystander.'

'Fair enough. It's nice to be able to scrub one name off the list. I'll call Gerrell.'

Fathers dialled direct, was swiftly answered and efficiently connected to Captain Gerrell. The name was pronounced with a hard 'g', but the accent was French rather than German.

'We're very grateful for your help, Captain Gerrell,' said Fathers.

'It is our pleasure. A picture is being sent, isn't it?'

'Yes.'

'That helps us, though Mr Pardoner described him very clearly. We are in the process of examining hotels to discover where Mr Granthelm may be staying. Do you know where?'

'No, though Brussels may help. They're calling us soon with what information they have and we'll pass on anything which will help you.'

'Good.'

'I am hoping, Captain Gerrell, that you will treat this as a matter of highest priority.'

'In the full spirit of cooperation, I assure you, Mr Fathers.'

'Sir Walter, you understand, is not a suspect. But he is involved in a murder enquiry.'

183

'I see. Yet he is an eminent man. His name is known here as a result of his financial business.'

'And of course,' said Fathers, 'his visit to Geneva may be entirely legitimate, though he should've told us he was going there.'

'I see.'

'Captain Gerrell, if I may put it like this, three things are imperative. First, that you maintain a constant watch on him. Everywhere he goes, everything he does, who he meets – everything.'

'I understand.'

'Two, that you keep a constant flow of information to us.'

'Shall we say every two hours, Mr Fathers? But of course, a dramatic development we shall report to you immediately.'

'Excellent. Three, that he remains unaware of your interest in him.'

'Ah, that is well understood. Your subordinate tells me also you wish to know any further flights that he books.'

'Yes indeed.'

'That is no problem.'

'Thank you very much, Captain Gerrell,' said Fathers, and after a further quick exchange of courtesies he hung up. As he sat in thought, Queen entered.

'Something to tell you, guv,' said the Detective Inspector, looking pleased with himself. He sat down opposite Fathers. 'I found out who Yarrow heard from about my little goings-on with Jacko.'

'Yarrow?' said Fathers innocently.

'Don't kid me,' said Queen. 'It has to be Yarrow. Kay, the grass, grew up in the same part of London as Yarrow. And it had to be someone on the squad, didn't it? I'm not daft, you know.'

'I've never thought you were. What about it?'

'I've fixed the little bastard. I remember him from—'

'You've what?' interrupted Fathers.

'I've hospitalised him,' said Queen calmly.

'And you reckon you're not daft. What've you done that for?'

'Better'n letting Jacko catch up with him.'

Fathers thought about it for a while. 'Go on,' he said.

'It took me all of two pubs to find out who'd been asking around about me. Stupid little sod's wandered into every boozer in the area asking if anybody knows about Jacko greasing me. I

184

reckoned it would come to Jacko's ears sooner or later – and either he'd pull out, which we don't want, or he'd go after the little bleeder, which would more than put him in hospital, or both. So I got in first, smacked him a couple of times and called an ambulance. Nothing to it.'

'Does Kay know it was you?'

''Fraid so. Only dodgy bit about it. I plain bumped into him as I was leaving one of his boozers on Saturday night. He scarpered so I collared him, took him round the corner and duffed him. We'll be safe as houses by the time anything comes of it, though.'

'You think so, do you? It'll be hard to hold Yarrow back now.'

'That's your job.'

'How long, do you think?'

'Some time this week. Jacko 'n' me set the figure on Friday. He'll need a coupla days to get it together. Then he'll get in touch and we'll set it up.' Queen looked at Fathers' worried expression. 'Don't worry,' he said. 'It'll be fine. Is that little squirt bothering you? Yarrow, I mean, not Kay.'

'You can never tell with Yarrow,' said Fathers. 'He doesn't like it one bit. He was going to look for his man over the weekend, so he'll have found him today in hospital. Either he'll come to me – or just as likely, he'll go straight to the CIB. Even if he comes to me, if I stall him, he'll probably tell them. Why couldn't you have left well alone?'

'You wanted Jacko to find out, did you?'

'I don't know. I just don't like it.'

'Well, I can tell you, with this sort of lark, once you're in, you're in.'

The phone rang. Fathers picked it up, and the Liaison Room duty officer told him it was the Brussels police on the line. Fathers put his hand over the mouthpiece and said to Queen, 'Go on, then. Just don't break any more bones.'

'Only if I have to,' said Queen rising. 'You make it sound as if I like it.'

Fathers looked at Queen in puzzlement as the Detective Inspector left the room. That was exactly what he thought of Queen. He took his hand off the mouthpiece and asked for the Brussels call to be put through. When it was connected, he introduced himself in French and immediately received a string of apologies with which he struggled to keep up. Finally he interrupted and suggested the man talked more slowly.

'It is, you see, like this,' said the Brussels police officer. 'We did not realise Sir Walter used the hotel service to change his flight and to book a hotel in Geneva. The Hilton, of course. He has a return flight booked for tomorrow evening.'

Fathers absorbed this information together with some more apologies, and then thanked the Brussels caller for his cooperation and concern. Then he phoned Captain Gerrell again and passed the information along.

'Thank you,' said Gerrell. 'We shall confirm that now and recall immediately if it is not borne out.'

After hanging up, Fathers decided there was no more he could usefully do. Before he left, he called Stevens into his office. 'How'd it go?' he asked.

Stevens lit a cigarette. 'Oh you know,' he said, 'I think it was all right, but I never like Boards.'

'You haven't missed one yet,' said Fathers.

'Always a first time,' replied Stevens morosely. 'I mean, there was nothing I couldn't handle, but you just don't know, do you? I don't know how many ups to DCI they're taking at the moment, or whether they're looking for something particular which I don't have.'

'James, what could there be that you don't have?'

Stevens smiled. 'I've not been good company at home, I can tell you. I think today's the first time Josie's ever told me to come in to work on a weekend. She couldn't bear it any more.'

'Always tough on the wife.'

'Isn't it? Still, if I don't get it I shan't mind too much.'

'Of course not. You'll keep the pleasure of my company, for a kick-off.'

'Oh, I hadn't thought of that. Maybe I will mind.'

'Get on with your work, James, you're becoming too familiar. What are you working on?'

'Lovely paperwork. Report on the Drews' fire.'

'Where's that got to?'

'Nowhere. He hasn't coughed, it doesn't look like insurance, I don't know. I know in my bones it's connected with my lorry-loving friends, but we're going to have to approach it from the other end. Alibis, of course, for the two firebugs who use that method.'

'Of course. Aren't there always? How about the kidnappings?'

'Nothing more. Engine's been idling a bit this week, to tell you the truth.'

'Never mind. Another Monday, another week.'

This thought did not seem to encourage Stevens as he returned to his paperwork. Fathers left for home straightaway: before Monday morning came Sunday evening.

CHAPTER 15

1

Fathers woke a few minutes before six. He turned over, snuggled against Sarah's warm body and closed his eyes, but couldn't get back to sleep. He lay on his back for a while feeling annoyed, decided that was a waste of time, and got up. He kissed Sarah's naked shoulder as he settled the bedclothes round her and smiled. He put on a dressing gown and tip-toed downstairs to the kitchen to make breakfast – healthy enough to earn Sarah's approval, except for the coffee he had with it. As he ate he made notes for the coming day on the pad they used for shopping lists and phone messages. By seven he had shaved and dressed. Sarah was still asleep, so he left a note for her propped up against the alarm clock and left for work.

The morning was chilly and overcast. He was barely conscious of it as he made the twenty-minute drive to the Yard. By the time the rest of his section began to arrive, he was making a series of telephone calls. From the general office the first-comers could hear his sharp, brisk voice through the open door as he rapped out requests and instructions. They looked at each other and nodded knowingly. When he walked quickly through the office to get himself a cup of tea, his cheery greetings were so efficiently made that he neither broke his stride nor seemed rude. His energy set the tone for the others as they settled to work, dominating their mood, without him saying a single word of encouragement or urging, or even being aware of the effect. During that morning, DS Gordon put two names together in a breakthrough which a week later produced three arrests in her antiques investigation, while Stevens snapped out of the previous week's slowness, rechecked his files and spotted the connection between the lorry hijackers he was after and Drew, the man whose timber warehouse had burned down.

At eight thirty a call came through from Milan. Via the interpreter, Captain Rutello explained to Fathers that Batesta, the dealer who had received the consignment of antiques from Homer the previous July, had driven overnight to Geneva. The Milan police had obtained clearance from the Swiss authorities to tail him into their country and two Italian detectives were now watching him there.

'Captain Rutello,' said Fathers, 'could I ask you to call Captain Gerrell of the Geneva Police Judiciaire and give him Batesta's description? There is a possible connection, and you should liaise with him on this yourself.'

Twenty minutes later, the phone went again. It was a woman from Gerrell's office, reporting, in the sort of unaccented English which reveals that it is not the speaker's first language, that Sir Walter Granthelm was at the offices of the International Commercial Credit bank, and that so far he had not changed his flight from the one to London he had booked for five thirty. Fathers thanked her and passed on Rutello's information. She returned the thanks and they hung up.

At ten, Fathers went to see Chief Superintendent Bastin, to show him the results of his morning's work and brief him on the meeting to review the Granthelm case set for that afternoon. Bastin looked over the sheet of paper Fathers handed him and smiled.

'Harry,' he said, 'this is brilliant. It's always been my view that your one weakness lies in your ability – or lack of it – to handle relations with your colleagues. But you've really excelled yourself with this. Brilliant.'

Fathers was forced to agree. What he had done was arrange for intensive surveillance of Mulholland, Rankley and, on his return, Sir Walter, while barely committing his own team to the task. The Drug Squad, the local CID and two of his own detectives would maintain the twenty-four-hour watch on Mulholland's flat. The manor would have extra men ready to tail both him and his wife while Drug Squad were putting two men on Rankley, and Guildford CID had a pair to follow Sir Walter on his return from Geneva. Moreover, Fathers had achieved this miracle while having everybody accept that he would remain in complete charge himself.

'I'll welcome your man Flores and the others this afternoon, but I'm afraid I can't stay for it,' said Bastin – to Fathers' unexpressed relief. 'It's the National Intelligence Scheme again: Seems to have broken down somewhere, so there's a committee to set it right. Meets at two thirty.'

Fathers left Bastin's office humming to himself. Mornings that went so well were a rare delight. But Yarrow followed him into his office. 'I'd like a word, guv,' said the detective constable.

'Can it wait? I'm going to the airport in half an hour to pick up our new friend. If you want to drive, you can tell me then, OK?' Fathers sighed: even the best of mornings could be spoiled.

2

Yarrow drove fast and angrily through west London. It was not until he reached the M4 that he broke the silence: 'My man got put in hospital Saturday night.' When he got no reply, he added, 'Not by Pascall's crew, though.' He took a quick glance at Fathers' face, frowning and staring at the road ahead. 'Queen went after him with a length of wood. Broke his nose, coupla teeth and a rib.'

Fathers spoke at last. 'I know,' he said.

Yarrow looked again at Fathers, longer this time. 'So now you both know who he is and you don't need me any more,' he said.

There was a silence between them. Yarrow concentrated on his driving, hurtling up the outside lane, watching for the airport sign. When he saw it, he waited till he had passed a lorry, then cut hard across to the inside lane and slowed. As he got into the slip road, he accelerated again, passing two cars with their left indicators going, getting by on the inside before they could leave the motorway. He braked and changed down to third gear as he approached the roundabout, then accelerated hard on to the approach road to Heathrow and moved up through the gears to fifth. As the car went into the tunnel he had to slow behind a taxi, thought about switching lanes and decided against it. Going at a more sedate speed, he turned once more to Fathers and said, 'What's going on, guv?' His tone was pleading, almost anguished, but tinged with anger.

'There are reasons,' said Fathers, 'good reasons, why you're not to take this any further.'

'Reasons. That's genuine GBH, what he did to my man, poor sod who's only passing the word about a bent screw. He should be had up for it.'

'Your poor sod was not only passing the word, he was also asking everybody and his second cousin about Queen and Pascall. Would you rather Pascall heard about it and got to him?'

Yarrow was silent.

'A nose, two teeth and a rib are not bad exchange for being in a

190

hospital bed, safely out of the way of Jacko's boot boys,' Fathers said.

The car emerged from the tunnel into the grey daylight and Yarrow concentrated on following the signs for Terminal Three. 'But what's going on?' he pleaded again as he pulled into the No Parking area in front of the terminal building.

'Listen,' said Fathers, unbuckling his seat belt and turning to face Yarrow. 'It's not your job to know everything that's going on in my section. It's mine. All right?'

Yarrow was silent, looking at the cars in front of him.

'All right?' insisted Fathers.

Yarrow nodded.

'I know what's going on and I'm looking after it,' said Fathers. 'Clear?'

Yarrow nodded again and cut the engine.

'Your job is to concentrate on the Granthelm business, not to poke your nose in where I'm telling you to keep it out of. Do you understand?'

'It's difficult,' said Yarrow. 'I didn't go looking for this or poking my nose in anything. I was phoned, I was told, I told you – and now my man gets clobbered.'

'He got clobbered,' said Fathers, 'because he was being stupid. Not because I worked out who he was and told Queen, but because Queen heard about him asking questions all over the place.'

Yarrow nodded. 'Yeah,' he conceded quietly, 'he was stupid.'

'And now I've told you two things,' said Fathers, 'and I'll repeat them. One: I know what's happening and I'm looking after it. Got that? It's as much as I'm going to tell you and it's as much as you need to know. Two: leave it alone. D'you understand?'

'Yes,' said Yarrow quietly.

'What?'

'Yes, I said,' Yarrow said more loudly.

'I don't want to hear anything more about it.'

'One thing – I promised Kay a century.'

Fathers opened the door and got out. 'Have you given him anything already?' he asked, bending down to look in at Yarrow.

'Coupla score.'

'OK, let him have another half monkey. A ton for his info, ton and a half for his trouble. Give it to him when he's discharged, all right?'

191

'Really,' said Yarrow, 'it's for his silence, isn't it?'

'You got it,' said Fathers, and straightening up he closed the door. A police constable walked up to him, ready to explain that neither parking nor waiting was allowed and ask whether Fathers could see the newly repainted double yellow lines. Fathers pulled out his warrant card and showed it to the constable who nodded and saluted.

Before going into the terminal, Fathers took a last glance at Yarrow. The young detective was sitting with both hands clasping the top of the steering wheel, gently butting his knuckles with his forehead. Fathers expelled a breath and walked in through the automatic doors.

3

Roberto Flores walked tiredly down the ramp to the immigration hall and looked at the two long and slow-moving queues for people who lacked the privilege of being British or EEC citizens. The men at the desks were taking their time, exploring the reasons for each foreigner's visit to Britain, trying to make sure nobody about to enter the country was planning to take a job, as if an economy with four million unemployed exerted a magnetic attraction on job-seekers the world over. A man in brown uniform with a security tag on his breast pocket was walking up and down the two queues, casting a suspicious eye at every face. He arrived at Flores just as he joined the line. He looked hard at him, moving closer until their faces were only inches apart. 'Flores?' he said. 'Roberto Flores?' Flores nodded. 'This way, please.'

Flores picked up his bags and followed the man. Behind him, speculative conversation began, wondering who had just been caught and what for. The side room into which Flores was taken was small and white. It contained a chair and a desk on which there was a telephone and nothing else. Three men were waiting for him. One was tall, smartly dressed in a double-breasted, speckled grey suit. A second was wearing a sports jacket over a pale blue sweater and the third was wearing a brown leather jacket and cords. The smartest of the trio stepped forward. 'Mr Flores?' he said. 'I'm Harry Fathers, we spoke on the phone.' He extended a hand in greeting.

'Passport, please, Mr Flores,' said the man in the sports jacket.

'Baggage checks,' said the man in the leather jacket.

Flores got out his ticket which had one label stapled on to it. 'It's a big red case,' he said, 'in that hard plastic or whatever it is.'

The man in uniform took the ticket. 'Samsonite?' he said.

'Samson?' said Flores. 'I don't know, it's pretty heavy, but I don't think you'll need him.'

The man in uniform looked at him uncomprehendingly. 'Big red Samsonite,' he said, and walked out through a different door from the one he and Flores had entered by.

'I don't think you need me any more,' said the man in the sports jacket, handing back the passport, and he followed the man in uniform.

'Where should we wait?' asked Fathers.

The man in the leather jacket took them to another room as white as the first. 'This'll do,' he said. 'I'll tell Jack you're here.'

When they were alone, Fathers apologised for the fact that no tea or coffee was provided. He asked Flores about the flight, warned him about the weather, asked if it was his first time in London and, through the small talk, assessed him.

Flores was about five feet ten, slim and fit-looking, with black, straight hair and a dark complexion. He looked Hispanic. He was about Fathers' age, and dressed in a lightweight, three-piece fawn suit. Fathers noticed his right ear-lobe was missing. Apart from that, he carried himself more like a lawyer than a policeman.

Fathers asked him about the unit he worked for. Flores explained that it was the latest in a series of efforts to put an end to, or at least restrict, the drugs trade in Florida. 'It's the major entry point for dope and coke,' he said. 'Billions of dollars worth come through each month. Light planes, choppers, small boats, cargo freighters, cruise liners, personal baggage, dead sharks – you name it, and somebody's brought it in that way. Every time they set up one of these special investigations, it proves two things. First, that the trade is bigger than anybody realised, and second, that it's grown during the period of the investigation. This one's been in business eighteen months. I guess we're making some progress. For instance, so far as we know, nobody's been suborned yet. A number of arrests, two major convictions, several little ones. But, you know, the trade's like that monster, what's it called? – you cut off its head and two more grow in its place.'

'Hydra?' suggested Fathers.

'Something like that. So we're not doing badly, and the cases have stuck in court better than previously, probably because we got more lawyers on the team this time.'

'Are you a lawyer?' asked Fathers.

'Originally, yeah. Criminal law in Tampa, mostly on the defence side, and the losing side, until the DA took me into a special task force on drugs he set up to get re-elected. Then I went to Washington to staff the Judiciary Committee in the House there. And when the governor promised a new crack-down in the run-up to the last off-year gubernatorial, I got drafted for it. I guess it's five years since I've really practised law.'

'So you don't do the actual investigating in this – what's it called?'

Flores grinned. 'It was going to be called the Special Narcotics Investigation Task Force, but then somebody pointed out to the governor that it added up to SNIT Force, so he decided to drop the Task bit, and went public with an anti-drugs effort called SNIF. That didn't help his re-election effort a whole lot, so then we ran through SNIB – B being for Bureau – and SNIC – C for Corps – before an administrative miracle produced the Special Narcotics Investigation Unit – SNIU, which sounds like an aborted sneeze but doesn't actually mean anything nasty.'

Fathers chuckled.

'Anyway,' said Flores, 'you were asking if I do the actual investigating. In lawyers' parlance, the answer is yes and no. I don't do a detective's work, but I keep in tight on an investigation, partly to make sure no corners are cut, there's no entrapment and everything's just hunky for getting it past the Grand Jury and into court. Partly, though we don't like to talk about it, to keep an eye on the real cops who're doing the real work, to make sure they don't get bribed.'

'And who keeps an eye on you?'

Flores looked at Fathers in surprise. 'I've never thought of that, you know. I guess somebody does. Huh, what a thought.'

The man in brown returned with Flores' case on a trolley and took them through the Green Channel and as far as the car where Yarrow was waiting, out of the car now chatting with the constable. He loaded the case into the boot, opened the door for Flores to sit in the back, went round to his side and slid into the drivers' seat, Fathers beside him.

'This is DC Yarrow,' said Fathers. 'He's working on the case.'

'Mr Flores,' said Yarrow, starting the engine.

'Please – Bob,' said Flores, reaching a hand forward to shake, but Yarrow was already easing the car out and looking for the exit signs. Flores withdrew his hand and slumped back in his seat.

On the way into London, Flores started to doze off. When Yarrow jerked him awake by braking sharply then accelerating and swerving into the outside lane, Fathers said, 'I've booked a meeting for early afternoon, but if you're a bit knocked out, maybe it's not such a good idea.'

'Yeah, I never can sleep on planes,' said Flores. 'But if I can get an hour's sleep and then some lunch at the hotel, I'll be OK.'

'Fair enough,' said Fathers. 'Then you can catch up with your sleep this evening.'

Flores looked out of the window. 'What's that sign mean?' he asked. '"No services on motorway."'

'Ah,' said Fathers. 'This is a very dangerous road, as you can tell by the way Yarrow's driving, and some people thought the power of prayer would help. But they cluttered up the road so much with their altars and stuff that it got worse, and we had to put up signs saying religious services aren't allowed.'

Yarrow's repressed laugh came out as an elephantine snort.

'You're fooling,' said Flores uncertainly.

'Yes.'

'Huh, I didn't think the English were that religious. Back home, of course, there's more'n a chance it really would be true.'

They left Flores at his hotel in Victoria, five minutes' walk from Scotland Yard. 'Why don't we phone you at one thirty to make sure you're awake?' suggested Fathers. 'Then somebody can come and get you at two, and we'll start the session just a few minutes late, OK?'

When they got back to the Yard and Yarrow had parked the car, he opened his mouth to say something. Fathers waited, expecting another comment about Kay and Queen, but Yarrow snapped his mouth shut without saying anything. 'Nice bloke,' he said finally as he switched the engine off. Fathers grunted agreement.

Even after Chief Superintendent Bastin had offered a flowery word of welcome to Roberto Flores and the man from Customs and Excise and left, the small conference room was crowded. Fathers sat at the head of the oblong table. To his right was Pardoner, then Yarrow with DS Cotton from Guildford the next one along. On Fathers' left was Flores, with DI Young and DS Larkin from the Drug Squad filling the rest of that side of the table. At the bottom sat DI Brain and the man from Customs and Excise – Ewart, a member of their cocaine target team. Behind Fathers was an easel with a flip chart on it.

It was not Fathers' way to delay business with decorous preambles. He had everybody introduce themselves and got straight down to it. First he outlined where, when and how the murders had occurred – 'I won't go into the issue of the locked room now,' he said, 'because that'll fall into place when we've got the rest. Our main problem is that we still don't have the second gun. In general, material evidence is important in this case only by its absence. So we've been approaching the problem via the motive. It's a question of going into the background, and then stepping on whoever looks good for it and hoping they'll crack.'

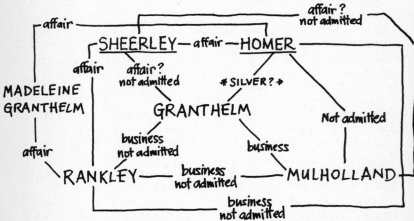

He stood up, tucked his chair under the table and turned to the flip chart. 'We have a lot of background. In fact, as you will see we have enough to make a pig's breakfast.' Folding back the cover sheet, he revealed the first page. 'Believe it or not,' he said, 'to those of us involved in this business, this makes things a lot clearer.'

His audience chuckled appreciatively. The names of Homer and Sheerley were in purple, the other names in red. The comments were in black and the lines connecting everything up were in blue.

'I'll just let you take that in for a moment,' he said, 'and if anybody can make head or tail of it, please explain it to me.' There were more chuckles. 'Right,' he continued, 'now what it shows is that at the core of the case we've got a fairly tight-knit group connected in various ways. As you can see there's a fair amount of sex flying around: the Granthelm woman with Homer and Rankley, the Sheerley woman with both of them, possibly Sir Walter and maybe Mulholland. Between the men, business connections – of which only the Mulholland–Granthelm one has been admitted in interviews. The others they didn't tell us about. In fact, they said there were no others. The Homer–Granthelm connection might be business apart from the silver. We've left off these charts everybody else – though with all that sexuality around the place, who knows but Lady Sarah fits in there as the jealous wife. Young Walter Granthelm and his boyfriend George Waterford seem to stand well to one side of the whole business. So far, there's no reason to suppose either is connected with the killings. Then there's the Briggs family – neighbours of the Granthelms – and the George-Watkinses – he's the US diplomat I told you about, Bob – and again we have no grounds for thinking any of them have anything to do with the killings. So, that's our basic group. Any questions?'

'Where does Brown Mulholland fit in?' asked Flores.

'She's taken as read under "Mulholland",' said Fathers. 'We don't know how their relationship pans out in terms of his connection with drugs. When we get to it, maybe you'll fill us in, if you can.'

Flores nodded. There were no other questions, so Fathers folded back the first chart to reveal a second, simpler one.

Standing so he blocked his audience's view of the second chart, he said, 'We think that out of that little lot we get three alternative motive sets. This is the first one: silver.' He stood aside to let them see the chart. 'Yarrow?'

'Last July,' said Yarrow from his seat, 'a load of antique silver was stolen from Granthelm House. Who did it, we don't know. But we do know that Homer shipped it to two dealers in Milan and Paris.'

<u>MOTIVE</u>

①

<u>SILVER</u>

HOMER ———⎡— GRANTHELM —⎤——— BATESTA
(+SHEERLEY?)   (KNEW? FOUND OUT?)

INSURANCE + MARKET VALUE
<u>CUT?</u>
(TWO-WAY OR THREE-WAY?)
DISPUTE??

He pointed to the chart. 'Batesta's the Milan dealer. He went to Geneva overnight, followed by the Milan police. Sir Walter Granthelm flew there last night as well. Just before we came in here, the Geneva police phoned. Batesta and Sir Walter had lunch together. They bugged it and the recording's being put on a plane this afternoon. They're not sure how good it'll be, but the fact that they met is enough, really.'

'This chart was redrawn in record time,' said Fathers. 'But how it works out motive-wise for the killings is not clear. Homer did or planned or set up the robbery. That much is clear. If Sir Walter found out afterwards, he might have done Homer in by way of revenge, outrage, what-have-you. If he knew about it beforehand, maybe there was a falling out over the spoils, which would not be small. Yarrow?'

'The insurance value was sixty-nine grand, which'd go to Sir Walter,' said Yarrow. 'But the market value could be twice that. Leaving some profit for Batesta, Homer might've grossed seventy grand or so himself. Sir Walter might've reckoned that was too much. Who knows?'

198

'What about Sheerley in this version?' asked Brain.

'Might've been involved too,' said Fathers. 'Maybe suggested it to Homer, even, or've been the one to put him and Sir Walter in touch.'

'Or,' suggested Pardoner, 'our motive sets might overlap: kill Homer about the silver, and Sheerley over the sex. If she and Sir Walter had had an affair, signs are it was over by Christmas.'

'So let's move on,' suggested Fathers, 'because sex is next.'

He flipped the page over, revealing the third chart. 'Motive number two,' he announced. 'In this set, we're down to basics. Rankley kills Homer because he's jealous of Homer screwing Madeleine, and kills Sheerley because he's through with her. Or Madeleine kills Homer because she's through with him, and Sheerley because she's jealous of her screwing Rankley. Or Sir Walter kills Sheerley because he's through with her and Homer because he doesn't like him.'

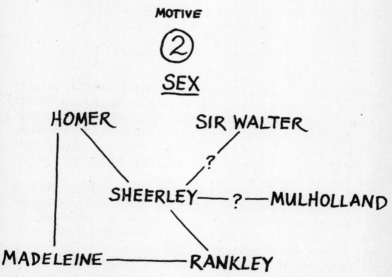

MOTIVE

②

SEX

HOMER   SIR WALTER

                    ?

          SHEERLEY —— ? — MULHOLLAND

MADELEINE ———————— RANKLEY

'Or because Homer tries to stop Sir Walter killing Sheerley,' suggested Pardoner.

'Or because of the silver,' added Yarrow.

'Any other options?' asked Fathers.

'Rankley had the hots for Sir Walter Granthelm?' said Flores, pronouncing the name wrongly. Amid the laughter there was a chorus of corrections.

'All right,' said Fathers, 'so let's try drugs.' He flipped the page over again.

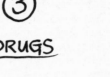

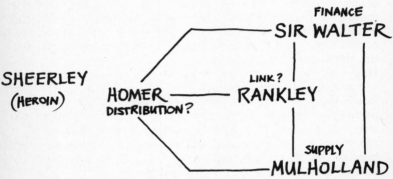

DI Young of the Drug Squad spoke up for the first time. 'Before you start,' he said, 'can you just tell us the basis on which you're about to construct another farrago of lies, insinuations and slander?'

'A flimsy one,' replied Fathers airily.

'Not so flimsy at that,' Flores put in.

'Michael George-Watkins,' said Fathers, 'the diplomat fellow, and a very reliable witness in my view, overheard a conversation on the afternoon after the bodies were found between Rankley, Mulholland and Sir Walter. Mention was made of Peru as the source of supply, the Bahamas as a handling point and perhaps also another supply source – there was something about they'd bought everything there they needed to – and London.'

'OK,' said Young, 'that equals cocaine. Or could do – especially if that's Mulholland's form.'

'Bob?' said Fathers. He pulled out his chair and sat down.

Flores pulled a folder from his attaché case. 'I can tell you a little more than I said on the phone,' he began. 'Number one: Mulholland's business expansion I mentioned was financed by a bank loan. That bank is on our list as probably mob-connected. Number two: we're pretty sure two of his freighter captains supply crack to the street dealers. It's possible they're bringing it in on their own account, but it's probable they're not. In which case, they're either ripping Mulholland off, or it's a form of bonus payment, or they double-up full-time as captains and dealers. To answer your question about Brown Mulholland, Harry, we have no indication she plays an active role in her husband's business, either the legitimate or the possible illegitimate side. She may do, of course, but we don't know that as of now. OK, if Mulholland is mob, he's middle executive level. Not the biggest fish in the water, but not one of the expendable, low level types. We couldn't go to the Grand Jury with him on what we've got, but the signs are good, and with what you told me on Thursday, Harry, we decided to move him up our priority list. Chances we'll succeed, I'd say, are reasonable. But if you wanna fry him this side of the pond, we shan't complain. My last point is that for the past two years we've been warning that American suppliers are targetting Europe. You've done good work keeping them out. It's not been perfect, but compared to what your problem could become, not much has come in so far. I read this as another attempt to break into the European market.'

'Crack's this cheaper type of cocaine, isn't it?' said Fathers.

'Cheaper, more potent, more addictive,' said Flores. 'Bit like free-basing. Smoke it instead of snorting, and estimates are that up to seventy per cent of first time users get hooked straightaway. Coke crystals are expensive – smart, jet-set people use it. Crack's your down-market alternative. Which also means a bigger market, bigger profits. And it's easy to make: just whip up a paste of coke, baking soda and water, let it harden and cut it into chips. Looks like white gravel.'

'Assuming Mulholland's a mob man,' said Young, 'do you think he only imports rock, or does he do dope as well?'

'Well, it's not rock he actually imports. He brings in regular white lady and the processing happens afterwards. But, no, we don't think he does dope as well – not now, anyway. Remember that, weight for weight, coke's worth about one hundred and sixty times as much as dope. You want bigger profits for less work – you trade coke.'

Ewart from Customs and Excise spoke for the first time: 'Is that file for general consumption? And does it tell us how and when Mulholland'll bring the stuff in?'

'Sure, it's for general consumption. As to how – I'd say he'll do it the way he knows best, in Customs-cleared containers along with a whole lot of fruit. When – no answer. But back home they're working on it.'

'If the food import deal is cover for the coke,' said Young, 'Sir Walter could actually be an innocent party in this.'

'So why did the three of them discuss the Peru-Bahamas-London route?' objected Pardoner. 'Does any fruit come that way?'

'Good point,' said Fathers, 'but it's possible Sir Walter doesn't know the details. Mulholland might've said that for Rankley's benefit. Maybe George-Watkins can help us out on that. By the way, what's that about purchasing everything they needed to in the Bahamas? Assuming it's a drugs deal, what're they buying there?'

'Influence,' said Flores. 'Protection. It's for sale.'

'How about motive?' asked Brain. 'I see the case for Drug Squad and Customs to get involved. But it's not necessarily anything to do with the kills.'

'Right,' said Pardoner. 'I mean, we've got Sheerley on the chart because she took heroin, but, in a sense, so what? Same with Homer: we don't know he's in the deal just because he's twice been seen near Mulholland's flat.'

'Same with Sir Walter, too,' said Young.

'So why was he in Geneva?' asked Brain.

'That was the silver,' replied Young. 'Maybe you've got him on that. Maybe we've got Mulholland and perhaps Rankley – though even that's supposition – for drugs. But who've you got for murder?'

The discussion circulated for a while round the welter of possibilities and connections until it reached virtual stalling point. A knock on the door rescued them and announced the arrival of the coffee trolley. 'This'll be good stuff,' said Fathers walking round to be the first in line. 'I told 'em it was Bastin's meeting, so we've got his personal hoard, not the usual muck.' He passed cups to Ewart and Flores, the only civilians present, took his own and left the others to serve themselves. 'But don't take the biscuits,' he added, 'they always bend in two places before you can bite them.'

As they got their coffee, DS Larkin of the Drug Squad, silent hitherto, approached Yarrow. 'How'd you get on to this Homer bloke and the antiques?' he asked. 'Out of interest.'

'Oh,' said Yarrow, 'we'd been looking for someone in the antiques line we only knew of as the Greek. Then these murders came up and, Homer being a Greek poet, we strung it together. Why?'

Larkin nodded with satisfaction. 'Yeah,' he said, 'Homer being Greek and all, it rang the same bells with me. I reckon he is – was – in on the drugs deal, if there is one.'

'Tell the boss,' suggested Yarrow as he sat down with his coffee.

'What's that?' asked Fathers.

Larkin waited till they had all returned to their places. Then he said simply, 'Homer was the Greek.'

Beside him DI Young banged his palm on to the table, hard enough to cause his cup to spill some coffee into its saucer. 'Shit,' he said. 'Brilliant.'

'Yarrow's, actually,' said Larkin.

'That's how we got on to him for the silver,' explained Pardoner.

'You have a Greek too?' said Fathers.

'We have a Greek too,' confirmed Young. 'On and off for about three years, not the biggest dealer in town, just the occasional transaction, but pretty big whenever he does it. We've been puzzling away now and again, but we never got a name or a description to go with the tag.'

'If it is Homer,' said Fathers, 'then he was a very clever operator indeed, into illicit antiques and drugs without any of us being any the wiser and with almost nobody knowing his name. My skipper – skipperene, actually – had to confront seven people with his name before she got confirmation.'

'So,' said Flores, 'Homer wanted in so they offed him.'

'Sheerley?' said Brain.

'Sex,' suggested Pardoner. 'Two birds with one stone.'

'Which rules out Mulholland,' said Flores regretfully.

'Not necessarily,' said Young. 'If he's hard enough, he could've put her away precisely in order to cover his tracks.'

'No,' said Fathers, 'it's good but it won't do. Homer didn't need to want in – he was already there, slipping Sir Walter's silver out of the country.'

'Assuming Sir Walter knew in advance,' said Pardoner.

'Good,' said Flores, 'but no cigars, huh?'

'Did Sir Walter know about the silver in advance, or didn't he?' said Fathers. 'Maybe that's the key to it all. What d'you reckon the chances are of successfully leaning on a merchant banker with friends in high places?'

'Worth a try,' suggested Young.

'My feeling too,' said Brain.

'Yeah, but you hate him because of the way he used the press to get after you when you didn't get his silver back,' said Fathers.

'True,' said Brain, 'fair comment, but what I mean is whether he knew in advance or afterwards, you must've got him for something, meeting that Batesta bloke in Geneva.'

'I s'pose he could be trying to buy it back,' said DS Cotton, his first intervention in the meeting.

'Too late for that,' said Pardoner. 'Batesta's sold most of it.'

'Could be *trying*,' insisted Cotton.

'Could be,' conceded Pardoner. 'I wonder what the recording will show?'

The group pondered that in silence for a while. Then Fathers said, 'Well, this and better may do, this and worse'll never. We shan't advance ourselves much going in circles here. Bob, you've got work to do with the Customs man and the Druggies. The rest of us can concentrate on the silver – though I think I'll think about sex. Still looks the best bet to me, whatever their other criminality. Anything else before we close?'

Yarrow coughed.

'Yarrer?'

'Well,' said Yarrow, 'I just wondered about one thing. I mean, it sounds simple, but what would they do with the cocaine once they got it here? Before they sell it, I mean.'

'They need to find a place to separate it from the other contents of the containers,' said Young condescendingly, 'then they store it some place from which they can distribute it.'

'Ah,' said Yarrow, slightly stung by Young's tone. 'A warehouse, for example?'

'For example,' said Young.

'So if Rankley had a warehouse, that might be interesting, then?'

Young looked open-mouthed at Yarrow. Fathers grinned: when Yarrow sounded his most simple-minded, he was usually about to bring a rabbit out of the hat. 'Does he have one?' asked Fathers.

'Ah,' said Yarrow, 'that I can't tell you.' He waited for the disappointment to sink in, and long enough for Young's surprise to change to irritation, before he added, 'But it looks like it.'

'What's the problem?' asked Fathers.

'Well,' said Yarrow, 'it's very difficult, what with Rankley being alive, you see. It's much easier to work these things out when a bloke's been swatted and you can have access to all his papers. I talked to a pal in Fraud and he was a bit of help, but it's not clear.' Yarrow paused and shrugged.

'Go on,' said Fathers.

'Well, a warehouse Rankley was handling for his company of property developers suddenly disappeared from the market at what seems like something below the right price. And it seems to have been bought by a company called Number Four.'

'So?' said Young.

'That's the shirt number Rankley wore when he played rugby.'

CHAPTER 16

1

After the meeting, they went their various ways: Flores, Ewart and the men from Drug Squad into session together; Brain and Cotton to Guildford, to finalise the details for following Sir Walter on his return to Gatwick; Fathers, Pardoner and Yarrow back to their desks. Fathers spent most of the rest of the afternoon with Stevens, discussing the warehouse fire and the hijackings. They were interrupted by a phone call from Captain Gerrell: Sir Walter had changed his flight plans again and would be returning to London via a two-hour stop-over in Paris. The rebooking had been done through the hotel. He had made another phone call – unfortunately, from the restaurant where he had lunch, and Gerrell's men had been unable to get close enough to overhear or bug his conversation. Gerrell added that Batesta had passed Sir Walter an envelope at lunch, which the financier had taken to a bank. Both the handover and the deposit had been photographed by a competent officer who was confident the pictures would come out well. Together with the recording of the Batesta–Granthelm lunch, they would be at Fathers' office early the next morning. Fathers thanked Gerrell, and then got on to the Liaison Room to approach the Paris police to watch and, if possible, electronically eavesdrop on Sir Walter. When he was through with Stevens, he called Malcolm Hardy to arrange a drink and contacted Michael George-Watkins to fix a meeting for nine the following morning.

Fathers was surprised by Hardy's choice of pub. Usually when they met it was in a crowded bar where no seats were free and every confidence had to be communicated at full volume. This time the pub was relatively empty.

'Now, what's all this about, Harry?' Hardy asked as they settled themselves in a corner. 'Friday I phoned and you didn't want a drink, today you phone and can't get round here fast enough. Do I smell a story? Is that the faint aroma of a little swapperoon of informations?' He took a long drink of his beer.

'That reporter's nose of yours, Malc – never leads you far astray, does it? How do you do it, I often ask myself during my endless hours of inactivity?'

'All right, all right.' Hardy pulled a packet of cigarettes out. Fathers reached over, deftly took one and waited for Hardy to light it for him.

'Our background research service has let us down in its usual way, so rather than haul you round to our cellars and beat the living daylights out of you, I thought I'd get you drunk and worm some useful blather out of your subconscious.'

'Happy to oblige. Is it about Granthelm?'

'Who else?'

'Got something in exchange, have you?'

'In principle, though I'll see the colour of your money first. But, you understand, not for immediate use. Usual thing.'

'Sure – background, but exclusive, I hope.'

'Of course. What've you got?'

'Granthelm: yeah, I've been looking into him, ever since he had that idiot Pindar phone me about you. For general background, I've got a hefty file of cuttings about the company, the silver robbery, the occasionally recorded social appearances of various family members, notably the delectable Maddy. I assume you're not interested in any of that. I assume too that you're well aware young Walter is a poof.'

'We don't use such language in the Met any more, but I just about remember its meaning from the dark days of yesteryear.'

'And you're not interested in my hunch about Sir Wally and his niece.'

'I'll come back to you on that one.'

'Which leaves us only with his financial difficulties.'

Fathers stubbed out his cigarette and pulled a packet of cigars from his pocket. He took Hardy's lighter and sat back with a contented sigh when the cigar was going. He didn't even object when Hardy stubbed out his cigarette and filched a cigar.

'Now you're talking. Tell all, and you will not go unrewarded.'

'The word is,' said Hardy, as he lit the cigar, 'that about a year ago he took a flyer on Brazilian coffee futures and came unstuck. Crop failure.'

'Badly unstuck?'

'To the tune of seventy or eighty grand.'

'OK. And this was his money, not the bank's?'

'Thass right. Apparently he was seen in his cups a fair bit, wondering what the hell he was going to do.'

'But he must be worth a fortune,' objected Fathers. 'Surely it'd be no big deal for him to raise that sort of money – bank loan, sell a few shares, couple of paintings.'

'Seems like it hit him at a bad time. The story is that he was also investing in a new company on the Stock Exchange, getting ready for the big bang – you know, last October when all the rules changed and a lot of the trading on the Exchange moved into the hands of the big companies. Anyway, it seems the group he was putting money into – personal money, mind, not the bank's – was under-capitalised and couldn't pay well enough to attract the bright young things who do all the actual buying and selling. I hear he put about sixty grand into that, and he couldn't get it out again 'cause nobody would buy.'

'So one way and another he was in very deep water with two big losses on his hands.'

'Well, not really. The broking company's been doing all right in AB One.'

'What?'

'AB One: first year after bang. This year.'

'Oh.'

'But the point is that he couldn't get his investment back then when he needed it, because it did look as if the company was going down the plug-hole. On top of all that, rumour has it he's been living beyond his means for years now, already selling the family silver to pay the tradesmen. So his personal reserves were pretty low.'

'Is this all common knowledge?'

'On the street, you mean? Yeah, though some people reckon his troubles weren't so great.'

'But none of it got printed.'

'Too hot. Blokes on the financial and society columns don't even need to be told to keep off something like that. Comes as second nature.'

'So what happened?'

'By all accounts, he was over it by the autumn. You can take it as an example of the miraculous powers of recovery of the ruling class, or as proof that there was no real problem in the first place. That's it, anyway. Any use?'

'Oh yes,' said Fathers reflectively, 'it fits very nicely.'

'So what've you got for me? Include another beer in it, why don't you?'

Fathers got up and bought two pints. He gave them both to

Hardy; his own was barely touched.

'Thanks, guv,' said Hardy, 'you gotta lucky face.' He drained half his second pint in one go. 'So?'

Fathers smiled. 'Not all of it, Malc,' he said, 'but a lot of it, and enough for your needs. But get back to me if and when it breaks and I'll give you the rest for post-trial coverage.'

'Whose trial?'

'That comes under the not-all-of-it bit.'

'Sod. What crumbs do I get then?'

'Malcolm, with your reporter's nose or whatever else you use for it, think hard about the relationship between selling the family silver and meeting an immediate financial need. Think about the best way to maximise your gains on the silver sale.'

Hardy thought for a moment. 'Fuck.'

'Neatly put, and an apt feed-in to the second part. They've all been screwing all round the place. Madeleine Granthelm . . .'

'. . . with that fart Wankley,' said Hardy.

'And with Homer, the dead man.'

'Kidding?'

'Not a bit of it. Rankley . . .'

'Wankley.'

'. . . with Ellen Sheerley, the dead woman, who was also doing it with Homer and probably Sir Walter.'

'Getaway. So my hunch was right after all.'

'I said probably – but it's only a fraction over fifty-fifty. Don't commit yourself on that one.'

'OK, thanks.' Hardy finished his second pint and relit his cigar. 'They've got some crust, haven't they?'

'The upper crust, oh yes.'

2

After the meeting, Yarrow spent the rest of the afternoon worrying away trying to connect Rankley with the company which had bought the warehouse through his property development firm. At seven he left to visit Kay in hospital and tell him that the offer was now two hundred and fifty pounds in return for keeping his mouth shut. Kay looked acidly out of his good eye and commented that if he went to the Police Complaints Authority, Queen would kick him in the balls – but two fifty would do very nicely. Then Yarrow called on Rita Thomas, their third evening together in succession. After a meal and a drink, they ended up at her flat at eleven. They talked till 5 a.m., at which point he summoned the courage to address what was dominating both their minds and suggest they go to bed together.

He got to work at nine on Tuesday morning looking contented, exhausted and unshaven. DS Gordon came over to sit on his desk.

'Well then, Elly,' she said in a loud voice, 'get your oats last night, did you? Nothing like it, eh?'

She nodded happily as a silly smile spread itself uncontrollably across Yarrow's features.

'Hey,' boomed Graves from behind his desk, 'Yarrer's got his leg over.'

'Up, up and had it away,' added Bunn.

Yarrow began to turn red, his eyes flickering from face to face, ceiling to floor, desk to filing cabinet, even more wildly than usual.

'And I thought you were saving yourself,' said DC Hands. She pouted. 'I'm distraught. I hope she's a nice girl though, is she?'

'Aw,' said Cathy Gordon soothingly, 'spoils the magic when all the world knows, doesn't it? Poor boy.' She grinned wickedly.

'Never on a weekday, Elly,' said Pardoner, 'not the first one anyway, not the one which takes you till dawn to commence and breakfast to consummate. Can't hide the signs, you see.'

Having done the damage, DS Gordon stood up and walked back to her own desk. Over her shoulder she said, 'Still, maybe it'll perk you up a bit. You've been worse'n death warmed up these last few days, not yourself at all. Haven't had a Holmes quote for yonks.'

'Back to work, children,' said Stevens from the door of his office. 'Yarrow, my heartiest congrats.'

'Oh fuck off,' mumbled Yarrow.

'I think you done that already,' said Graves.

'Where did Holmes say that?' demanded Pardoner.

Fathers returned from the Embassy at ten. He called Pardoner and a now shaven but still tired-looking Yarrow into his office. 'What's wrong with you, Yarrer?' he asked. Pardoner made a show of opening his mouth ready to explain.

'Shut up,' said Yarrow quietly to Pardoner.

'Oy,' said Pardoner, 'you're not a skipper yet, mate. Time enough for that kind of talk when you've made the grade – the other grade, I mean.'

'Touched a raw spot, have I?' asked Fathers innocently. Pardoner made as if to say something.

'Shut up,' Yarrow said more emphatically.

'Only raw through over-use, I should think,' Pardoner murmured.

'All right,' said Fathers, 'leave the lad alone.' He looked at the folders on his desk. 'Hope she's a nice girl, though,' he said quietly. He looked at Yarrow over the top of his reading glasses. 'Not telling me to shut up, are you?' he enquired.

'For fuck's sake,' said Yarrow in exasperation.

'I think,' said Pardoner, 'that if you changed your expletives, you might find the rest of the morning a little easier.'

'Well, let's help by getting down to business,' said Fathers. 'First things first: is Sir Walter back in the country?'

'Yeah, last plane from Paris to Gatwick and drove back to Granthelm House,' said Pardoner. 'He's at his office now. Drove up this morning. Brain's boys are camped across the street from him and everything's wired for sound.'

'Have the pictures and transcript arrived from Geneva?'

'Right here,' said Pardoner, passing a folder to Fathers. There were three pictures of Batesta handing an envelope to Sir Walter: one showed him taking it out of his pocket, the second Sir Walter taking it from his outstretched hand, and the third Sir Walter tucking it into his inside jacket pocket.

'Handy things, motorised camera drives,' commented Fathers.

Five more pictures showed Sir Walter first entering a bank, then standing in front of the teller with the envelope in his hands, next pulling a document out of the envelope, then handing it to the teller and finally getting the receipt.

'Can't mistake that,' said Fathers. 'Obviously not a cheque – banker's draft, I expect. How many copies do we have?'

'Four of each,' said Pardoner.

'Right. And this is the transcript?'

'Yup.'

Fathers skimmed through the typed pages. 'Here we go,' he said, and began to read aloud, using a stage Italian accent for Batesta and a BBC voice for Sir Walter:

'"B: I do not understand why the middle man is not here, why you have come yourself.

'"G: Don't concern yourself with that. It's between him and me. Did you do as I asked?

'"B: Of course. Here it is in full. This settles all.

'"G: Quite so. It was simply more convenient for me to do it, that's all.

'"B: There are no complications at your end?

'"G: None.

'"B: Because as I told you the police have been asking me questions. The situation borders on the delicate, though I am essentially confident. But they know it is your silver and are seeking to recover it.

'"G: Then perhaps I'll get it back. An added bonus.

'"B: For you perhaps, but it reduces my profit margin, so this payment is less than we first estimated. But that is as we agreed by phone.

'"G: Quite."

'Shame they didn't use Homer's name,' said Fathers taking off his glasses and tapping them on the transcript, 'but you can't mistake what's going on. Anything else?'

'An interesting little report,' said Pardoner, 'from the watch on Mulholland's pad.' He opened another manilla folder. 'Seven p.m., Mrs Mulholland left in cab. Followed to Ritz Hotel. Met man in bar, approx. seven thirty. After drinks, went to Lee Ho Fook – interesting name, that – restaurant in Soho south, approx. eight fifteen. Ate full meal, returned Ritz, approx. ten fifteen. Pair went to room 617, stayed night. Took breakfast in room, approx eight a.m. Mrs Mulholland left approx. eight fifty. Arrived home nine twelve. Man identified as Royston Curry, American citizen, presumed tourist.'

'Tell Young and Flores,' said Fathers.

'Already done it. Flores is calling Miami as soon as they're awake and Young's phoning the Drug Enforcement Administration.'

'And what did Mister do while the lady was out playing?' asked Fathers. 'A lot of it about, eh?'

'Thereby hangs a tale,' said Pardoner. 'Approx. eight p.m. cab arrived target. Woman got out, subsequently identified as Madeleine Granthelm.'

'And she stayed the night?'

'Liberated lot, these Mulhollands,' said Pardoner. 'Left this morning at eight thirty.'

'All timed to the minute,' said Fathers. 'Well I never.'

'Not as often as they do, anyway,' suggested Pardoner. 'Better modify our charts a little. Anyway, that's all I've got. Did you get anything from George-Watkins?'

'A bit. He's in no doubt that whatever deal was being discussed, Rankley, Mulholland and Sir Walter were all part of it. He thinks it was Mulholland who mentioned the Peru–Bahamas bit. He says Mulholland and Rankley were quite calm and smooth, but Sir Walter was pretty edgy. He put it down, he says, to the invasion of the family home by murderers and policemen.'

Fathers leaned back in his chair, putting his feet on the desk. 'Right, next steps. Any suggestions?'

'I think it's time to move on Sir Walter,' said Pardoner.

Fathers leaned back in his chair and inspected the ceiling. 'Maybe. Yarrer?'

'Still can't pin down who's behind this company, Number Four, guv. I think we should have a chat with Rankley – not about the warehouse, mind, but about him and Mulholland. I also wondered if it'd be worth having a go at that Madeleine bird,' said Yarrow.

'Bird?' said Pardoner.

'Gets around a bit,' said Yarrow.

'Granted.'

'Sex,' said Fathers. 'Yes. Well, I want to think about this for a while. I'm going to read through everything. Then I'll decide. We may be hobbing with the nobs this afternoon, Yarrer. Till then, keep on this Number Four of yours. Skip, have a go at Paris to find out what Sir Walter did there last night, will you?'

Pardoner left but Yarrow remained in his seat. As the door closed behind the Detective Sergeant, Yarrow leaned forward and said, 'Guv, Cath's asked me to come back in on the antiques thing. 'Parently she reckons she's on the way with it. But she's put it under Queen.'

'Yes, I saw. OK, she can have Bunn instead.'

'Thing is, don't tell her I asked 'cause she might think it's that I don't want to work with her.'

'You and she don't have trouble, do you?'

'No, not at all, far from it.'

'Then she won't think that. She is a very secure person, our Cath. But I'll tell her it's because you're fully tied up on this. OK?'

'Thanks. Um, Kay's happy with the two fifty. Says that Queen'd have his balls if he made a complaint.'

'Probably not far off the truth,' said Fathers cheerfully.

'I'm trusting you,' said Yarrow. 'It is all right, isn't it? Like you said.'

'Like I said.'

CHAPTER 17

1

'Put another way,' said Yarrow, 'the more we think you got something to hide, so the more suspicious we are, the harder we dig and the more we uncover. You can stop us by just telling the truth. Which means the whole truth and nothing but.'

Madeleine Granthelm looked with visible distaste at the young detective. His superior was bad enough – cool, distant and insistent. But at least he had an air to him of a man who understood – some things, at any rate. She assumed he had a university education and his accent, if not polished, was not exactly uncut like the proletarian Yarrow's. Fathers looked as if he was just doing a job, and even the way he sat suggested he'd rather be doing something else. Yarrow, on the other hand, sitting forward eagerly on his upright chair, his eyes sweeping up and down over her body as she leaned back in her sofa, was like a child gleefully pulling the wings off a butterfly, carefully listening to find out if its agony would be audible.

'I've nothing to add,' she said.

'How long have you been doing it with Mulholland, for example?'

Madeleine Granthelm responded with an angry glare and a blush.

'We know you're doing it,' said Yarrow, 'but we want to know exactly when it began.'

'What is this?' she demanded. 'You sound more like a gutter press hack than a detective.'

'Oh I haven't started yet,' said Yarrow calmly. 'We also want to know how you were introduced, how you came to get into the sack with him and how often you do it.'

'Are you going to permit this?' she asked Fathers.

'Miss Granthelm,' said Fathers smoothly, 'I think I've explained adequately that, given the place, time and manner in which the murders occurred, the relationships between those present that weekend are of prime interest to us. It is material, I assure you.'

Madeleine Granthelm did not look any happier.

'Last night, f'r instance,' said Yarrow, 'did you know before

215

that Mrs Mulholland would be out till morning, or did he call you up to tell you?'

She remained silent.

'Mr Rankley, now,' said Yarrow, enjoying himself, 'does he know you're having it away with the American, or will it be a surprise when I tell him?'

'We have an understanding.'

'I bet you do. Like with Mr Homer, I suppose. When did you tell Mr Rankley about him? While it was going on or after it ended?'

'This prurient moralising—' began Madeleine Granthelm.

'Your father, of course, knows everything,' Yarrow cut in.

She looked at him with obvious horror, mingled with repugnance, and then pleadingly at Fathers.

Fathers shrugged theatrically at her.

'We'll be seeing him some time,' said Yarrow, 'and I'll happily fill him in then. Probably be easier coming from an outsider rather than you having to tell him.'

'You little fucking oick,' she said, but the anger was acted – it was the fear that came through the insult.

'Go easy now,' warned Yarrow. 'There's always what you call the gutter press to think of. I know a bloke'd give his right arm for a story like this. Nothing they like better than kicking the rich and powerful when you're already reeling.'

She shook her head violently. Fathers decided her distress was genuine. 'Yarrow,' he said sharply, 'I think you've made your point. Now look, Miss Granthelm, none of this need be necessary. Everything can be discreet. You can remain in charge of when and what to tell to whom. The point is, if you tell us, Yarrow cannot leak it without being disciplined – severely, I assure you. But if you don't tell us . . . Well, it's just that the information we hold is then not privileged in the same way.'

He hoped Madeleine Granthelm's knowledge of the law of criminal procedure was hazy enough for her to believe him.

Evidently it was, for she eyed him gratefully, then cast a sidelong glance at Yarrow and another appealing look at Fathers. 'It's so difficult,' she said. 'It's not that I'm ashamed, of course, but . . .' She let her eyes slip Yarrow's way again. 'It's so difficult,' she repeated.

'Yarrow,' said Fathers. 'Wait in the car, will you?'

Yarrow shrugged and got to his feet. He turned to Madeleine

Granthelm, pointed his pen at her and opened his mouth to say something. Then he thought better of it and walked out of the room, out of her flat and down the stairs to the pavement. He leaned against the car and whiled away the time doodling on his pad.

Twenty minutes later he was joined by Fathers looking grim. They got into the car in silence. Fathers looked at Yarrow for a while. 'Well done,' he said at last, 'very nice.'

'Artful sods, ain't we? Stupid how often they fall for the hard-soft number. She talked, did she?'

'Did she ever? Mulholland since late January. Because Rankley asked her to, would you believe?'

Yarrow whistled. 'What about Homer?'

'June to October last year. Not the odd time, but regular. Rankley knew all about it. Had her describe it to him, then did it with her the way she'd just done it with Homer. I'm glad to get out of there alive.'

Yarrow started the engine. 'Looking good on the sex motive front,' he said.

2

It was almost three thirty when Yarrow parked the car round the corner from Rankley's office. As Fathers got out of the car a uniformed constable approached him. Expecting to be told to find somewhere else to park, Fathers reached for his warrant card, but the constable held up a hand. 'It's all right, Mr Fathers,' he said. 'I just came to say he's still in there.'

Fathers looked at him and eyed his hair. It was long for a copper on the beat. 'Drug Squad?' he asked.

The constable grinned by way of reply. 'We borrowed this get-up for the day. Nobody suspects a bobby, after all. I'm just hoping nothing happens that needs me to act like a beat man. I've got some cover in mufti, though. Feels strange to be back in clobber, I can tell you.'

Fathers chuckled. That was a smart move by Young.

Yarrow got out of the car. 'Demotion, Dave?' he said. 'More dope gone astray and they've finally nailed you for it?'

The uniformed plainclothes detective grinned again. 'Better

plod about me lawful business,' he said, and walked off with the measured stride of the beat policeman, hands clasped behind his back in the classic position. At the corner he was approached by a woman in fur. He looked at his watch and said something to her, then pointed to the clock across the street. As she ran off, he turned and winked at Fathers and Yarrow.

'We'll do it the same way,' said Fathers. 'Keep it straight till I scratch my nose, then rile him with the uppity pleb number.'

'D'you reckon it'll work so well with him?'

Fathers shrugged. 'I think you'll get under his skin just as well, but he may not trust authority as instinctively as she did. Anyway, part of the point is just to shake the trees and see what falls out. Don't necessarily have to get him to cough.'

Yarrow had described the company Rankley worked for as property developers. It occupied the bottom three floors of a large City building and exuded prosperity and established success. Fathers and Yarrow went to reception, introduced themselves and asked for Peter Rankley.

'Do you have an appointment?' asked the receptionist.

'He's expecting us,' replied Fathers ambiguously.

'Second floor, then, his door's just to the right as you come out of the lift.'

Behind Rankley's door they found a neat office containing an attractive secretary. They introduced themselves again, and she explained that Mr Rankley had a client with him. She looked worriedly at the diary on her desk and commented that they did not have an appointment.

'Please just tell him we're here,' said Fathers, politely but firmly, 'and that we're not inclined to wait. Thank you.'

She looked likely to object but Fathers gestured to her telephone and she picked it up and pressed a button. 'There's two police officers here to see you, Mr Rankley,' she said. 'They say it's most urgent . . . All right, fine, I'll tell them. Thank you.' She put the phone down. 'He'll be five minutes. Will you have coffee while you wait?'

'No, thanks.'

'I think I'll just wait in the corridor,' said Yarrow.

'Good idea,' nodded Fathers.

After more like ten minutes, a door with no name on it opened and Rankley came out with another man. They shook hands, exchanged goodbyes and then Rankley saw Yarrow. He came over. 'Ah, Jarrow, is it?' he said. 'Sorry to have kept you waiting. I'm ready for you now.'

'It's Yarrow.'

'Ah. Where's the other one?'

'Mr Fathers is in your secretary's office.'

Rankley shut the door which led direct into his own room and walked ahead of Yarrow into his secretary's office. 'Mr Fathers.'

'Mr Rankley,' said Fathers, pleased with himself that, even after the session with Madeleine Granthelm, he managed not to use Hardy's version of the former rugby player's name.

Rankley went into his office and sat behind his desk, the window behind him so the light played on the detectives' faces but left his in shadow. Fathers took a padded upright chair opposite him, while Yarrow found another set against the wall and sat down. He pulled out his pad and pen.

Before Fathers could say anything, Rankley held up a hand. 'I have just received a phone call and I understand you have been harassing Miss Granthelm, which is not at all in order.' His voice remained smooth, but there was an edge in it which was meant to communicate severe displeasure to the policemen. It was a tone which assumed superiority. It annoyed Fathers but it didn't intimidate him.

'Asking questions is not the same as harassment. Refusing to answer them is what is not in order.'

'We'll see,' said Rankley.

'Certain difficulties have arisen about your evidence to us in your signed statement,' continued Fathers, 'and I wish to go over them and clear up some areas of doubt.'

He waited for an answering shot from Rankley, but none came.

'For example,' he continued, 'you told us you were not doing any business with Mr Mulholland, but in fact you are. Would you care to amplify?'

Rankley maintained his silence, but Fathers waited him out. 'It's not true,' said Rankley at last, 'that I have business dealings with Davis Mulholland. I don't know what makes you think otherwise.'

Fathers sighed elaborately. 'You should be more careful how you park that nice car of yours,' he said. 'Would you like to try again?'

'I have no business dealings with him,' insisted Rankley. 'He's an acquaintance whom I occasionally visit. Parking round there is

219

very difficult, so I've picked up a ticket virtually every time I've been there.'

'Would you care, then,' said Fathers mildly, scratching his nose, 'to explain your business dealings with Sir Walter Granthelm?'

'I have none.'

'Bullshit,' said Yarrow.

Rankley looked at him in annoyance.

'What're we putting up with this for?' snapped Yarrow. 'Waste of time.'

Rankley tried an angry glare, but Yarrow was now talking to Fathers: 'What's the word?' he asked. Fathers looked at him. 'Procuring, that right?'

'I think that's right,' said Fathers.

'How much'd he pay you?' asked Yarrow, turning his eyes on Rankley. The flickering gaze was openly scornful now.

Rankley's mouth opened and closed a couple of times, but he seemed lost for words.

'Go on,' insisted Yarrow, 'how much'd he pay you when you tossed your girlfriend his way?'

Rankley brought an angry fist smacking down on the desk. It juddered under the impact. He was a large and strong man.

'Done it before, have you?' sneered Yarrow. 'Is that why Madeleine laid Homer?'

'This has gone far enough,' said Rankley loudly, not quite shouting. He stood up.

'Oh, I'm just getting warmed up,' said Yarrow. 'You lot make me sick. This is a murder enquiry, not some rugby club jape where you've nicked a Belisha beacon's yellow hat and the beak'll fine you all a tenner, or let you off on a promise of good behaviour if he happens to be president of the club. This is the real thing, mate. This is where it counts when you tell downright lies.'

Still standing, Rankley placed both fists on the desk and leant on them. The impression of his looming bulk was menacing. His face and neck were red. 'Mr Fathers . . .' he said.

'Apart from providing Mulholland with your girlfriend,' said Yarrow, 'what other business do you do with him?'

'This is outrageous,' said Rankley, straightening up. 'If Miss Granthelm is seeing Davis Mulholland, that is entirely her affair. I will not permit you to drag her name through the muck—'

'There is that, of course,' interrupted Yarrow sharply, silencing Rankley. He turned to Fathers. 'There's an industry in muck-raking not far from here. What say I call in on that chum of mine on our way back to the Yard? Then this git'll know all about dragging things through the muck, once it hits the front page.'

'Mr Fathers, this is utterly intolerable. You cannot permit this, this thug, to threaten me like this.'

'Or Sir Walter,' continued Yarrow. 'I wonder how he'd like it. I could tell him first, give him a couple of days to think it over, then splash it over the tabloids.'

Rankley sat down, his face still red, his fists still clenched.

Yarrow made a visible effort to calm down, and when he continued it was in a quiet, almost chummy tone. 'Look, Peter, answer the questions, and there's no need for anyone else to know.'

At the familiar use of his first name, Rankley jumped to his feet again. 'I think this has gone far enough,' said Fathers. Rankley looked at him with pleasure and sat down, casting a scornful glance at Yarrow.

'I'd nick this git here and now,' said the detective constable. 'Obstruction.'

'Technically, that is right, Mr Rankley,' said Fathers. 'Pressing a bit hard, perhaps, slightly out of place to do it with you, maybe, but we really can't sit here all day and wait for you to make up your mind to answer our questions honestly. Yarrow, would you go downstairs and warm the car up? There's a good fellow. Mr Rankley, I'm afraid that if you don't start being a little bit more cooperative, we are going to have to adjourn to the Yard.'

Yarrow stood up, pocketing his pen and pad. He muttered something which sounded like, 'I'll have him yet,' and walked out, slamming the door behind him. When he was in the corridor, he grinned. He felt nothing but contempt for Rankley, his bluster so easily silenced, his confidence so easily shaken, and apparently his attitudes to sexuality so strange. Nailing him would be a great pleasure. He tripped lightly down the stairs and out on to the street. Waving at the Drug Squad man he went to the car and started it. Just in case Fathers had to go through with his threat, he drove round to park outside Rankley's office building, the engine idling. While he waited, he used the radio to make sure that Sir Walter Granthelm was still at his office.

Fathers arrived fifteen minutes later. He got in and banged the car door shut. 'Granthelm's,' he said. Yarrow pulled out into the stream of traffic.

'Pack of lies,' Fathers continued, 'interesting, but lies. Still insists he's not doing business with Mulholland. I threatened him with a witness, without naming George-Watkins, but he shrugged it off. He introduced Madeleine to Mulholland but says he didn't toss her to him. His affair with Sheerley was longer than he let on, several months, but he was only playing it down because he thought it wasn't relevant. He apologised to me, and I apologised on your behalf.'

'So he thinks you've swallowed it,' said Yarrow.

'That's right. He was shaken, obviously, though with a man like that it's anger which comes out first. His first line of defence is to come the bully. But now he's recovered himself a bit, so I don't think we've disturbed anything but his peace of mind. Having fun, aren't you?'

'Well – he's such a prat.'

'True enough. Pull in over here. Sir Walter's place is just round the corner.'

'I checked, by the way. He's still there.'

'Good. The thing about him is that, on the one hand, we've got more definitely against him than anybody else. I mean, Madeleine you were just teasing about her sex life, and we don't know for a *fact* that Rankley's in drugs with Mulholland. Whereas we do know Sir Walter's gone in for a bit of insurance fraud. On the other hand, by rights he should be much tougher than the other two – older, more experienced, more powerful. I'll see if I can get him going a bit. If I give you the nod, jump in really hard. Otherwise, maybe I'll do the understanding don't-really-want-to-trouble-a-man-in-your-position bit and you can be the invisible subordinate. I'll make it up as I go along. Maybe we won't get much out of this immediately.'

'But this time we know there's some really rotten apples in the trees, even if they take a day or two to fall.'

'Exactly.'

CHAPTER 18

1

Everything about Sir Walter Granthelm's spacious, comfortable office spoke of wealth and power – from the leather armchairs and sofa, to the massive desk behind which the financier sat, to leather-bound volumes on the wall shelves, to the two oil paintings, to the deep pile carpet. Sir Walter's merchant bank was housed in the heart of the City, and this room was the heart of the bank. This, thought Fathers, is the establishment. He sat opposite Sir Walter, a manilla folder on his lap, with Yarrow off to one side, silent, pen and pad again at the ready.

'We have some points we'd like to clear up, Sir Walter, so we can eliminate a few possibilities and continue with a better sight of the road ahead.' His tone was respectful without being deferential.

'Please proceed,' said Sir Walter. 'But bear in mind I have an appointment at five.'

'Yes, of course, thanks for seeing us anyway. One thing – you really should have told us in advance that you were going to Geneva.'

'Yes, well, I do apologise, but it came up rather suddenly out of the conference in Brussels – a need for a face-to-face with a colleague over there. I saw no harm in it and no point in trying to contact you at the weekend.'

'You actually booked the flight on Friday evening,' said Fathers mildly, 'as you checked in at the hotel. That's also when you booked the hotel room in Geneva.'

'Yes, well I did have forewarning, and made the bookings in case they were needed. One cannot be perfectly sure of getting the right flight if one leaves it entirely to the last minute.'

'So it didn't actually come out of the conference. You knew beforehand.'

'I knew of the *possibility* beforehand, and it was confirmed at the conference.'

'Ah, I see, and I suppose it was the same thing with calling in at Paris?'

'That's right. That came out of the meeting I had in Geneva.'

'You really should have told us,' said Fathers with gentle reproach.

'As I said, I saw no harm in it, and I didn't want to disturb you at the weekend.'

'Oh, there's always somebody at the Yard.'

'I didn't think. I apologise.'

'And you actually flew to Paris on the Monday.'

'Yes, but it was only the merest delay in my trip home. Same sort of thing can happen because of strikes or weather, for heaven's sake. I'm back now anyway. It was only one day longer than I told you.'

'Yes, I suppose so. Still, until this business is over, please do tell us *all* the details of any trips you make. It makes things so much easier.'

'Yes, of course, now that I know the drill,' said Sir Walter.

'Well, that's enough of that, anyway. How's the fruit deal with Mr Mulholland going?'

'Eh? Oh, fine, fine. There's been a slight delay. At my request, really – I wanted to get this whole sorry affair out of my hair before seeing a new enterprise through to standing on its own two feet.'

'Yes, of course. What's Mr Rankley's role in this deal?'

Sir Walter frowned. 'He has no role,' he said.

'Are you sure, sir?'

'Quite sure.'

Fathers frowned with puzzlement and looked at Yarrow who shrugged ignorantly at him. 'That's not what we've heard,' said Fathers.

'Oh? And from whom, may I ask, have you heard to the contrary?'

'Um, well, that's privileged information,' replied Fathers. 'Not gossip, though. You know – reliable.' His tone remained respectful.

'Unreliable in this instance,' said Sir Walter with smooth confidence. 'A misunderstanding perhaps.' He relaxed. It seemed this policeman was not such a threat as he had feared, though his knowledge about the Geneva and Paris visits was annoying – probably shouldn't be surprising though.

'Yes, perhaps,' said Fathers. 'Perhaps the three of you are involved in some other business arrangement.'

Sir Walter shook his head, his eyes wide open, round and frank under his bushy eyebrows.

'Or just you and Mr Rankley.'

The financier shook his head again and smiled.

'Mr Rankley and Mr Mulholland?'

'Not to my knowledge. You must ask them.'

'Yes, I must. Oh well. Yarrow, note that, will you? We should really sort this one out.' Yarrow dutifully made a note. 'Um, what was next? Oh yes. You and Miss Sheerley: what was your relationship?'

'She's my sister-in-law's daughter,' replied Sir Walter.

'Yes, well I know that. Apart from that, I meant.'

'I'm afraid I don't quite catch your meaning.'

'Well, Sir Walter, you know, how close was it?'

'She was often at my house, as you know, with her parents abroad over the past few years. It was an affectionate relationship, I suppose one would say. Very fine girl. I liked her a lot.'

'Yes, and when did your affair with her start?' asked Fathers, still in the same respectful tone.

Sir Walter gave little outward sign of any reaction to the question – a frown which might have meant irritation or surprise, a look in his eyes which might have meant calculation or anxiety, and then a smile. 'Really, Mr Fathers, I think the misinformation you've been collecting is getting a little out of hand.'

'Oh. But she saw you often and was constantly telephoning you, both here and at your various homes.'

'Well, we were in regular contact, but I can assure you there was no affair.' There was no emphasis in Sir Walter's words, no sign of irritation or insistence. He was merely correcting a mistake.

'It seems to have been everybody's impression.'

'Well, I'm sorry to hear that, but they are mistaken.'

'What was it all about, then?' asked Fathers. 'All these telephone calls.'

'Well, you know, family matters, and arrangements, and often she wanted loans.'

'Loans,' repeated Fathers.

'Yes, you know the sort of thing, young woman in London, terrible expenses.'

'And after Christmas, why did your relationship with her deteriorate?'

Sir Walter paused a beat before answering. 'Again you've been misinformed,' he said. 'It did not deteriorate.'

Fathers shrugged and turned to Yarrow. 'That's an awful lot of witnesses we're going to have to put right,' he said.

'Seven or eight,' agreed Yarrow. 'Can't all be wrong, can they?'

Fathers waited.

'Well, perhaps it did rather fall off,' conceded Sir Walter at last. 'The loans, you see. I felt she was getting too much in the habit, so I had to refuse a couple of her requests, and she did pester me a bit about it. Credit cards all used up, and so on. But you can't go on for ever relying on somebody else's generosity, can you? Especially since the loans were really gifts – the chances of being paid back were minimal to zero. Quite large gifts, too, I may say. So I felt I had to put an end to it, and she – well, she didn't like that.'

Fathers nodded understandingly. 'Of course, I see the difficulty,' he said. 'Well, that's cleared up, then. I'm glad at least some of our information is accurate.' He smiled with self-deprecation. 'Mind you, I expect you'd understand her position very well, what with your own problems last spring.'

Sir Walter looked at him.

'The Brazilian coffee, I mean,' said Fathers conversationally, 'coming on top of your investment in that broking company which looked as if it was a lost cause. Still, it's flourishing now, and you seem to have pulled out of whatever difficulties you had well enough.'

'I did,' said Sir Walter shortly. He leaned back in his chair. 'You seem to have been doing rather a lot of snooping in my affairs.'

'It's our job actually,' said Fathers waving his hand apologetically. 'A good working definition of detective work is snooping around.'

'I suppose so,' said Sir Walter graciously, before adding with a touch of acerbity, 'but you need to be sure your information-gathering doesn't descend to the level of gossip-mongering.'

'Oh, but out information's usually pretty reliable,' responded Fathers evenly. 'For example, you've admitted we were right that your relationship with Miss Sheerley fell off a bit, and we know all about your personal finances, and the trips to Geneva and Paris, of course.'

He looked levelly at Sir Walter and smiled again. The financier held his gaze for a moment and saw nothing there to disturb him. 'Is that all?' he asked.

'Just one last thing. The silver.'

'The silver?'

'Yes. Seems pretty clear that Homer either stole it or set the job up.'

'Good heavens, the little blighter.'

'But you know that, don't you?' added Fathers.

'Know it?'

'Well, you had lunch with Signor Batesta from Milan, didn't you? While you were in Geneva. And in Paris, at the airport – what's the name of that bloke, Yarrow?'

'Languedon,' said Yarrow, pronouncing it Lang-yew-don.

Sir Walter looked at Fathers with a bland face, his mind working fast. What did this policeman know?

'Didn't you?' repeated Fathers, his tone still gentle and respectful, all shades of insistence and disbelief carefully ironed out of his voice.

Sir Walter remained silent. 'I do think you owe us an answer, sir,' Fathers prompted him.

'I – well, yes, you're right, of course.'

'Of course,' said Fathers. 'You were followed, you see.'

'Followed?'

'Yes. I expect you didn't spot them, because they're rather proficient at it, and you've no training in that sort of thing. What did you talk about?'

'Well, Signor Batesta contacted me from Milan and said he'd come across some silver which he recognised as part of my collection, and, well, he'd heard it was stolen, and, since the need to go to Geneva came up, I phoned him from Brussels and asked if he could get up to Geneva – which he did.'

'Exactly where did you phone him from?' asked Fathers casually.

Sir Walter thought quickly. They would have the records of calls from the hotel. 'From the conference centre,' he said.

'Public call box?'

'No. Telephones are part of the conference facilities. Quite standard.'

'And Monsieur Languedon,' asked Fathers, pronouncing it correctly. 'He contacted you too, did he?'

227

Again Sir Walter thought quickly. 'No, Batesta told me about him. He didn't say how he knew – heard it on some trade grapevine, I suppose. Anyway, I called Languedon from Geneva and arranged to meet him. If you were having me followed, you probably know that I made a call from the restaurant where I lunched with Batesta.'

'You'd already booked the flight,' commented Fathers.

'Yes, I had, because Batesta told me on the phone from Milan that there was this chap in Paris, so I booked a stop-over in Paris just in case, and after conferring with Batesta I called Languedon and took the booking up.' He relaxed as he finished.

'What if you hadn't needed to see Languedon?' asked Fathers. 'You'd've had a wasted trip to Paris.'

'I could always have changed it back. It's not hard to change flights, you know.'

Yarrow flipped back through the pages of his notepad. 'But from Brussels,' he said, 'you booked well ahead of time because you couldn't be sure of getting the right flight otherwise. That's what you said, anyway.'

Sir Walter looked at him. 'It varies with the routes, you see. Some are easy to switch bookings on, others are more difficult. When you travel around Europe as much as I do, you get to know.'

'I'd've thought Geneva–London on a Monday would be just as busy as Brussels–Geneva on a Sunday,' said Yarrow thoughtfully.

'Well that shows how little you know,' said Sir Walter snappily.

'I suppose I can check,' said Yarrow.

'Anyway,' said Sir Walter, 'if there'd been a problem about rebooking I'd have wasted two hours at Charles de Gaulle – not such a tragedy.'

'No,' said Fathers, 'I'm sure not. Not very public-spirited of Batesta, was it? Waiting all this time to tell you about the silver.'

'Well,' said Sir Walter recovering his poise after Yarrow's too accurate nit-picking, 'I suppose it only just came into his possession.'

'No. Like Languedon, he received the consignment from Homer in July.'

'Well, maybe he'd only just seen a description of my silver.'

'Yes,' said Fathers, 'I suppose that's possible. How much did they pay you?'

Sir Walter jerked forward in his chair. He recovered himself, but took too long before he spoke again. 'What're you talking about?' he said.

Fathers opened the folder on his lap and pulled out two photographs. He pushed them across the desk to Sir Walter. 'There you are,' he said, 'receiving an envelope from Batesta, and there, you're depositing it in a bank. How much was it?'

Sir Walter sat silently, his face white, his eyes hopelessly searching the photographs for a way out. For once in his life, he was in a situation he could neither control nor comprehend. It was the other two men who had the experience, who knew what to do, which rules applied and which didn't. He looked bleakly at Fathers and saw him scratch his nose.

'Right,' said Yarrow, standing up abruptly and moving towards Sir Walter, 'let's have him in.'

The financier jumped to his feet and backed away. His hands were shaking and it seemed to him as if his surroundings were physically collapsing about him.

Yarrow kept on advancing. 'Insurance fraud,' he said. 'Charge him, get his two mates charged with receiving, and then we can open up all the records, including in Switzerland since part of the offence occurred there.' He rounded the desk. Sir Walter moved away round the other side, towards Fathers. 'And then he can tell the truth about him and his niece, and cough up about the deal with Mulholland.'

'Yarrow,' said Fathers sharply, standing up and putting a hand on Sir Walter's shoulder. The financier jerked at the touch. 'I think you've overreached yourself, lad. We're not quite ready for that yet.'

Yarrow looked at his boss sulkily. 'He knows what business Mulholland's in,' he said. 'I can smell it.'

'Wait outside.'

Yarrow shrugged. 'I'd nick him right now,' he said angrily and, dismissed for the third time in the afternoon, went through the outer office and into the corridor. He aimed a punch at Sir Walter's nameplate on the door, stopping a fraction short of its target, and grinned.

Inside, Fathers was all solicitude. He led Sir Walter back to his seat and gently pushed him into it. Then he headed for a cocktail cabinet set into the bookshelves and opened the glass-fronted door. 'Whisky, I think,' he said. He poured a generous measure and returned with it to Sir Walter. He picked up the financier's hand and wrapped the fingers round the glass. Then he perched on Sir Walter's desk, moving the telephone and a picture of Lady Sarah, Madeleine and the younger Walter Granthelm out of the way.

'Well,' he said quietly. 'What am I to do with you? Technically, Yarrow's right, of course, and I should have you down the Yard this minute and book you. Your story doesn't stand up for a moment. I should add that we have a recording of your conversation with Batesta, so don't bother concocting any lies about it. We also bugged your little chat with Languedon, though I've not seen the transcript of that yet. So it's really pretty much a cut-and-dried case. And, of course, to an observer – to a jury, say – it must look a little bit like you fell out with Homer over this whole thing and bumped him off, then added Ellen Sheerley to get rid of the nuisance she'd been making of herself after your affair ended. I think we have a motive pretty well sorted out for you, we have the means and opportunity. I can't see what's missing. In fact, if we go with the insurance fraud, we'd pretty much have to throw in murder for good measure or it'd seem odd. But for reasons which I'm sure I don't need to explain, I'd much rather not see a man like you in that position. Have some of your drink.'

Fathers' manner and tone were still quiet, but all respect had dropped out of his voice. This was a tone of command. He was talking down. Sir Walter felt humiliated and empty as he nodded and drank some whisky from the glass the detective had placed in his hand.

'Then again,' continued Fathers, 'I can't just write it out of the records. I've my own position to consider too – not as elevated as yours, of course, but worth something, to me at least. And there's Guildford to consider as well. You rather lorded it over them, I'm afraid, about the silver robbery and they're a little eager to get their own back. But I'd like to find a way out.' His tone now had picked up an edge of chiding: the financier had become the irritating source of a problem which would take some inconvenience to resolve, a small boy in front of his headmaster at prep school.

'And of course,' he went on, 'there's the Mulholland deal. That is very serious, much worse than insurance fraud. But it may be your way out.'

Sir Walter emptied his glass. 'What can I do?' he asked.

'The usual arrangement,' said Fathers, 'is by way of fair exchange.'

'What d'you mean? Money? No, I'm sorry I said that.'

'I should think you would be. Lucky for you Yarrow's outside. Offering money to a policeman in front of a witness is easily enough to add a charge of B and C to the insurance fraud and double murder.'

'What then?'

Fathers took the glass from Sir Walter and returned to the cabinet, pouring another large shot. When he had given it back and sat on the desk again, he said, 'Usually we trade information.'

'What sort of information?'

'What sort d'you think?' asked Fathers impatiently. 'Come on, damn you, you're in the shit and it's up to you to pull yourself out, or I'll close this case right round you.'

'I didn't kill them.'

'But I can make a case against you and I will. I wasn't kidding you when I said everybody thought you were having an affair with Miss Sheerley. They do think that, and they'll testify. And they'll testify to your relations with her getting difficult. Then there's your money problems last spring and the silver. Then there's getting the money from Batesta. It all adds up.'

Sir Walter remained stubbornly silent.

'Ah, the hell with it,' said Fathers suddenly, getting off the desk and pulling the phone over, 'I give up.' He began to dial.

'Who're you calling?'

'Getting a van round. I'm going to take you in.'

'No!'

Fathers put the phone down and made a gesture as if beckoning Sir Walter towards him. 'So give,' he snapped.

'I didn't kill them.'

'Who did?'

'I don't know,' said Sir Walter miserably. 'I don't know. You must believe me.'

'Why?'

'It's the truth.'

'Ha,' sneered Fathers. 'The truth. That's no problem. What I'm concerned about is the evidence.' He reached for the phone again.

'Mulholland and Rankley,' said Sir Walter quickly.

'They did it?'

'No – well, I don't know. I didn't mean that. I don't know.'

'What do you know?'

'They're involved in a deal, and they've been trying to pull me in, but I've refused.'

'Cocaine,' said Fathers.

'You know,' said Sir Walter slumping in his seat. His glass tilted in his fingers and drops of whisky spilled on his trousers.

'Not everything,' said Fathers. 'Try me. Start at the beginning. Start with Ellen Sheerley.'

Sir Walter recovered himself, gripped his glass more firmly and drained it in one go. He started to talk while Fathers went to refill it.

'You're right, of course. Along with many others, I was my niece's lover. A couple of times in the year before last, and then more frequently last year. I kept her well looked after and she came to my flat once a week, sometimes twice.'

'Sugar daddy,' said Fathers, pouring the whisky. His tone was friendly even if the words weren't.

'I suppose so,' said Sir Walter. 'She was very free with herself, with her body, and she received quite a lot of presents, I suppose.'

'One way of making a living.'

'Yes, when I thought about it, I realised that was how she made her living.'

Fathers handed him the fresh whisky and he drank before continuing: 'She became a bore and I called it off in November. She wasn't pestering me about that, though. It was about money, like I said, because her lifestyle was getting more expensive.'

'With the heroin.'

'She insisted she wasn't addicted, but it couldn't really be true, could it? When I refused she forced it out of me anyway. She swore she'd tell my wife not only about us but about the silver.'

'You knew in advance, did you?'

'She introduced me to Homer, then when this Brazilian business blew up I was really stranded. You may find it hard to understand, but I was at my wits' end to know how to make good the damage. There was money owed, you see, for work done on the house the previous winter, and other things, and I'd used all my disposable assets for the broking investment. Of course, if the coffee had paid off I'd have settled the bills and had plenty in hand.'

He paused to sip more whisky. He was steadily becoming drunk. After a while, thought Fathers, he'll go through the talkative stage and get to the morbid silence bit. I hope he doesn't hit maudlin first.

'So Homer suggested a way out,' said Fathers.

'Peter bloody Rankley, actually, the shrimp-brained whale who put me on to the coffee in the first place. I should've known better – Christ, how I should've known better.'

'Rankley showed you the way out, then.'

'Yes, he suggested it and explained that Homer was the kind of man who could fix it.'

'What was the deal?'

'I got the insurance money and fifty per cent of the net take.'

'Net take?'

'Well, the sale price in Milan and Paris less his expenses. Then we each took fifty per cent.'

'And he rooked you?'

'No, it all went very smoothly, but when he was dead, well, I saw a chance to step in and pick up all of the last two payments we were owed.'

'Very smart. Go on.'

'Well, that's that on the silver, actually.' Sir Walter finished off his whisky and waved the glass at Fathers.

Like an obsequious butler, Fathers took it wordlessly and went to refill it. 'Cocaine,' he said.

'That's another story. Rankley decided that after the silver business, I'd developed a taste for the shady. They kept on and on – him and Mulholland – and Homer wanted in but they wouldn't have that. Christ, what a bloody, bloody mess. I suppose they fell out. I don't know. I'm not part of it.' He took another mouthful of whisky. His fourth glass, thought Fathers. Not long to go now.

'What do you know about the deal?'

'Mulholland's the supplier, Rankley's handling distribution.'

'What did they want you for? Finance?'

'No, Mulholland's got all the ready cash they need.' Sir Walter frowned, concentrating. 'The idea of investment from the bank was mostly so it would handle the profits, transferring them to dummy corporations abroad. We work with very liberal regulations these days, and the operation wouldn't be illegal, not in itself. I wouldn't involve the bank in anything that wasn't legal, of course.' The last word, thought Fathers, sounded suspiciously like 'coursh'. 'But, when they told me what the deal was, I wasn't interested.'

Fathers grasped Sir Walter's chin and turned his face towards him. 'You must learn to tell me the truth,' he said quietly. 'You are supplying the exit route, aren't you? And some finance for the cover – the fruit.'

Sir Walter's eyes slipped out of focus. He said nothing. Fathers let go of his chin. 'Why did they want Homer out of the way?' he asked urgently.

'Out of the way?' repeated Sir Walter, catching the phrase. 'I don't know. They didn't trust him. They didn't want to do business with him.'

'Who did it? Who did the killing?'

Sir Walter shook his head. 'I don't know. I do not know. Sshame, lovely girl, did you shee her? Lovely.' His words were slurring, but as Fathers picked up his manilla folder and made to go, the financier suddenly snapped upright in a poor imitation of his earlier confident pose.

'So I can rely on you, can I?' he said slowly and distinctly. 'You'll do your part?'

Fathers, at the door, turned and looked at the wreck. 'Can I rely on you? Will you do yours?' He opened the door and slipped through it.

'Good man,' said Sir Walter as the door closed.

As he rode down in the lift with Yarrow, Fathers summarised the result: 'Yes to Sheerley and him. Yes to the silver – he knew in advance. Says he's not involved in the cocaine.'

'Did he do it?'

'Says not. Says he doesn't know who did. Maybe. He's talked himself right into the perfect motive for it though.'

'One thing, I thought,' said Yarrow. 'It wasn't Rankley who tossed Madeleine at Homer. It was her father. He's the one who introduced them, that time that Madeleine says was a cocked-up lunch appointment.'

'Oh yes,' said Fathers slowly. 'Makes sense.'

'They use sex, don't they?' said Yarrow. 'They use it to tie somebody in.'

'That's right.'

234

'But his own daughter. Is nothing sacred to that sort?'

'Money,' said Fathers as they stepped outside, 'privilege, position. A way of life.'

2

Before Fathers and Yarrow returned to the Yard, Pardoner received a phone call. 'Yeah,' he said, 'speaking . . . Who? . . . What? . . . What? . . . I thought you said that but I couldn't believe it. What's going on down there? . . . Yeah, yeah, I know . . . OK, so what're you saying now? . . . Sure about that, are you?' After the other party had hung up, Pardoner held the phone in his hand for a while and regarded it with a dazed look.

DS Gordon, who sat opposite him at the double desk, had watched with amusement as the tone of his voice and his facial expression ran through the gamut from boredom to surprise, shock, anger, sarcasm and finally total wonderment. 'Something up?' she enquired.

Pardoner put the phone down with elaborate care and looked at her. 'Well, well, well,' he said.

'*Bien, bien, bien,*' she suggested.

Pardoner scratched his head. 'You know that silly joke about there were three holes in the ground?' he asked.

'No,' said Gordon, in a way which revealed she didn't want to.

'Well, well, well,' said Pardoner, ignoring her tone. 'Once when we had a French *assistant* at school for conversation classes, this twit tried to tell it in French. *Il y'avait trois troux dans la terre. Bien, bien, bien.*'

'David, what are you talking about?'

'Shell shock,' said Pardoner. 'Don't worry about it. I'll be back in the trenches in no time.'

Fathers and Yarrow walked quickly through the office on their way to Fathers' sanctum. Yarrow was talking excitedly, and Fathers' adrenalin seemed to be pumping too.

'Oh dear,' said Pardoner, rising heavily from his seat, 'oh deary me. The bringer of bad news.'

By the time he got into Fathers' office, his boss had pulled his private bottle of Scotch out of the bottom desk drawer and was pouring small doses into each of two plastic cups held by Yarrow.

'Skipper,' said Fathers, 'you'll join us?'

'I think I'll need to,' said Pardoner. Fathers picked another plastic cup out of his drawer and tossed it to him. Pardoner caught it neatly and came forward to get his measure. 'I gather you've had an exciting time,' he said.

'Sir Walter's cracked,' said Yarrow. 'Rankley's trying to brazen it out and Madeleine performs for Mulholland to the big prat's instructions.'

'Sir Walter's cracked?' echoed Pardoner.

'On the silver,' said Fathers. 'Says he's not in on the coke, didn't do the murders and doesn't know who did.'

'Not out of the reckoning yet, though,' said Yarrow, 'not by a long chalk, though I like Rankley for it – weird bloke that, really filthy.'

'We'll fill you in,' said Fathers to Pardoner, 'but what've you got for us?'

'Ah yes,' said the skipper. 'I'll work up to it, I think – or down. Um, Curry's nobody – you know, Mrs Mulholland's night-time pal – well, he's a film producer, which isn't nobody, but he's clean for drugs, so say Miami and Washington. Flores is checking Los Angeles now. Number two, Flores got a call saying that a freighter of Mulholland's left the Bahamas early last week but hasn't arrived in Miami. His mates are doing a check now of the likely Caribbean ports, but obviously there's the strong possibility it's heading our way.'

'And number three? There's some reason why you're looking so glum, skip. Out with it.'

'Yes, well, out with it, as you say. Don't put the Scotch away yet. Godalming Ballistics just called. They've checked the results they sent us, and they were wrong. Both the bullets came from one gun.'

Fathers and Yarrow looked at him with open mouths. Wordlessly, Fathers unscrewed the top from the whisky bottle, poured them each another shot, and screwed the top back on. He looked into the cup, swirled the liquid about, and finally tossed it down in one swallow. He wiped his mouth with the back of his hand and looked first at Pardoner, then at Yarrow.

'Bloody hell,' he said.

CHAPTER 19

1

'Nowhere,' said Fathers. He took a sip of his whisky and sucked on his cigar. 'Not as far as square one. Not even on the board.'

Sarah looked across at him, slumped morosely in his favourite armchair, one leg hooked over the side. He had phoned to say he'd not be back till midnight or later, then turned up just after nine o'clock. Waving aside her offer of supper he went straight for the whisky bottle and cigars, turning a look at her which stifled any reproof she might have been about to voice. Then he joined her in the sitting room in front of the television to watch a crime thriller. After a while she had switched it off, partly because he kept interrupting with his usual pedantic objections to the writer's understanding of police procedure, but mostly because he made random remarks from which she gradually gathered that the Guildford investigation had quietly blown up in his face.

'But you've got the silver and the cocaine,' she objected.

'We've got the silver and almost got the cocaine,' Fathers corrected her. 'But on the case we went in for, nothing.'

'But you just said Sir Walter thought they were both murdered.'

'That's right, but it's not a lot. Number one, the local plod told him that to explain why we were coming in on it. Number two, even if he knew it anyway, nobody'll put up their hands for it on that basis. I can just see it: "Excuse me, Mr Mulholland and Mr Rankley, but Sir Walter thinks somebody murdered Mr Homer over a drugs deal we're not one hundred per cent sure is coming down. Does either of you gentlemen have anything to say which can help us with our enquiries?" Fat chance, I should co-co.'

'So, do you think Homer did kill himself then?'

'Fortunately not, no. Because when we talked it over just now, we realised he couldn't've topped himself and dropped the gun where it lay when Brain's lads found it. Not physically possible. So it was two murders with one gun, one faked to look like suicide but clumsily done. No – it's just that everything we've got adds up to a good deal less than circumstantial.'

'Why fortunately?'

'Eh? Oh, because we don't have to admit publicly that the ballistics lab let us down. That would be rather uncomfortable.'

'But you couldn't be blamed for that.'

'Bringer of bad news,' he said, reaching for the bottle he had positioned on the coffee table beside him. 'I just don't like the feel of it. With no definitive material evidence, and if they all stay tight, we're less than nowhere with it. Like I said, not even at square one. Not . . .'

'That can't be true,' Sarah interrupted impatiently. 'Not really. You've been working on it over a week and you haven't narrowed it down at all? I don't believe it.'

Fathers looked at her for a while and then refilled his glass. 'Well, yes and no,' he said finally. 'You see, a lot swings on whether one person did them both in or not.'

'Do I have it straight that she was killed first, then Homer?'

'Yes.'

'So you're saying maybe whoever killed him hadn't already killed her? How come?'

'You see, my Yarrow brought up the revenge motive again this evening. Homer offs her and then gets his from whoever – from someone who's murderously upset about it. Follow?'

'I think so.'

'The advantage of looking at it that way is we don't have to find one killer with one motive embracing both killings. Nor explain why there was no third person in the trees where she got shot. OK?'

'And what's the disadvantage?'

'Well, we've got nobody who fits the bill – no sign that any of them would respond like that. Nor can we figure out a reason why Homer would've knocked her off. And anyway, how did X get the gun off Homer without a fight? Of which there were no signs.'

'All right,' said Sarah, her head beginning to ache at the convolutions, 'so what happens if you drop that idea?'

'Then we do have to explain why there's no third person in the trees, and find a motive embracing both kills. Not Lady Sarah – the girl perhaps, but not Homer. Madeleine maybe, but I don't think I can get that to wear somehow. His Nibs more likely – her to be rid of a nuisance, and him to get the extra money on the silver. Rankley or Mulholland: for Homer over the drugs – but not for her unless it was a favour to Sir, though that sounds a bit unlikely.'

238

'Sir Walter's your best bet, then.'

'Sort of looks that way, but if Wally's our man it means I didn't step on him as hard as I thought this afternoon, because he passed the parcel their way as neat as you like. Saying they'd fallen out over something. On the other hand, if he wasn't trying it on, maybe that's the key: get at whatever they fell out about.'

'You're beginning to lose me.'

He smiled at her. 'I'm beginning to lose myself. Going in circles.'

'Ever diminishing ones.'

'But in no position yet to scatter shit and derision at my pursuers.'

'Bad case, second whisky, bad language. Time for a quiet exit.'

'Fifth,' said Fathers. 'Three at the Yard.'

'Then it's worse than I thought. I'm going to read in bed. What's your plan?'

'Drink and think. Dammit, I know there's something there in what we've already put together, something which'll make the rest click into place.' He waved the glass at Sarah. 'You'd be amazed how much this helps straighten the old grey matter out.'

'You're right. I would.'

2

Sir Walter Granthelm sat at his desk in his library. Outside, through the uncurtained window, it was a still, clear night. The lights in the library were switched off; only the desk lamp cast its limited pool of light. He took his cut-glass tumbler in his hand and looked at the pale amber liquid. He had had enough of that today, too much – no, yesterday, for it was after midnight, the witching hour – and he no longer needed its help to see his way through to the decision to which he was slowly coming.

When the policeman had left him in his City office he had sat for a while at his desk, finishing the last glass of whisky the man had pressed on him. After a time his secretary entered, but he waved away her words of concern, and she had withdrawn. He was feeling desperately tired. He pulled himself from his chair and went to the sofa, kicked off his shoes, lay down full length and slept.

When he awoke, his watch showed it was past nine o'clock. His mouth was dry, his head heavy. He sniffed the air and tasted the stale whisky odour. When he tried to stand up his head swam, and he had to sit on the sofa's edge to recover his balance. When he tried again, the dizziness was still there, but manageable. But he had to get down on his knees to hunt out his shoes, and the room spun round him again. His fingers fumbled to undo the laces, then tie them up when he had slipped his feet into them. Suddenly be began to feel sick. He got to the door of his private washroom with his hand to his mouth, jerked at the door handle, stumbled through, reaching vainly for the light switch, gave up on his second attempt at opening the door to the lavatory, and finally made it to the basin as the vomit surged uncontrollably out.

Long after his stomach was empty he continued to retch. At last, the motion calmed itself. He filled a tumbler with water and took a cautious sip. The cool taste eased the soreness of his throat and his mouth's parched dryness, but he resisted the temptation to gulp the refreshment down for fear it would start him vomiting again. He washed his hands and rinsed his face in cold water. His senses were beginning to return to normality, and his step was firmer as he turned his back on the smell of the washroom, gathered his attaché case and coat and left his office.

Sitting in the library of Granthelm House, Sir Walter had no clear memory of his drive home. He remembered only two things from the first part of the journey: the abiding, inert sadness which weighed down on him with such oppression that he sat behind the wheel with his shoulders hunched and his head tilted slightly; and the moment when he had first glimpsed a route out of this terrible mess. Perhaps his mind, functioning on automatic, had already caught sight of it, for he had had no thought of returning to the house near Regent's Park – which would have been the rational decision in his condition – and he had not consciously decided to drive to Surrey. As he left the A3, it was not yet eleven o'clock. He had no desire to get home while his wife was still up. He turned into Guildford and cruised slowly down the hill in the centre of the town. He realised he was hungry and found a simple restaurant open, an Indian one. There were a few customers there, finishing their meals, and the waiters did not seem pleased to have this late-comer. But he explained that he wanted a quick, small and simple meal, and they brought him a plate of plaice and chips. Indian – but they did all sorts of cooking. He drank water with the meal and didn't touch the chips.

Eating, he tried to recall what the detective had said to him, and what confessions had spilled hopelessly out. He was fairly sure he had retained enough control not to let it all fall out, despite the appalling urge to please Fathers and purge himself. He ate and pondered calmly. He could even admire the skill with which the detective had set him up, letting him believe that all the little lies were working – the ones thought out in advance, and the ones he'd had to make up on the spot – assuming the tone of a man who knew he was speaking to an obvious superior, and all the time relentlessly tracking his quarry through the labyrinth of half-truths till the moment came to spring. So confident had the detective been that he was able not only to swallow his pride and play the fawning fool so perfectly to bait the trap, but even to explain every detail in case the whole dismal picture might not be clearly understood. Sir Walter knew he had been played like a salmon – the line let out, reeled in, out again, until finally he was pulled ashore. And the young one – what was his name? – Barrow, Harrow, whatever – he had shown a dramatic sense of timing with his sudden dart towards him, threatening arrest. He must have earned his superior's approval for that performance – and good luck to him, for merit deserved to be rewarded, and he had played his part in landing a great prize.

And, as they must have known it would, Sir Walter reflected with rueful detachment, it had thrown him into an immediate funk. What was the phrase – a post-war funk? Where did that come from? But for him, the war was not over, and he had a sudden flash of insight into how a general feels facing an enemy who outnumbers him, who is equipped with superior weapons, and not only that, but also with a better strategy and more proficient general staff. He can be overwhelmed by a frontal assault, or outflanked, or taken in the rear. He does not know when or how the attack will come, but he knows it will be devastating. He has already tangled with his opponent, only a skirmish – but it was bloody, and only the beginning. That feeling that the general must have: it was Hitler in his bunker, it was Mark Antony facing Octavian, Macbeth at Dunsinane.

He put the glass of whisky down untouched on the library desk and clenched his fists. Play the Roman fool, he thought, play it.

From generals facing inevitable defeat to incompetent insubordinates and inadequate allies. But as he returned to his car from the Indian restaurant, his mood allowed him no anger at

Mulholland and Rankley. If they could have cut Homer in, the deal would have gone through untroubled. He would never have had any further cause for financial worry. There would have been no further investigation of the silver robbery. He would not now be making his sad way home.

And why not cut Homer in? He was the one who knew how to market the stuff, after all. He was the man with the contacts and experience. Mulholland didn't know London; no more did Rankley – not in that sense. He was only the fixer, the man who put the parties in touch with each other. But he didn't like Homer – and there was some reason why Mulholland didn't trust him either.

The hell with it. It had happened. They had made the mistake. There was nothing more to be done. Why be angry? The fact is accomplished.

When his car arrived at the top of his driveway, Sir Walter had seen but not noticed the car parked on the other side of the road some yards along. He had not seen the man sitting in the back seat who, as the Rolls-Royce swept round the corner, leaned forward to see the number plate, then picked up his handset and confirmed that Sir Walter, who had been tailed as far as the turn-off in the village below, had arrived home.

The outside light was on above the door when he pulled up in front of the house. He let himself in. The hall and stair lights were on but a quick check in the main parlour and music room showed nobody was up. So much the better. He left his case and coat on a chair in the music room and went to the drinks cabinet where he poured himself a glass of his best Scotch. The cabinet seemed much depleted. Presumably, Lady Sarah was still taking all of this just as hard and drinking her way through it. Certainly, she had been doing too much of that in Brussels, to the point that for the first time he had wondered about the wisdom of taking her on business trips. But then he had scoffed at his doubts; this was, after all, a particularly difficult time all round, and he'd had every expectation that it would all settle down. That was before he realised the extent to which Fathers had out-thought him, out-planned him and out-gunned him.

Eventually he arrived at his desk. He took a cigar from the box on the top, cut it, putting the end in the ashtray he had collected from the music room, and lit it. He smoked with relaxation, occasionally fingering his whisky glass, but not drinking. He had no reason to sit there except that it was the smallest, narrowest, most cocooned place he could be in a house where cosiness was an absent, even undreamed-of concept. At previous times when he needed the solace of his own silence, the small parlour was the room to which he withdrew. Not now. He thought of Ellen, of her corpse lying on the sofa nine days ago, her beauty, her apparently carefree ways, the frankness with which she offered her body when she realised that he, suddenly recognising she had long since become a woman, was ogling her and casting a fantasy around her every moment they were together. The frankness, too, with which she came to a business arrangement with him: his money, her favours. And the frankness – call it that – with which she threatened to tell all to Lady Sarah if he did not continue to make gifts, even after he broke off their liaison.

From there his thoughts drifted back – to Ellen coming to visit as a little girl, Madeleine and Walter playing with her, him playing with his children, his wife as a young and beautiful mother, his courting of her, all the unending memories that a family brings. But now, he thought, they are grown up. There are no more memories to come. It was ludicrous for a man only in his mid-fifties, at the peak of his powers in the public world, with a successful family life, to draw a line under his personal life and have that thought – the end.

He set his cigar meticulously on the ashtray and leant down to his left. A small room between the hall and the kitchen held the shotguns. After pouring his whisky, he had gone to it, unlocked the cupboard with the key which Bolt always left above the lintel, and selected and loaded one. He had brought it, breech open, to the library desk and laid it carefully down beside his chair. Now he picked it up. He snapped the breech shut, and rested the stock on the floor between his feet. He pushed his chair back a little to find the right position, then leaned forward with his mouth open, poised above the barrel. He gripped the barrel with his right hand, and with his left thumb felt for the trigger.

This too is ridiculous, he thought. He shut his mouth and rested his chin on the end of the barrel. Fathers has battered me down. Damn it, he has not destroyed me. I will not let him have the day. Even if he puts me in the dock, I shall fight him. A good QC – the best – will wreck his circumstantial evidence for the murders. That's all nonsense and he knows it. Mulholland said he'd have the first delivery delayed and he and Rankley will pull their horns in and wait a while. Only the fraud will be left – the ill-conceived measure of a man in desperate straits. The sentence will not be harsh. I will survive it. I am of the class which always survives. In fact, once Mulholland reactivates the plan, I shall prosper.

I have looked over the edge and there is nothing worse for them to offer me. I shall confront it. I will not play the Roman fool.

He began to straighten up. As he did so, he brought up his right hand. The shotgun came up and the trigger met the pressure of his left thumb. Parts of Sir Walter's brains and fragments of skull spattered the ceiling.

CHAPTER 20

1

'In the end, sitting up into the wee hours, I couldn't see that it makes any difference,' said Fathers. He was in his office with Pardoner, Yarrow and Young. 'The drugs and the silver are obviously still on. That we got on to them because of a technical error made by some apprentice boffin is just one of life's little ironies. As for the deaths – well, there's the position of the gun, and the way Granthelm talked all the time as though he knew for a fact that they were both murdered.'

'Maybe he knows,' said Pardoner, 'and knows they're down to either Mulholland or Rankley or both – but doesn't know which.'

'Maybe,' said Fathers.

'You didn't push him on it, though,' said Young.

'No. First, because my plan was to shake the trees and see what fell out. Second, because I wanted to nail him on the silver, and then come back at him on the murder. I'm also going to break him open on the coke – I *know* he was lying about that. I'll do it today. Anyway, tell me, who d'you like for it?'

'Mulholland,' said Young. 'The Miami drug world is hard. A man who's successful there could handle this kind of thing without blinking. He's the only one of them we can say that about for sure. But I'll bet the other two are in it one way or another.'

'Me too,' said Pardoner, 'but I'm not sure they'll wear it in the end.'

'Oh?'

'I have a suspicion we'll line them all up for the drugs and throw the silver at Granthelm. But if we set them up for murder and conspiracy, the jury'll chuck it out – partly because we've no way of showing which *one* of them did it. No matter, they'll go down on the other charges. We can make them stick.'

'Could be. Yarrer, any bets? Or do you still fancy the butler?'

'I've been thinking,' said Yarrow. 'I reckon Homer didn't want in – like you said before, guv, he was already there.'

'But they wanted him out,' said Fathers.

'Yeah, or Rankley did, so's he could run the distribution. Unless he's another pusher Drug Squad don't know about . . .'

'No way,' said Young, embarrassed.

'. . . how could he run that unless he got all Homer's contacts? So I reckon he conned Homer and then dunned him.'

'And Sheerley?' said Pardoner.

'There's two possibilities there,' said Yarrow.

'Yes,' said Fathers. 'Either Mulholland, having dallied with her, didn't trust her . . .'

'Or Sir Walter wanted her out of his hair,' Yarrow continued, 'so they put them both into one package, so to speak.'

'There's another possibility,' said Young. 'She could've been just caught in the crossfire. They offed her to make Homer's suicide look more convincing.'

'So no sex angle,' said Pardoner, looking at Fathers.

'I got an idea about that too,' said Yarrow. 'I reckon Homer was conned so far, Mulholland or Rankley had convinced him that if he topped her, he'd be in the deal. Then he had sex with her for old times' sake, shot her, and carried her into the house – at which point one or the other took him out too.'

'Bit fanciful,' objected Young.

'But it does explain why there were no signs of anybody else out in the trees where she was shot,' commented Fathers. 'Right, so that's the betting. Let's get to it. Stay close, Yarrer. We're talking to Sir Walter again this morning.'

The phone rang. Yarrow, closest to it, picked it up. 'Serious Crimes, DCI Fathers' phone,' he said. 'What? . . . Christ . . . I'll tell him.' He put the phone down and looked bleakly at Fathers. 'You won't talk to him today,' he said. 'That was Guildford. Sir Walter's dead. Suicide, according to Bolt when he called it in.'

Fathers thought for a minute as the other three exchanged looks. 'Right,' he said to Young, 'I suggest you treble your watch on Mulholland and Rankley. Whatever else, the trees are well and truly shaken, so watch out. I think you should take particular care with Mulholland – overlapping independent teams. He's got experience. So far as we know, Rankley hasn't.'

'Sure,' said Young. 'His idea of subtlety would be the Maori side-step: not round your man but straight through him.'

'Skipper, I want you here in case anything breaks. While away the time checking round the ports again. So Yarrer, that means you go to Guildford, OK?' They rose, but Fathers stopped Yarrow. Pardoner and Young left. 'Yarrer, old sparrer, don't go

246

with the presumption that it's suicide.'

Yarrow nodded.

'And while you're down there, be a skipper. You know what I mean?'

Yarrow nodded again.

2

Brain leaned against the end of the stack of shelves. His arms were folded, his face set in grim stillness. He suppressed the urge to take another look over his shoulder at the gruesome, half-headless corpse beside the desk. Today, even Dr Albert seemed subdued. He worked quickly and deftly, without his usual running commentary. A shotgun blast through the head at close range leaves a very different result from a dainty .22 calibre slug.

The emergency call had been received at 10.47. Brain was told two minutes later, left instructions for Fathers to be informed and was at Granthelm House at 11.10. While he waited for the pathologist to arrive, he found out why it was so late in the morning before the body was discovered. Bolt had been up at his usual early hour, and Mrs Carrock had arrived almost simultaneously with Anna Dark at 7.30. The instruction from Lady Sarah the night before was to wait until she awoke before preparing breakfast; Sir Walter would be staying in town, she expected. But the Rolls-Royce had been parked in front of the house, and Bolt had noted the attaché case and coat in the music room. The door to the library was shut, as it had been last night before he had gone to bed. Sir Walter, presumably, was in bed. The three staff had breakfast together and then set about their work. Anna had completed some light cleaning in the music room and the main parlour when Lady Sarah descended a few minutes after ten o'clock, wearing a dressing gown over her nightdress and looking as fuzzy-headed as she felt.

She had gone to the breakfast room where Bolt gave her the morning paper and took her order for breakfast. A large jug of orange juice, black coffee and two thin slices of brown toast. 'Yes, madam,' he said, 'and what will Sir Walter be taking?'

'Sir Walter?'

'Or perhaps he is still asleep?'

'No, he didn't come back last night.'

'Oh yes, madam, he did. The car's outside.'

She frowned and stroked her fingertips across her forehead, erasing the lines of the frown. Then she looked up at Bolt. 'Oh,' she said. 'Well, he didn't sleep in my bed.'

'Perhaps he didn't wish to disturb you,' said Bolt smoothly. 'I'll see to your breakfast and then perhaps check the other bedrooms.'

'Would you, Bolt? Thank you so much.'

He went to the kitchen and passed on the breakfast order to Mrs Carrock. Remembering the previous spring when Sir Walter's troubles had weighed him down and he had taken to heavy drinking for a week or two, Bolt visited the cellar to see if his master had collapsed there again while seeking a fresh bottle. When he returned to the kitchen, Lady Sarah's breakfast was ready. He took it through and buttered her toast, then made his measured way up the stairs. Just to be sure, since Lady Sarah's testimony was not necessarily reliable on the morning after an evening such as she had spent, he began by checking her bedroom. She had been right, however. He went from one bedroom to the next, always knocking on the door and waiting some moments before entering. When he had checked all ten bedrooms and four bathrooms he came slowly down the stairs. He paused in the hall. Sir Walter was not in the main parlour or the music room which left only the small parlour – surely unlikely – and the library. A sudden thought led him to check the downstairs lavatory first, and then he made his way through the music room to the library. He entered, walked to the alcove where the desk was – and stopped. He put a hand on the shelves to support himself, fighting to control his nausea.

He could hear Anna calling him and he turned. Anna came quickly into the library, almost running. 'Mr Bolt,' she said, 'Lady Sarah says not to open the small . . .' He moved to try to block off her line of vision, but she caught an unmistakable glimpse over his shoulder. She looked angrily into his eyes, held them for the merest fraction of a second, and then let go a terrifying scream.

He took her shoulders, spun her roughly round, and walked her briskly out of the library. He sat her down on the nearest chair in the music room and poured her a brandy. As she took it, the smell tickled his nostrils and the nausea became overpowering. He pushed past Mrs Carrock at the door, ran across the hall, ignoring Lady Sarah at the dining-room door, into the cloakroom and was violently sick in the lavatory bowl.

He returned to the music room. Mrs Carrock was kneeling beside Anna's chair, muttering quiet, soothing words. Lady Sarah stood irresolute a yard or two back. She took a pace towards the open library door, but he laid a firm hand on her shoulder. 'No, madam,' he said and gently turned her round and walked her back to the breakfast room. 'Get her to the kitchen,' he said over his shoulder to Mrs Carrock.

He guided Lady Sarah to her chair and pushed her delicately on to it. She looked up at him.

'Yes, madam,' said Bolt, 'it is my . . .' He paused for a long silent moment, then wiped the back of his hand across his mouth and re-formed the sentence. 'I am very much afraid that Sir Walter is dead,' he said. 'I shall call the police.'

She raised her hand in what might have been about to be a gesture of assent, dismissal or disagreement. Then she let it drop.

'Anna found him, did she?'

'I found him, madam, but Anna also saw.'

'And it is not a nice sight.'

'No, madam.'

'Call the police.'

As he left the dining room, she added, 'Call the rotten bloody stinking police.'

When Bolt had made the 999 call he phoned Mrs Briggs, explained the situation and she promised to come immediately. Next he called Madeleine Granthelm, who also said she would come straightaway, and then her brother who was out so he left a message. He phoned Carrock the gardener and summoned him to the house as well. He went and closed the library door. He went to the lavatory to clean it. He went to his flat to wash, clean his teeth and change his clothes. He arrived downstairs in the hall in time to answer the door, first to the police and then to Mrs Briggs.

Brain had brought with him two plainclothes women police officers, as well as DS Cotton, several uniformed constables and two scene of crime men. He was relieved Bolt had thought to bring in somebody to be with Lady Sarah, and that Carrock was already in the kitchen chatting about nothing and something with his wife and a pale and silent Anna Dark. He left his women officers in the kitchen and took Bolt out into the fresh air where Cotton made notes as the butler gave his orderly account.

He went and took a look at the body. He came out looking pale, despite his hardening years of experience. To Cotton he said, 'I don't think I ever want to hear anybody refer to me as Brains, ever again.'

Cotton nodded and gave his boss a small brandy. Brain sipped it until Dr Albert arrived, then he screwed himself up to go back into the library. The pathologist took one look at the body and gave a quiet little groan that combined distaste, sadness and sympathy. Then he set to his work and Brain positioned himself where he needn't watch.

Dr Albert emerged, stripping off his surgical gloves. 'Obviously shotgun,' he said. 'Death between midnight and, say, two a.m.'

'He arrived home just after midnight,' said Brain.

'Probably around one o'clock, then. Why don't you open a window. This place smells like a morgue. I'll be ready for him when your boys have finished. My God.' The doctor shook his head and left.

3

Yarrow arrived. He went into the library to peer over the shoulders of the scene of crime officers. He took a slow look at the remains of the powerful financier and walked heavily out. As he emerged into the music room, Brain was waiting with Cotton who held a small glass of brandy.

'Here,' said Brain, 'on the house.'

'Thanks. Can we go outside?'

They stood beside Sir Walter's Rolls-Royce, facing the besmirched cherub in the centre of the forecourt and began to talk the case over.

'Sir Walter coughed for the silver yesterday,' said Yarrow.

'Knew in advance, did he, or found out afterwards?'

'In advance. His cut was fifty per cent of the proceeds after meeting Homer's expenses, plus the insurance money.'

'What a bastard,' said Brain angrily. 'Going after us like that in the local bloody press.'

'Do you think it's suicide?'

'Looks that way, doesn't it? No note – but that doesn't mean much. Let's sort out the movements. We've got some of them: the maid left at eight, the cook got home at eight thirty. Nobody arrived during the evening until Granthelm turned up about midnight.'

Yarrow noted that for Brain, as for the detectives at the Yard, Sir Walter had become plain Granthelm. It's difficult to use a criminal's title.

'Bolt's the steadiest of them right now,' said Brain. 'Let's get the rest from him for the moment, leave the lady till later.'

Cotton found Bolt and brought him out to the forecourt. By his account neither Anna Dark nor Mrs Carrock had returned after finishing work – why would they? Lady Sarah had watched television for two hours, drinking steadily, and he had helped her to her bedroom at ten to eleven. He had gone to bed at eleven thirty. He had not heard Sir Walter's arrival, and definitely had not heard anything like a shotgun blast. But then, it was an old and solidly made house. Lady Sarah, he added, would almost certainly not have heard either car or shot: not only was her bedroom at the other end of the house from the library, and the other side from the forecourt, but with the amount she had drunk her sleep would have been very sound.

They thanked Bolt and dismissed him. Before he left, he asked if they would like some lunch in a little while. They shook their heads decisively.

'Who did you have on the place last night?' asked Yarrow.

'Man in a car by the entrance,' said Cotton. 'Changed the watch every two hours through the night.'

'Nobody down this end of the drive?'

'No – didn't want the dogs to get him, you see.'

'So somebody could've sneaked in somewhere else.'

'Except for the dogs,' said Brain.

Yarrow nodded. 'Yes, but Homer dealt with the dogs one time. He might've told somebody how he did it – Rankley, for example.'

'Well, he's under the druggies' beady eyes, so why not ask them?'

'They'd've said already.'

'There's always Lady Sarah to think of.'

'Hallo,' said Cotton. 'Who's this?'

Madeleine Granthelm's Ferrari pulled to a stop on the far side of the forecourt. She got out, swung the door shut, gave them a scathing look, jerked her gaze off them and walked briskly into the house.

'Ouch,' said Cotton.

'Now you know what it's like to be cut,' said Brain.

They chatted desultorily until one of the scene of crime officers came out to report on their progress.

'Well,' said Brain after hearing the report, 'it doesn't look physically possible for it to be anything but suicide. But let's try Lady Sarah anyway. She's had enough time by now. Skipper, get one of the girls to accompany us, will you?'

Brain, Yarrow, Cotton and a woman detective found Lady Sarah, Madeleine Granthelm and Susan Briggs in the dining room. They were sipping tea and talking quietly and intently of anything but Sir Walter and the last ten days.

'Lady Sarah,' said Brain gently, 'I'm afraid we must ask you a few questions. I do apologise, but it is necessary.'

Madeleine Granthelm rounded on him. 'Why is it necessary?' she snapped. 'Aren't we going through enough without having you torment us? And haven't you done enough damage already?' she added to Yarrow.

He raised his eyebrows at her and sucked in his breath, casting a quick glance at her mother and then back to her. She glared at him furiously but her righteousness wilted under his knowing look.

'Just one thing, Miss Granthelm,' said Yarrow politely. 'When Bolt phoned you, did you call anybody before leaving – Mr Rankley, for example?'

'Yes,' she said quietly. 'I also called my brother, but he was out so I left a message.'

'Thank you.'

Lady Sarah put out a hand to her daughter, mutely protesting being left alone with the detectives.

'Do we have to go?' asked Susan Briggs. She was a straightforward, practical-looking woman of about forty.

'I'm afraid so,' confirmed Brain. 'It won't take long, and it's best to get it out of the way right at the beginning.' He moved over to her and said very quietly, 'Best for her. Do it now, and then she won't have the thought of us hanging over her, you know? There'll be a woman officer here, just in case.'

Susan Briggs saw the practicality of that. 'Come on then,

252

Maddy,' she said firmly. 'They can have fifteen minutes. We'll see how lunch is getting along.'

Madeleine Granthelm cast another angry look at Yarrow as she swept out. In the hall, she shuddered with fury and repugnance. It was intolerable that such a man should know what he did about her, outrageous that he should feel free to wave his knowledge at her like a magic wand. She hoped his come-uppance would not be long delayed. Peter had promised to fix him if he got half a chance – though whether there was more than blather to that, she didn't know.

Twenty minutes later, Brain, Cotton and Yarrow were back in the forecourt. Lady Sarah had been entirely convincing about last night. It was not dignified to claim to be in a more than half-drunk sleep at the time your husband committed suicide in the same house. Nor was it much of an alibi. For both those reasons, it had the air of truth.

From the maid and the cook they got confirmation that Lady Sarah had drunk half a bottle of wine with the meal, as had become her habit, having already had several sherries. From the angle of the shotgun blast and the way the fingerprints showed Sir Walter had been holding it, it was inconceivable his death had happened without his volition, unless he were unconscious before the blast. The *post mortem* would tell them about that, but there were no signs that anybody else had been with him.

'Well,' said Brain after they had gone over it all one more time looking for loop-holes, 'why don't you come back to the station? We'll have a spot to eat, a drink, and see how far we can get towards wrapping this thing up.'

'Thanks,' said Yarrow.

'I have to say it looks as if you and your governor pushed him over the edge,' Brain said gently. He laid a hand on the young detective's shoulders. 'Don't feel too bad about it. The bloke was criminal anyway: his cocaine would've done as much damage to thousands of kids as he did to himself.'

'I know,' said Yarrow, 'I've heard it lots of times. His choice to take the wrong road, not ours. His decision to cheat his way to the top of the shit heap, not ours. His lies which forced us to put the pressure on him. I know it all. Still doesn't feel nice though.'

Yarrow arrived back about six thirty to find Fathers' section enjoying some sort of celebration. There were cans of beer, bottles of Scotch and even some champagne. Graves pressed a plastic cup of lukewarm champagne into his hand and invited him to join in. 'Stevo's cracked it,' he boomed.

Yarrow stood on the sidelines, feeling disorientated and in no sort of mood to participate. The cup slipped out of his fingers and champagne splashed over his shoes, trousers and the floor. He walked over to his desk, pushed DC Bunn off it, opened the middle drawer and slipped into it the folder he had brought back from Guildford. Looking up, he saw Fathers approaching. 'Come into the office,' said his boss.

He closed the door and sat down. Fathers was smoking a cigar and carrying a cup of champagne.

'What's going on?' asked Yarrow.

'Stevens heard about his promotion for one thing.'

'Oh great.'

'And the Post Office verdict came through. Got the lot. Loader included. Have a drink.'

'No thanks.'

'Sounds like you had a rough time.'

Yarrow shook his head – not to deny Fathers' comment, but to emphasise its accuracy. 'It's suicide,' he said. 'Position of the gun. Nobody with him. Conscious the moment before death. Put his chin over the barrel and let go.'

Fathers grimaced. 'Anything else?'

Yarrow shook his head again.

'Maybe you should get out of here.'

'I think I'll go to the gym,' said Yarrow. 'Get it out of my system. Anything I should know?'

'Mulholland's ship is due in tomorrow at Tilbury. Rankley knows Granthelm's dead . . .'

'Yeah, Madeleine told him.'

'. . . and he's told Mulholland. He was in a fit but the Yank calmed him down. They were talking very carefully, as if they knew they were being bugged. We're keeping a very tight watch on them. The paging system's on the blink again, so give us the number you'll be at, and we'll call you in if anything breaks.'

Yarrow pulled out his membership card for the police athletics club where the gym was and copied the phone number on to a scrap of paper. He gave it to Fathers who said, as he took it, 'You'd better call in your new number when you leave.'

'OK. Thanks. See you.'

Fathers accompanied Yarrow back into the general office. As Yarrow walked through it, Queen weaved up holding a bottle and a cigarette in one hand, but he caught Fathers' swift shake of the head and let Yarrow go.

5

He was doing press-ups when the call came, sweating the day out of himself. It was a quarter to eight. He was wearing his tracksuit top with the bird and fist emblem on it, tracksuit trousers which didn't match and training shoes. Underneath he was wearing a cotton polo-neck. He went to the office by the changing rooms and took the phone. It was Pardoner. 'Rankley's gone to ground,' he said. 'They've totally lost him. The Yanks're on a rabbit. Everybody in.'

He hung up and ran into the changing room, grabbed the car keys from his trouser pocket and, dressed as he was, ran out to the car. The gym he favoured was in Holloway. He broke the speed limit flagrantly along Camden Road, beat a series of lights on the amber and headed down for Euston. As he rounded Mornington Crescent, a thought struck him, and he pulled the car over. There was a phone box fifty yards back and he ran to it. He had no change on him but he could reverse the charges. It was out of order. Cursing, he looked round for another one. None in sight. He ran back to the car and started up again and moved off. He could go to Euston Station, but there might be queues for the public phones and he felt with urgent certainty that there was no time to waste. Sod it, he decided, I'll have to risk it.

6

Davis Mulholland heaved the two suitcases on to the scale as his wife handed their tickets to the woman behind the check-in desk for first class passengers. She examined them and tore out the pages she needed. 'That's all your luggage, is it?' she asked, and tapped expertly on the keys of her computer terminal: 'Smoking or non, Mrs Grey?' she asked.

'Definitely non,' replied Brown Mulholland.

Tap-tap on the keys.

'Window seats or centre?'

'Window.'

More tapping and then the woman waited. With a chugging, grating whine the boarding cards emerged from the side of the machine. She tucked them neatly and deftly into two clear plastic wallets with the pages taken from the tickets. Then she tagged their cases with the destination code and attached labels on thin elastic, tore off half of each label and stapled one to each ticket. She leaned over on to the high desktop, handed the tickets back and tapped the plastic wallets with a biro.

'Seats 4A and B, Gate B37, boarding in sixty-five minutes, go through passport control when you're ready, it's upstairs, escalator just along here to the right, have a pleasant flight,' she said with a polite smile and without taking a breath.

'Thank you,' said Brown Mulholland. She swung her bag on to her shoulder, her husband picked up his attaché case, and with arms linked they walked along the line of the check-in counter.

'So far so good,' she muttered as they stepped on to the escalator.

'No problem,' said her husband. 'Like I told you, I fixed this up months ago. Open ticket on SA Airways, the passports are top quality, we go on from Cape Town to Buenos Aires in a coupla weeks and get back to Miami with our own passports showing we've been in Argentina for the past three months.'

'The stamps for Argentina are fixed as well, are they?'

'Everything's fixed. Look, we lost the guy in Piccadilly and he didn't pick us up again when I got the cases out at Victoria. They've no reason to think we're on our way. They don't even know we had luggage at the station. They'll just go back to the apartment and wait for us there.'

'And when the London police call Miami and the local blues get on to us?'

'The company'll pay 'em off,' said Mulholland as they stepped off the escalator, 'and they'll report back it must've been a different Mulholland in London. Relax, there's no problem. Peter can take any shit coming his way. Homer was his friend, and Ellen his girl. Or else they'll give up and put it all down to Sir

Walter, now he's dead and can't answer back. We're out of it. And either this deal will work, in which case fine, or it won't – and next time the company wants to break into the UK market they'll send somebody else.'

'I'm worried about what the company will say. And do.'

'No sweat. I told you, I checked back last week – going ahead was their decision. But look, if you're worried, we'll talk about it in South Africa. We wanna go to ground, we can do it. We're stacked with cash and I can call up some company resources before they find out. We got the option. We can chew it over.'

'OK,' said Brown Mulholland. 'Shall we go straight through immigration?'

'Sure.'

They showed their boarding passes to the security man who nodded and waved them on. They showed their passports at the second barrier. A brief look, another nod and they walked on. As they approached the security checkpoint, two men came up to them.

'Mr and Mrs Mulholland?' said the older one, holding out some sort of identification. 'I'm Detective Inspector Young of Scotland Yard. This way please.'

'Nice try, Mulholland,' said the other in a distinctively American accent, 'but no cigars – not for a long, long time.'

CHAPTER 21

1

Yarrow stopped the car round the corner from the warehouse owned by the company called Number Four. He opened the car door, closed it quietly, walked to the corner, took a cautious look round it and crossed the road. A few yards down the alleyway beside the warehouse a car was parked. The Morgan. Just beyond it was a side door into the warehouse.

Yarrow tip-toed down the alley, saw the side door was ajar, carried on past the car and along the path, following it round a bend till he came to two three-foot-high concrete posts. They left enough room for cyclists or pedestrians to get by, but not for a car. He ran back up the alley, stole past the car again, crossed the street and got into his own car. He started the engine and, keeping the revs as low as he could, edged out across the street and into the alleyway. Rankley now had no way out by car. Yarrow switched off his engine, left the gears engaged in fourth, put the hand-brake on, pulled the steering wheel hard over and put the security lock on it. As he got out he shut the door as gently as he could and locked it. He checked the passenger door and boot were both locked and pocketed his keys.

He thought about the warehouse. It had big double doors on the main street. There was the side door into the alley. Further down that path he had seen a door in the wall, possibly another exit via the back yard. When Rankley wanted to leave, he would see his way by car was blocked. If he then went straight off on foot, Yarrow could follow him. But if Rankley was clever – and if he guessed whoever'd put the other car there was alone, as he might do because it was not an official car – he would go back into the warehouse and wait a few minutes before leaving. Then, whichever door Yarrow watched, it was a risk it would be the wrong one. How clever was Rankley? Let's not under-estimate him, he said to himself. He would have to get in there so he could see which way Rankley left by.

He put his mind to the task of entering. First he checked the big double doors. Locked – presumably from the inside. Two windows on the ground floor had thick security glass. A first floor window was broken but he could see no way to get up to it. He tip-toed back down the alleyway past the Morgan. The door in the yard wall was also locked. The wall was high and had barbed wire on top. So – only one way in.

He crept back up the alley and pushed gently on the side door. It began to squeak. He froze. There was a grunt from quite close by and heavy footsteps. He ducked round the far side of the Morgan and crouched down. Looking through underneath the car he saw the door swing open. Two feet appeared, visible thanks to a light inside the building. They stepped out into the alleyway. Then they walked towards the road. Rankley had seen the white sports car parked at the end and was going to investigate. Yarrow watched him stride towards the Nissan, bang angrily on its roof, then squeeze past it out into the street. Yarrow could make him out looking this way and that, apparently seeing nothing. Rankley came back and tried the Nissan's doors. He gave another bang on the roof when he was frustrated. Then he turned and searched along the bottom of the wall. Whatever he was looking for, he found and picked up. Something heavy it looked like – a brick or a chunk of concrete. Rankley smashed it against the window on the driver's side and the glass shattered. He knocked out the glass, leaned in and evidently released the handbrake, for when he pulled his large trunk back out he went to the front of the car and pushed. It didn't move. He went back to the door, leaned in and Yarrow assumed he wrenched the gear stick to neutral. He returned to the front of the car and gave another heave. The car lurched backwards and swung into the wall. Again Rankley returned to the driver's door and leaned in. His body thrashed around a bit. Yarrow watched gleefully. Presumably Rankley was discovering that the security lock was on tight and the steering wheel would not shift more than a millimetre. The big man re-emerged from the car, stood up straight and crashed both fists down on the Nissan's roof. He picked up the chunk of masonry he'd used before and smashed the windscreen, then he crashed it down on to the bonnet, and again on to the roof. Yarrow's glee evaporated as he watched Rankley's rage wreck the car.

Finally, he stopped. He went back to the street again, another quick look and then ran down to the warehouse door. He ducked in and then quickly back out, casting a look down the alley the other way. He disappeared inside, leaving the door wide open. Time to go in, thought Yarrow, and crossed the threshold.

There was a narrow ill-lit corridor, strewn with rubbish. He picked his way carefully along till he reached the point where the corridor gave on to the main body of the warehouse. He stood with his back to one wall and looked out into the large area. He was looking towards the front of the warehouse, towards the street. There were no lights on. He moved to the other wall and looked down to the back. There was a light there, coming not from the main room, but from one at the side. He eased himself out and round the corner, flat against the wall, moving as carefully and as quietly as he could. On that side there was a series of offices, each with a window. The light came from the second one down. Presumably Rankley was in there. Yarrow paused, wondering what to do. He had found him – and the man knew he had been found, unless he might unreasonably and wishfully think the Nissan was parked there by accident. He had come back into the warehouse, probably to get something before he left. Yarrow could follow him further. When Rankley finally stopped somewhere, then would be the time to get to a phone and call Fathers.

There were several piles of industrial palettes and packing cases on the warehouse floor. The nearest was not five yards away. His mind made up, Yarrow darted for one of them, to hide behind it and wait for Rankley to come out from the office.

'Well, well, bloody well.'

Rankley's voice sounded ten times as loud to Yarrow as it really was.

'What've we got here?' the assured, confident voice continued. 'Looks like an oily oick. How pleasant.'

Yarrow turned. Rankley was walking towards him from the front of the warehouse where he'd been hiding in the dark, waiting for whoever had followed him to appear.

'I'm glad it's you,' he said, 'very glad, because I'm going to take particular pleasure in wiping you on the walls. Your boss would've been fun, but you're a real bonus.'

He was carrying a crowbar, the sort used for opening heavy packing cases. As he emerged into the pool of light from the corridor, Yarrow could see it was blue, claw-ended and heavy. Rankley hefted it in his hand.

'I expect you're getting a taste for it,' said Yarrow. His voice did not quaver, he was relieved to hear, despite his racing heart. 'Like a dog what's bit a sheep – got to get more blood.'

'A dog what's bit a sheep,' mimicked Rankley, in an accent at the other social pole from Yarrow's. 'I arrest you in the name of good taste for violent assault on the English language. I'd smash your brains out for that alone. But you're also a nuisance, and a lot more dangerous than you look.' As he talked, he advanced on Yarrow who had not yet moved.

'One thing,' said Yarrow, 'before I shuffle off this mortal coil. Why'd you kill Sheerley? We know why you done Homer in, but what was the problem with her?'

Rankley took a practice swing at a tea-chest as he passed, crumpling it. 'I think this'll do nicely for opening your skull,' he said. 'What do you think?'

Yarrow moved away from the pile of palettes. Rankley looked at him with pleasure. Despite his show of bravado, the little man was so scared he was hopping from foot to foot.

'A touch of jiggety-jigs?' said Rankley. 'Can't sit still? Want to use the loo? Pissing your pants?'

'Go on,' said Yarrow, 'last request and all. Why Sheerley?'

'Oh she was getting to be a nuisance,' said Rankley, following slowly after Yarrow as the policeman backed away. 'Like you.'

'Blackmailing Granthelm, you mean?' asked Yarrow, shaking his hands in front of him to loosen them up.

'That – and Homer talked too much to her about the deal – as if the little fart was going to get in on it. Once I'd wheedled his best addresses out of him, he'd no chance. Bumptious credulous crud.'

'Wasn't that overdoing it a bit?' asked Yarrow, backing further off. 'I mean, you'd'a been raking it in. You could easily afford another partner.'

'Mulholland,' said Rankley, moving quickly to close the gap on Yarrow, 'runs what he calls a tight ship. No loose ends. And when he was in the sack with the girl, he decided she was a very loose end indeed. We'd no further use for Homer and none at all for her. It was also a good way of tying Sir Walter in closer.'

'Of course,' said Yarrow, snapping his fingers, 'with the murders done in his house, he was yours for life. Lovely – so the exit route'd always be there. He could never close down on you. Brilliant.' He backed off again, half stumbling on a plank of wood, then recovering.

Rankley used the opportunity to get closer. He was no more than six yards off now. The little man was still hopping from one

261

foot to another as he backed away. Not for long.

'I made a bet,' said Yarrow suddenly. 'You can tell me if I won.'

'Go on, little man, little dead man.'

'I reckon Homer topped Sheerley and carried her in, fixing to make it look like suicide. I reckon you conned him into it, saying he could come aboard if he did it. Then you whoffed him and made it look like he'd done her in and topped himself.'

'Brilliant,' sneered Rankley, 'but it won't do you any good now. Too late to be a smarmy little worker bee.'

'They'll get you,' said Yarrow. 'We saw through the fake suicide in no time flat. You think you're so clever.'

Rankley stayed silent as he continued to track Yarrow towards the back wall.

'Did he actually help you?' asked Yarrow. 'Sir Walter, I mean. Or was it your bird give you the key from his desk?' He kept shifting backwards with his strange little hopping dance-step.

'Why don't you just stand still?' suggested Rankley as Yarrow backed off further. 'You'll be at the wall in a minute, and you'll have to then.'

Yarrow was now two feet from the wall. Rankley hefted the crowbar again and rested it on his shoulder. The fist in which he held it was large and strong and white at the knuckles. He moved in to be three yards away from Yarrow, striking range. Yarrow shifted left, Rankley went with him – right, Rankley went with him.

'It was Sir Walter, of course,' said Rankley, hoping Yarrow would lose concentration and stay still for a second. But Yarrow continued to bounce this way and that, the other mirroring him with a shuffle and a slide. They made a strange, mismatched, but almost balletic duo.

'You lot make me sick, you do,' said Yarrow, trying to concentrate equally on Rankley's face, crowbar and feet. 'The way you use anyone and everyone. You all just reckon you can do anything and get away with it.'

'We can. We've done it for generations. You're not going to stop us.'

As they talked they concentrated fiercely on each other's moves.

Bounce, hop – shuffle, slide.

'You'll have to catch me first, you great clumsy git.'

'Don't worry about that,' said Rankley, his knuckles going yet whiter as he tightened his grip on the crowbar.

Bounce, hop – shuffle, slide.

Yarrow realised he couldn't keep this up for much longer. The day had taken too much out of him. The moment had come.

'Look at Homer. First he screwed her, then he shot her. I call that sick. Course, it wouldn't shock you, not with the way you let him and that Yank have your bird and . . .'

'You little turd!' screamed Rankley as he swung the crowbar in a huge vicious arc at Yarrow's head.

But Yarrow was no longer there. The crowbar swung right through to the ground and Rankley's momentum took him crashing into the wall, banging his head. As he regained ·balance there was a stinging blow on his right elbow, another on his hand and he dropped the weapon. As he righted himself he saw Yarrow's foot flash out and managed to half block the third blow as it landed on his thigh. He steadied himself and looked at his still bouncing opponent.

'Come on, you great git,' Yarrow taunted him, still in his little hopping step, backwards and forwards, side to side, 'twice my size and half my brains. I'll have you for supper.'

Rankley bellowed again as he threw himself forward. Something hard thudded into his chest and stopped him short. He didn't see what it was, nor the next blow into his ribs which knocked him half a step to his right. He staggered, his left hand up to clutch his rib-cage in the reflex response to pain. He shook his head to clear it and saw Yarrow's left foot flash out towards his crutch. He half turned to his left and swung his right arm down to block it, but it was the right foot which crashed into its target. Rankley screamed and clutched himself with both hands. He felt as if his insides were falling out. Through the pain he did not see Yarrow's hand stab out, straight fingered, but he felt it land and flung one hand up to his eyes. As he reeled with the impact and the sickening pain, he wanted to beg there should be no more, and then his temple exploded in agony as if a hammer had landed by his right ear. He collapsed to the floor, barely semi-conscious.

Yarrow paused for a moment over Rankley's prostrate body. He knelt, found the pressure points behind the ears, pressed in with his thumb knuckles and Rankley lost consciousness entirely.

He stood up and gave a slight half bow towards his beaten opponent – marking a respect he did not feel with a ritual that had been trained into him over the years. He frowned self-critically as he responded to another item of his training – the self-assessment. Rankley, of course, was easy meat. Over-confident, unaware of Yarrow's skills, used to relying on his weight, unfit, slow in reflex and movement, and with his temper wound up to breaking point. But the first side-kick Yarrow had landed on his weapon arm should have been more telling. It shouldn't have needed a second one, and that had succeeded more by luck than judgement. Against a more formidable, quicker opponent, he could have been in trouble. The third kick, a roundhouse, had been entirely wasted; instead, he should have stepped in with a lunge punch to the throat and then finished him off. The side-kick to the chest, however, and the roundhouse into the rib-cage – made without pausing to recover balance – had been quite satisfying. The feint and snap kick to the groin did its job, and the straight fingers into the eyes were smoothly delivered. But the hammer fist was a fraction off target. Middling, thought Yarrow, middling. I must put in more time.

He looked at the body again. It was big and heavy. Now I've got you here, he wondered, what do I do with you? I can put you down, but I can't pick you up.

Behind him there was a cough and Yarrow whirled. 'Very impressive,' said Graves emerging from behind a pile of palettes. 'Very impressive, indeed.' The heavy detective sergeant walked forward puffing on a cigarette. He stood in front of Yarrow and tapped the bird and fist emblem on the younger man's jacket. 'Nice badge, nice skill. Comes in handy, the old kung-fu, doesn't it?'

'Karate,' replied Yarrow. 'Wado-ryu, basically, and kick-boxing.'

'Third Dan, isn't it?'

'Yeah, but it's getting a bit rusty. I don't get time to put the hours in nowadays.'

'If that's what you call rusty,' said Graves.

'What're you doing here anyway?'

'Listening and watching. Peaking through the pallets.'

'You heard him, then, what he said.'

'Oh yuss, every word.' Graves dropped his cigarette and stepped on it. 'Nicely done. Why'd you string it out of him, though? Didja know I was there?'

'No I bloody didn't. I was just winding him up and getting him where I wanted. How come you didn't lend a hand?'

'Well, I've not seen you in action before. Only heard about it. Wanted to watch – educational, like.'

'Fuck off.'

'Wait'll you're a skipper for that sort of talk, laddy boy.'

'Why you here, anyway?'

'Oh we're all over the place. Daddy's watching the exit.' Graves looked at Yarrow's expression. 'Oh yeah, if you can work it out so can he, mate. Don't go getting uppity now, just because you're the king-fu. It was time to move, you see. Mulholland's been picked up at the airport – thought he'd lost his tail, and so he had, but only one of them. Pardoner went down to this prick's flat. We came here, and I came creeping in, saw you were engaged and settled myself at a convenient vantage point. Don't worry: if he'd spattered your brains on the floor I'd've had him.'

'Thanks for Fanny Adams. I reckon you bottled out.'

'Steady there, matey. No Sloane's ever gonna be a problem for me. Nor for you neither. I had other things to do.'

'But Rankley really did drop his tail, did he?'

'Yeah. Dunno how. Maybe he's not so daft as he sounds. What a wally, eh? Be the greatest pleasure to see him in the dock. And I bet they'll be nice to him when he's doing bird.'

Yarrow looked at Rankley again and then at Graves. He raised his eyebrows suggestively.

'Yeah, all right,' said the big detective sergeant, 'let's have him out of here.' He rearranged Rankley so he lay on his back, propped him into a sitting position, took him under the arms to heave him to his feet, then spun him round and bent down so the unconscious man folded over his shoulder. He picked up the crowbar and straightened up without much effort. 'How long'll he stay this way, d'you reckon?'

'Few more minutes,' said Yarrow.

'Right, let's be off then.'

As they got into the alleyway, Yarrow saw Fathers lounging in the shadows. He approached them. 'Ah, all done then?'

'Yeah,' said Graves, 'kung-fu kid here finished him off in about two seconds.'

'Put him in the van then,' said Fathers, 'and take him in.'

'Book him, Danno,' said Yarrow, 'murder one.'

'Oh that's right,' said Graves. 'I forgot to say. Sherlock teased a confession out of him. I heard it. In fact – sorry I forgot to

265

mention this, Elly – I taped it. Modern methods, don't you know, ho-ho.' He patted his jacket pocket, turned and walked out to the street.

Yarrow called after him, 'You should get him into casualty, skipper.'

Graves waved the crowbar in acknowledgement.

'Shame about your car,' said Fathers to Yarrow as they got to it.

'Violent idiot,' said Yarrow, stroking the dented bodywork. He began to shake.

'Drink?'

'Yeah.'

'You deserve it. Talking of idiots, though, detective constables who go tearing in without calling in often don't go any further. Not because they don't get promoted, but because they're no more.'

'Tried to call in, when I thought of the warehouse, but I couldn't find a phone that worked. I was just going to check it out, but he was here, so I was going to follow him on foot after I'd blocked his car, but he spotted me so I had to take him on.'

'Nice work anyway,' said Fathers, 'stupid, but nice. But be careful next time. You'd only have to slip once. It's not just the Rankleys of this world who can be over-confident.'

They arrived at the car Fathers and Graves had come in. Behind it was a van with two uniformed constables. As Fathers slid in behind the steering wheel and pulled the door shut, Graves loomed up. Fathers wound down the window. 'Take a ride back in the van, will you, skipper?' he said. 'See to the paperwork. I'll call the others in on the radio. We'll line a drink up for you.'

'Okey doke,' said Graves.

Fathers started the engine and then turned to Yarrow with the engine idling. 'I owe you an apology,' he said.

Yarrow looked at him.

'I decided I couldn't tell you about Queen's little operation, because I wasn't sure I could trust you for total discretion. So I had to let you think what you would and stall you. Sorry.'

'What was the operation?'

'Suckering Pascall into trying a bribe. Set it up, wire Queen for sound and bingo. He pulled Pascall and three of his crew in this afternoon. That was the other part of the celebration. Along with Stevens' promotion and the PO job.'

Yarrow nodded, leaned his head back and blew out a long sigh of relief. 'Shame for Kay,' he said.

'Well, it's Queen's way, isn't it?' said Fathers as he engaged the gears.

'I trusted you,' Yarrow said as the car started to move. 'You could've trusted me.'

Fathers shrugged. 'Hard to know who to trust,' he said. 'Did you trust Queen?'

Yarrow's nod acknowledged the accuracy of the jab. 'You did though,' he said.

Fathers shot a quick glance Yarrow's way. In the light from the dashboard his smile glinted. 'Did I?'